What It Takes

FICTION

What It Takes

FICTION

Lola Akande

TUNMIKE PAGES

Published by
TUNMIKE PAGES
20, St. Finbarr's College Road

Akoka, Yaba

Lagos, Nigeria

E-mail: tunmike.pages@gmail.com

© Lola Akande

First published by Kraft Books 2016

This impression 2018

ISBN 978-978-965-747-6

Cover design & Formating by Kayode Odukoya

DEDICATION

for A and G, my children, my friends.

AKNOWLEDGEMENTS

I am most grateful to the Almighty God for all. My special thanks go to Adewale Maja-Pearce whose assistance in editing the novel is invaluable. I thank him also for his professional advice. I owe a debt of gratitude to Odia Ofeimun for granting me access to his library, encouraging me to write, and for counselling me to brave the odds. I thank Remi Anifowose, Taiwo Obe, Lanre Idowu, Teju Olakiigbe, Samson Olusola, Wale Motajo, Demola Ogunlowo and Patrick Emoukhare for their compassion, support and encouragement and for being so kind with their time and resources. My appreciation also goes to Bunmi Ishola, Anote Ajeluoruo, Abubakar Adam Ibrahim, Kayode Ketefe, Yinka Oyegbile, Denrele Adeniyi Abdulmumin Balogun, Auwal Sa'id Mu'azu, Maxim Uzoatu, Sola Balogun, Seun Bisuga, Bunmi Oludiran, Michael Jimoh, Hannah Ojo, Osby Isibor and Ngozi Emedolibe. Thank you all for your love, support and encouragement.

One

SEPTEMBER, 1998

I stand in front of the large mirror and beam; a pretty, smooth-faced woman smiles back at me. I giggle in ecstasy, marvelling at how youthful I look at thirty-eight. Wow! I'm still young and beautiful, I whisper tenderly, admiring the way my mouth curls when I smile. Holding my PhD admission letter in my right hand, and ready to explore a new path in my life's journey, I'm unable to contain my excitement and sense of accomplishment, my body tingles with renewed excitement as I gaze endlessly at my reflection. I'm a beautiful woman, without doubt. Standing tall at 5ft: 10 inches without slouching, I turn my face slightly to get a side view and then change my posture to search for wrinkles on my left temple. There are none. I breathe a sigh of relief. I shift anxiously to check my right temple, still no wrinkles. I move closer to the mirror to scrutinise the area around my eyes. No lines at all. I sigh in relief. I'm delirious with joy. I'm absolutely stunning and thoroughly graceful!

The mirror in front of which I stand is not the only one in my bedroom. In spite of my precarious financial situation, I have bought two additional large ones within the last two weeks to counter the psychological warfare my subconscious relentlessly wages against me. I take time to stand in front of them in turn, assessing and reassessing my face, figure, poise and general physical appearance as objectively as I can and taking delight at my positive findings each time. The mirrors are not even my only source of self-appraisal; I have taken another quick step aimed at putting my self-proclaimed youthful looks to the test. Yes, I leave my car at home daily now and use the public transport popularly known as danfo to execute my itinerary.

Lagos residents are familiar with the hilarious, yet mischievous way bus conductors remind commuters of their age. If a woman looks old in their reckoning, they address her as 'Mama' or 'Iya'. I see women protest vehemently against being so addressed but such protestations only serve to reinforce the bus conductors' conviction. 'Anti' or 'Sista,' is used for women deemed to be youngish in looks. Such women have every reason to put on their dancing shoes and rock because there can be no greater affirmation of their youthfulness. I share in the palpable pain of my fellow women who I witness being mercilessly condemned to the age of Methuselah by these wickedly funny bus conductors, particularly because they always seem to be correct. There is another categorisation for those who appear stylish, sophisticated, trendy, upbeat and classy; conductors address them as 'Maama,' and to be so addressed is capable of catapulting any female to a state of delicious delirium in Lagos.

So, I deliberately make danfo my choice of transportation within the city; and, every day as I climb into the bus, I ensure that all my senses are hyper-alert, my hearing more acute but my subconscious is always fraught with nerves. Sometimes, when I'm lucky, I have the pleasure of being addressed as 'Maama'. I savour such moments. Even more reassuring is the way some of them wink seductively at me, as if they knew I truly needed their weird encouragement. As mischievous and insensitive as they are, Lagos bus conductors are of immense value in helping to strengthen my psychological balance and I'm thankful.

My mind drifts to the time when I didn't used to worry about how young or old I looked because I occupied my time with productive engagement. I was gainfully employed in the federal civil service and led a relatively settled life. Then, suddenly, about six months ago, a rationalisation exercise hit the ministry where I worked like a thunderbolt and swept many of us away, leaving many families in indescribable anguish. That was sad; but what was sadder was that, barely two months after the exercise, news of the sudden death of some of my former colleagues began to make the rounds. The news reminded me of the outbursts of many of them as the sack letters were being distributed. They openly predicted their death, although no one paid them any attention. They said they would not be able to carry on with life without employment. How right they were. And how did they know? While many engaged in hysterics, cursing and abusing the government for gross insensitivity and irresponsibility, some simply sat rooted to their seats, staring vacantly at some unknown object. But there were those who seemed to have anticipated it and were prepared. There were also those who received the news of the cessation of their hitherto source of livelihood with shock but also with equanimity. Reminiscing about it probably puts me in the last category because I'm also one of those who believe the loss of a job ought not to be synonymous with the loss of one's hopes.

I remember the tragic story of one of my superiors, Mr Simeon, who used to pass through my street every Saturday during his bicycle-riding morning exercise. When he stopped coming around about a month or so after our disengagement, I thought he was taking time off to plan his next course of action. But I got slightly worried when he still didn't show up three months after so I enquired after him. It came as a rude shock when some of my former colleagues wondered how I didn't know of his sudden death two months into our forced retirement. I was devastated because Simeon was ebullient and full of life. How did his wife take his demise? How would his young children fare since their mother had no employment? No one had any answers.

"Mummy, what are you still doing in front of the mirror?" Deyemi's voice drags me back to the present. I whirl around to smile at her.

"Mummy is looking at herself."

"You are very fine," she says.

"Thanks, sweetheart," I mumble, feeling reassured as I take another quick look at my reflection to check for gray hairs. Not a single strand. I beam at my daughter. It's the beginning of a new era for me, I mutter under my breath, and begin putting a few items together in readiness for my journey to the National University of Nigeria, Abuja, where I have just secured admission for a PhD programme in literature.

Two

I decide to leave Lagos late in the afternoon so as to arrive in Ibadan in the early evening. I want to spend a night with my mother before proceeding to Abuja. I want to explain the circumstance of my sudden loss of employment, to let her know that I wasn't sacked because I committed an offence, or was negligent in my duties; that the decision to relieve my colleagues and me of our duties was taken by the management of my ministry, which also acted on instructions from the federal government. Most importantly, I want to assure her that, as is often said in popular parlance, losing my job is a huge blessing in disguise because I'm now a doctoral student in one of Nigeria's most prestigious universities.

My mother is not literate but she never ceases to amaze me with her demonstrable knowledge of the goings-on in governance, economy and even the social scene. I think it's because she's an avid listener to the radio. She is aware, for instance, that people with doctoral degrees are addressed as 'doctor' and that they hold prestigious teaching positions at the highest educational level - the university. Every mother wants the best for their children and mine is no exception. She would be overjoyed to see her daughter being addressed as Dr Funto Oyewole. The thought brings a smile to my face, but realising that I'm travelling in a public bus, with seventeen other passengers, I attempt to smother the grin that is now threatening to split my face in two.

My journey to Ibadan is smooth, fast and hitch-free. There are no broken-down, heavy-duty vehicles on the expressway and no accidents. Happily, too, policemen who usually adorn every five kilometres with check points causing long queues of vehicles and extorting motorists are virtually nonexistent. I take a bus from Challenge to Beere, where my mother's yam flour stall is located. The stall is also within walking distance of her residence. My mother is a very strong woman. In spite of having lost my father over twenty-five years ago, she is steadfast in her motherly affection and lending support to her four children including me, the eldest. I do my best to support my siblings, too. I funded, single-handled, my youngest sibling's secondary and university education and, prior to my sack, we were all happily employed in different sectors of the economy.

I meet my mother chatting excitedly with Mama Sikira who also sells yam flour and whose stall is third to my mother's. They are age-mates. I genuflect as soon as I get to them and my mother's face lights up in surprise. Then, she seems to suddenly come to a new realisation and her expression darkens.

"Funto, aren't you supposed to be at work? Today is Tuesday." I take a deep, steadying breath and curl my lips in the semblance of a smile.

"I came to see you for an important discussion," I whisper. My mother's friend takes a cue. She smiles sweetly at me, telling me to make sure I see her before returning to Lagos. She hurries off to her stall. My mother gazes at me intently, her face etched with concern. I look away from her to watch a cloud passing in front of the evening sun. The shadows spread across our faces, momentarily obliterating our features. I use the opportunity to take another deep breath and prepare to make my mission as easy to understand as possible.

"We've not had enough rain this year," she says and I nod

in agreement. "I think it's going to rain tonight," she adds. I say nothing.

"Come, Funto, help me put my wares in the stall. I might as well close for the day." Still I say nothing but I do as she requests and soon we are walking home. Why have I suddenly become taciturn?

My mother is dressed in a patterned blue wrapper and I observe that she is still curvy. She looks absolutely gorgeous and smashing for a fifty-eight year old. As we do the less than five minutes walk to her residence, I'm absorbed in a mental organisation of my presentation to her. As soon as we reach home, she wants us to talk first, before cooking dinner. I start by telling her that I'm going to spend the night in Ibadan with her. I see the surprise and unasked question on her face but I pretend not to notice.

"There has been an unexpected development," I begin, trying to keep my voice as calm and controlled as possible. I watch as her brow furrows and continue. "I implore you, Ma'ami, to be understanding and supportive as you have always been because, in the final analysis, this development is a very positive one."

I pause again but my mother urges me with her eyes to continue. I resume.

"There has been a rationalisation exercise at my work place."

"What does that mean?"

"It means a situation has arisen that has made it mandatory for the government, through the leaders in our ministry, to find ways to reduce their spending. You know Nigeria is going into a democratic experience next year after several years of military rule. Therefore, in order to make governance easy for the civilians who will take over the mantle of leadership, it has become necessary to take a dispassionate look at the size of the civil service. The result of that appraisal is the sad but compelling downsizing of the workforce of some ministries. Unfortunately - but fortunately in another sense - I'm one of the people affected by the exercise."

She narrows her eyes and looks thoughtful but doesn't speak. I try to do a mental appraisal of my delivery. Perhaps, I was a bit too vague.

"Talk to me, Ma'ami," I beseech her.

"What's the matter with you, Funto? I have watched your lips move and heard your voice but you haven't been talking to me."

I open my mouth to say something but, not knowing what to say, I close it. My mother fixes me a hard look. I lower my gaze.

"Since when has it become impossible for you to talk to your own mother in a straightforward manner?"

I open my mouth to speak again but she holds up her hand. I obediently shut my mouth. She continues.

"What is this matter that overwhelms you so much that you are going round and round in circles?" she queries, eyes wide open in alarm.

"Ma'ami, I didn't mean to confuse you or overstretch your patience." I pause, searching for the words. She is gazing intently at me. I take a deep breath and swallow hard.

"What I am trying to explain is that they have sacked some people in my office and I am one of them." I say it in a rush as if I'm desperate to be rid of it. I take a furtive look at her, trying to decipher the weight of what I've just said on her. Her expression is now desolate.

"Ah, ori mi o, t'emi bami, owo ota bami/ Oh my creator, I'm in trouble, my enemies have gained an upper hand." She starts to pace about the room. Beads of sweat suddenly form on her forehead and descend rapidly to her temple.

"Ma'ami, there are no enemies. It's an official decision and it isn't the end of my life."

"You are ignorant of the world and the wickedness of people who inhabit it. How can my eldest child suddenly lose her job?"

"If only you will calm down and let me explain, Ma'ami. This development is a blessing in disguise, just listen to me."

"Blessing in disguise, Funto? How can losing a job be a blessing in disguise?"

"I have a plan that will take me farther than a career in the ministry can."

"What plan?"

"I am going back to school."

"What school? You went to the university before you started working."

"Indeed you are right, but I'm going back to the university to study again so that I can get an even better job."

"That's no plan at all. You are confused."

"Ha-ah, Ma'ami, why do you talk like this? You sent me to school, remember? You laboured to train your children because you believed going to school was a good plan."

"Yes, I sent all of you to school and you went, Funto. You have a master's degree. What more education can anyone hope for?"

"I can go back to get a doctorate."

"Don't be foolish. You want to engage in a white elephant project, isn't it?"

"No, don't talk like that."

"Well then, teach me how to talk since you think my not going to school makes me deaf and dumb to happenings around me."

"What are you talking about, Ma'ami? What's happening?"

"You think I'm not aware that people spend as long as ten

years trying and, in some cases, failing to get a PhD?"

"You got it all wrong, Ma'ami. PhD is a three-year programme."

"Now I know you are the ignorant one. You know Agbeke, don't you?"

"Agbeke," I echo, slightly confused.

"Yes, Agbeke, the one whose stall is fourth from mine?"

"Oh yes, of course I know her, Mama Tunde?"

"That's her, it's the same Tunde I have in mind. He's been trying to get a PhD for the past eight years without success. He came to visit his mother last week and after he left, I asked her how far her son has gone and she said the story is the same."

I shift uncomfortably on my seat, perching at the edge of the cushion chair. My mother ignores me and continues talking.

"I asked Agbeke when her son will become the Doctor she has repeatedly boasted to us about. She said she asked Tunde the same question and his response was that no one is ever able to predict the finishing date of a doctoral programme."

"Which university is he, Ma'ami?"

"How will I know?"

"You see?"

"Which university do you intend to do your own PhD?"

"National University of Nigeria, Abuja."

"Listen to me, Funto," my mother says harshly. I flinch. "I can see you don't want me to advise you," she adds sadly. I shake my head in protestation.

"You are my mother, why wouldn't I want you to advise me?" I query, trying to sound as convincing as possible and wishing desperately that she won't try to dissuade me.

"Good. Did they pay you a reasonable amount of money as compensation?"

"Well, eh-r, yes."

"How much"

"Two hundred thousand."

"How long did you serve them?"

"Eight years."

"Will they pay you monthly pension?'

"No, a worker is entitled to pension only if they spend up to ten years in service."

"That's sad. You needed to have spent just two more years to qualify."

"Yes."

"The first step I think you need to take is to leave Lagos."

I gasp and my mother curls her mouth in a reluctant smile. "I'm not saying you should come and live in Beere here with me; but Lagos is an expensive city and not good for a woman with responsibilities but without a job. Believe me, Funto; it makes no sense to continue to live there. Come to Ibadan," she says with the conviction of one who has all the facts and figures at their finger tips. I gape at her. Why do parents often fail to recognise and come to terms with their children's chronological growth and even maturity? My mother wants to tell me where to live at thirty-eight? I'm pissed.

"Is a job waiting for me in Ibadan, Ma'ami?" I ask, sounding belligerent and angry.

"Be patient, let me finish," she says, scowling at me.

"I'm sorry to interrupt," I say sulkily.

"With less than fifty thousand naira, you will be able to rent a large and spacious flat at Bodija GRA. If you pay for two years, you will still have more than one hundred thousand left and you can invest the amount in a profitable and moving trade. I suggest you go into poultry business. Part of the reason why you will need to rent a big flat at Bodija is so that you can carve out sufficient space to use as farm house where you will keep your

11

birds. You and Deyemi don't need more than one room, so if you have a large apartment you can do what you like with the rest. I tell you something, we are in September; if you hurry and come quickly, houses are everywhere at Bodija with house owners jostling to attract tenants. If you buy day-old chicks before the end of this month, they will be ready for sale at Christmas. You'll be amazed at the huge profit you'll make. I'm not trying to make you relocate to Ibadan in order for you to look after me. You can see that I'm able to look after myself but you mustn't forget that you are a single mother. You have a daughter who is barely ten years old. Her education and upkeep must be paramount in your plans, not how to acquire a PhD degree that may turn out to be a mirage. Do you want her to suffer because her father is not even aware of her existence? You must be alive to your responsibilities, and it's your responsibility, not anyone else's, to feed, educate and generally look after her in every way a responsible mother looks after her child. You cannot afford to be foolish by starting a programme that has no completion date when you know you have nobody to lean on for support."

By the time she finishes my mood has moderated. What I feel now is confusion, doubt, and..., yes, fear. How wise is my decision to pursue a doctorate in view of my enormous responsibilities? I want to look directly at her, search her eyes for something I'm not quite certain about: support, assurance, wise decision, clue to the way forward, what? I make my eyes search hers and finally our eyes lock but I can't find my answer, maybe because I don't know what I'm looking for. Her gaze is intense, yes, but what I see is only motherly concern and fear.

As I continue to stare at her, my subconscious begins to mirror her feeling. Muscles deep in my belly clench. I tear my eyes from her scrutiny and stare blindly at my feet. My heart is pounding. My breathing is aggravated, loud and shallow; my scalp prickles; my mouth is dry; I feel faint. No, I mustn't permit any negative emotions, I whisper to myself. I straighten up and shake my head to gather my wits.

"I know you mean well for me, Ma'ami, I mean, you've always been the best mother anyone could wish for but I urge you to look at this matter from my perspective."

"Fine. What's your perspective?"

"I have nothing against poultry, or any form of farming for that matter. If I consider that a former head of state of this huge country is a farmer, who am I to insinuate that farming is beneath me or not a worthwhile venture? As noble and lucrative as farming is, however, it's not what I want to do."

"You want to be addressed as Dr?" my mother snarls and my heart sinks but I manage to ignore her sneer.

"Some of my colleagues who were also sacked have since taken up stalls at popular markets in Lagos such as the Tejuosho and Balogun. Some have even gone ahead to stock their shops with a variety of wares and are happier for it, so I don't reject trading as a means of survival.

"Your colleagues are not only reasonable; they are realistic. Can't you see?"

"I understand your point, Ma'ami; it's just that different people tend to have different dreams and different ways of responding to similar situations. We all can't be the same or do the same things."

"Who looks after Deyemi while you embark on a long journey that may lead to nowhere?" she asks and I understand her pessimism about PhD. Who in heaven's name has been feeding her with such a negative notion about the noblest aspiration? Do I stand a chance of ever being in a position to convince her to see it differently? A feeling of frustration and resignation threatens to overwhelm me but I don't allow it.

"It takes only three years for full-time students to start and complete a doctorate." I deepen my stare at my mother, my fears gone. She is watching me, eyes wide, bemused. She obviously doesn't see things my way and I'm angered by her lack of understanding. Tears prick and pool in my eyes. I dash the tears angrily with the back of my hands, glaring at her. She seems to have realised she was making me miserable because her gaze suddenly softens.

"Don't cry," she says, her voice soft, warm and full of love."

"Oh Ma'ami, there's so much I want to say." She brushes my face with her hand and I start to relax.

"Go on, talk to me, olowo orimi," she coos.

"I have secured admission to the National University of Nigeria at Abuja. I'm going to Abuja tomorrow, from here. I want you to support my decision, to believe in me and wish me well, Ma'ami,"

"You know I'll always support you. I wish you well all the time. I'm only concerned but you know these things more than I do. I'll continue to pray for you." She gives me a reassuring smile and I smile back my appreciation, feeling genuinely at ease.

"You know you can still relocate to Ibadan." I pout. Not again. "Your school is in Abuja and..."

"I know, Ma'ami, I want to remain in Lagos"

"Why? Won't it be easier for you to shuttle from Ibadan to Abuja rather than all the way from Lagos, especially giving the notoriety of the Lagos-Ibadan Expressway?"

"I know about all that but Lagos is where things happen."

"What things?"

"Everything – the terrific, the fantastic, the spectacular and the horrific, but I do and strive to choose only the good things at all times, Ma'ami. My chances of survival are better in Lagos."

"Is there a man in your life in Lagos?" I take my time to

answer as my mind goes to Shettima and his proposition. Shettima wants me, I'm aware, but I'm even more aware of my resolve not to let him or any man come into my life. Not again.

"No, there is no man in my life." I mumble.

"You haven't told me how you intend to take care of Deyemi while you are in school."

"Oh, Deyemi has just gained admission into Maryland Secondary School. She is in the boarding house. I have also used a substantial part of my gratuity to cover the initial three years of her secondary education. I will obtain my PhD at the same time that she will be completing the junior level. People with doctoral degrees don't lack employment. I'll secure a respectable job as a university lecturer before she starts her senior secondary school and life will be sweeter than honey for all of us. I only need you to bear with me during these three years. I promise to make it up to you."

"Don't' worry about me at all, olowo ori mi, I'm worried about you. I don't want you to make more mistakes. I sincerely hope you are right this time, Funto. I hope you have made a truly right decision. Oya, let me pray for you." I sink on my knees. I know the mistake my mother has alluded to is about Deyemi's father, but I choose not to pursue the subject.

I met Deyemi's father, Isaac, eleven years ago. I was twenty-seven, a university graduate without a steady relationship and anxious to marry. What set him apart from other men I had met was that he was devastatingly handsome. He simply took my breath away. I was in his sexual thrall and I believed he was in mine as well. We started what I imagined was a relationship. He told me he had lived his entire adult life in the United States and that he barely knew Nigeria. I was further enthralled. I wasn't quite sure whether it was because I found him a very beautiful man, or because I was mesmerised by his eloquence and manners, or perhaps, my desperation got the better of me because I began to dream of marrying him. Truth was, it was as if my life was in black and white before I met him. With him, my whole life was richer, brighter. I was soaring in his dazzling light and I couldn't imagine life without him. I gave him my love, my body, my dreams, my world and in my delusion that he loved me as much and would marry me, I failed to ascribe meaning to expressions such as, "This is going to be quick, baby," and, "We don't have long, come on," which he mumbled regularly, especially whenever we were making love.

I was operating in the clouds, transported beyond the realms of the real. I can't recall how many times we made love but the entire affair lasted just six weeks. I woke up one morning to the realisation that he had returned to the US without so much as a goodbye or a forwarding address. I discovered I was pregnant three weeks afterwards. Who could I accuse of being responsible for my woes? I had acted foolish and got what I deserved, so I moved on quickly and became a man to myself. Although part of me longed for the fabled trembling knees, heart-in-the-mouth, butterflies-in-my-belly moments, I couldn't find anyone who I was attracted to. Who could match the gorgeous looking man that Deyemi's father was?

I chose to concentrate on the fulfilment and joy of motherhood. I also resolved not to make the circumstance of my daughter's conception a subject of discussion with colleagues, friends or even relatives, apart from my mother. Whatever happened or failed to happen about my love life were my issues and I ought to be entitled to my private life. Mercifully, Deyemi wasn't in the habit of asking about her father. Once, when she was about five, she suddenly stopped on the road as I accompanied her to school one morning, peeked up at me and asked: "How did you get me?" My heart skipped a beat. I felt world-weary, but

I recovered just in time. Smiling sweetly, I said: "God gave you to me." She laughed a long, throated laughter and we resumed our walk. I heaved a long sigh of relief. As for Shettima, we met only recently and although he seems a nice person and has not minced words about how he feels about me and how he wants to be the man in my life; my response has remained an emphatic no. My experience with Deyemi's father suggests to me that I don't know what to look out for in a man. It's often said that women hardly know what they want, and may be the assertion is correct. Perhaps, I don't even know what is good for me. What I do know, however, is precisely what I don't want – I'm not interested in how genuine or otherwise Shettima is. What's the point?

"I think you need to shower before you eat." My mother's voice pulls me back to the present and my excitement blooms, eclipsing all other feelings.

Three

I'm in a state of delirium as I board a bus from Beere to Iwo Road Motor Park where vehicles are filling up for different destinations, the motor park touts jostling for passengers. I soon locate a rickety Toyota Hiace bus bearing a carved piece of wood on its roof with the inscription Ibadan – Abuja. Five people are already in the bus. I climb in and take a seat beside a young woman who is busy chewing gum noisily.

"Good morning, Anty," I greet cheerfully. My excitement is refusing to stay repressed.

"Morning," she grunts but I don't take offence. I smile sweetly at her. Our bus is filled and the journey begins. We make a brief stop at Ife Junction, where a large number of women and young girls selling bean cakes swoop on our bus.

"Hot akara, fresh akara, buy o," they sing ceaselessly. I beckon one of them but four literally race to my side of the bus. How do I make them all happy? My plan was to buy twenty naira worth of bean cake, not because I'm hungry but simply to feed my joyous mood. With four of them beseeching me, all wanting me to patronise them and unwittingly heightening my sense of importance, I ask each of them to give me twenty-five naira worth. Sadness can take care of itself, but to get the true benefit of joy, one has to share it is a popular saying and it finds perfect relevance to my situation. Besides, my mother often says that it's always good to extend an act of kindness to others so that we may also receive same wherever we turn.

I go straight to the post-graduate school on my arrival in Abuja and I'm directed to Room 001 when I explain my intention to commence registration for a doctoral programme. I check my bag to ensure my money is intact as I take long, urgent strides towards room 001. I meet two young men standing behind a fairly long counter.

"Good morning, my brothers," I greet breathlessly.

"Good morning," they chorus.

"I'm a new PhD student in this great university and I'm here to start my registration."

"May I see your admission letter, madam?" the taller of the men asks. I open my bag, bring out my letter and brandish it to him. He takes it and glances at it. My heart pounds away for no apparent reason but I maintain an outward serenity.

He looks up from my letter and I breathe an involuntary sigh of relief.

"Okay. What you have to do now is go to your department. You cannot start your registration until you have found a supervisor, a lecturer in your department who will agree to work with you because PhD is a mature programme. When you find a lecturer who wishes to be your supervisor, they will give you a written consent which you will submit here at the PG School. It's only after you have done this that registration forms will be issued to you. Do you understand?"

"Very well, thank you," I say, nodding vigorously.

"By the way, remind me of your department."

"English," I say and turn on my heels.

"Best wishes, madam." He says to my retreating back.

"Thank you," I say without looking back.

"Excuse me, did you do your master's degree in this university? Are you our product?" he shouts after me. I'm slightly irritable. Why does he want to waste my time? I whirl around reluctantly to answer his question.

"No," I say simply, hoping he'll let me go this time.

"In that case, you need to go to the office of the Head of Department of English first. He'll give you all necessary assistance toward getting a supervisor."

I'm slightly confused and a bit apprehensive but I park these thoughts.

"Thank you very much," I say, smiling and feeling genuinely thankful. I hurry to the English Department, where I easily locate the HOD's office. After I answer a few questions from the secretary, he lets me into the HOD's office. I sit in front of him and drink in his features from beneath my lashes. He has a handsome profile with a square jaw.

"Congratulations, Mrs. Oyewole," he says after looking briefly at my admission letter.

"Ms, sir," I correct him with a smile.

"Oh. Sorry, Ms," he murmurs and I smile.

"Yes, Ms. Oyewole. I want you to listen very well so that you don't misunderstand what I'm going to tell you."

I straighten and fix him a stare.

"You may not be pleased with what I'm about to say but part of my duty as the HOD is to let students know the truth at all times and assist them as best as possible."

My heart skips a beat as I shift uncomfortably in my seat.

"It's fairly difficult to find a PhD supervisor due to a mirage of problems confronting universities in Nigeria. The number of academic staff in every university is grossly inadequate; hence, what has to be done is left in the hands of few academics who can only struggle to cope. This situation has continued to have grave consequences on current and prospective students. Surely, you're aware that lecturers are overworked, Ms. Oyewole?"

I shake my head this way and that in confusion.

"University authorities can always employ, sir," I mumble for want of a more suitable response. He gives me I-know-you-wouldn't-understand kind of smile and I feel foolish and ignorant. "You forget about funding, Ms. Oyewole. You employ people only when you have the resources to remunerate them."

I avert my eyes from his amused gaze and stare at my knotted fingers.

"Added to these problems is the long-standing university policy that limits the number of PhD candidates an academic can supervise. No lecturer is allowed to accept to supervise more than a stipulated number of PhD candidates. The result is that there are many PhD applications that have to be turned down, in spite of the qualification and suitability of applicants. For example, I have the maximum university approved PhD students under my supervision as we speak, so I can't accept any additional student. The university authorities wouldn't let me, even if I wanted to."

I swallow nervously as I begin to process the information he's reeling out. I feel the beginning of a headache. Why is he discouraging me?

"All the same, I don't want to discourage you," he says, as if reading my thoughts. "I merely want to equip you with the necessary information and prepare your mind, so that if you approach a lecturer and they decline to supervise you, don't take it personal and don't be discouraged to try another one. Eventually, you will find someone to supervise you because the university wouldn't have offered you a provisional admission if they knew there might be no vacancy. Good luck to you Ms. Oyewole."

I nod uncertainly, tucking in a stray strand of my hair behind my ear. My mood changes, beads of sweat cascade down my face.

I attempt to wipe them with my palm. I feel an overwhelming urge to cry as a sad and lonely melancholy tightens around my heart but I don't succumb to these negative emotions. I manage to pull myself together. Sounding braver than I feel I ask:

"Would you kindly suggest names of lecturers I could try, sir?"

"Eh-r, it's difficult to say. Uh-mm, let me see, are you in language or literature?"

"Literature, sir."

"May be you should try Dr Kolade Durojaiye. His office is on this floor, just two or three offices from the general office. You will find his name on the door. Good luck." He says the last two words in a rush, as if to dismiss me. I climb warily to my feet, mumble a few words of appreciation and head out the door. I easily locate Dr Durojaiye's office and I meet him standing outside, talking to a group of students. He dismisses them as soon as I announce I wish to see him. He saunters into his office and I follow in tow. Dr Durojaiye is tall; his shoulders are broad and he has an athletic body. I notice he has prominent teeth. I immediately become aware of his eyes regarding me. I swallow nervously and fidget. He tells me to sit and I do as he says, murmuring my thanks. I no longer feel the confidence to introduce myself as a new student. Instead I say:

"I'm a prospective PhD candidate in this department, sir. I'm here to request you to kindly be my supervisor."

He regards me for some moments. I feel ill at ease and surreptitiously gaze at him from beneath my lashes. He's looking at me but saying nothing. I become even more uncomfortable. Perhaps he doesn't have space to accommodate me as his student.

"What's your name?" he finally asks.

"Funto Oyewole, sir."

"Are you married?"

What has my marital status got to do with anything? I wonder silently, but to him I say:

"No, sir,"

"Are you engaged or in a serious relationship?"

"Eh-r, no, sir, but I have a ten-year-old daughter, sir."

"I see," he says and resumes gazing at me in a way that makes me feel ill at ease. His lips curl up in a wry smile. Where are we going with this? I wonder but say nothing. He rises from his seat and strolls majestically toward me. He leans over. I lower my gaze. His arm brushes against me - accidentally, I imagine. Oh yes, it must have been accidental because... well, Dr Durojaiye hasn't said or done anything out of place. He has asked about my marital status merely because he wants to know more about me, yes, perhaps he wants to accept me as his PhD student. His other arm is now resting on the back of my chair, touching my back. This makes me uncomfortable so I sit up, not leaning against the backrest. I attempt to swallow hard, but my mouth is dry.

"How does a beautiful, mature woman like you cope without a man?" he asks, his lips inches from my ear. I don't know the appropriate response to give so I say nothing.

"You need a man," he breathes into my ear. My skin crawls at his proximity. "Don't you think so?" he adds. Still I say nothing. I decide the best thing to do is to ignore him although he's still leaning over me and all my senses are hyper-aware. Why is he acting this way, in heaven's name? His behaviour is awkward and embarrassing and inside I'm screaming, back off, but outside I remain calm. He's playing with my braids now, running his hand over them. I cringe, gritting my teeth. What's going on? I glance nervously at the door; he follows my eyes with his and says: "It's locked." An alarm bell sounds in my head. What does he want? Suddenly, he cups my chin in his right palm, raising my face so that we stare at each other. His eyes glow with amusement. "You want to pretend that you don't play?" he asks, pointing his chin at my breasts. My stomach somersaults in a weird way

"Excuse me, sir?"

"You don't play?"

"Play what, sir? Chess, scrabble?"

"Why are you acting like a kid? You are a mature woman; you have a daughter. So, this isn't the first time a man is trying to play with you."

"This is rather awkward sir." The words are out of my mouth before I can stop them.

"There's nothing awkward about anything but I see you are uneasy. Come, get up from there and come and sit on the couch. Let's talk like the adults that we are." I rise from my seat and walk slowly to the couch. Dr Durojaiye mirrors my action; he sits beside me, encroaching into my space. I shift uncomfortably, perching at the edge of the couch. He gets up swiftly and walks toward the door, turns the knob to ensure it's locked, then removes the key, puts it in his right pocket, and comes back and sits beside me. I look questioningly at him but he says nothing. A wicked smile etches at the corners of his mouth. He turns to face me, resting his head on his right hand and propping his elbow on the back of the couch.

"I like you," he says, smiling mischievously. "I am willing to accept you as my PhD student but you must also be prepared to play the game by the rules."

Game? PhD is a game? I wonder silently but say nothing.

"You are not a small girl. You ought to understand that I'm a man with needs. I feel sexual urges and need to satisfy them."

"Aren't you married, sir?"

"What has being married got to do with it? Of course I'm married, but you are aware that a man is a natural polygamist. Besides, if you knew my wife, you would wish I didn't marry her.

Oh, that woman is a thorough nag. She accuses me of drinking excessively, womanising, not loving her and every imaginable misdemeanour. And what do I do? With my status and stature in society, am I going to sue for divorce? That would be ridiculous, to say the least, so I manage and, yes, I make myself happy anyway possible. I look elsewhere for compensation, for the sake of my physical and mental wellbeing; otherwise, I probably would have been locked up in an asylum by now."

I sigh and smile weakly at him because I can't think of what to say. He leans back. My personal space seems safe.

"You are a beautiful woman. Do yourself a favour by agreeing to work with me. You are extremely lucky to have someone like me showing interest in you and, if you agree, I give my consent this minute and put it down on paper."

I can't let him go on like this, giving him the impression that I'm encouraging him or that I'm not sure what I want. I find courage and mumble a demurral but he ignores me. I watch, open-mouthed, as he clasps my hands, giving them a gentle squeeze. Then he starts to caress my cheek, running his fingers down to my chin, which he grasps between his thumb and forefinger. Not satisfied, he leans forward and attempts to plant a kiss on my lips. That is it, I can't take any more. I leap to my feet, yanking him off. I start to pace back and forth, a defiant look on my face.

"Am I rushing you?" he asks but I say nothing. I'm trying hard not to be rude to him, not to insult him, but he's pushing me too hard.

"Okay, I'm sorry. Sit down and relax," he coaxes but I ignore him and head toward the door. I'm aware it's locked but my state of mind makes me bereft of logical reasoning. He comes after me, placing his hands on my shoulders, turning me to face him.

"Am I repellent to you?" he asks.

"No," I mutter, awash with embarrassment.

"Sit down." I do so, this time on the chair directly facing his table, but he insists I return to the couch. Reluctantly, I obey. He takes his seat beside me again.

"There's nothing strange about what I'm trying to do, or you want to tell me you've never been kissed before?"

"I'm not saying it's strange, sir. It's just not appropriate."

"What's inappropriate about a man kissing a woman?"

"Actually, I'm married, sir," I lie.

"You are married? Didn't you tell me earlier you are not?" he asks. I'm exasperated. How do I handle this situation, dear God? How do I respond to this man? What will happen to my ambition, my hopes? It's all so confusing.

"I said that only because I want my certificate to bear my maiden name, sir. I'm married, sir, and I can bring my marriage certificate as proof. I mentally pat myself on the back for my ingenuity.

"Well, you may be married if you choose. You may even have a thousand men in your life if it makes you happy. All I ask of you is a piece of the 'action' and you'll get my consent to supervise you in return. Fair bargain, isn't it?"

I glance up at him. He looks cool and calm. Muscles clench deep in my belly. How do I respond to a prospective randy supervisor? I knot my fingers, staring at them hard, trying to gather my ravaged senses. Again, I'm aware of his eyes on me, regarding me. I peek up at him and watch as he unbuttons his shirt at the top so that I can see a sprinkling of hair. I gape at him in embarrassment. I'm still looking at him, wondering why he's gone this far, when he suddenly loosens his trouser button and, and, what! Am I in the real world or a trance? Have I levitated? Dr Durojaiye has his manhood out of his boxers, holding it to me and muttering, "Rub it for me, baby, come on now, suck me, sweetheart, it won't bite you, play with me, darling."

My mouth drops open. I squeak. I try to keep my revulsion in check. Averting my eyes, I rise and attempt to walk to the door. I have only taken a few steps when he comes after me, lounges at me, pushing me against the wall, his erection pushing, pressing into my belly. He's muttering, "Come on now, you've seen my own, I've got to see yours too, you must suck me, you have to suck me, damn you." Is he raving mad? I claw ruthlessly at his exposed chest like a vicious hyena, digging my nails deeper and deeper into his chest until I feel his hitherto turgid manhood shrink dramatically.

He scampers to safety and I stand menacingly, daring him to come closer. I cast a quick glance at his lower region and find the bastard possesses miserable dog-size manhood. Bloody fool! He must have had too much to drink. How could a supposed academic act so barbarously? My heart rate has gone through the roof. I'm panting as though I have run an uphill race. I'm in shock; I arch him a perfect eyebrow and he stands rooted to the spot, looking beaten. He turns his back to me and pretends to stare out of the window, but I'm aware he's trying to repair his trouser. I wait. There is a knock on the door. He turns abruptly and swiftly brings out the key from his pocket to open it. A young woman of between nineteen and twenty-one walks in. I breathe a sigh of relief; but I obviously need not worry because, within seconds, I watch and marvel as Dr Durojaiye returns to his seat and transforms into a formal persona. What a mask, what a show? I marvel silently as I straighten and sit directly opposite him. I have my back to the young woman.

"Oh yes, Tinuke, you'll have to come back in an hour's time. I have somebody with me, as you can see. She is a senior student."

Tinuke grunts a "yes, sir" and I involuntarily whirl around to take another look at her. She winks at me and skips off.

"I'm a very busy person, Funto. Do you want to do your

registration or do you want to play the rebellious little child?"

I swallow a lump in my throat.

"I can't agree to your proposal," I say simply.

"Very well then, you may leave my office, but if you change your mind before it's too late you'll be lucky," he says dismissively.

I feel weak, exhausted and mortified. I head out the door, closing it behind me as gently as I can. I walk toward the HOD's office as tears start to fall. I choke back a sob. Soon, tears are streaming down my face but I really don't understand why. Why am I crying? I ask under my breath. Dr Durojaiye is very clear about what he wants. I'm also holding my own. So, what are the tears in aid of? Maybe I'm just overwhelmed. Oh, calm down, Funto, you're not going to allow this to traumatise you. I admonish myself as I wipe my tears with the back of my left hand.

I soon arrive at the HOD's office. The secretary says he is busy attending to some students. I wait. I'm thankful as this provides me with an opportunity to pull myself together. The HOD's door opens shortly and students file out. Tinuke is one of them. She greets me cheerfully. I return her greeting with forced excitement, planting a false smile on my face. I'm stunned when she grabs me by the wrist and pulls me up to my feet as if we were long-time friends. She drags me out the door and I let her, bemused. The girl sure has got some nerve, I murmur to myself.

"Are you alright, madam?" she asks breathlessly as soon as we are on the corridor,

"I'm fine, thanks," I say with genuine bemusement.

"You don't look okay to me. You look troubled, and I..."

"Oh, but I'm fine, sincerely," I say in a rush. How is it her business what or how I feel? I don't know her and don't wish to. The only person I wish to see right now is the HOD and I'm in no mood for...

"See, madam," Her voice cuts into my reverie. "I have an idea of what may be the problem here."

"I see, what do you think?" I ask, sounding irritable.

"Every student in this department knows that Dr Durojaiye demands sex from the female students who tickle his fancy. He doesn't pretend."

"Well, thanks, he hasn't asked me for sex, and he's not likely to," I mutter sullenly but Tinuke doesn't allow my irritability to deter her.

"I know what I'm talking about, madam. Successive students eventually come to the realisation that it's best to give him what he wants."

The girl sure won't give up. I resolve to listen to whatever crap she wants to tell me without further interruption.

"I'm a 400-level student, offering one of his courses this semester. It's a compulsory course, not an elective. He told me after our very first interaction that he wanted sex from me. To tell you the truth, madam, I have been obliging him. Does that remove a strand of hair from my body? I came to his office when you were there because my class is scheduled to have a test in his course tomorrow and he promised to give me the test questions a day before to enable me practise and write well. I'll go and meet him now and he'll give me the questions. Then, at about 8.00pm, I'll go to his office, he'll be waiting for me and I'll give him what he wants. He has never invited me outside the campus; we do it in his office, on his table, and so it's convenient and fast. It doesn't stop me from having a boyfriend and I do have one. My boyfriend can't ever find out. I'm not the only student Dr Durojaiye sleeps with but he's fair to every one of us. If he sleeps with you, he also finds a way to help you pass his course so that you don't feel aggrieved. I decided to help you because I noticed you looked confused and worried, and especially because he mentioned that you are a PhD student. You'll get your PhD in time and put Dr Durojaiye behind you, if you cooperate with him. Think about it, madam." Tinuke finishes her speech and without waiting for me to respond, skips off like a ten-year-old, leaving me standing. I turn and walk to the secretary's office.

"May I see the HOD now, sir?" I ask the secretary.

"He's free, you may see him," he says and I enter. The HOD smiles kindly at me, pointing to a chair opposite him. I sit and swallow nervously.

"How did it go, Ms Oyewole? Did he agree?

"Eh-r-r, no sir, n-not really, sir."

"Poor you." The HOD's voice is quiet and soft. I'm completely stumped. He gazes at me and furrows his brow. Does he know what I know? How do I recount my experience to this kind-looking man? Is he aware of Dr Durojaiye's mistreatment of his female students? Should I tell him about it? Perhaps he's not aware. Maybe he is but what if he himself is also like that? I feel nervous, off-balance.

"Sir, Dr Durojaiye said that, eh-r, actually sir, he explained why he can't agree to be my supervisor. He said that eh –r, well, I think, eh-r…" I can't even string a sentence together. I give up the effort and take a deep breath. I can't seem to steady my nerves. My heart is pounding and my breathing is shallow. The HOD looks kindly at me and there is a hint of pity hidden in the depth of his eyes.

"Go and try Prof Lara Owoyemi, woman to woman, I'm sure she will assist you," he says. Really? There is one of my own in this department and it takes the HOD this long to let me know? I jump to my feet, energised and freshly hopeful. I forget to mutter words of thanks.

"Ask anybody where her office is. Best wishes, Ms Oyewole," his voice rings after me as I race out the door. My mind goes to Deyemi as I go in search of Prof Owoyemi. She must be in class now, being taught along with her classmates, or, she's on break and playing with the new friends she must have made. I can't wait to have her home in December when the term will come to an end. Why do I miss her so much? We are still in September and she left home just last week. I stop in my tracks to say a prayer under my breath for my adorable daughter, then, I quickly resume my walk.

Four

The story of women is the story of compassion and empathy. Women are innately sympathetic because they are bearers and conduits of life. They are nurturers. They see things in their pristine, peaceful and harmonious mode, just as they are wired to feel disharmony when it occurs. When a woman enters a room filled with five hundred crying babies, she can decipher the cry of her own. It's a unique phenomenon. I smile a knowing smile as I go in search of Prof Owoyemi. She is a woman like me and, because she possesses an innate capacity to discern, will sense my anguish upon setting her eyes on me. With her, I will find succour. I sigh in relief when I locate her office and knock timidly on the door.

"Yes, come in," she answers. I open the door and ease myself in.

"Good afternoon, ma," I greet. Her office is spacious and elegantly furnished. Immediately to my right is a large cardboard attached to the wall; there are photographs everywhere on the cardboard. My eyes flick over the cardboard briefly and settle on her but I'm immediately taken aback by her looks. I don't know what I had expected but she doesn't fit into my mental picture of her. She is sitting behind a large wood desk looking lean, pale, dull, almost haggard, dishevelled and uncared-for. Her eyes are hollow and flat, as if there is no life in them, and her cheeks are sunken. Why does she look like this? My heart goes out to her. She seems to be the evidence of the HOD's remark about how university teachers are over-worked. Why would a professor look like this? I want to hug her, comfort her and urge her to take a greater interest in her wellbeing and appearance.

"Yes, how may I help you?" she asks curtly. I lower my gaze. Her curtness unnerves me and I'm momentarily fidgety. She rises to pin yet another photograph to the cardboard, gives me sufficient time to find my voice.

"Yes, madam, what do you want?" she prompts as she walks back to her seat.

"I'm a prospective PhD candidate in this department, ma. The HOD says he would be delighted if you would kindly agree to be my supervisor, ma."

"I see, what's your name?"

"Funto Oyewole, ma."

"Well, I think I can accommodate you."

I beam as my subconscious stirs in jubilation.

"As soon as you finish with your registration, you will bring to me the proposal you submitted to the PG School and we will take it up from there. In the meantime, you will prepare three possible topics on which you may base your thesis. You will do a presentation of the three topics before me, justifying your rationale for selecting the topics and I will approve one of them, eventually."

"Yes Prof, thank you very much, I'm very grateful. Prof, I'm required to obtain a consent letter from you which I'm to submit at the PG school before I can have access to registration forms."

"Oh, sure, I'm aware of that," she says and pauses as if contemplating something. I'm expectant and a little edgy.

"What do you do for a living?" she asks suddenly, fixing me a hard stare. I'm thrown.

"Eh-r…, actually, Prof, I don't have a regular employment at the moment," I explain and her expression clouds.

"I see. What do you do for a living then, business?"

"Not really, Prof."

"What do you mean not really? You must have a means of livelihood."

"Well, yes, I was gainfully employed by the Federal Ministry of Home Affairs until six months ago, but I was affected by the rationalisation exercise at the ministry. However, my dream has always been to retire as an academic. When I lost my job, I saw it as an opportunity to fulfil my age-long dream."

"Very impressive. You are married?"

"No, I'm not."

"How then do you intend to finance your programme? Perhaps, you have a huge savings account, boyfriend or wealthy and supportive family behind you?"

"N – n – not exactly, but I'm positive God will see me through."

"That'll be leaving things to chance and somebody who aspires to run a doctoral programme ought to have more intelligence than that."

"I'm a very optimistic person, ma. I truly trust in God also."

"Don't delude yourself. There are practical things you will require as you go along. You'll need books and other study materials. What has God to do with that, or are you a religious fundamentalist? Where are you from?"

"I'm from Ibadan, Oyo State. I'm not a religious fundamentalist, ma."

"Tell me truthfully then, do you have people who can support you financially?

"I have my mother."

"Good. What does your mother do?" she asks and I'm exasperated. Does she have something in mind that I'm yet to decipher? I try for comportment.

"She sells yam flour at Beere market in Ibadan," I explain calmly, but this only elicits raucous laughter from her, making me flinch. Is she mocking me?

"If that isn't interesting, tell me what is." The sarcasm in her voice ravages my soul, I cringe. You want to do a PhD?" she asks and I nod. She resumes talking. "You are a terrific dreamer," she says with a throated laugh. My heart sinks. Unbidden and unwelcome tears pool in my eyes. Prof Owoyemi looks directly into my eyes, our eyes lock, mine frosty and hers intense.

"I'll be straight with you, umm – what's your first name again?"

"Funto," I mumble.

"Yes, Funto, you don't talk like someone who's ready to embark on a PhD programme. An unemployed, husbandless, middle-aged woman whose only relation sells yam flour in a local market seems more suited for a tramp. When did loafers become qualified to dream, let alone aspire for a doctoral degree?" She queries, fixing me with a stern gaze.

I can't believe she said those words. I'm neither a tramp nor a loafer, but I try not to be angry. I remind myself that women are also the worst critics of other women and that educated women prefer to talk about logic and rationalisation. The more educated some women are, the more they tend to distance themselves from their knowingness, from themselves, thereby losing their innate quality of empathy. Some educated women tend not to think in kaleidoscopes; they lose their ability to recognise multiplicity of colours and see things in black and white only. Has education injured Prof Owoyemi's innate female attributes? I stare quizzically at her but she ignores my expression and continues talking.

"You've just told me you are required to obtain a consent letter from your would-be supervisor before you can start your registration. Did you think I would write such an important letter just like that?"

What? Is that all there is to her ranting? A lump forms in my throat. I swallow it. Prof Owoyemi is looking at me. Her look is serious, almost strained because her jaw has suddenly clenched and her eyes appear tight. Is she angry, upset or shocked that I dare to aspire to embark on a PhD without a huge bank account? What's going on? What have I said or done to warrant the sudden hostile atmosphere that I'm beginning to sense between us? I can't believe what she's telling me. All my senses are hyper-alert.

"I ride a V-Boot at the moment. I know people like you would regard it as a status car but it's not so to me because it's not padded. I want to buy a padded V-Boot. I'm a full professor, for crying out loud, and mere senior lecturers are riding bigger and better cars." My jaw drops, I stare at her in astonishment. She seems to be reading my mind.

"You don't think I deserve a padded V-Boot, do you? Fine, think about this, I'm presently accommodated on campus; tell me, where do I move to when I retire if I don't build my own house? Do you honestly believe I can build a decent house from my meagre salary? Do you know how much a professor earns? Do you know my salary with all my years of training and absolute devotion to research and writing?" The atmosphere between us has changed completely. It is now charged with pure hostility. I groan in frustration, rolling my eyes heavenward.

"My world and desires are very clear, my dear PhD-aspirer; my world does not resemble the mysterious, vague hues of many of my colleagues. I make my stand known to my students, especially my senior students, the class you wish to join. I demand financial compensation from them because I work hard to impact knowledge unto them. Haven't you heard the proverb, where one works is where one eats? If the government does not have a sense of fair play to remunerate me properly, the students who are the direct beneficiaries of my high intellect must compensate me. It's a fair deal, if you ask me. My relationship with my students is strictly official, though cordial. I teach them well, I don't miss classes. I work hard and insist on being adequately compensated. If you are serious about becoming a PhD candidate under my supervision, you must have thirty-thousand naira to get the consent letter you are required to submit at the PG School. After your registration, I will spell out other terms of engagement to you."

Prof Owoyemi is clearly the limit, I realise sadly. A part of me wants to laugh at her crudity, another part is horrified, but there is also a part that is seething with humiliation at the undeserved insult she's been hauling at me. This part wants to dominate my psyche right now because hot tears stand in my eyes but I don't succumb. I blink back the tears, glowering at her. My blood is boiling with uncontrollable rage. Damn Prof 'Cash and Carry'! Anger is good, I tell myself firmly as I embrace it and prepare to give it full expression. Isn't it better to be angry than tearful? I turn my gaze from her and scan her office as I organise my response. Maybe I should calm down, I tell myself. Is it worth joining her in a senseless tirade? Perhaps I should demonstrate maturity. I manage to put my anger in check.

"Thank you very much, Prof. I guess I need time to process all the information you've given to me," I say as calmly as I can.

"How much time do you think you've got? It's either you have what it takes or you don't."

That's about all I can take. Prof 'cash and carry' sure wants to have it from me and I will have no choice but to give her an overdose of her own medicine.

"I'm appalled by your crudity, Prof," I lash out, feeling very good with myself. "I came to you full of hope, especially as you are a woman like me. I thought women were more compassionate, empathetic and mature. I thought women were not driven by blind, obsessive and dangerous ambition. I thought women didn't make unreasonable demands from anyone and especially not from..."

"Shut the hell up and get out of my office!" she roars. "I know your type," she continues contemptuously. I laugh melodramatically. I'm determined to engage her, foolish woman.

"I know your type," she repeats but I say nothing. In the meantime, I concentrate on arching my eyebrow at her. "You are among the ignorant women who foolishly condone and encourage male domination by believing that women don't deserve the good things of life. Why should my gender prevent me from enjoying what my other colleagues enjoy?" she asks shamelessly and I realise it's pointless arguing with her. The woman's foolishness is beyond compare. I get ready to leave but not before I give her a parting shot.

"You are right about one thing, Prof, I don't wish to be your student and people like you ought to be flushed out of our country's revered ivory towers

"Get out! I don't need an insolent bitch like you as my student," she retorts, scowling at me, fury emanating from every pore. I rise swiftly to my feet and head out the door without another word or backward glance. Nonsense!

I'm back in the HOD's office. I sink into a chair, hunching my shoulders. My world seems to be slowly but steadily crumbling around me. Why, in heaven's name, are my hopes and dreams being cruelly dashed? No, no, Funto, don't think like that. I self-admonish as I await the HOD's attention. He's busy looking into a file. A second later he glances up and his eyes meet mine.

"Were you in luck with Prof Owoyemi?" he asks in his characteristic soft voice.

"No sir, she's rather occupied," I say with the boldness and bravery of someone who has had a little alcohol.

"In that case, you will go and try Dr Raphael Douglas, and if he declines, your last resort may have to be Prof Charles Ephraim."

I turn this over in my mind briefly. My last resort, what does that mean? Anyway, I thank him and take my leave.

I find Dr Douglas in his office talking to a middle-aged woman whom I presume is also a lecturer. He gestures for me to take a seat on a cream-coloured couch. I sit and wait. They end their discussion and Dr Douglas turns to me.

"Are you okay, madam? You look worried," he observes. I lower my gaze. This is a new experience. It's good to know that there is a lecturer who can decipher a worried look from a student.

"I'm fine, sir," I mutter, clasping my hand for distraction as I'm aware of his eyes on me.

"Alright then, madam, how may I be of use to you?"

I like the way you talk to me, sir, I mutter under my breath, but to him, I say: "I am interested in running a PhD programme here, sir, and I'm in search of a supervisor."

"Ah, sorry, my sister, you are two weeks late. I accepted two new PhD students two weeks ago. Take a look at this, he says, pointing to an office file sitting on his crowded desk. "It's the file containing the work of one of my students, a very hard-working lady. Oh, I would have taken you straight away but with the two students I accepted two weeks ago I now have the maximum number of PhD students permitted by the university, unless you can wait until at least one of them graduates."

My heart clenches anew and releases a fresh wave of silent sobbing. Why am I so unlucky? Here is a man whose attitude and disposition to students is pleasantly different. What can I do to ward off the ill-luck that seems to be dogging my every step?

"Try some other lecturers in the department." His voice distracts me from my gloomy introspection.

"You are the third lecturer I have approached, sir, and it's been rejection all the way," I blurt out in frustration.

"Don't be so discouraged, my sister, I'm sure you will find a supervisor soon if you persist in your efforts," he says kindly.

"I'm losing hope, sir. What am I doing wrong?" I cry, thoroughly exasperated.

"Take it easy, my sister, most of the things we worry to death over are hardly worth the effort we dissipate on them. We are often obsessive in chasing after vanity without realising the foolery of our action." Is he trying to preach at me? I wonder silently, looking at him. He's still talking.

"I was interacting with a 400-level student who came to my office last week. I said to him: 'Lukman, you are almost through with your degree programme,' and he said, 'yes, sir.' I asked him, 'what plan do you have after graduation?' He said he would go for national service. I asked, 'after NYSC, what will you do?' He said he would get a good job and settle down. I asked, 'after settling down, what will you do?' He said he would find a beautiful woman to marry. I asked, 'after getting married what will you do?' He said he would start a family, raise his own children. I asked, 'after raising your own children, what will you do?' He said he would train them as best as he could and they would be very successful. I asked, 'after training your children and they attain utmost level of accomplishment, what will you do?' He fell silent. I said, 'Lukman, you would die.'

"You see, my sister, we all came to this world with a death sentence hanging over our head. We are required merely to do our best at all times and spread goodness to others. All the stress and strain we put ourselves through are needless, wasteful. You'll find a supervisor, don't give up, but don't injure yourself with worry, okay?"

I nod vigorously.

"God bless you, madam," Dr Douglas says solemnly as I rise to leave.

I don't go back to the HOD. Hasn't he told me that one Prof Ephraim may be my last resort? I may as well take my chances with him without further delay. I search hastily for his office. Thankfully, he's in. He responds to my greeting with warmth and offers me a seat. I begin to relax.

"I'm a prospective PhD student in this department, sir, and I would be grateful if you would kindly supervise me," I say without preamble, but I'm sure my erratic breathing must be audible.

"I would be delighted to be your supervisor," he says with a wry smile, rising to his feet. Did I hear right? I've got a supervisor at last, without conditions, no bargaining and no hassling? Goodness! I'm on top of the world! I observe that Prof Ephraim's office is elegantly furnished. I touch the dark wood table in front of me and tingle as if it has life. Prof Ephraim is still standing. He has his back turned to me as he searches through a book shelf containing mostly Bachelor and Master degrees bound essays. I concentrate my gaze on his features. My supervisor is a man mountain, statuesque, massive, dark-skinned and balding and seems possessed of groggy energy. His hands and feet are fat and he has high-rounded buttocks. I drag my gaze from him and momentarily settle on his desk which is stacked with piles of paper. The desk is also massive. There is a pen in a matching stand, an ivory letter opener and a silver name-plate similar to the one on his door.

"The PG School requires me to obtain a letter of consent from you, sir. The letter is a condition for the issuance of registration forms, sir," I add by way of explanation.

"No problem, but you will have to come back for the letter."

"Sir?"

"I said you will have to come back for the letter as I'm not in the mood for writing a letter right now."

"I came from Lagos, sir."

"You came from Lagos?"

"Yes, sir."

"Are you going back to Lagos today?"

"Yes, sir, I have nowhere to pass the night in Abuja, sir."

"Hmm, in that case, you will go back to Lagos and come back before the end of the week."

My heart somersaults. Prof Ephraim speaks gently and calmly but in spite of the gentleness of his words, there's something faintly bullish about him. In his manner perhaps, or his posture as he stands, maybe in his broad body, his huge hands, I don't really know. I listen, confused. He's still talking.

"Alternatively, you can find a hotel to lodge and come back tomorrow from two o'clock in the afternoon."

My brow creases as I continue to stare at him. He turns to face me and I surreptitiously lower my gaze.

"Have you told me your name?"

"Ah, I'm sorry, sir, my name is Olufunto, Oyewole, but people call me Funto."

"Are you married?" Why is my marital status so important to everyone?

"No, sir, but I have a ten-year-old daughter who has just started secondary school in Lagos. I enrolled her in a boarding school last week, sir."

"What do you do for a living?" Another sore point? I roll my eyes in exasperation.

"Nothing at the moment, sir, I want to devote all my energy and resources at my disposal to working on my PhD, sir."

"That's okay, Funto."

"Eh-r, excuse me, sir, I don't have enough money to take up hotel lodging. I'll go back to Lagos today and come back in two day's time. That'll be Thursday sir, today is Tuesday."

"That's alright." I breathe a long sigh of relief.

"Let me warn you from the beginning," he says and I panic. What have I done now?

"I'm a no-nonsense person. I don't compromise standards simply because things are not the way they ought to be. I always let my students know this so that they'll understand why I may have to discipline them as necessary to ensure that they understand my role as their supervisor and theirs as my student." My face clouds in confusion but I'm silent. He stares fixedly at me. I struggle to calm my nerves. "You may leave now; have a safe trip back to Lagos."

"Thank you, sir. I rise clumsily and head out the door. The HOD is in his office.

"Prof Ephraim has agreed to supervise me, sir," I announce.

"Congratulations! I'm very happy for you." I smile weakly, unable to hide my lack of excitement. "You will do precisely as Prof tells you, okay? Once you are able to do this, you'll have no problem with him."

What exactly is the HOD telling me? I don't even know how to tell him to clarify his statements. My mood darkens and I look sad and morose.

"Alright, I'll be specific," he says in answer to my unspoken question. "You see, it's not in my place to tell you these things but, given the trouble you've gone through, I'm moved by compassion to let you know that there are three things you must have if you want to work with Prof Ephraim. The first one is patience, the second is patience, and the third is patience. If you are armed with patience, patience and patience, you'll have absolutely no problem working with Prof. Good luck to you on your programme, Ms. Oyewole."

I listened to him with utmost attentiveness but failed

miserably to make sense out of his speech. What has the HOD told me? I feel completely numb. My subconscious appears to have also emigrated or been struck dumb. I walk out of his office and stand in the open office, momentarily pacing about. What do I do? I dash into the secretary's office.

"Well done, sir, would you do me a favour, sir?"

"Yes, what do you want?" he asks without looking up from the file he's peering at. "Could you kindly link, I mean, introduce me to a PhD student in this department, any one at all? I'm in dire need of some guidance. He looks up. He seems to be turning it over in his mind. I stand calmly, trying to mask my anxiety. A man in his mid-thirties walks in and stands still, looking at the secretary and at me in turn. The secretary's face lights up and I feel my nerves calm instinctively.

"Akpabio," the secretary addresses the man, "this lady needs your help." Turning to me, he says, "Madam, this man will guide you as you wish."

"Akpabio, you want to see me?"

"Yes, sir, but I guess I should carry out the assignment you've just given to me. I'll be back to see you, sir."

Akpabio and I walk out and stand on the corridor, our hands on the rails.

"I'm a fresh PhD student. I want you to give me information about anything and everything about the programme, the department, the lecturers, anything at all, please," I plead, my voice bordering on hysterics. He regards me with amusement. He appears to find my confusion mildly entertaining.

"You have to be specific now. What do you really want to know?"

"Okay, tell me about my supervisor, Prof Ephraim."

"Prof Ephraim is your supervisor? Ol' girl, you are unlucky o." My heart skips a beat.

"I'm unlucky? Why did you say that?"

"You didn't find out about him before you approached him to be your supervisor?"

"Did I need to?"

"Of course you did."

"Well, I didn't."

"Then, I'm afraid it was a mistake on your part. You are supposed to be a research student, for goodness sake."

"Never mind my mistake, just tell me about him." I'm perspiring and my head is in a whirl. Akpabio sighs, clears his throat and starts talking.

"Prof Charles Ephraim is an exceedingly hostile man with infinite capacity for hate. He hates his colleagues in the academia because he regards them as being arrogant. He hates the senior non-academic staff because they are not cerebral. He hates the lower cadre non-academic staff because they are poor. He reviles all students for lacking in intelligence, although students of his own ethnic group are exempted from this hate. He hates the poor, the sick and the needy for constituting a nuisance to what would otherwise have been a clean and decent society. In particular, he is contemptuous of women, except, as I pointed out earlier, those of his own ethnic stock. His attitude to members of his own gender is somewhat more complicated. Undergraduate students avoid taking his courses except when he handles compulsory courses. I think Prof Ephraim also hates himself for reasons only he can fathom."

"Stop!" I cry. "Sorry for interrupting you. Is that the reason why the HOD advised me to be patient with him?"

"You mean Dr Okoroafor already told you about Prof Ephraim?"

"Who is Dr Okoroafor? Is that the HOD's name?"

"You mean you didn't even know your own head of

department's name? Are you sure you are a student of this department? Look, all your senses must be alert. Research is the name of the game here, baby, and you are not going to be conducting research in your topic only. You will also be researching into personality types and idiosyncrasies of all the lecturers and even non-teaching staff of the department and outside of it. You have a lot to learn. They are a curious lot and you are in for surprises. Most of these surprises, I must warn you, will be very unpleasant. Welcome to the National University of Nigeria. By the way, what's your name?"

"Funto Oyewole."

"You are Yoruba?"

"Yes."

"Ah, you don't stand a chance with Prof," he says darkly. I wince involuntarily.

"Why not?"

"Why ask me? Haven't I told you enough? Anyway, there could still be a chance for you."

"Really? How?"

"If you quickly change your name, if you took a name from his ethnic stock. Prof would be happy with you."

"You are clowning," I accuse.

"Clowning? Okay, we shall see."

"Where is he from?"

"Why are you asking me? He's a Nigerian and you are a research student. Why not find out?"

He turns abruptly and walks into the secretary's office. I stand immobilised, paralysed by his unflattering remarks. Finally, I put my head down as I proceed to the gate, keeping my eyes on the ground, blurred by my watery tears.

Five

I don't stop over in Ibadan to see my mother in spite of the promise I made to her. I just wish to be on my own now. I need time to process all the information Akpabio has given me. Even more importantly, I need to reconsider my decision regarding my ambition to embark on a PhD. Isn't it better to back off and consider other means of survival rather than throw myself into a quagmire? There are indications that the journey toward attaining a PhD might be tortuous. Do I possess the physical and psychological will to undertake, let alone accomplish it? I'm a psychological coward and will do anything to prevent pain. Wouldn't I be knowingly, wilfully bringing pain on me by starting the programme in view of the scenarios Akpabio has very vividly painted? Do I take my mother's advice and jettison my dream? Life as a poultry farmer seems more alluring now. I turn this over in my mind but the thought makes me recoil. I'm in dire need of advice, I resolve. My mother? No! I know who to see; it's my friend, Folake. Perhaps my mother is right, but it would be foolish to go and recount the unsavoury tales of my first day as a PhD student to her when I'm aware of her pessimistic disposition toward the idea. How I wish my daughter was not in a boarding school. Her presence alone could go a long way in giving me succour. "I miss you, Deyemi." I mutter under my breath. Thank God for Folake.

Folake'll be at her boyfriend's house. She deserves her

privacy but the seriousness of my situation demands her urgent attention and I trust she'll be willing to grant me audience. Folake is thirty-two, six years younger than me. She's single, gainfully employed as a relationship manager in a fast-growing beverage company. If I know her as well as I imagine, she's not desperately searching for a spouse. She doesn't fret or push; she lives in the moment and takes each day as it comes. She's not likely to fall into the kind of emotional pitfall I have fallen into. She's warm, caring and very accommodating. We've become so close that we are almost like sisters. We are different in a number of ways but we feel and profess genuine affection toward each other. Whereas I'm circumspect, she's a talker and quick to friendship in a way that I am not. She's gregarious and has a lot of friends but she's content with only one boyfriend at a time. She's currently dating Geoffrey and their relationship appears to hold promise. She complements me and I enjoy her friendship to no end. Two is better than one is a widely accepted cliché and since my mother's bias makes her unsuitable for my purpose, Folake, who's not only educated but can also be regarded as my contemporary, is the person I need to see and talk with, I resolve firmly.

Five hours later, I step into the Lagos heat like I'm wearing it, it saps everything, especially as it hasn't rained for some days. I alight at the Bar Beach bus stop on Victoria Island and start walking toward Geoffrey's house. I tell myself for the umpteenth time that I'm not going to get worked up about the issues at hand. They are clear enough and all I require from my friend is practical advice. Geoffrey lives in a compact bungalow that sits squarely overlooking the Bar Beach. He's one of the 'Lagos Big Boys' dealing in automobiles. I breathe a sigh of relief when I meet his younger brother a few metres away from the house and he tells me Geoffrey has gone out with a friend but that Folake is in. For reasons I don't quite understand, I always feel awkward whenever I visit Folake in Geoffrey's house. Does he resent me or my occasional intrusions into their privacy? I can't tell but there's something about his behaviour whenever I visit that makes me feel unwanted, as if I'm some kind of parasite.

I try not to pursue these thoughts; rather, I try to convince myself that I'm being unnecessarily presumptuous and possibly unfair to Geoffrey. Anyway, I'm very certain about one thing: Geoffrey loves Folake to distraction and I'm glad that my friend is happy. As I press the bell at the gate, my stomach begins a fresh whirlwind, churning with all the information and confusion I want Folake to help me deal with. She comes running out as soon as she hears my voice. Again, I warn myself silently not to get emotional but a huge lump suddenly forms in my throat as I hug her. I know she's surprised at my unusual theatrics. We are not used to hugging each other when we see. I try to hold myself together but fail miserably as tears pool in my eyes and I sob quietly.

"Awww, Fun-un-to," she croons, disentangling from me and holding me at arm's length. She regards me for a second and heads inside without another word. I trail after her. We pass into a corridor, a series of grey painted doors on either side, before she opens one of the doors to usher me in. I have come to meet her at Geoffrey's a number of times, but she has always entertained me in the sitting room. She has apparently sensed the seriousness of my situation and wants us to talk in utmost privacy. This is the best place to talk. The furnishings are ultra-modern, very now.

"What's up with you, Funto? I thought big girls don't cry," she says, trying to sound nonchalant. I glance down at the Formica tabletop, tracing a pattern on it with my index finger before glancing at her.

"I'm in fresh crisis, Folake," I blurt out and proceed to give her as much detail as possible of my experience in Abuja. She smiles when I finish but her eyes crinkle at the corners with concern.

"You exaggerate; I thought there was a huge problem."

"I exaggerate? How can you talk like that?"

"Nigeria is warming up for a democratic experience, I think you'd do well in politics considering the number of hyperbolic expressions you've used while recounting your experience in Abuja."

"Politics?"

"I was only pulling your leg, but you amuse me by the way you magnify issues and give people credit they don't deserve."

"Why don't you stop rambling and say something sensible," I chastise, beginning to relax.

"You should have chosen the one that asked for sex."

"What! Are you out of your mind? Thank God Geoffrey is not here to hear this."

"Let's leave Geoffrey out of our conversation. On a serious note, Funto, it won't be fair to abandon your dream. Even at the risk of praising you, you're a bright, young woman; you can't allow obstacles, doubts or self-esteem issues to stand between you and your goals. You have more than what it takes to embark on a PhD programme. It's unfortunate that people find it convenient to trample on others openly and brazenly in order to be happy. In my view, the randy professor might be easier to deal with than the sadist, but it's a choice between the devil and the deep blue sea, really. Besides, everybody can't be like the young, unfortunate undergraduate who, sadly for our country and our future, has mastered the tricks of a coquetry and seduction and is able to apply it to her lecturer's pleasure."

"What do I do?"

"You've chosen the sadist, you can't pull back, go on, work with him, and I'll stand behind you every step of the way. I'll support you in every way possible. Dr Funto Oyewole!" She hails and genuflects in mock obeisance. I can't help but smile at her, in spite of my poignant sadness. My elegantly sophisticated friend is right, the PhD journey has begun and there can be no turning back.

"Give me five, joor!" Folake enthuses. Our palms slap together and slide across each other. I'm energised by her boundless enthusiasm. I come to a quick decision; I'll have to sell my car and commit the proceeds to funding my programme – frequent travels to Abuja, books and other study materials. Folake agrees with my plan and suggests we give the car to Geoffrey so as to get a good price.

As I prepare to leave, Folake hands me a hand pack, says it's for my dinner. As I search my brain for kind words to express my thanks, she places her hands on my shoulders.

"Funto, I think you and Deyemi should move in with me at my Bode Thomas home in Surulere."

My mouth falls open. "Are you kidding me?"

"I'm not. I don't want you worrying about house rent for the next three years while you run your programme. Deyemi is in boarding school; she'll be coming home only on holiday and I spend most of my weekends here with Geoffrey. Why do I have to keep a two-bedroom apartment under lock when I have a friend who is temporarily financially constrained?"

"I don't know what to say," I whisper.

"Good, so, don't say anything. Move in with me and save the money you would otherwise have to spend on rent. I promise I won't disturb your writing when I come around." I feel a freshness of relief overwhelm me.

"Yes, Folake, I agree to your proposition and I'm deeply grateful," I murmur. "But what about Geoffrey?"

"Yes, what about him?"

"Do you think he'll like the idea of me and Deyemi moving in with you? I mean...,"

"I know what you mean; I'm not married to Geoffrey. He doesn't control me. Besides, you seem to think that he doesn't like you and I believe you are not being fair to him. He may not want to get involved with girls' talk but he thinks highly of you. Why don't you try to get to know him closely and discover who he truly is?"

"I admit my failings. I must work on my thought process."

"I will talk to Geoffrey too, to change his attitude."

"May be you should leave him alone for a moment. Let's see how far my reorientation can go."

"It will go far, trust me. Geoffrey is a cool guy."

"Before nko, on whose side will you be if not that of your bobo?"

"Yes o. I no deny at all." She says jocularly.

"Oh, well, what can I say? Thank you, again," I mumble.

"It's you I have to thank for accepting my offer, Funto. I think you should run along now, before the evening traffic traps you." She says, changing her expression from jovial to serious.

"You are damn right." I skip off without another word. As I walk to the bus stop, my mind goes back to the argument I had with my mother over my insistence on staying in Lagos. I was right after all, I mutter under my breath. In which other city would I have found a friend who would literally beg to accommodate not just me but also my daughter? I burst into a song as I walk.

Ni'lu Eko yi l'emi ti ri ranlowo o	*It's in this Lagos that I find help*
Mori ran lowo to'gbemi ga	*I find help that lifts me to greater heights*
Ni'lu Lagosi l'emi ti pade ore o	*It's in Lagos city I find a true friend*

Ore ti oun f"aiye mi fun re	*A friend that wants improvement in my life*
Af'ole l'ole pe Eko odun	*Only an indolent says Lagos is not sweet enough*
Af'ole Eko dun ojoyin lo	*Only an indolent because Lagos is sweeter than honey*

"Obalende, CMS, Obalende, CMS!" an excited-looking conductor hanging dangerously on a danfo shouts. I wave down the bus and run happily toward it. I find a space by the window and sit, humming and smiling as the bus gathers speed. Ni Ilu Eko yi...

Six

I'm in front of my supervisor's office, waiting, because he is not in. He's probably in one of the lecture halls, teaching. I ask a bored-looking man in the departmental office if he has seen Prof Ephraim today and he says no. I'm pacing about the long corridor now, allowing my eyes to settle on each closed door for some moments, trying to memorise the lecturers' names. I'm a research student, I echo Akpabio's admonition. I wish I can find a place to sit outside my supervisor's office. I've been standing for a while and my legs are beginning to tire. It must be because I haven't eaten and it's past two o'clock. I glance up and sight rolls of benches across where I stand and contemplate going there to sit, just to rest for a while. I perish the thought when I realise I may not be able to see my professor from a sitting position across his office. What if he walks in without my noticing him? All I need is patience so that I'll be the first to see him as he approaches. It's been two whole days since my last visit and I have no doubt in my mind that he would have written the consent letter which he will simply hand over to me and I'll scurry off to the PG School for submission and issuance of registration forms. I glance up instinctively and there he is. I beam at him as he reaches his door and searches in his trouser pockets for his key.

"Good day, sir," I breathe, expanding the grin on my face.

"Good day," he answers curtly. I look down at my feet, trying to stifle my goofy grin. He opens his door and walks in. I remain standing outside, ostensibly to allow him some moment to settle down. I wait for some time but he doesn't invite me to come in even after a considerable length of time. I move closer to the entrance of his office and tilt my head to one side so that he can catch a glimpse of me. As if on cue, he raises his head and our eyes lock but he says nothing. I stand for a few more minutes and repeat my performance but still he says nothing. I summon my courage and walk briskly into his office, taking a seat directly opposite him.

"Well done, sir," I murmur. He's silent

"I've come to collect the letter of consent, sir." He's mute still. What can I do or say to make my supervisor talk? I search my brain frantically for ideas.

"I must really thank you for agreeing to supervise me, sir. I'm truly grateful, sir, and only God can adequately reward you. You are a wonderful and extremely kind-hearted man, sir. You are a rare gem." He seems to be enjoying the encomiums judging by the way he moves importantly in his seat. I pause and wait.

"Eh-r, I have not written the letter so you will wait while I scribble something on paper right now." I roll my eyes at him knowing he isn't looking at me. I say nothing and the silence between us stretches. Finally, he picks up a pen and a piece of paper and begins to write. I celebrate quietly. He finishes writing, folds the letter neatly into three, puts it in a white long envelope, seals it and hands it over to me. I take it in both hands and climb quickly to my feet.

"Thank you, sir, I'm very grateful, sir," I say breathlessly and head out the door.

"Funto!" he calls. I stop in my tracks and turn around to look at him. "Don't fill the registration form on your own. Bring it here so that both of us can go through together and fill it accordingly."

"Yes, sir," I say happily and leave.

I'm back from the PG School. I'm sitting facing my professor. I place my registration form on the table, a pen dangling between my thumb and my forefinger.

"What's the first item?" he asks.

"Name in full, sir, surname first.

"Right. Next?"

"Age, sir."

"Ah, how old are you?"

"Thirty-eight, sir."

"Interesting, you are thirty-eight in 1998. You were born in 1960?"

"Yes, sir."

"Were you born in October too?"

"No, sir, I was born in April, April 20."

"Well, you are still a child of independence; you heralded it so to say. Next?"

"Address, sir."

"Ok, where do you live?"

"Lagos, sir."

"I mean your permanent home address?"

"It's Lagos still, sir".

"Are you from Lagos State?"

"No, I'm from Ibadan, Oyo State but I live in Lagos permanently, sir."

"You are a Lagos woman?"

"Yes, sir, proudly so, sir."

"That's alright. Next?"

"Sponsorship, sir."

"Yes, who is your sponsor?"

"Nobody, sir, I intend to sponsor myself, sir."

"Alright then, write self in the column. Next?"

"Type of programme, we have full-time or part-time in bracket, sir."

"Oh, yes, write part-time."

"Sir?"

"I said; write part-time, so that you will have no problem if you are not as productive as the university wants you to be."

"On the contrary sir, I shall be very productive. I shall devote my energy, time as well as all my resources to the programme, sir. I'm interested in running a full-time programme, sir."

"Well, what you've expressed is a mere wish; there are no guarantees in life. What's the guarantee that you'll succeed at being as productive as required of a full-time student?"

"I promise to be productive, sir. I want to run this programme on full-time basis, sir. I'm not doing anything else, sir."

"Well, I'm your supervisor and I want you to be a part-time student. You will do as I say. Fill part-time in your form."

I gape at him in disbelief, my eyes frosty. When our eyes meet, it dawns on me I have no choice but to do as he commands. He looks stern. Dear God, what have I got myself into? I manage to pull myself together and resume the task at hand. Soon, all the columns are filled and I'm ready to submit. I thank him profusely and make to rise but he appears to want to say something. I relax, placing the form back on the table.

"Let me give you one or two guidelines for your programme."

"Yes, sir."

"When you submit your form and pay your fees, it does not mean that your programme has commenced. Well, yes, it has commenced officially, but you are not to start writing immediately. Remember, this is a PhD and not a master's programme; it's in your own interest not to run too fast. Therefore, you are not to put pen or paper for the first one year of your programme." My heart starts to pound again and the room begins to spin. I grip the edge of his table for balance, take a deep, steadying breath and resume staring at him.

"I don't want to read anything from you for the first one year of your programme and I don't want you to write anything. However, this does not mean that you will stay idle for the period. Rather, you will start reading from tomorrow. You will need to buy a lot of books, but you will also need to borrow more books than you buy. Let me tell you, no PhD candidate can afford to buy all the books they require for their programme, no matter how rich or financially comfortable they may be. You would have to take a World Bank loan if you wanted to buy all the books and materials you would need. Borrowing is indispensable to doing research of this nature. You will read widely any book on any subject but since you are a literature student, your take-off point will be literary theory. You will familiarise yourself with the ideas of the various theorists because it is at the end of your reading that you will be able to identify the particular theory or theories that go with your research topic. Then of course, you'll read all the literary outputs of all ages and I'm talking about the poetry, the prose and the drama of all centuries. What this means, therefore, is that you do not yet have a research topic. What you have in your PhD proposal is only a tentative topic which is bound to change after you have read widely. During this period too, you will make yourself available in the department at least every fortnight for the departmental seminar. Attendance is compulsory for all PhD candidates. Academic papers are presented by students and lecturers during the seminars and you will have the privilege to learn and gain greater insight into how academic papers are written, not only through the presentations but also through the reactions that follow the presentations. At the end of the first one year of wide consultation with scholarly materials, you will present three topics to me, including your justification for choosing each of the topics. I will approve one of them and you will start writing. Note that, as you write, you will also be attending seminars and you will continue to do so till the end of your programme. You will discover, as your work progresses, that you are to deliver your own seminar papers, too, but as I pointed out earlier, you have not reached that stage yet."

As I watch him speak, I feel a tiny stab of disappointment that I'll not be able to work with the kind of speed I had envisioned but I detect honesty in his mien. He seems to have reeled out the guidelines quite diligently and I imagine him a meticulous scholar. I resolve silently to buy as many books as I can afford. I decide also to spend the entire two years' rent Folake has saved me to buying books as a demonstration of my commitment to the programme. Then I'll borrow as extensively as possible in line with my professor's advice. There is one psychological step I need to take quickly, I tell myself silently. I must embrace the reality that my programme will take four years and not three, with genuine grace rather than preoccupy my mind with how my earlier calculations have failed. I recognise that I may have challenges paying Deyemi's school fees and mine for the fourth year since I haven't made financial provision toward it, but with Folake's promised assistance, which has already begun to manifest, I feel confident that I will overcome the odds. Finally, I resolve to surprise my supervisor with hard work, exceptional intelligence and knowledge acquisition.

"I'm very grateful to you, sir, for your time and patience in explaining these things to me. I promise to be a worthy student to you by taking all your guidelines very seriously."

"That's okay," he says. I rise and head out the door, feeling absolutely ready to prove my academic worth. I return to my department after submitting my registration form and begin a door-to-door visit to lecturers, seeking audiences with them.

"Good day, sir, I would appreciate any material that might be useful to my research sir."

"What's your topic?"

"Oh, well, I only have a tentative topic for now. The Poetics of Nigerian Literature, sir."

"I do have books and journals that may be relevant to your research but I don't loan them or any other materials to students because they don't return them. I have lost countless books and journals to students and, each time I remember, I feel like killing someone."

"I'm very sorry, sir, but there shouldn't be a problem with me because I'm going to leave my handbag, wristwatch, necklace and earrings with you while I rush quickly to make a photocopy of the materials you give me, sir. I'll pick up my items when I return the original, sir."

"Your handbag will be just fine."

I repeat the same method in the office of every available lecturer in the English department but I'm careful not to knock on Professors Kolade Durojaiye's and Lara Owoyemi's doors. I'm amazed at the piles of materials I'm able to gather just hours after the official commencement of my programme. Soon, I become aware that I may tamper with my transport money back to Lagos. I halt the exercise.

Two days later, on Saturday, Folake comes to assist me to move my things to her Bode Thomas, Surulere home. We pay for a lorry to move the heavy items like furniture and my large mirrors while we use my car and Folake's to convey the smaller items, driving in a convoy. She'd suggested I sold off my beds, chairs and even my large mirrors but I vehemently refuse. In the end, we find a place behind her house to drop most of the items, excluding my mirrors, all of which I place at strategic corners of what has now become my room. Geoffrey promises to send someone to pick my car during the week so that he can scout for a buyer. The next day, Sunday, I pay Deyemi a visit at her boarding school to update her on all the happenings so far. The vanity of children! Deyemi is excited at the news that she'll be spending her next holiday in Folake's obviously more exquisite home. I'm elated and pleased with the turn of events. Everything in my life is on course and I raise my head heavenward, muttering words of gratitude to the creator.

Before I make my debut presence at the departmental seminar, I visit the University of Lagos library where I succeed in gathering a lot more materials and photocopying them within the library. I contract a furniture-maker to make a book shelf for me in which I proudly display my academic acquisitions. My reading begins in earnest. My professor advises that I start with the literary theories. I begin with: What is Literary Theory? I move to humanist literary theory: Plato, Aristotle, Horace, Sir Philip Sidney, Sir Francis Bacon, Joseph Addison, Edmund Burke, Samuel Johnson, Sir Joshua Reynolds, William Wordsworth, Samuel Taylor Coleridge, John Keats, Edgar Allan Poe, and Matthew Arnold. I delve into Practical Criticism and New Criticism, Formalism and early Structuralism - French Structuralism. I read the ideas of Ferdinand de Saussure, Claude Levi – Strauss and The Structural Study of Myth. From there, I move to Post-Structuralism, paying particular attention to the ideas of Derrida. Then, there is Deconstruction, Psychoanalysis, Feminism, Queer Theory – Gay and Lesbian Studies, Flexible Sexuality, New Historicism. I go on to engage Ideology and Discourse – Marxist Theory, Race and Post-Colonialism – Colonialism and English, Henry Louis Gates, Jr. and the Signifying Monkey, Post-Colonialism and Orientalism, Homi Bhaba and 'The Location of Culture,' Gloria Anzaldua and 'Borderlands / La Frontera.' Finally, I come to Postmodernism

– Modernity, Jean Baudrillard, Jean-Francois Lyotard, Gilles Deleuze and Felix Guattari.

Sometimes, my head whirls as I read and there are times when I feel I'm on the brink of a mental breakdown. Folake has taken to spending more time at Geoffrey's apartment so as not to distract me, but I crave her company when my head starts whirling. Her presence gives me an excuse to stop reading when I know I truly deserve a rest. The truth is that when my zeal and enthusiasm to achieve keeps pressing me to keep myself on track but my brain gives signals of fatigue, her company offers me distraction and comfort at the same time. What would I do without her? She's the angel sent direct from heaven, the only person I know who can brilliantly deadpan a joke. Ah, thank goodness, Deyemi is home on a long holiday after successfully completing her JSS1. I have a real reason to lock up my books in the shelf and spend quality time with her. She has lots of stories to tell and I'm willing to be her audience and playmate.

Seven

SEPTEMBER, 1999

I wear a face-splitting grin as I knock gently on my supervisor's door. How can I contain my excitement? It's been exactly one year since starting my programme. I have spent the whole year reading voraciously as my supervisor instructed; I'm on campus today to begin my registration for a new academic session and to officially obtain his approval to start writing my thesis. In the last one year, I have diligently attended all departmental seminars without fail. On occasions when my supervisor didn't attend, I took the additional responsibility of writing and presenting to him the titles of papers delivered, as well as the most important contributions made by the audience without his requesting it. Apart from my desire to impress him and demonstrate, in real terms, how hard-working I am, my almost overzealous attitude to my programme is largely a definition of what I represent. It's in my nature to work like I'm going to war. I bring intensity to everything I do and my PhD programme can't be any different.

I find my supervisor in his office. He answers with a, "Yes, come in." I open the door gently and ease myself in. He glances up at me briefly and lowers his eyes immediately. I take a seat directly in front of him, frantically searching my brain for the best way to introduce the subject of my visit. I have no reason to be apprehensive, really; both of us have agreed on my research topic and I have obeyed all his instructions to the letter. It's just that my interaction with him in the last one year suggests that he suffers from perennial mood swings, so I try to watch out for his mood at every meeting we have. There have been instances, for example, when he appears deep in thought, radiating a deadly brooding silence and I'm often perplexed and helpless at such times. I'm still racking my brain for ideas when I hear a knock on the door. He answers the same way he did when I knocked. I turn around to look at the new entrant. It's a young woman in her mid or late twenties, average looks and cheerful disposition. She is wearing black pant trousers with a cream, long-sleeved fitted shirt. She wears her hair in braids but the braids are neatly packed and bound up, giving her a neat, country look. She smiles luxuriantly and he's obviously delighted to see her, judging by the way his face lights up. The young lady walks in briskly and drapes her arm around his shoulder in a casual display of affection. My professor explodes in laughter. I'm feeling slightly embarrassed but I can't help it and I'm laughing too. The young woman draws the chair next to me and sits down. They gaze at each other for a few moments, during which they seem oblivious of my presence. They ignore me completely and start a conversation.

"How may I help you, young lady?" my Prof asks, cupping his jaw with both palms, still smiling.

"I've come to fill my registration form," she says simply.

"Then what are you waiting for? Go right ahead and fill it." She takes the form from her handbag and places it on the table. I peer at it surreptitiously. It's the same one I filled out a year ago. I smile and lean back in my seat. It doesn't seem as if Prof will attend to me until he finishes with his 'young lady.' She fills in her name – Surname: NOAH, First Name: AGNES, Other Name: ELLEN. The process continues until she gets to 'type of programme.'

"Type of programme?" she whispers, raising her face to smile at Prof, who smiles back sweetly.

"What type of programme do you want to run, young lady?" he asks.

"Full-time."

"Then full-time it is for you," he says, his smile broadening. Did I hear right or was my imagination playing tricks on me? Isn't it also in her interest not to 'run too fast?' What's going on at National University of Nigeria? Wrapping my arms protectively around myself, I take a deep breath and keep my head down. She finishes filling her form and rises, telling our supervisor she has other things lined up for the day. I feel a stab of envy as she leaves. I sigh resignedly and as I get ready to broach the subject of my visit, I realise that my supervisor has resumed his distant, uptight persona. How can he switch so quickly? He is certainly the most capricious person I know. My blood is pounding in my veins. Why am I so nervous?

"Yes, how may I help you?" he snaps. I swallow nervously.

"Yes, sir, I'm here to obtain your permission to start working on my thesis, sir."

"You started working on your thesis a year ago when you started reading, that's if you've truly been reading."

"I've been reading, sir. I have read the works of nearly all African writers to date, sir. I have consulted encyclopaedias as well as countless other literary and non-literary materials, sir. I feel quite equipped and ready to start writing, sir."

"You may claim to have read widely but there is only one way to find out. I'm going to put you to the test right away."

A large lump forms in my throat.

"Okay, let's have it. Tell me about two literary theories you've read. No, I take that back. To give you the privilege to choose is to encourage you to cheat because you may have read only two so I'll test you on two theories of my choice. Now, do a brief presentation on Deconstruction and Postmodernism, in that order."

I take a few moments to calm my nerves before launching into my presentation. "Deconstruction is a set of signifier that points to a complex and often confusing set of ideas, concepts and practices. I'm fascinated by the ideas of the leading figure in Deconstruction, Jacques Derrida, who insists that Deconstruction is not a theory per se but rather a set of strategies, or ways of reading. He says that every philosophic system, every attempt to explain the relations among the mind, the self and the world posited some sort of centre, a point from which everything comes and to which everything refers. This centre may be the concept of God, or the human mind, or the unconscious, or space aliens depending on whose system you're talking about. Deconstruction asks some questions that are very intriguing. Among them is that Western thought is constructed in terms of binary opposites e.g. light/dark, day/night, up/ down, right/ left, male/female, white/black. Why is it that one part of the pair is always given a higher cultural value than the other? In other words, one part is marked as positive and the other as negative. Hence, in western philosophy, we get pairs like good / evil, where good is preferable to evil. Whereas it is pretty easy for us to understand why good is better than evil, but why is male better than female, or white better than black? What would happen to the structure of western thought if we took the binary opposite apart? These are the basic questions Deconstruction is asking and they are absolutely interesting." I pause to regard him but his expression is inscrutable. My heart constricts.

"Go on, what about postmodernist theory?"

"There is no way we can talk about postmodernist theory without first talking about modernism and modernism…"

"Okay, stop. It's good to know that you've been reading. Did you say you read the works of many African writers?"

"Yes, sir."

"What about English writers, Can you mention some of the English writers whose works you've been exposed to?"

"Charles Dickens, Thomas Hardy, D.H, Lawrence..."

"Literature of the Black Diaspora?"

"Richard Wright, Tony Morrison, Frederick Douglas…"

"Very well, Funto, you may start writing," he says curtly and I rise warily, more exhausted by his unfriendly manner than the test, but thankful for the leeway regardless.

"Thank you, sir," I murmur.

"That's okay." He grunts and I head out the door. I go in search of Agnes and find her talking with two other girls on the corridor, her back to me. The girls' appreciative expression alerts her to my presence. It must be Folake's plum dress which I'm wearing today that is doing the magic. I mutter under my breath. Yes, I have taken to being attired mostly in Folake's dresses partly because most of mine are old and I haven't been able to buy new ones, and partly because she doesn't mind me wearing them. As soon as she discovered that I was lacking in trendy dresses and shoes, she told me to feel free to pick whatever I want from her wardrobe.

"Whatever belongs to me is yours as well, I expect you to know that Funto," she'd said earnestly and I haven't disappointed her ever since. Today I know I look hot. As the girls gaze at me appreciatively, Agnes turns and addresses me.

"You want to see me?" she asks.

"Oh yes, please, if you don't mind."

"Okay, girls, catch you later," she says, waving playfully at them.

"My name is "Funto Oyewole, a PhD Candidate, like you. I

find we're both under Prof Ephraim and I'm curious about a few things. Do you mind shedding some light?"

"Oh, by all means, go ahead," she says genially. I'm encouraged.

"Um, you seem to be a fresh student. Have you just been offered admission, I mean, are you doing your first registration?"

"You are absolutely correct; I'm just starting."

"I see," I say, smiling. "Eh-r, I hope you don't mind my presumptions, it seems to me you are a special candidate." I pause to regard her. She looks neither angry nor surprised. I continue. "I say this because Prof gave me some tough instructions before I did my first registration last year but I didn't see him do the same with you."

"Instructions like what?"

"Well, that I was not to start writing immediately, for example. I just got his nod today to start."

She looks confused. I wonder if what I'm trying to do wouldn't put me in jeopardy. It's already too late to back off, I might as well take my chances.

"Pardon my inquisitiveness. I was just wondering if he gave you a similar instruction, earlier, perhaps."

"No, not at all, he hasn't told me not to write and he's not likely to. I'm a full-time student, which means I've got only three years to finish. Why would anybody tell me not to write during the first one year - or anytime at all?"

"I understand what you mean and that takes me to my next question. I was amazed at how quickly he acquiesced to your decision to run your programme on full-time basis."

"Why should that surprise you? I'm the student and I determine the pace at which I work," she says with confidence. My smile dissolves.

"This is what baffles me, really. Do you possibly know why

he insisted I filled part-time in my own form even when I pleaded with him I wanted full-time?"

"I'm sorry to hear this, madam, but I have no idea." She looks genuinely concerned. Why am I taking the poor girl to task?

"I'm so sorry, too, to bother you, but just one last question. Are you related to him in any way? I'm sorry to ask but I noticed a familiarity between you, I'm just curious."

"Oh, you are right about that, Prof is my brother." she says, her eyes glinting with pride.

"I see, brother as in …"

"We are from the same town."

"I understand now, I murmur.

"Prof is a very nice person," she says.

"Yes, he is," I acquiesce, blinking back the tears that have formed in my eyes and anxious to end our conversation.

"He wants me to get a job in the university, that's why he's encouraging me any way he can. He says he'll get me a teaching position in the Spatial Learning College of the university as soon as I complete my registration."

I squeak, but Agnes doesn't notice as she continues. "You know, one of the conditions of engagement is to be a registered PhD candidate. Prof says I'll teach at the college for three years while I do my doctorate and that as soon as I finish, he'll use his influence to get me fully integrated into the main scheme of things as lecturer in NUN. My sister, I can't wait to see these good things happen to yours truly."

"You deserve it," I manage to say before adding quickly; "thank you very much for talking to me, I want to see them at the departmental office." I give her a side hug and scurry off. She's too absorbed in her exhilarating world to notice the many changes in my countenance and I'm thankful. Poor Agnes, what has she done to deserve my misplaced animosity?

Mr Oragui is a clerical staff in the departmental office. He's thickly set with clownish features. He peeks up at me when I step in; there is clear admiration in his eyes. Folake's dress is truly plum, I smile secretly.

"Well done, Mr. Oragui."

"Welcome, madam."

"Thank you, I've come to obtain an advancement form which I understand is mandatory for all PhD students to fill and submit annually from their second registration."

"That is partially true, madam."

"Pardon?"

"I said the information you've been given is not entirely true because filling the advancement form does not determine the rate of your advancement in your programme."

"I don't understand."

"In that case, I will tell you, but do not say I told you, you hear?" he says, lowering his voice to a whisper. I nod frantically

"Your supervisor is the only one who determines your progress. The advancement form is a mere formality, totally irrelevant to students' actual progress because nobody bothers to look at it. You will make progress if your supervisor wishes you to, irrespective of whether or not you fill the form." I feel beads of sweat break out on my forehead.

"Damn!" the word escapes from my mouth before I could stop it.

"Take it easy, madam, I'm only trying to assist you."

"I'm sorry, Mr Oraqui, it's just that I find frustration everywhere I turn in this university."

"Things are not as bad as you make them seem. You haven't understood the system, that's all. Once you understand how things are done, you'll blend with the crowd and there'll be no anguish whatsoever."

"What may I do to earn my supervisor's favour?" I ask.

"That's the question you should have asked. See ehn," he glances around furtively and beckons me closer. "You'll buy him gifts from time to time, you'll palm him envelopes lined with naira notes as often as you can afford to, you'll find out the number of children he has and their ages because you must keep showering them with gifts. If you can do all these and more, you will make rapid progress."

"What about the form?"

"Oh, you may fill the advancement form if it's convenient for you and, well, you know as they say, to fulfil all righteousness."

"You mean a university don would condone the kind of illegalities you've just described?"

"Why do you talk as if you are not a Nigerian? Is the University different from the larger Nigerian society? By the way, who is your supervisor?"

"Prof Ephraim."

"You mean Prof Terror?"

"I beg your pardon?"

"This woman, your drama is too much. Why do you beg my pardon? You want to tell me you don't know your supervisor's nickname? Madam, e be like say the things wey you no know plenty small o."

I frown and he laughs light-heartedly.

"Okay, I'll tell you. Your supervisor doesn't make demands on his students but he takes whatever they give him. I think you understand me?" he asks, and I nod. He swallows and continues talking.

"The problem with him is that, whether you give him gifts or not, he won't be nice to you unless you speak the same language with him. Ethnic affinity is the only way to escape Ephraim's wickedness. However, it's advisable you buy him gifts to mitigate your suffering."

"This is preposterous!" I cry.

"Leave big grammar alone, madam, let me give you one quick example. A PhD student like you came to look for him recently but Prof Ephraim had come earlier that day and said he was going out and would not come back to the office. He's a mature person, just like you. I told him Prof had gone out and would not come back. He said he came from Maiduguri. I asked him if he wanted to leave a message, he said, 'Yes'. Then, he counted two thousand naira and gave me. I was looking at him and wondering where his action was leading. My guess was right. He gave me a sealed envelope containing fifty thousand naira, telling me to help him give it to Prof. I looked at him with pity. I asked him if he wouldn't mind if I advised him; he told me to go ahead. I said, 'Okay, you see, sir, if I delivered this money to Ephraim as you gave it to me, it would take you more than ten years to finish your PhD.' He opened his eyes wide and asked me why? I said because Prof Ephraim would know that I knew you gave him money. He asked me what he could do since he came from a far distance and would not be able to come back soon. I said, 'Calm down, sir, you are looking at an experienced man. I have spent more than twenty years in this university; I am not a stranger to its ways.' I said, 'Sir, do you have anything in printed form in your briefcase, anything at all, like handout or something a little bulky?' He said, 'Yes.' I said, 'Well, I will give you a large envelope. You will put the money in the middle of the handout, and then you will put the handout inside the large envelop and address it to Prof Ephraim. You will give it to me and I will keep it for him. When he comes I will tell him one of his PhD students came looking for him he said I should give you this envelope that contains his work. He said he has already discussed it with you.' The man opened his mouth and thanked me. He did as I instructed; I did as I promised. Do you know what Prof Ephraim told me after he opened the envelope and found money?"

"No."

"He walked casually into this office, his two hands in his pockets, telling me the man actually told him he would be bringing his chapter two and that was what was in the envelope, as if he needed to explain anything to me. Imagine the cock and bull story, madam, but of course I understand the game, so, I said, 'Well done, Prof,' I continued with what I was doing. I'm sure both of us must have looked like two old fools trying to outsmart the other. That's the system, madam."

He makes a sudden grimace of disgust. Wondering why, I let my eyes scan through him and settle on Dr Rotimi, who has just sauntered in.

"Good day, sir," I murmur,

"Good day," he mumbles as he checks his pigeon hole and retrieves some documents. "Has anybody asked of me, Mr. Oragui?"

"Nobody," Oragui responds without interest. As soon as Dr Rotimi leaves, he whispers to me, conspiratorially, "He's a very wicked man."

"Really?"

"I don't like the way he treats his undergraduate and master's students. Anytime he gives them assignment, he gives them a deadline within which to submit."

"What's wicked about that, Mr. Oragui?"

"Can you exercise some patience and listen to me?"

"I'm sorry, go on."

"He gives an instruction as to what time to submit, say 2pm, not only to the students but also to me, warning me that any student who brings their assignment one minute past 2pm,

I shouldn't collect. What's my own? I carry out his instruction. But do you know that one month, two months, sometimes three months after he has asked the poor students to submit and I have dutifully refused to collect the scripts of those who brought theirs late, Dr Rotimi is yet to pick up the same assignment from me? The students' scripts are here, gathering dust, and I'm wondering why he instructed me not to take from those who submitted late when he knew he had no intention to grade the scripts early. I tell you, madam, sometimes Dr Rotimi completely abandons the scripts with me throughout the semester. How does he grade the poor students for their continuous assessment?"

My mouth falls open.

"Now, I can see you are surprised," he says self-righteously.

"It means the lecturers in this English Department are really bad?"

"It's not just about the English Department. I told you earlier that I have been working in this university for over twenty years. There is no faculty in NUN that I have not worked. The story is the same in all. Many of those lecturers you treat with respect are demons. A few of them are good, though, like Dr Abdullahi who, anytime she wants to travel abroad, tells her PhD students and asks them if they would like her to help them buy books they can't find in Nigeria. She's very motherly; she encourages her students to work hard and doesn't waste their time - except those who clearly don't want to work. You know, as we have wicked and insensitive lecturers so do we have unserious students. There are many so called PhD students who register for the programme only so that they can boast that they are PhD students. You see, such students come around at the beginning of every session for registration; they dash money to departmental staff, drag their feet around for a while and disappear till the beginning of another session, when they come again for the same ritual. Let me not talk too much but I hope I have been able to help you understand the terrain a little."

"You don't know how much you've helped me. I'm very grateful for all the information. I promise I shall process and use it well," I say, feeling thoroughly exhausted.

"You are welcome, madam."

I palm him a five hundred naira note. He smiles shyly and I head out the door.

"By the way, Madam, I hope you know the meaning of PhD?"

I turn round, slightly confused.

"Of course I know. Who doesn't know the meaning?"

"Okay, what does it mean?"

I smile a self-righteous smile before muttering, Doctor of Philosophy."

"You see, I thought as much. There are many things you don't know, Madam."

I'm angry but I don't show it. What does he take me for?

"In Nigeria, PhD means, Prostrate, Hard work and Dobale. You are Yoruba; you know the meaning of Dobale. It means you'll prostrate to them, you'll work hard and you'll prostrate yet again. It also means you'll do more of prostrating than hard work."

I open my mouth to say something, words fail me. I shut my mouth and turn to leave then remember the advancement form.

"The advancement form, please."

"It's the PG School that issues and keeps records of the form. Collect it from there, fill and return to them. Good luck, madam."

I silently resolve I will fill the advancement form every year regardless of what Mr Oragui has told me. What a system, what a world. Is there a chance that I will survive in it, let alone thrive?

Eight

Deyemi has since gone back to school; Folake is with Geoffrey, so, I'm all alone. But in spite of my aloneness, I awake this morning in a state of excitement and I know exactly why – my former colleague, Boluwatife, will be visiting at ten o' clock. When last did I have the privilege of playing host to someone in my home? I can't remember when last I entertained a quest. But I haven't forgotten how, only years ago, my house was a beehive of activity where multitudes of friends and relatives thronged, especially at weekends. It's amazing how life sometimes tosses us an unpleasant deal. However, there are people who have long discovered this truism about life and living and have taken steps to curb unpleasant surprises. One of them was our former vice-chancellor, who was said to have instructed his three children to hurry up and find spouses whilst his tenure as VC lasted, warning them that it was the only way to guarantee that their weddings would pull the kind of memorable crowd they desired. He was a wise man.

The thought brings a smile to my face and my mind drifts back to the present. Oh yes, today promises to be very interesting, I mutter aloud, as if to reassure myself. Boluwatife and I worked in the same department for a few years and, we lost our jobs the same day. The unhappy circumstance under which we parted, and the fact that we immediately became wrapped up in our separate struggle for survival did not allow us to re-connect until our chance meeting the other day in traffic. She did not look quite good when I saw her and I wondered why. Anyway, I'm elated at the prospect of having an old friend visit me. I'm really looking forward to receiving her.

It's twenty-five minutes after ten when Boluwatife arrives. I rush to welcome her, grinning from ear to ear.

"Did you find it hard to locate this place?" I ask, unable to hide my excitement. She ignores my question but appears to be as excited as I am.

"Funto! Is this you?" she exclaims as we hug. I don't like the feather-like feel of her body. I move back to take a close look at her. Yes, it's obvious that she has emaciated considerably. This is not the Boluwatife I knew, my vivacious, charming and cheerful colleague whose hips were boldly outlined in her fitted skirt. How I used to envy her curves. Is this what it really means to lose one's job? Am I as shrunken as my former colleague? Perhaps I have also lost weight in all the wrong places and only people who once knew how I used to look would notice the difference. But what I find more worrying is not merely her weight loss. She also looks strangely pale. I stand rooted to the spot, astounded by my old colleague's disheartening physicality. She is moving about in the room now but her gait is stiff and it seems she has difficulty lifting her legs. I notice she is also taking a long, hard look at me; a small smile stretches across her lips. What's she thinking about me? I wonder silently. I turn quietly away, trying to decide whether or not to verbalise my observations. Why should I pretend? Boluwatife was an interesting colleague and our relationship was cordial. I turn boldly to face her; there's no need to act as if I haven't noticed the changes.

"What happened to you? You look too dry for my liking." I say in a rush. She smiles, but sadly, which only aggravates my fears.

"I don't like the pimples on your forehead. Even the foundation you applied is not helping much. Why do you allow our loss of employment to blight your radiance?" I stop, realising that I'm sounding stupid. Who wouldn't be negatively affected after losing their means of livelihood? Unless they have someone to lean on, someone like Folake? What would have become of me if I didn't have Folake? When our branch manager told us during a routine staff meeting many years ago to take our jobs seriously, we didn't know the importance of his words. "If you lose your job, you will also lose your friends," He warned but we just giggled, making light of what we didn't reckon could turn out to be a prophecy.

"Come, let me get you something to eat," I say softly and turn in the direction of the kitchen.

"It's a long story, my sister," she mutters darkly after we have emptied our plates of rice and plantain. I look at her quizzically.

"Are you sure you want to hear it?" she asks. I nod vigorously. She sighs heavily and starts to talk.

"Things became very hard for me after we were sacked," she begins as we hold each other's gaze. "Life became so difficult to the extent that I couldn't pay my house rent. You know that Lagos landlords are completely lacking in human compassion. My landlord didn't waste time issuing me a quit notice. I was about to be homeless and I didn't know what to do." I shook my head in grave understanding and urge her, with my eyes, to go on talking.

"The only option open to me was not an option at all – packing my bags and returning to my village. God forbid! I would sooner go and take up residence under the bridge in Oshodi than go back to Ekiti to have my relatives make fun of me. Anyway, I had a boyfriend who I thought then was a godsend. He gladly took me into his house, including the girl that was staying with me. You know I had this girl, Mope, who is my friend's younger sister and who had been staying with me for more than three years before I lost my job. In fairness to my boyfriend, Oladapo, he was kindness personified. He fed, clothed and generally took responsibility for virtually everything I needed. I was living far better than when I was working. He regularly counselled me to trust God, telling me he was convinced that God would provide another job for me someday. He even promised to set me up in any business venture of my choice if I failed to find another job after two years. As for sex, hmm, you know how it is with men and sex; I didn't starve him of my love. What greater thing can a woman give a man who solves nearly all her problems if not her entire body? So, I gave Oladapo my body, even at times when he didn't request it. I cooked his meals, washed his clothes, kept the house and generally acted like the dutiful and loving wife. I thought that would be enough to make him happy. I even permitted myself the fantasy that he would propose marriage. How wrong I was."

"So what happened?" I ask impatiently.

She sighs and I take a cue reflexively. I don't know the problem yet, but I think I'm already feeling her pain.

"Talk to me, Boluwatife." I coax.

"I went out one day only to come back and meet my man doing it with the young girl living with me. He was sweating profusely and gliding down recklessly, like someone possessed of a strange energy. I swear, Funto, I had never seen him sweat so, not even during the best of our love-making sessions. To say that I was furious was to understate my feeling at that moment. I was murderously enraged. For how long had they been doing it behind my back? That was the first question that ravaged my soul. To think that I was a mere fool in a relationship I thought was the best to have ever happened to me was more than I could accept. But then, what was there to do under the circumstance? Take a walk? To where? I was in a quagmire."

"What did you do?" I ask; unable to suppress my impatience. There's something in her manner that suggests to me that she probably didn't handle the situation with sufficient tact. I cast an appraising glance over her once again and my mood further darkens. She looks so thin and sickly. What did she do that has left her looking this severe? Or is it just the emotional and psychological trauma created by a feeling of betrayal? I try to think how I would have reacted but my mind is blank. I shoot her another glance. She looks drained and there are dry patches under her armpits. What a life?

"What did you do?" I probe. She smiles a quiet smile that doesn't reach her eyes before she resumes.

"I did a few things, Funto. First, I sent the girl packing that very day. There was something about the way they were doing it that convinced me that they would never have been able to put an end to it if I allowed the girl to continue to stay with me. Besides, I no longer had the grace to continue to live under the same roof with her, and I knew I couldn't afford to leave Oladapo. I had nowhere to go. Oladapo didn't raise any objection. Perhaps he thought that was the worst thing I could do but I proved him wrong. I plotted my revenge."

"Revenge? You got yourself another boyfriend?"

"I did worse than that. I got myself a younger lover; someone who was more than ten years younger than me."

"To prove what?" The words were out of my mouth before I could stop them.

"Well, he cheated on me with a girl that was far younger than me. So, it's an eye for an eye."

I gasp.

"You haven't even heard the worst part," she says. I take a

long breath and straighten my shoulders.

"I'm listening"

"Well, I know you are going to blame me for this, but I organised for my new, younger lover to come and make love to me in Oladapo's house - and on his bed. I also made sure that Oladapo caught us in the act exactly the way I caught him."

My jaw hits the floor. I stare at Boluwatife in horror. She meets my stare for a long moment, neither of us speaking. After a while, I readjust myself in my seat and force a wry smile to perch at the corners of my mouth. I'm determined to just listen, smile and agree with everything Boluwatife tells me from now on. What would be the point in my making any comment? She has done what she considered was right, and I'm merely an audience to an awry tale. She seems to be reading my mind and ready to resume talking.

"Revenge is sweet," she says with a tinge of sadness. "I had my revenge. I enjoyed it while it lasted but I couldn't have been prepared for what happened after. Oladapo threw me out with the speed and brutality I never knew he was capable of. The effect, for me, was like the aftermath of a senseless drinking expedition. My senses were speedily restored but it was already too late to make amends. It dawned on me that I went too far and I regretted my action. I tried to beg him. There was nothing I didn't do to appease him but he wouldn't forgive me. He wouldn't even look at me, let alone consider giving me another chance. He insisted that I had to leave his house, even when he knew that I had nowhere to go. In the end, I had to leave. That was when my real nightmare began. I took refuge with a distant male cousin who was living in a one-room apartment. I'm still living with him as I speak, sleeping on the bare floor. Life has been very tough on me, Funto." She pauses. I stretch my hands toward her. Tears pool in my eyes, but I don't want to shed them so as not to make her cry. I blink them back, lowering my face. By the time I look up, Boluwatife is staring at me, her eyes frosty. I tear my gaze from her. Thankfully, she seems to have something more to tell me.

"Occasionally, I run into some of our former colleagues and a good number of those I have seen seem to have succeeded in finding their feet. A few of them have assisted me financially. My cousin also tries to provide for me but he is a motor mechanic. Then, one morning, I was brushing my teeth in the outer compound and suddenly I began to feel an excruciating pain on one side of my body..."

My heart starts to pound. What else is she about to tell me? Why is Boluwatife's visit turning into an ordeal? How I have looked forward to this visit, expecting us to have fun! I'm perspiring and, it seems, I'm beginning to feel pain all over my body. Boluwatife senses my discomfort. She resumes talking.

"The pain soon became so unbearable that before I could finish brushing my teeth, I had to call my cousin's attention. That was it. That was the last thing I remembered clearly. Every other experience became hazy. By the time my cousin got me to the hospital, the doctor said I had suffered a mild stroke."

"Ah!" I scream. My heart begins to pound furiously. Poor Boluwatife. I don't know what to say or do. I look blankly at my former colleague, my heart going out to her, yet I don't know the appropriate response or action to take. I sigh, resigned.

"I have been an extremely fortunate person," she says, her voice reaching me from a distance. I muster all my psychological strength to go on listening to her. It's the least I can do in the circumstance.

"My recovery was unbelievably rapid. I didn't even finish my medication before I got back on my feet," she says smiling. I manage to smile back. Then, silence stretches between us. She appears to have completed her story but I still don't know how to respond.

"So, how have you been making out financially?" I ask after a while.

"Life is tough but I'm coping very well, thanks to my son."

"Your son? I didn't know you have a child." My mood brightens.

"Oh yes, I do have a son."

"Great! Good to know!" I'm jubilant and thoroughly excited now. My day is finally coming along well. Wow!

"I just made sure nobody knew about him in the office then," she explains and I nod vigorously. "You know how these men are. Once they know you've had a child, they conclude that you are already blemished and start to disrespect you. Our men tend to think that a woman who has never given birth is somehow 'purer' than the one who has. I think it's unfortunate that they reason that way but then you can't change it, so you try to make yourself as desirable as you can."

I don't know what to say. I smile.

"I got pregnant when I was in secondary school."

"Really? He must be grown by now."

"Oh yes, he is, but I'm careful not to let people know about him so as not to jeopardise my chances of getting a suitor."

"I see," I murmur.

"He's in his twenties now."

"Wonderful! Where is the young man?"

"He was about to graduate from the polytechnic when they sacked us."

"Great! He'll sure look after his mum. Has he found a job yet?"

"Eh-r, well, he was offered a job as a marketer by a commercial bank shortly after completing his national service but he declined the offer."

"Really? Why?"

"He said he can't join them in the business of wearing suit and tie every day. He said he found the prospect absolutely boring."

Boluwatife is at it again. What exactly is she trying to say? Anyway, I think I have had enough shock in one day. I try for indifference.

"What's his preference?" I ask, sounding as casual as I can.

"You know this thing they are doing now? That's what he is doing." Boluwatife and her theatrics, I have no clue what she's talking about.

"I don't know what you are talking about. Why don't you just tell me?" I blurt out, exasperated.

She lowers her voice to a conspiratorial tone before muttering, "Yahoo-yahoo."

I gasp, horrified.

"Your son is a yahoo-yahoo boy?"

"Yes o, my sister, what's so bad about that? He's making good money from it, and I mean the kind of money he can't possibly make from any bank job."

I glower at her in both anger and disbelief. How come I never knew this aspect of her all through the years we worked together? It's obvious I never truly knew her.

"Why then are you still staying with your cousin and sleeping on the floor?" I snigger. "I'm sure your son can rent a befitting apartment for you. Or, better still, why aren't you living with him?"

"I can't stay with him."

"Why not?"

"He lives with his friends. You know they work together. And he doesn't want me to stay on my own yet because of my health."

"Is that so?" I sneer, but if Boluwatife notices the disapproval in my voice and countenance she pretends otherwise. She just wants to talk.

"That boy is really trying for me o. Some months ago, there was this family wedding I needed to attend. You know how family ceremonies are, compulsory for every member to partake. The aso-ebi we were all to wear was thirty thousand. I was still wondering where and how I would get the money when my son paid me a visit. He was even the first person to broach the subject. You know what he told me?"

I shook my head and it was all she needed to continue talking.

"He said to me, 'Mummy, you will be the first person to buy the aso ebi in the family.' I didn't believe him but to my pleasant surprise he gave me the money that very day."

I'm aghast but I try not to show it. Instead, I smile brightly, a wave of relief suddenly flooding through me. I would have been unhappy not being in a position to assist her financially if she had told me only the story of her illness. But now that she has fed me with this other one, I realise I don't have to worry or feel bad. And when she asks me how I have been coping and what I have been doing, I'm unable to talk about my ambition to get a PhD. I don't know how she will feel about it and I don't want to bore her. We are now talking about Lagos - parties, clothes, jewellery, shoes, food, everything and nothing. Our conversation is flowing and I'm finally having the much anticipated fun.

Nine

NOVEMBER, 2000

Today is an important day for many reasons. It's been fourteen whole months since I got my supervisor's consent to start writing, meaning that I'm now a little over two years into my programme. It excites me no end that time is gradually slipping by and in less than two years from now I will obtain my doctorate. Who wouldn't be excited? Even more heart-warming is the successful completion of the second chapter of my work which I'll submit to my professor in a matter of hours. I gave him the first chapter eight months ago but he has neither returned it to me nor said anything about it since then. Although I have been persistent in respectfully asking for his response, he has also been consistent in telling me to go ahead and finish the second chapter, which I told him I had started. I'm dressed in Folake's sleeveless pink cotton dress and my hair is neatly wrapped in her large pink scarf. I look at the large mirror in my room as I prepare to set out for Abuja and my joy soars.

When I arrive in Abuja, I knock on my professor's door but there is no response. I take a deep, steadying breath and knock again. Silence. Perhaps he's in one of the lecture halls, teaching. I hesitate for a moment and turn the door knob and am pleasantly surprised when it opens. Wow! My Oga is in. He is sitting calmly behind his massive desk but he's not alone. Sitting directly opposite him is Agnes. A file is open in front of him, which he appears to be using to explain something to her. They pause in their discussion as soon as I enter and Prof Ephraim gazes impassively at me.

"Good morning, sir, how is your family, sir?" I greet with bated breath.

"Good morning," he grunts.

"Agnes, how are you?" I murmur.

"I'm fine, Madam," she answers politely. I feel awkward and out of place. There's something in their manner that suggests that I'm an intruder.

"It appears you are busy, sir," I say cautiously.

"Yes, I am," he says. His tone is harsh. I don't give up.

"When may I come back to see you, sir?"

"I don't know, keep trying until you find me on seat."

God help me, my Oga is downright irritable. I mutter under my breath.

"Okay sir, I shall keep trying, sir," I say, putting as much cheerfulness as I could muster into my words.

"That's alright." He smiles enigmatically. My soul is slightly ravaged but I allow myself to hope that all is well. I have every reason to be hopeful, I say firmly to myself. In the over two years that I have known him, I have also come to understand that. although he's closed and complicated, engaging him in mundane discussion puts him in a playful mood. Perhaps I need to put this knowledge into use in order to get him to attend to me. In the meantime, I try to be hopeful in spite of the fact that my mind is beginning to boil with unanswered questions. I don't want to examine my feelings in relation to what I think I have just discovered because I'm terrified what answers I might find. My professor and Agnes appear to be busy discussing her work. Is this true? If it's true, is it the first time he's giving her such devoted attention or has this been going on for some time? Has Agnes, who registered a year after me, made more progress? How far has she gone? Is our supervisor privileging her over me? Questions and more questions are agitating my mind but I can't find answers. All the muscles clench deep in my belly and my senses are disconnected but I struggle not to pay any heed, at least, not until the big revelation. I take consolation in the knowledge that in spite of my supervisor being difficult to keep up with because he can be friendly one minute and formal and stiffly the next, I can put him at the best of his moods whenever he grants me audience.

In the long corridor outside his office, I begin to pace back and forth, unable to decide what to do to while away the time. I start to sing my version of Enya's new song, Only Time:

> *Who can say where the road goes*
> *Where the day flows –*
> *Only time*
> *Who can say why your heart sighs*
> *As your dream flies –*
> *Only time*
> *And who can say why your heart cries*
> *As your hope dies –*
> *Only time*
> *Who knows – Only time*
> *Who knows – Only time*

At the seminar hall, I'm seated between Mrs Lawal and Mrs Korede. Mrs Lawal is a much older woman; she's over fifty and I derive tremendous inspiration from her. How many people of her age would willingly surrender to the brutish and demeaning treatment our lecturers flagrantly subject us to? Mrs

Lawal regularly sinks to her knees to greet lecturers, including her children's contemporaries. She runs after them, trying to hold conversations because they don't stop to talk to students. It is said that if they do so they debase their position and give students the opportunity to undermine their authority. Mrs Lawal runs like an undergraduate student to keep pace with her lecturers. When she meets them on the way, she relieves them of their bags, books or any baggage on them because it is also said that a PhD student must seek the favour of all lecturers, irrespective of their department or faculty because they have no way of knowing who their internal assessor would be. Besides, stories abound about how PhD students easily fall into disfavour with their supervisor over alleged insolence or lack of reverence to the supervisor's friends or colleagues. Mrs Lawal doesn't take chances; she respects, honours, begs and works hard, very hard. Mrs Korede, on the other hand, is younger than me; I reckon she's in her early or mid thirties. She looks respectable, stylish, elegant and sophisticated. They are both language students but we meet and interact from time to time, especially during departmental seminars. They are engrossed in conversation when I arrive but they quickly create a space between them and I sit, hoping for some relief from them.

"How are things going with you two? How is the almighty national university treating my ladies?" I ask, laughing boisterously to mask my inner turmoil. They exchange glances as if contemplating how much to divulge. I pretend not to notice.

"I brought my chapter two for my supervisor but I'm having difficulty getting him to grant me audience," I say.

"Has he read your chapter one?" Mrs Lawal asks.

"I imagine so. It's been with him for eight months," I explain. They erupt in a convulsive laughter. I frown.

"You know, your childlike innocence intrigues me to no

end, Funto," Mrs. Lawal says, looking genuinely amused. I feel suddenly bereft of hope. A lump forms in my throat.

"Arrrgghh! H-o-w, w-h-y?" I stutter, confused.

"What do you mean, why? What's eight months? Do you know how long my thesis has spent with my own supervisor without a response from him? Eighteen months!" I gasp. "This is my fifth year on the programme and it was only last week he finally told me he is preoccupied with other things and has no time to read my work."

"Meaning what?" I ask, staring at her, wide-eyed.

"Listen now," Mrs Lawal says, charging at me angrily as if I was in connivance with her supervisor. Mrs Korede seems to find Mrs Lawal's action quite entertaining as she quirks up her mouth in apparent amusement. My gaze darkens. Mrs Lawal resumes talking.

"He then directed me to Dr Meniru, you know him?" she asks. I shake my head.

"I don't know most of the lecturers," I explain.

"That's true, since you have no direct relationship with them, being in literature. Anyway, Dr Meniru just got his PhD and he's probably interested in joining the department as a lecturer."

"Your supervisor directed you to Dr Meniru," I echo, eager for her to continue.

"Yes o, my sister, my supervisor told me to give my thesis to Dr Meniru to help me read and correct."

"What's his job as your supervisor?" I ask, scowling at no one in particular.

"Who am I to ask him that kind of question but you haven't heard the full gist yet."

I roll my eyes in anticipation.

"He told me I will pay Dr Meniru for his services."

My hope vanishes and my lower jaw practically hits the

table. Get a grip, Funto! I admonish myself. I adjust my sitting position, straightening my crouched shoulders and peering at the two women in turn from behind my lashes. What a supervisor, what a university and …yes, what a country!

"I beg your indulgence, Mrs Lawal. Can you tell me precisely how he communicated his directive to you? He couldn't have been so shameless as to verbalise it, I'm sure?" I query.

"What do you mean? He told me, whoa! He didn't mince words. Well, he started by telling me that although he hasn't had the time to look at my work, he's certain it would contain a lot of grammatical and other errors. Then, he said he has a lot of sympathy for me being an older woman with failing health. You know, I had this dreadful illness last year which required surgery. He said he sympathises with my poor health and the fact that I have spent nearly five years on the programme. He said because he has not had and will not have time to look at my work in the nearest future, he would suggest I gave it to Dr Meniru; that he already mentioned it to him and Dr Meniru agreed to be of assistance but that he had to be remunerated if I wanted to finish."

"Have you gone to see Dr Meniru?"

"Of course! I went to see him immediately. He wanted to know the length of my thesis. He said he would charge me per page but that he needed to take a preliminary look at it to determine how much work he would have to do, which in turn would determine how much he would charge per page."

I laughed a horrified laughter. Turning to Mrs Korede, I ask, "I hope you are luckier than Mrs Lawal."

"That depends on your definition of luck, Funto, but if you consider that I started my own programme when you started, that is, two years ago, and that the only chapter of my work that my supervisor hasn't read and approved is the one I haven't written, then, you might conclude that I'm luckier than Mrs Lawal."

"Ha-ha, lucky woman!" I exclaim as my mood moderates instantaneously and I slap Mrs Korede's back playfully, refusing to take my hand off. "You are definitely a lucky woman," I repeat, feeling a faint stab of envy.

"You haven't asked me how I achieved the feat."

"Very well, then, give me the magic wand," I tease.

"My Oga and I are intimate," she whispers, lowering her voice.

"What!" I scream, but realising the implication of what I have just done, I cover my mouth with both hands, glancing furtively around to see if anyone is paying us attention. I lower my voice still.

"It's not right, Mrs Korede. You are married."

"I'm married, so? What would you suggest I do when my supervisor insisted it was either I yielded to his sexual demands or I asked my husband to give me a PhD? Look, Funto, what someone doesn't know doesn't hurt them. My husband accompanies me when I come to see my supervisor at times but he can't find out because we comport ourselves in his presence. I do what I have to do to get to where I want to be. What crime am I committing?"

I open my mouth to say something then close it. I stare at my feet. When I raise my face moments later, I fix my gaze on Mrs Lawal. Her revulsion at Mrs Korede's story is held in strict check. The line of her jaw is strained and there seems to be tension around her eyes. I shift my gaze to Mrs Korede, looking questioningly at her; she shrugs in a nonchalant way. I allow my feeling of disappointment to linger for a moment.

After the seminar, I go in search of my supervisor but fail again to secure an audience. The number of visits I have made to his office is innumerable but each time he tells me he is busy. Finally, I ask him if he wants us to reschedule for tomorrow and he agrees. This doesn't discourage me still, because I no longer return to Lagos the same day whenever I come to Abuja to attend a seminar. I take my time to visit the library and interact with lecturers and fellow PhD students. I have, therefore, become a regular lodger at Satellite Hotel and Folake picks the bill each time. With my gratuity exhausted, I practically live off her now and she takes good care of Deyemi and me, doing so cheerfully. I used to feel uncomfortable by her incredible generosity and kind-heartedness but she gets livid with me each time I make a demonstrable show of appreciation. She takes Deyemi as her daughter, making me feel completely at ease. Where would I be without her?

In the morning, I stand beneath the shower at Satellite Hotel, absentmindedly washing myself though careful not to wet my tied-back hair. I'm contemplating yesterday, about all the people I interacted with: my supervisor, Mrs Korede, Mrs Lawal… I'm scheduled to meet my professor at 11'oclock. I finish and dress up quickly. May today be better than yesterday, I supplicate silently as I make my way to the campus.

I knock gently on his door but there is no response. I try to open it but it's locked. I stand by the door to wait for him. He doesn't come until 12:30pm but I wait calmly.

"Good morning, sir," I greet, collecting the files he's holding and helping him place them on the table when we enter his office. I don't think he responded to my greeting but I remain hopeful, taking a seat directly opposite him, regarding him and trying not to appear impatient. We stay like this for some time then I clear my throat.

"I had an interesting encounter as I was leaving the campus yesterday evening," I begin, watching out for his nuances.

"Tell me about it," he says without interest. I don't let his lack of encouragement deter me.

"I saw a young man and a young woman holding hands and breathing into each other. As I moved closer, I was just in time to see the young man gently stroking the girl's cheek with the back of his hand and telling her he would be with her forever, come rain, come sunshine. Old memories came flooding through me and I stood mesmerised by their display." I peer at my supervisor from beneath my lashes. He has the most ludicrous grin on his face. I'm buoyed by his reaction and mentally pat myself on the back before launching into further details about the fictitious love birds. "As they got even more absorbed with each other, the lover boy took the girl's chin in his hand and tilted her head up to reach his eyes, whispering some inaudible sweet nothings. I was again enthralled by the spectacle. Finally, they appeared to have had enough fun for the moment and they disentangled, each facing a different direction. As I recovered and made to proceed on my journey, the girl called out to her lover softly and he turned to her immediately, no hesitation. Then, the girl asked, 'Would you come tonight as promised?' And the boy responded, 'Sure, of course, if it doesn't rain.' He resumed his walk swiftly, totally oblivious to the sudden change in his lover's countenance."

My professor erupts in a long, throaty laughter and I join. Soon, we are both laughing heartily.

"Did you say the love birds brought old memories of your own experience back to you?" he asks and I'm further convinced I'm doing well at my game.

"Oh yes, sir, I had a fair share of fun with..., well, with boys, especially during my undergraduate days. I went to parties, clubs and did all the funny things younger people do now."

"Really? Tell me about it."

"Ah, Oga, I had fun o. I remember that clubbing and partying held special allure for me then, if you know what I mean," I say, laughing with deliberate exaggeration.

"How would I know if you wouldn't tell me?" he says, eyes glinting with excitement. This Oga truly likes useless stories o, I say silently but. addressing him, I say with seriousness:

"I mean, sex is sweet on its own but it's a lot sweeter on a dance floor," I giggle and shake like a teenager. My professor is reeling with excitement. Wonderful!

"There's something magical about dancing with the opposite sex in the dark or when the light is dim. It has the power to make the most frigid female succumb helplessly to the spell of the moment," I say, alarmed at my own whimsicality.

"We thought the fun we had was the real thing. We believed people of your generation missed out on a lot of things," he says unabashedly. I'm intrigued.

"No, no, sir, you people got it wrong. We had more fun than you did," I cry in pretended protestation. "Let me prove it to you, sir. I remember this particular day. I think it was in my 300-level. We, I mean all the four of us in my room, attended an all-night gig and what happened there was an unusual experience for one of us. When we returned from the party, she whispered to her bunk mate that the boy she danced with at the party took her, right there on the dance floor and she felt remorseful about it. You know, it was a private confession aimed at achieving some sort of inner peace, but her bunk mate roared with uncontrollable laughter, outing her to the rest of us and assuring her that she had only just started living. Can you beat that, Oga?"

My professor loses control; he throws his head over his seat laughing uncontrollably. I join in the laughter and I'm happy, happier that I'm achieving my aim of putting him in a mood that would make him amenable to my purpose. I feel confident that my professor is now where I wish him to be. I clear my throat, ready to broach the subject of our meeting.

"Yes, sir, this is my chapter two. I promise to make the

necessary corrections to chapter one, which you are giving me today so that I can move on to chapter three very quickly, sir. I appreciate your hard work and I'm very grateful for everything sir," I say, placing my chapter two on his desk and looking imploringly at him. As soon as I mention my work, Prof Ephraim closes down. His countenance changes from jovial to angry. He frowns, his face darkens and his mouth presses into a thin, hard line. I'm rattled by his reaction. I stare at him for some moments, waiting for him to say something, wishing, hoping, praying that the expression I think I see on his face is a figment of my imagination. No, I must be mistaken. Is this not the same man who, only moments ago, was laughing like an exuberant, happy teenager? Is it wrong of me to want to make progress in my work? Isn't that the basis of our relationship? I'm waiting but he's saying nothing. I look at him again and now he's scowling at me. No, I'm not one to be easily intimidated by an indolent supervisor, so I prompt.

"Yes sir?"

"I haven't looked at your work," he snaps, his voice colder and scolding. What wrong have I committed? I stare down at my feet. I feel sick but I'm determined to wait for him to say something more reasonable, perhaps offer some kind of explanation for not having read my work and, yes, make a concrete promise regarding what he intends to do or when he plans to look at it. I wait for moments on end but he says nothing. I'm forced to look at him. He is glaring at me now, the silence stretching between us, but I'm keeping my own counsel.

"I'm busy doing other things," he says finally. My eyes are frosty and he's still talking. "By the way, I don't like the speed at which you are writing. How many times do you want me to warn you that this is PhD, not a master's degree programme? You have to take things really easy and work as slowly and as diligently as possible. I don't appreciate it when my students rush their writing because there is no surer way of compromising quality. Let me sound a note of warning yet again. In the business of doctoral thesis, it's not about how fast but how well. You have to take your time. In fourteen months, you have produced two chapters. Do I need to remind you that the first two chapters are the most crucial to your thesis? Okay, tell me, where do you do your research and how do you source your materials?"

"I do my research at the University of Lagos, sir. I'm a regular face at the university library. In addition, I have made a deliberate effort to cultivate the acquaintance of almost all the literature lecturers in this department and a majority of them are kind enough to grant me access to their personal library, sir. More than that, I buy books and any material I find relevant to my research, sir."

"Well, I don't know about the long story you've just told me. I ask you that question because I'm aware that books and other research materials are hardly available in Nigeria. Most of the books that are relevant to your work are obtainable abroad. You've not travelled out since the commencement of your programme, to the best of my knowledge. Now, if you tell me you get books from people's libraries, I know the kind of books you are getting. They're books published in the 1980s and 1990s. This is the beginning of a new millennium, my dear student. You've got a lot of problems on your plate. Your research will not only be shallow but also outdated and completely out of tune with present reality if you rush to use those old materials."

He stares impassively at me, his face unreadable. Don't be easily thrown, I mutter under my breath and to him. I say:

"Yes, sir, I appreciate your observation. I'm sorry I have neglected to mention that I also use the library of this great university, sir. Every fortnight when I come for departmental seminar, I sleep over and visit the library as well as the major bookshops in Abuja so as to lay my hands on any new material available, sir. I have been doing this diligently and without fail, sir. Perhaps if you find it in your heart to be kind and to look at what I have written, you might be in a better position to evaluate what I have done and the relevance or otherwise of the materials I have consulted, sir."

He's simply gazing at me, his expression unfathomable

"Eh-r, excuse me, sir. I was really hopeful yesterday, sir. I mean, I had high hopes that you might have actually looked at my work when I saw you and Agnes discussing what seemed to me to be her work, sir."

"What I was discussing with Agnes is her seminar paper which she intends to present at the next seminar."

Oh no, my mouth dries as I digest his words.

"All is set for Agnes to deliver her first seminar paper, sir?"

"Yes."

"That means she has made appreciable progress in her research, sir?"

"Yes."

"When would you want me to deliver my own first seminar paper, sir?"

"You can't present a seminar paper until I read part of your work and decide that you are worthy to be a PhD student."

"How soon are you likely to make this assessment, sir?"

"You are not on my radar now. That's why you have to slow down, take things easy and work at a very slow pace; the pace I want you to work at. You can't get a PhD in a hurry. I repeat, you cannot get a PhD in a hurry."

It's time to talk with courage, I resolve.

"I appreciate your diligence and meticulousness, sir, but as I mentioned to you a little over two years ago, I'm very single-minded. I focus and put my best to everything I do at any given time. The only activity I'm engaged in at the moment is my research work. I don't want you to misunderstand my commitment and devotion to my research as a sign of being hasty or shoddy. I'm a born hard worker and I shall appreciate your effort at encouraging and supporting me, sir. God will bless you and your family beyond compare."

He looks blankly at me, leaving me in no doubt that he's through with our meeting. He isn't going to say any more and he's definitely not used to being challenged. This is a discovery and it's revelatory and unnerving. I rise warily to my feet. My senses are thoroughly ravaged. The only thing I'm capable of doing at the moment is hum a sad melody of fading hope

I sob quietly as I sing and head out of the campus.

Ten

I owe my mother a visit. I have deliberately avoided stopping over to see her during the last couple of journeys, hoping to be able to give her some good news about the progress I'm supposed to be making in my programme. In view of the current reality, however, I can't continue to avoid her. Even if I don't have money or material gifts to bestow on her given my circumstance, it's incumbent on me to continue to pay her regular visits, at least to reassure her of my love.

I'm in Ibadan but my mother is not in her stall. I walk the five-minute-distance to her house, taking long, quick strides. She's not at home. I stand impatiently in front of the house awaiting her return and wondering where she could have gone. It's a long wait because she doesn't return until sunset. When she does, she's brimming with joy but her expression changes as soon as she sees me. I genuflect courteously before her, relieving her of the polythene bag she's holding.

"Dide, dide, nle, agbeke o, agbeke ogo, omo a jogo mago denu, omo eru ni won fin … nile baba yin, omo ti mobi lojo oja ti mio jeun epo. Oh, how I enjoy my mother's praise chants, and today's own is special. Does she have an inkling of what's going on in my life? She props me up and I rise, blinking back my tears and making sure I keep my head low so she doesn't see the outline of my face. Mothers and their instincts! She knows I'm troubled in spite of all the precautions I have taken. How do they do it?

"Tell me whatever is bothering you. I'm your mother and I deserve to know everything. Besides, you and your younger ones are the reason why I live. Tell me, oko mi, olowo ori mi."

"I'm fine, Ma'ami." My voice wavers as I see the concern on her face but I manage to hold myself together, pasting a false smile on my face as we enter the house. Within minutes, she presents me with a steamy yam flour meal, adorned with ewedu soup and beef. Deep down, I know I'm hungry but, right now, my stomach is tied in knots. I'm sitting across my mother, uncertain about how to tell her that I have neither succeeded in understanding my supervisor nor made any progress in my programme. She knows it's been over two years since I started; I'm sure she hasn't forgotten how I boasted to her that it would take me only three years to finish. Does my situation promote a healthy appetite? I look dubiously at the food whilst carefully weighing my options. Finally, I resolve not to mention my travails. I must insulate my mother from unpleasant thoughts and experiences, I tell myself firmly as I start to eat.

"You didn't ask me where I went," she accuses playfully.

"That's because I knew you would tell me," I murmur defensively. The truth is that I've been too wrapped up in my own misery to remember the basic niceties of our relationship. I haven't even enquired after her well-being, much less her business. My mother and her theatrics! I smile wryly at her.

"So, where did you go?"

"Your cousin, Bidemi, is getting married soon." My heart summersaults.

"How soon?"

"Ah, very soon o, you know how they do it these days; she's heavy with child already." I squeak.

"Just like that? I mean, no prior notice?" My brow creases.

"Ha, ha, what more notice does anyone need? Isn't it better to hasten things up before the man comes up with another story? You should be happy for her," she chastises and I'm overwhelmed with a genuine sense of remorse. My mother misunderstands me and it hurts because I can't explain my perspective. Of course, I'm truly happy for Bidemi, who is twenty-eight and long overdue for marriage going by the dictates of our culture. What worries me is my financial predicament knowing the implication of a wedding ceremony involving a close relation. There'll be a mandatory aso-ebi with all the paraphernalia to go with it. Can I afford it? Well, Folake may rise to the occasion. The greater challenge is about the actual ceremony when tradition demands that I do some elaborate cooking and invite a large retinue of guests to the feast. To our people, doing this is the only way to demonstrate respect for the bond of kinship between us. Bidemi's mother and my mother are sisters and I'm aware that Bidemi would have done the same at my wedding if there had been one. The only money I have left in my bank account is the proceeds I received from the sale of my car which I have been careful not to spend so that I can use it to fund Deyemi's Senior Secondary School education. Folake has been my pillar of support at ensuring that the money remains stashed away untouched when my supervisor insisted that I registered for a part-time rather than a full-time programme. What would I do without Folake's support? She not only feeds me, I wear her clothes, shoes, jewelleries and all and she funds my endless journeys to Abuja. How do I tell her that I'm compelled by tradition to spend at my cousin's wedding and that she has to pick the bill? Or, how do I explain to my mother and other members of the extended family that I would be jettisoning our age-long tradition because I have no job and I'm running a PhD programme? What do I do? Do I rush to the bank, withdraw my life's savings and jeopardise my only child's education in order to do right by my natal family? Why is my life becoming more complicated by the day? My mother can't understand me. How can she when even I can't understand me? It's better to plead guilty to envy than to ruin my ambition and aspiration.

"It's not like that, Ma'ami," I mutter sulkily.

"Don't worry, one day soon your own man will come and marry you," she says soothingly and I don't argue. I knew it would come to that eventually. I allow my mouth to curl in the semblance of a smile.

"You've not told me the full story," I say as cheerfully as I can.

"Oh yes, what happened today was the traditional presentation of kola by the groom's family to formally declare their intention to marry Bidemi and to interact with members of our family. You needed to have been there to see your pregnant cousin. She was very happy." I'm struggling to hide my exasperation.

"When will the wedding hold?"

"Next month. She is heavily pregnant, as I mentioned, and the wedding has to hold before she puts to bed. The aso-ebi will be unveiled next week."

I pout. How could I have forgotten that it's also my responsibility to buy my mother's aso-ebi? What do I do? My visit is ruined. I don't talk to my mother for the rest of the evening and in the morning I return to Lagos sadder than I had planned.

Back in Lagos, the apartment is empty. Folake is at Geoffrey's. Deyemi is in school. I turn on the television so there's noise to fill the sitting room and provide some semblance of company, but I don't listen or watch. I sit and stare blankly at the wall. I'm numb. I feel nothing but confusion and pain. How long can I endure this? My mind drifts to Shettima. I remember seeing him the other day at Allen Avenue roundabout. "For how long are you going to keep running from me?" He asked, looking solemn. I didn't know how to respond because I knew he would not understand. The truth is that my refusal to yield to his entreaties has nothing to do with him. It's about my own demons which I admit I don't have the courage to confront. But how am I supposed to explain it? I ignored his question and tried for politeness. "I won't give up on you." He threatened. I waved him off playfully. I don't need a man in my life. I reaffirm silently and my resolve drags me back to the present. I rise to look at the calendar. Deyemi is not due home for the next four weeks. No, I can't go on like this. Tomorrow I'll go to see Folake at work to plead with her to come home for a few days at least. How can I go on like this? I can't read or write in my present frame of mind. Besides, I have to let Folake know that I will need her financial assistance in respect of aso-ebi for my cousin's wedding. Well, that's all I can allow my mind to accommodate at the moment.

I pay Folake a visit at her work place and insist she comes home at the close of day. She doesn't argue. She's home now although I'm beyond fatigued by the time she arrives. I welcome her back home with my arms outstretched. As soon as she's in my arms, I burst into tears. She feels so good and I lose control. Reluctantly, I relinquish her, quickly reeling out my tales of woe accompanied by torrents of tears. She listens without interrupting. When I have finished, she says:

"How many times do I need to tell you, Funto, that you are a bright, beautiful woman and that you mustn't allow doubts to destroy you? Ignore the antics of your nepotistic supervisor. You will get your PhD if you hold on to your dream and continue to work as hard as I see you do. Yes, it may take you a little longer than his cherished Agnes, but what difference would it make at the end of the day other than to put him to shame? The fact that he has neither sense of shame nor justice and fair play makes him a pathetic wretch. I don't know how else you want me to say this. I will support you every step of the way. As for your cousin's forthcoming wedding, I will inform Geoffrey at once and both of us will deploy all necessary resources to ensure that you are not put to shame."

I watch Folake in awe as she speaks, allowing myself to feel a modicum of excitement.

"See your flat nose," she teases. "Come with me joor, I bought you a gift." I jump up in excitement.

"A gift? What gift?"

"Come now, it's a surprise. Don't you know how surprises work?" She arches a perfect eyebrow at me and saunters out of the sitting room. I smile at her retreating back before skipping off to join her. The gift is well wrapped and sitting delicately on the back passenger seat of her car but I know what it is by merely looking at it. It's a large mirror.

"You are nuts, Folake," I scold playfully. "Why waste money on another mirror when you know there are more mirrors than I need in this house?"

"It's not a waste. I know how much you enjoy admiring yourself, so there goes a beautiful mirror for an even more beautiful friend."

We laugh boisterously as we take it in, each of us holding either end. By the time we succeed in creating a space for it in my room, almost every space in my room is now taken up by mirrors. I stand in the middle and see my reflection everywhere. A song breaks out from my mouth involuntarily:

Ore l'onpani, Ore l'ongbani, Ore l'on s'orisirisi fun ni/Friends can kill, friends can save, and friends can do all manner of things to their friends. I start to dance as my excitement blooms, eclipsing all other feelings. Soon, Folake joins me. Ore l'onpani,

Ore l'ongbani, Ore l'on s'orisirisi fun ni. I'm enthralled by Folake's competent dancing steps. As we dance, I start to mirror her steps and, in time, it becomes effortless for me to follow. We dance until beads of sweat break out on our foreheads. Then, suddenly, we remember that we are hungry. We play-fight as we walk into the kitchen. I bring out okra from the fridge for Folake to chop while I slice onions. Folake chops each finger of okra into more than a dozen pieces. Yam flour is our choice any day because it's smooth, light and easy to swallow. My mind drifts to my supervisor as we cook but all I do is smile at the memory of his harsh words.

"I have been thinking, you know," Folake says as she retrieves the chicken from the deep freezer. She pauses to eye me mischievously and I smirk at her.

"Are you smirking at me?" she challenges.

"I know you are up to something foolish whenever you look at me that way," I say aggressively.

"I don't care what you know, Funto. I won't let you intimidate me."

"Very well, out with it," I murmur, giving her an encouraging smile.

"Let me say this for the umpteenth time, Funto, you are an amazingly exquisite woman. You are beguilingly beautiful and..."

"Why don't you spare me the praises and simply go straight to the point? What are you up to?" I ask, feigning exasperation."

"You need to loosen up a little. Allow a man to come into your life." I saw it coming. I hiss.

"Why don't you want to give me a chance to at least express my view? Why are you always uptight and impossible each time I broach the subject?" she accuses, eyeing me the way a mother does a querulous child.

"Don't preach at me. Folake," I warn, looking menacingly

at her.

"It's no preaching and you know it. Look, I understand it when a woman closes up after having had an unpleasant experience with a man, but…"

"Stop! Just stop, okay? You described what I went through as an unpleasant experience? What happened gave me maximum heartache, for crying out loud. What am I supposed to do after that? You want me to throw myself at another man who would probably disappear after one week? Oh bloody hell, no!"

"I like your choice of word, 'probably'. You have become so self-possessed that you don't realise how you deny yourself a chance to be happy by shutting the door to possibilities. Look at Shettima, a man so honest and so consistent in his desire to have a relationship with you. No, you wouldn't even let him try. All you want is to go on punishing yourself."

"What do I know about Shettima?"

"Fine. You don't know anything about him, but what can be wrong with giving yourself a chance to find out/"

"I know where you are coming from, Folake. You talk like this because you have a man who adores you but you forget that every man is not like Geoffrey."

"And every man is not like Deyemi's father," she says softly, placing her hands on my shoulders and forcing me to face her. Our eyes lock and I feel the weight of her insistence. I drag my gaze away from her, turning to check for the chicken on the stove.

"I'll be straight with you," I say without looking at her. "I have resolved to spend the rest of my adult life avoiding any extreme emotion. I haven't shut the door to possibilities, as you describe it, but I feel ambivalent about male/female relationships. I haven't found anyone I'm attracted to."

"That's only because you've been closed, too much so. Look, it's reasonable for you to be guarded, but it's even more sensible that you don't deny yourself a chance to be happy. And I don't believe that you don't feel attracted to Shettima. It's obvious you are stubbornly struggling to keep to your needless resolve."

"Okay o, Madam Preacher," I tease.

"That's my babe! Give me five, joor." We slap our palms together and allow them to slide across each other. Our amala is ready; we devour it in companionable silence.

My cousin's wedding day arrives and we travel to Ibadan in grand style. Geoffrey doesn't go with us but he gives us a driver and, on Folake's insistence, we cram the boot of his Mercedes Benz with assorted party paraphernalia. A week or so before we travel, she had procured souvenirs bearing the inscription: 'Bidemi weds Bodunde, Happy Married Life.' Beneath is written: Courtesy of Funto Oyewole, Bride's Cousin. We don't cook in Ibadan but we have sufficient cash. Folake tells me to ask my mother to introduce us to professional caterers. We have assorted drinks and beverages in surplus. No one in my family has an inkling of my financial stress. Sophisticated jewellery and accessories make us stand out in the crowd even though we are dressed in the general aso-ebi for the occasion.

There is a band stand on display and we dance and sway tirelessly to the renditions of the lead musician and his band boys. Olufunto mi l'onjo, awo Folake mi aguleyinju/It's Olufunto that is dancing, the one who is affiliated to beautiful Folake. I'm drunk with excitement and I go gaga, literally swaying vigorously like someone possessed. This is my own area of specialisation. I enjoy dancing to high-tempo traditional music and I always revel in demonstrating my talent at every opportunity because it never goes unremarked upon. Even Folake can't hide her admiration.

It's now time for the couple's dance. As they make their way to the floor, the MC announces to all of us to join the couple as a mark of honour. Folake pulls me up immediately and we are the first to join the couple. We start to spray them with naira notes and the musician begins another round of praise singing. We move over to him and spray him also. He croons: Olufunto mi l'on nawo, awo Folake mi aguleyinju/It's Olufunto that is spraying money, the one who is affiliated to beautiful Folake. As we dance, I notice that a certain man has been eyeing me all evening. As soon as Folake and I return to our seat, he emerges from nowhere, wends his way through the crowd and is suddenly standing next to me, greeting me and laying his hand on my arm. I peek up at him; he has a spell-binding look. My heart summersaults and starts to pound furiously. It's another beautiful man, my subconscious announces darkly. I tear my gaze away from him, muttering to myself, no, I won't fall into the same trap again, I can't handle it. I shake my head vigorously this way and that way. I opt for distraction by starting a chat with Folake. The man reads my mood and walks away. I breathe a sigh of relief.

Eleven

I'm standing by Folake's chest of drawers, staring at her mirror, trying to comb my hair into some semblance of a style. I'm dressed in her jeans and T- shirt, ready to travel to Abuja for our departmental seminar. After gazing at my reflection for the umpteenth time, I'm convinced that I'm good to go.

I arrive on campus with a modicum of excitement as I look forward to the day's presentations. There are usually two presentations at every seminar and I often find commentaries and critiques of papers delivered sometimes far more insightful than the actual presentations. People ask questions that throw up more questions and others proffer answers that are very illuminating. I don't expect today to be any different. I hastily scan the hall for either Mrs Korede or Mrs Lawal, or the both. Neither seems to have come yet and my eyes settle on Agnes. She looks unusually officious. She is chatting with a man sitting next to her. Our eyes meet briefly and we smile our greetings. I find a seat, but just as I'm about to settle down I feel a sudden urge to pee. I fling my handbag in the locker and make a quick dash toward the rest room. I climb down the staircase and pass through a corridor leading to the rest room. I must have been either self-absorbed or in a haste because I nearly bump into my professor without noticing he was coming. I stop in my tracks.

"I'm sorry, sir." I mumble apologetically.

"Wow, Lagos woman! You look great!" he exclaims

dramatically, wide-eyed. I'm thrown by his unusual grace. Since when did my supervisor start paying me such a glorious compliment? I peek up at him through my lashes. There is genuine appreciation on his face. Wonderment! So my professor can be this gracious? He seems to be in extraordinarily joyous mood. I push my chances even further.

"Why did you call me Lagos woman, sir?"

"Because you have the Lagos look about you. You no see as I be?" What? My professor is speaking pidgin to me? Is it really about me or about him? I wish I brought my chapter three today, which I have already finished writing but have been afraid to present to him lest he accuse me of wanting to get a PhD in a hurry. Anyway, it's nice to have my professor notice my appearance. Folake and I will definitely drink to this. I cock my head to one side and smile contentedly.

"You look great as well, sir," I breathe.

"Thank you and, eh-r, where are you going? The seminar will begin shortly."

"Yes, I know, sir, I will be back soon," I say, stepping aside to let him pass. I stand immobilised for a few moments. That's another surprise. My professor is urging me not to be late to a seminar? He hardly attends them himself. Has he attended up to three in the almost three years that I have been on the programme? I don't think so. I try to solve the jigsaw but I can't wrap my head around it. Well, suffice it to know that Professor Ephraim is not as difficult to gauge as I imagined. I relieve my bladder of the pressure. Mrs Lawal is in the hall now. We exchange courtesies. There is no sign of Mrs Korede. There is silence because a presentation is already in progress. The central idea of the paper is about the soul. It says the soul is beyond and older than the person. It cites, as an example, the African-American which, it says, captures the African imagination involuntarily. The paper insists that in spite of our introjections of Christian and Islamic values, the market remains a spiritual, metaphysical and ritual space.

"I don't feel the presence of the gods in our churches and mosques," the presenter shouts into the microphone and the hall erupts in prolonged laughter. I nod my head enthusiastically and write down as many points as I can of the various submissions, arguments and counter-arguments. The first presentation ends. The presenter takes a bow and returns to his seat amidst whispers and murmurs.

My supervisor emerges from the right front corner of the hall and walks briskly to the lectern. A hush descends as all eyes turn to him.

"I say good evening to colleagues and students here present."

"Good evening," the hall responds.

"I want to congratulate all those who have assembled here today because you are very lucky people. You are lucky because you are going to have a spectacular time. Those of you who know me will agree that I'm not loquacious and I don't describe people in flowery language. I'm a plain man and I go straight to the point. However, when you find yourself in an extraordinary situation, you can't but step out of the box to act in an extraordinary way. The next paper shall be delivered by a young lady who is exceptionally brilliant. Now, you know why you are lucky. This is a lady who deserves to have gotten her PhD at nineteen if she had applied herself to it. She has waited until she reaches nearly her late twenties before realising her potential but the delay has only further sharpened her exceptional intellect. I don't want to waste your time because it's not part of the process of seminar presentation to make speeches but, as I pointed out earlier, we have a distinctly unique situation in our hand and it cannot be out of place to celebrate our rare find. Ladies and Gentlemen, Ms

Agnes Ellen Noah presents."

Everyone in the hall is gaping at him with…what? Surprise, amusement or confusion? I don't know. My brain whispers at me that my professor has gone nuts but I dismiss the thought. He can't even be bothered by the audience's apparent disapproving reaction. He smiles warmly at Agnes who walks over to the lectern and places her paper on it as my professor returns to his seat. I watch in utter embarrassment as people make repeated efforts to stifle yawns as Agnes makes her presentation. Finally, it comes to an end. There is palpable relief in the hall. The seminar coordinator calls for responses from the audience and Prof Brown's voice roars from behind the hall. There is absolute silence as he rises and begins to speak.

"I don't know what is going on in the English Department these days," he says calmly. All eyes are turned toward him with necks craning from different directions. "I don't know in particular what my colleagues in literature are doing with their time. It's absolutely absurd for anyone to write and, worse still, have the nerve to stand here to deliver a paper that fails to use at least one literary theory to foreground their paper. What I find truly amazing is that such a paper gets the approval of a member of our highly esteemed department. We don't allow this kind of abnormality in language and it's unfortunate that people are allowed to compromise standards in literature. I'm saddened by the conscious and steady bastardization of our educational system by those who easily sacrifice standards at the altar of interpersonal relationships. Honestly, we need to be ashamed of the wrongs we flagrantly commit. What kind of certificates are we dishing out to our so-called graduates at all levels? I'm saddened because when you point out these absurdities to my colleagues who are not unaware of the grave implications of their wrongdoing, they label you as their enemy and target you for thoughtless vengeance. I weep for our disgraced and thoroughly shamed educational system. I weep for my discredited fatherland. Above all, however, I wail for beneficiaries of a circumvented system. I sympathise with those who obtain unearned degrees and certificates. Let them continue to gloat at the supposed magic their godfathers, godmothers, concubines, mistresses and kinsmen can shamelessly spin for them. At the peak of their undeserved glory, their fall lies in wait and it is only a matter of time before they fall irretrievably in."

Prof Brown is heading toward the door, my supervisor has leapt off his seat and is desperate to say something; the seminar coordinator is trying to restore order; everybody is talking at the same time.

"It's not a language/literature problem," someone says beside me. "There is favouritism and nepotism everywhere," he adds. No one responds. Order cannot be restored. Prof Brown is effectively out of the hall now; my supervisor is fuming. Some people are beginning to walk out. Soon, everyone is leaving and I can't but do the same. At the door, I find Akpabio beside me. I'm happy to see him.

"Caught you at last," I beam, putting my hand on his shoulder.

"Olufunto, the queen," he hails and my smile booms.

"Look, I have been searching for you all over the campus. Glad to find you."

"I'm glad to see you, too. How're you doing?" he asks but I don't answer. Instead, I drag him from the crowd.

"I need to talk to you," I murmur.

"Not now," he says.

"Why not? Are you going somewhere?"

"No, it's you."

"Me? What about me?"

"You can't afford to talk to me or anyone for that matter now."

"Are you okay? You confuse me, Akpabio."

"Don't be confused. What you need to do right now is to follow your supervisor to his office or wherever he may be heading if you are halfway serious about getting a PhD."

"What do I have to do with two feuding lecturers?" I query, confused.

"You don't know? Prof Brown has just given your supervisor a blow below his belt and you stand here and say it doesn't concern you? Na wah o. Run along now, okay? Show solidarity. It's as important as writing your chapter one."

"But I want to talk to you," I insist.

"I'll be waiting for you in front of his office. It's more important than anything you want to discuss," he says dismissively.

I take Akpabio's advice and skip off. Soon, I find myself behind a column. I notice that my professor is in front and all of us are following him like a group of mourners. We move in the direction of his office with Agnes walking closely behind him. When we arrive, Ephraim opens the door and we all file in, quietly. He sinks into his chair and for some moments we all just stand and stare; his eyes are intense, threatening even.

"Sorry about Prof Brown's ranting sir," somebody says.

"The man is too forward for my liking," another offers and it appears that's all my professor needs to explode.

"Who the hell does Brown think he is? Who the hell does anyone think they are?" he thunders, throwing fist into the air. We all cower under his roaring and he resumes his vituperations.

"They run the system as they like, and why shouldn't they when they are supposedly the major tribes and languages? They call us the minority, what trash? We are going to show them in this country that we are as important as any single tribe or ethnic group, be it major or minor. We'll put our people in strategic places and catapult them to the highest echelons. Only then will they reappraise their jaundiced categorisation and classification. Minority my foot! Don't we have Hausa helping Hausa, Igbo helping Igbo, Yoruba helping Yoruba in this university whether or not they merit such help? It's wrong only when the so-called minorities do it. They have continued to persecute us and deny us our inalienable rights. We shall see. This is the National University of Nigeria, it belongs to all of us, and we are all equally entitled. I repeat, equally entitled! Even if our minority status makes us minors, has it ever happened that the minor members of a family are denied certain privileges? Why am I sitting behind this damned desk, by the way? I ought to go look for Brown and talk some real sense into his dull skull."

He rises with the kind of swiftness that is not usual in a man of his massive frame and makes to leave but is restrained by a multitude of hands placating him. Just then, I remember Akpabio's warning. Perhaps he hasn't noticed my presence. Isn't this a good opportunity for me to let him know that I'm also part of the solidarity train? I clear my throat and shout above the group with drama.

"We love you, sir. You are a distinguished scholar and no one can diminish you." It works! The group erupts in a sing song: "We love you, sir! We love you, sir! We love you, sir!"

A face-splitting smile breaks out on his face. As if on cue, we throng out of his office, satisfied that we have stroked our professor's ego.

I find Akpabio waiting patiently outside.

"How did it go?" he asks.

"It went as you predicted. But how come you know so much about these things?" I ask, my tone is playfully accusatory.

"Because I have been around for a while. This is my sixth

year as a PhD student, so I ought to know."

"Anyway, I wanted to tell you what transpired between Ephraim and me when I tried to give him the chapter two of my thesis. Perhaps you can advise me."

"Answer this question before you tell me what happened. How many times have you bought him a gift since you started?"

"I haven't at all."

"What? Okay, but you've been giving him cash periodically?"

"No, I have never."

"Funto, you disappoint me. I'm sorry but…"

"Don't spare me; tell me precisely what I've done wrong," I plead.

"You don't look like someone who is cash-strapped to me, but even if you don't have money, as I don't, there are other ways you can make your Oga happy and thereby accelerate your progress. For example, I go to my supervisor's house every weekend to help with household chores. I wash his car, do his laundry, run errands and do sundry other things. I'm practically at his beck and call. I do all these things to make up for my financial limitations."

"Honestly, Akpabio, I feel very bad that you have to remind me of this. I just haven't given it any serious thought."

"You must bear in mind at all times that university lecturers are very powerful. They act like demigods, and indeed they are as far as getting a PhD is concerned."

"I think you are right."

"You think? Of course I'm right. You may not like their ways but you've got to follow the dictates of their whims if you want a PhD."

"Okay, Akpabio, I'll do as you say."

"One more thing, Funto, don't make it a one-off thing. It must be sustained because that's the only way it can work in your favour. You don't do it once, twice or even three times and stop. You must keep doing it until they let you go."

"Akpabio, you are the best! What would I do in this campus without you?"

"Leave the encomiums for now, this is a good time to start. Do you have some money?"

"Uh, no, I mean, yes. If I look into my bag, I'm sure I'll get something."

"Good. Your supervisor has four children, three boys and a girl. The girl is about ten, she's the youngest and he adores her specially. That makes her the first beneficiary of your gifts. I'm sure you know the needs of a ten-year-old girl."

"Okay, I'll do that tomorrow before going back to Lagos."

"Very good. Did you bring your car?"

"Um-m no, I came by public transport."

"Do you drive?"

"Yes, I do."

"In that case, I'll let you use my car."

"Wow! That's very kind of you"

"I'll be in the department from 9 o clock in the morning. I may accompany you if you don't know your way around town."

"Very well then, see you tomorrow," I say cheerfully, but my mind is in a whirl. How could I possibly turn down Akpabio's advice and magnanimity? The truth, however, is that the only money I have is what Folake gave me for my transport and lodging. There are only two options now, it's either I use the money to pay for my lodging as planned, or I expend it on procuring a gift for my professor's adorable daughter. It's absolutely inconceivable to go by the earlier plan in view of the reality before me. Akpabio is right. I want to get a Ph.D. I have to be prepared to give as much as I can to achieve my ambition, but where do I pass the night? I have no relative in Abuja, no friend and no acquaintance. The only place I know in the city is the university. I come to a quick decision. I'll go into a classroom and sit until daybreak. I know the implication of what I'm about to do. It means not only will I not be able to have a bath in the morning. I won't be able to brush my teeth or change my clothes. Well, the situation is a test of my determination to achieve my dream and I might as well give it my utmost. I mutter under my breath as I take melancholic strides toward one of the cafeterias on campus for an early dinner.

When I have eaten, I buy a bottle of water to accompany me through what promises to be a long night. First, I go to the library to read but it closes at 10pm, then I head for one of the lecture halls. Mercifully, there is electricity. I sink into a seat and bring out the photocopy of a book I made at the library. I place it in front of me and pretend to be reading, but I'm looking blankly at it, my mind travelling far and wide, capturing old memories, both sweet and sour. I recall a particular experience that left an indelible mark on my psyche.

It happened during my master's degree programme which I obtained from Western University of Nigeria. One of my lecturers then, Professor Bamijo, took a liking to me and told me he wanted me to be intimate with him. I told him I appreciated his interest and that I was humbled that a university don could find me attractive. However, I also politely pointed out that I felt no romantic inclination toward him and would be grateful if he would only regard me as the normal student that I was. Probably because of my extreme politeness and respect with which I communicated my lack of interest, he didn't threaten me. He acted gallantly and even earned my respect further. Our relationship throughout the semester was characterised by cordiality and respect - or so I thought. I didn't know I was living in the proverbial fool's paradise until our results were pasted on the board at the beginning of the second semester.

It was with confidence that I strolled to the board to check my results. Why wouldn't I be confident? The course in question was a compulsory one, and we knew it was a must pass course without which we would not graduate. We studied hard for it. It was also an interesting course. Anyway, I went to the notice board and what did I find? It was unbelievable. I saw 0- 0-0. Continuous Assessment = 0, Examination = 0, Total Score = 0. My first reaction was to laugh. I meant it simply couldn't be true. I laughed and laughed and laughed like one who was freshly possessed of madness. When I recovered, I took another look. Perhaps I had looked at someone else's matriculation number. I took a second look, then a third and fourth until I realised that it was indeed my matriculation number. My brain whispered another rationalisation. It was an honest mistake. Oh yes, that must be the true explanation. My lecturer must have got things mixed up. With this thought, I headed for his office. I knocked and he told me to enter.

"Excuse me, sir, I saw 0-0-0 against my name, sir."

"Congratulations! You got 0-0-0," he says simply.

"I thought there has been a mistake, sir."

"What do you mean by there has been a mistake? What you saw is precisely what you got."

"I beg your pardon, sir, but it can't be true because I was not absent at the examination, sir. Besides, you gave us a test and we also wrote a term paper for our continuous assessment. How is it possible that I would score zero in the test, zero in the term paper, sir?"

"What impudence! You stand in my office and call my integrity to question? Do you think I'm a yesterday Professor? I became a Professor when you were probably in your diapers, if your mother had the good fortune to be able to afford them?"

"Excuse me, sir, I'm very sorry, I didn't intend to upset you sir. I just thought there had been a mix-up that was not intended and I wanted to respectfully call your attention to it, sir."

"Leave my office this minute! You deserve to get zero and you got it, period."

I walked out confused, angry and sad but after consultation with a few of my classmates I was advised to write a letter of complaint to the Head of Department. I took their advice seriously because this was a first semester course. We were already in the second semester and if the issue was not resolved it would give me an undeserved extra semester. I wrote a letter to the Head of Department, explaining as succinctly as possible my shock find at the notice board but leaving out the dirty details of Prof Bamijo's earlier amorous intentions toward me. I submitted the letter to his secretary and waited for his response. Four weeks went by with no response. Meanwhile, I went to see the secretary nearly every day, asking if the HOD had responded to my letter and urging him to help me remind him. Five weeks after the submission of my petition without a response, I walked boldly to his office and insisted on having a one-on-one discussion with him. The secretary tried all he could to dissuade me, telling me the HOD would send for me if and when he chose to but I stood my ground. After engaging him in a protracted argument, the secretary saw that I was prepared to create a scene and granted me access.

"Good day, sir, my name is Funto Oyewole. I wrote a letter concerning…"

"Oh yes, you did. Sit down, please," he said kindly. I sat bold faced, straightening my shoulders and looking directly into his eyes. He looked uncomfortable, slightly off-balance and appeared to search for something to say. Our eyes locked for long moments and I kept my counsel. He blinked several times before clearing his throat.

"I got your letter," he began and I started to relax. "I'm sorry I haven't got back to you. I was trying to find a way to solve the problem amicably. I tried to talk to Prof but he was difficult. He said you humiliated him and he wasn't going to forgive you."

"Humiliated him? How?"

"That's what I should ask you, really, because when I spoke to him, he was vehement. He swore to deal with you."

"I don't know how I have humiliated him, sir, but what I requested you to do in my petition, which is what I still ask, sir, is that my exam script, the test script and the term paper I wrote in respect of the course be reassessed by another lecturer."

"Um-m, I hope you don't mind my asking you this, Ms Oyewole are there any social issues between the pair of you that need to be resolved?"

"With due respect, sir, I don't want us to dwell on social issues. I'd rather we concentrate on intellectual issues that are germane to this discourse. I feel very strongly that Prof Bamijo has not treated me fairly, sir, and I want the department to organise for my script to be reassessed. If the new assessor hands me the same score, I shall accept it in good faith, sir."

"Unfortunately, Ms Oyewole, things are not as straight-jacketed as you imagine. There is no lecturer in this department who would be willing to re-grade a script that Prof Bamijo has previously graded, for whatever reason."

I was jolted, but I didn't betray any emotion.

"I feel convinced that I'm being persecuted, sir, and as a legitimate student of this department, don't I also have a right to request the department to look into my situation, sir?"

"You do have the right, Ms. Oyewole, and please believe me when I say that I genuinely sympathise with you. I asked you if there were social issues between you and Prof because I wanted and still want to assist you in the only way possible. Take my advice, young lady, go and meet Prof, resolve all outstanding issues between you and all will be well. That's the easier and better way to resolve it. However, if you insist on following the formal procedure, there's only one way to do it."

"I'm interested in the official procedure only, sir."

"Very well, write a letter to the Postgraduate School, they will instruct the department to release your script to them and then arrange for an independent academic from another university to re-grade it. That's the only way you can get justice. But if you would do me the honour of listening to me, I would advise you to take the first option, find a way to placate Prof. Give him what he wants and let him reassess your script. Prof is one of the oldest lecturers in this department. Nobody can confront him, not me, sitting on this seat and certainly not any other lecturer. He's an institution, a colossus, an enigma that we all hold in awe and high esteem. If you truly want to seek justice, write to the PG School, the process will be long but justice is assured at the end. Go home and consider both options, whatever you decide to do, you have my best wishes and, once again, I'm very sorry for not getting back to you. I couldn't quite figure out what to do."

I thanked him profusely and took my leave. I had made up my mind about what I would do and did not need to weigh my options. I would write a petition to the PG School and, no matter how long it took I would wait and insist on a thorough investigation of the matter. To my utmost surprise, however, another professor in the department suddenly requested to see me that same day. I went to see him and was totally thrown off-balance when he broached the subject of my dispute with Prof Bamijo. I didn't quite know what to make of his involvement. When and how did he get to know about it? Why was he interested? Why did he want to get involved? My mind was boiling with unanswered questions.

"Do you believe in God?" he asked me. I was shocked. What has God to do with the matter under discourse? I was aware of his eyes on me. Why was he looking at me as if I were a querulous child? I hadn't had any close interaction with him since becoming a student. I felt petulant and aggrieved and my head ached. I didn't know what to say so I said nothing. He continued.

"Look, I sent for you because I want to help you. I have observed you in this department and you don't look like a troublesome person to me. If you write to the PG School, you will get justice but you will also become controversial. Other lecturers in the department will team up with Prof Bamijo to deal with you ruthlessly because you will have humiliated him. They will work in concert and solidarity with him. Suddenly, you will be failing all your other courses and you will not be able to understand or explain why. How many lecturers do you want to accuse of deliberately failing you? They will make sure you don't get a certificate from this university. That's why I asked you if you believe in God because if you do, I would advise you to take your grievance to Him and let Him be the ultimate judge. Leave Prof Bamijo to God. Prepare your mind for an extra semester. The HOD will ensure that the course is allocated to a neutral person so that you'll have no further dealings with Prof."

Well, I took Prof Bayonle's advice in the end. I reasoned that Bayonle meant well for me and that it would be equally reasonable if I acquiesced to his wise counsel, not because I believed or was afraid of other lecturers teaming up with Prof Bamijo to victimise me, but as a gesture of gratitude for his peace efforts. I went through the agony of an undeserved extra semester and, as was promised by Bayonle, the course was given to another lecturer who treated me like a regular student. It was not until much later that I got to know that Professors Bamijo and Bayonle were first cousins. Perhaps he dissuaded me from taking the action only because he was interested in protecting his relative from what would have probably been the most calamitous event of his career. With the benefit of hindsight I would have defiantly turned down Prof Bayonle's advice and would have gone ahead to push for …"

"Madam, Madam, Madam!" A middle aged woman wearing a green-white-green overall and holding a broom in her right hand distracts and brings me back to here and now. It's daybreak. Wow! Did I sleep? I can't tell. I climb clumsily to my feet, pick my handbag and head toward the department to await Akpabio's arrival.

"You look sort of odd," he comments as soon as he sets his eyes on me.

"Well, I, I…" I can't put a sentence together.

"Your eyes are red, you didn't sleep well? And you've not changed your clothes." I look down at my feet, awash with embarrassment.

"Actually, I slept in one of the lecture halls. I sat throughout the night," I blurt out eventually.

"You did what? You could have been attacked and assaulted. There are bad boys on campus, you know."

"Well, I guess that's a lesson for another time. For now, I have saved the money I would have used for lodging and I can use it to buy a gift for my supervisor's daughter." He gives me his car key and walks with me to the car without another word. As I drove out of the campus, in company of Akpabio, I sing silently to myself: I'll get a PhD. Oh yes I'll get a PhD….

Twelve

Deyemi wants us to go shopping today. I don't really feel like it but bow to her wish regardless, knowing that it doesn't always have to be about me. Besides, I'm trying to key into her exhilarating mood realising that it's her holiday. Not only is it normal for her to want to make the most of it; it's also my responsibility to make her occasional home-coming as fun-filled as possible. I'm not worried about money. I have made my budget. One thing I continually pat myself on the back for is my ability to anticipate my daughter's material needs and meet them. I'm often reluctant, for instance, to frontally ask Folake to help me with Deyemi's school fees. I'm aware, though, that by taking care of nearly all my financial needs, Folake is also indirectly responsible for my daughter's upkeep. But the more I think about it, the more convinced I become that I would be disrespecting my daughter if I openly pushed her to Folake for her needs. I would be abdicating my maternal responsibilities. Anyway, I'm financially ready to take Deyemi out for shopping today.

"Deyemi! You'd better be ready or I'll change my mind," I threaten mockingly.

"I'm ready, Mum. I just want to add to my list."

"Keep adding to your list, you hear? I suppose you think I'm the Central Bank of Nigeria."

"It's only three more things I'm adding."

"Let me see it when you are done."

"Okay Mum."

She gives me the list. Her eyes are dancing with excitement. I scan through it – shoes, underwear, dresses, jean skirt and trousers, tops, wristwatch, school sandals, socks, mosquito net, earrings. I smile.

Five hours later, we return home, both of us feeling very happy for different reasons. Deyemi is excited by per purchases and I'm basking in the euphoria of having satisfied her. I tell her to take a rest before we start preparing dinner. I'm about to drift to sleep when she practically races into my room, alarm all over her. I jump.

"Mummy, Mummy, come and see." I leap off the bed, my heart somersaulting.

"What is it? Is it a fire? Did you light a match near the cylinder?"

"No, Mummy, there's something in my pants."

"Your pants? What's in your pants?"

"I don't know. I just went to the bathroom to pee, and … and … I saw it. Oh mummy, it's so terrible, black and dirty." Tears stream down her cheeks. My heart constricts. I know what it is; my little angel is a woman. My heart is beating even harder now. This is a moment I have looked forward to. I even believed it would give me great joy and a sense of pride when it arrived. Now, it has arrived and I'm suddenly overtaken by fear. Why? I don't know, but perhaps my subconscious thinks my daughter's new status will also be burdensome. But to whom? I don't know. Dear God, help my little angel to cope with the challenges of womanhood, of which the monthly menstruation is but a small part.

"Mummy?" She distracts me from my introspection.

"Sweetheart, what you've just seen may seem dirty but

it's not dirty at all. Eh-r-m, I mean, in terms of its usefulness. It's a symbol of beauty, Deyemi. It connotes womanhood, responsibility, wholesomeness, chronological maturity. Above all, it is a call to personal discipline and self-restraint. It is what I have been talking to you about, telling you to expect. It is your menstruation, commonly known as period."

She frowns. I give her a warped smile. There's confusion in her eyes when I meet her gaze.

"Oh, Mummy, is it what you said I will need sanitary for when it comes?" she asks solemnly.

"That's my girl! I trust your retentive memory!" I cry with exaggerated excitement, giving her a playful push. "Come on now, let's go get the pad. I'll show you how to use it."

"You told me to expect blood, Mummy, but what I'm seeing doesn't look like blood. It's too dir…"

"Don't use that word, sweetheart. I already told you, it's a beautiful thing. Yes, it doesn't look clean now only because it's just about to start. It will get clearer as it flows. By tomorrow, it will have become bright red," I explain in a grandma-like tone.

Inside, my head is whirling. I'm not sure about what I'm saying or what I ought to be telling her. Teach me how to help my daughter, God, I mutter silently. I'm trying to rack my brains for other important information I should be giving her but her voice distracts me.

"You mean I will still see it tomorrow?" she asks. I nod solemnly. "Will I remove the pad when I'm going to sleep at night?"

"No, darling. You will have to continue to have it on throughout the days the 'period' lasts."

"What?" She glares at me then heaves a sigh. She suddenly looks pale and forlorn. I take a deep breath and pat her reassuringly on her shoulder.

"The blood will run for about five days, darling, but I assure you that it's not going to be difficult for you to manage. Besides, I'm here to support you, show you how to cope. It's a monthly visitor and your mummy has been playing host to it for many years now. So, you are far from being alone. Come on, let's get the pad so that you don't stain your dress." I stare at her for a moment then exhale abruptly.

"Okay, Mummy," she mumbles. Her voice is flat. I feel drained and world-weary.

"You can ask me any questions at all. I promise to tell you everything and by the time you've done it for three months, it'll have become so much a part of you such that you'll no longer feel uncomfortable about it, okay?" I give her a solid hug and that gets a genuine smile out of her. I draw a deep, shaky breath, my insides still trembling.

Back in my bedroom, I bring out a pack of sanitary pads from the wardrobe, open it and begin to demonstrate how it is placed on the panties. I cast intermittent glances at her as I demonstrate. Her expression relaxes somewhat. She even manages a smile as she watches me.

"If you place it like this, and you pay attention to the magnitude of blood flow such that you visit the bathroom and replace the used pad with a new one as frequently as you need to, you will always feel free and no one will know that you are in your period. However, if you are not careful with the way you position the pad, blood can escape from the side of your panties and your dress gets stained, even though the pad is not yet fully used up. Also, if you neglect to replace an already soaked pad, you inevitably direct the blood to your dress. And it can be really messy, so you don't want that to happen."

"Okay, Mummy, I promise I won't get stained," she says with a hint of humour in her eyes.

"I trust you, sweetheart." I slip my arm around her shoulders as I embrace the temporary relief that floods through me.

"Later this evening, I will tell you everything about the real meaning and implication of 'period' in a lady's life. I will also tell you about the dangers inherent in becoming a grown woman." She nods uncertainly.

Finally, we finish with the intricacies of using a sanitary pad. I nudge her to return to her room to take a nap. She doesn't argue. The truth is that I want to be alone for a moment to gather my wits. I don't even know how I'm feeling right now. As soon as she turns her back, I stretch out on the couch and my head begins to swim. I close my eyes, resting my arm across them. I feel oddly disconnected, as though my head has been severed from my body. A chill of apprehension runs through me. Am I overreacting? How on earth am I going to deal with Deyemi as the adult she is fast becoming? Raising a child is definitely not the same as raising a teenager, and to think that I'll have to do it all alone? No, this isn't fair. Why, in heaven's name, did her father treat me the way he did? Isaac, why did you impregnate me only to abandon me to my fate? I query him in absentia. Then, my subconscious reminds me that it was my own fault. It was never his plan to do so. He's not even aware that he has a daughter by me. It was my foolishness that landed me in trouble and the least I should do is admit that I acted stupidly. But then again, the conception and birth of my daughter should never be regarded as trouble. Deyemi is my profit. She is the invaluable reward from my life's travails. It shouldn't matter how foolish I acted in the process of having her. It's just that I wished I had someone who could help me guide her in life instead of having to do it all alone. I sigh. My pulse has slowed and the dizziness has abated but the ache constricts my throat still.

"Where are you, Isaac?" I cry out in distress, tears streaming down my cheeks. Then I stop, realising that I might wake Deyemi. But Isaac's image appears before me, looking as dangerously handsome as ever. I stare at him, not in fury but with resigned supplication. "Deyemi is your daughter. I'm aware you don't know about her but she's yours regardless. You've got to lend a helping hand. You have to assist me in raising her, okay?" He doesn't respond. He just stares blankly at me. Still feeling weak, I continue to stare at him in my mind's eye. I manage a hint of a smile, to encourage him to say something, but he doesn't. Finally, he nods at me. I nod back at him. I move my arm and open my eyes. Tears slip down my temples and move rapidly down my neck. I think I'm overreacting but I feel more emotionally raw than I have for a very long time.

My mind drifts to the woman I met some time ago who recounted her ordeal at the hands of her teenage daughter. She said she went out for a few hours only to return and find that she had invited a boy to their home and had cooked for him. "Only God knows how many times that boy had been to my house and what he and my daughter had been doing," she lamented. On this particular day, however, she said it took her daughter an unusually long time to open the door when she knocked. That didn't arouse her suspicion, she said, adding that she thought her daughter was busy in the kitchen or something. It was the expression on her face, the way she fidgeted and stuttered while responding to a normal enquiry that gave her away. Even then, she said, she still couldn't make sense out of her daughter's strange behaviour. Then, suddenly, there appeared to be some movement behind the big settee in the parlour. That was when she discovered him, another teenager, probably her daughter's age-mate, lying almost prostrate and breathing uneasily. He was a youth, no doubt, but his face had all the angles and planes of a man's, especially with his jaw line defined. He was staring at her, perplexed and now motionless. She said it was more than a little frightening to find that her daughter had been interacting with a male on such a complicated level and even had the audacity to invite him to their home. Still dazed, she said she glanced through the room momentarily and her eyes settled on the plates of half-eaten rice and plantain, a bottle of Coca-Cola beside each one. It was at that point that she lost control, imploring the world to come to her rescue.

"Egbami o/ Save me!" she cried. Neighbours rushed to her home in a jiffy, but what could they do? Well, they sent the boy away after extracting a promise from him never to greet or acknowledge greeting from the girl again, let alone visit her at her residence. Upon interrogating the girl, she admitted that she and the boy had been seeing each other for some time and that the day in question was not the first time she had entertained him. She also claimed to be in love with him and that thoughts of him made her happy. However, she insisted that they had never gone beyond kissing.

"So much has changed between my daughter and me ever since the ugly incident," the woman intoned grimly. For a long time, she said, she battled with conflicting emotions, believing and not believing in her daughter. She even contemplated taking her for a virginity test but her husband would not hear of it.

"What would we do if we found out she was not a virgin?" he queried.

I sigh. My own Deyemi will not behave like the woman's daughter, I tell myself firmly.

Over the years, I have trained myself not to entertain negative thoughts about my daughter. Yet, there have been occasions when an insignificant incident has triggered an awful sinking sensation, like the day I caught her stealing fried fish. In spite of such minor incidences however, I have always managed to remind myself that Deyemi is a good girl and that I'm also living my life fairly admirably, setting a good example. I don't even know if I want to describe what she did as stealing really but she took the fish without my permission. She was seven at the time. I remember beating her and warning her never again to take anything that did not belong to her. Nothing like that ever happened again. Deyemi becoming a woman is, however, a new reality and that's why I'm paranoid. A new wave of panic rises in me. I'm just overreacting, I mutter under my breath for the umpteenth time. I close my eyes again. I don't want to dwell on how motherhood completely changes the course of a woman's life.

The sound of Deyemi's footsteps commands me to open my eyes.

"Mummy, is it time for me to change the pad now?" She's standing directly in front of me, waiting for an answer. Our eyes meet and we hold each other's gaze, hers inquisitive, mine slightly confused. You are the only person who should know when to change the pad because you are the one wearing it. You are the one from whose body blood is dripping. I say all these in my head but to her, I say:

"Sweetheart, let's go to the bathroom together to assess the pad." I rise swiftly and lead the way, possessed of a renewed energy to courageously steer my daughter as she matches into womanhood.

Thirteen

SEPTEMBER, 2001

It's been three years now since I started my PhD and although I have finished writing my thesis, I'm afraid of letting my supervisor know because I'm almost certain that he would prefer otherwise. It wouldn't be in my interest to take any steps that might infuriate him, I tell myself over and over again as I dress and contemplate how best to approach him today. I need not be told that I must tread softly, pay utmost attention to nuances emanating from him and act in accordance with his wishes. My professor has become a god who I must not only hold in reverence but in absolute obeisance. The realisation intrigues and saddens me at the same time. It's curious how fast I'm learning things I never imagined would be part of my repertoire as an adult. How amazing it is that we are in a perpetual learning curve. When I set out to pursue a doctoral degree, I envisioned a process that would guarantee me a meal ticket, make me proud and more knowledgeable, but I find myself learning more about the complexity of human nature than scholarly postulates and submissions. It's intriguing because, in many ways, my experience unwittingly brings me closer to my field of study.

Literature deals with man in his environment, illuminating his needs, problems, achievement and failings and in a fascinating way; my professor has become the principal character in the world of my doctoral programme. I study him closely, carefully, frighteningly. How more interesting can it be? What I find disheartening is how it seems essential that I relegate my thirst for academic knowledge to the background and super-impose how not to offend my supervisor on my psyche. How would I have known that the fear of stepping on powerful toes in my university could take centre-stage in a supposedly academic pursuit? I have since learned, for instance, that one of the worst mistakes a PhD candidate could make is to concentrate solely on how to advance their academic knowledge and ignore the dynamics and treachery of human relationships. Whilst it is absolutely foolhardy of anyone who aspires to a PhD degree to cultivate the friendship of only a few in the university community, it is risky to ignore those that might want to act as enemies. Enemies are a luxury only foolish PhD candidates can afford. Nobody is a permanent friend of a PhD candidate, not their supervisor who has the power to do and undo, not other lecturers who can pull surprises by any means, not even the junior non-academic staff who overtly and covertly demand their own appeasement. For any right-thinking PhD candidate, the rule is simple - everybody is a potential enemy but even as you keep those you regard as friends close, keep your enemies even closer. I give myself a mental pat on the back for having learned these lessons and for continuously striving to put them to good use.

I have my plan in place now. I will submit my chapter three only. Also in school today, I will pay my fourth and what I fervently pray will be my final school fees. I awake today with renewed hope for a positive turn-around in my supervisor's attitude toward me and my work. I assure myself that 2001 is a significant year for me at a deep, elemental level. It's the year the Nigerian government introduces the Global Mobile Telecommunication System otherwise known as GSM. Deyemi completes her junior secondary school education this year and is moving on smoothly to the senior level. These are positive developments around me and they are strong enough to provide the anchor for my optimism that 2001 will also be the year that I will become Dr Funto Oyewole.

Folake asks me how much I require for my registration. I tell her and she gives me the entire money, like a dutiful parent. I don't know how to react so I say nothing. I'm in my room, putting finishing touches to my dressing, preparatory to leaving for Abuja. I'm sitting directly in front of one of my large mirrors. I don't wear makeup as a rule. What do I need it for? I'm naturally beautiful and smooth-faced. Sometimes, though, I permit myself the frivolity of wearing accessories, especially when I'm in a super-terrific mood - as I'm now. I currently have an artificial weave-on fixed on my hair which falls in soft waves around my face, spilling over my shoulders, almost to my breasts. I tuck one side behind my ear, revealing Folake's big earrings which she bought only a week ago. I gaze satisfactorily at my reflection and my hope soars. I look trendy, gorgeous, exquisite and good for the red carpet. As I take what I hope will be the final look at myself in the mirror before leaving, I remember to take my handset which Folake bought for me.

When she gave it to me, she also gave me another for my mother. I was stunned but when I opened my mouth to speak she held up her hand. I don't remember now what I wanted to say. Anyway, my mother has since been given her handset after painstakingly teaching her how to use it, which consisted mainly of showing her how to press the green button, and how to position the phone to receive her calls. She hasn't had problems answering her calls since then, and if she needs to initiate a call, which is rare, she gives the phone to a literate person to help her locate and dial the required number. Things are definitely looking up for Nigeria, as they are for me. I smile happily as I finally set out on my journey.

I go in search of Akpabio as soon as I arrive on campus. I haven't thanked him enough for letting me use his car the other time - and even more for his company. Most importantly, I must thank him for his advice. It turned out that he was right about the necessity of me buying a gift for my professor's daughter going by the reaction of him and his wife.

When we got back to the campus after buying the gift, Akpabio told me to take an intra-campus cab to my professor's house to deliver the gift rather than use his car. He said it was important that I went alone, promising to wait for me at the university gate for feed-back and to wish me a safe journey back to Lagos. I did as he advised. I chartered a campus taxi and did not object when the driver offered to drive me up to my professor's front door. I knocked softly on the door and a young girl of secondary school age opened it, ushering me into my Oga's palatial sitting room. Huge doesn't describe it. I felt out of place. My supervisor sat on a couch, watching a football match on the television screen. He acknowledged my greeting but did not show surprise at my unscheduled visit, just as he pretended not to notice the neatly wrapped gift item. I placed the gift on the square-shaped dark wood table in the middle of the room before taking a seat on the couch next to the one he sat on.

"I brought this little gift for your adorable daughter, sir," I said, trying to put as much cheerfulness into my voice as I could. He glanced briefly at it and smiled.

"That's very gracious of you," he said, turning to look at me briefly and shifting his gaze back to the screen. I glanced down at my hands in embarrassment and started to twist the small gold ring on my middle finger. The truth was that if my supervisor had no sense of shame, I did on his behalf. The first time I entered

Folake's sitting room, I thought it was exquisite; when I came in contact with Geoffrey's, I thought it was the zenith of splendour, but both places looked like a junk yard in comparison to my supervisor's. Why does he need to accept gifts from his students? It is true that he did not request it of them, but it's also true that he neither rejects nor discourages them. Why not? Why isn't he protesting about the one I brought? I thought about the smile on his face when I announced that the gift was for his daughter and bile rose in my mouth. What he seemed to have said with that smile was that I had just awoken to my responsibilities as a student.

Or was I mistaken? Maybe he would admonish me for buying the gift. I waited for him to tell me it wasn't necessary. That what I had done amounted to corrupt inducement and that if I tried it another time he would not accept it from me. I waited and waited but he didn't say so. Instead, he called out his daughter's name and she came. He told her "auntie" had bought her a gift and she should say thank you to her. The girl said a hurried, "thank you," and scurried off, taking the gift with her. There was something in the girl's manner that suggested she was already used to such. Her "thank you" was perfunctory. It was said with the air of someone who thought it was the duty of the gift-buyer to buy and her right to receive. The buyer had not and probably would never give anything that would warrant a genuine, heart-felt thank you from her. I was still in my seat, contemplating these thoughts when my professor's wife appeared from the corridor.

"Good day, madam" I mouthed.

"Good day, my sister. I saw your package for my daughter o," She said with a smile.

"Don't mention, madam." I said, then paused and frowned. Don't mention what? She hadn't thanked me, she merely said that she saw it, so, what was I asking her not to mention? I took a deep breath and shifted. I was now perched on the edge of my seat, looking amused. Appearances could be truly deceptive. I was anything but amused. I felt resentful toward my supervisor, his wife and even their innocent daughter. Was it really necessary for me to have sacrificed a whole night's sleep and put my life in jeopardy just so that someone would tell me it was gracious of me to have brought his daughter a gift and another would say she saw my package? I rose to my feet and bade my professor a hasty goodbye. He responded without taking his eyes off the TV screen. I felt angry.

Anyway, that was last session and my mood has since moderated. Now, I go in search of Akpabio, not only to thank him but also to congratulate him on his monumental success. He has defended his PhD thesis and promptly secured an appointment as lecturer II in our department. His success reinforces my hope, although I can't help feeling apprehensive when I consider that it took him six years. I pray silently that mine would not take as long, anchoring my hope on the thought that he's in language whilst I'm in literature. I will spend only four years, I reassure myself again. Akpabio doesn't have an office yet, so I'm searching frantically for him and, when I find him, he gathers me in his arms and hugs me tightly. I surrender to his hug, feeling happy to be in his embrace. He smells clean, divine and thoroughly Apkabio. I'm shocked at my feelings for him because I don't cultivate friendship easily. With him, however, I'm a different person. I like him. He seems kind, reliable and loyal. He's also humorous and knows a lot about how to get a PhD. He has an avuncular appeal to me.

"World Akpabio!" I hail, then quickly correct myself. "Dr Akpabio Asuquo! You have now joined the league of the powerful. I bow to your mightiness," I quip, raising my arms in the air.

"My hard working student!" he teases as we hug again.

"I want to congratulate you warmly and thank you for the last time," I say breathlessly.

"Don't mention, Funto, we are together. By the grace of God, you too will join the league of the powerful at the end of this session."

"Amen o," I say, raising my arms heavenward as if in supplication to some invisible forces.

"Have you seen your supervisor?" he asks.

"No, I decided to look for you first," I say, giggling.

"Very kind of you but you have to go and see him now. I pray his mood is good today."

"I pray so, too," I say, determined to maintain a positive disposition. I insist Akpabio show me the office he says he's sharing with another lecturer so that I don't have to be searching for him all over the place. He reminds me that we are now in a brand new world of GSM and easy accessibility and I can always call him to ask where he is. We exchange numbers. As I turn on my heels, he calls me back.

"Funto, did you come with recharge cards for your supervisor?" I frown.

"No. Why?" I ask.

"Why do you always ask these questions? Why, what?" he retorts and my frown deepens. Akpabio is beginning to get on my nerves but I struggle to keep my counsel.

"I bought his daughter a gift the last time, for crying out loud. I did so at a grave personal cost, remember?" I ask with a slightly raised voice.

"Yes, you did, but do you really need to be tutored that it has become part of your responsibility as a PhD student to help your supervisor recharge his phone now that there is GSM?" he asks, looking me straight in the eye. I'm riled.

"He earns a salary, I don't. I have no job, Akpabio, can't you get it?" I say in exasperation but he's adamant. It's obvious from his countenance that he's not sympathetic to my cause.

"It's not about whether or not you earn a salary, Funto, it's about what you have to do if you want to get a PhD."

I open my mouth, then close it again and scowl at him. He, too, glares at me and the atmosphere between us changes from warm to frigid. I stand, arms akimbo, fixing him with a piercing look. He's getting on my nerves.

"Your supervisor uses MTN, in case you don't already know. Go and buy three thousand naira worth of recharge cards. Give them to him before you mention your work," he says and stalks off. I laugh to hide my horror. Akpabio is clearly insane. The euphoria of having just acquired a PhD must be putting ideas in his brain. Does he think I pluck money from the tree? Nonsense! I turn and walk in the direction of my supervisor's office. Damn Akpabio! I fume as I walk. I reject excessive corrupt inducement of supervisors. Why do my chances of being able to get a PhD have to depend more on what I give my supervisor rather than the quality of the thesis I write? A doctoral dissertation is a contribution to the body of knowledge. I'm determined to make my own contribution and that is what should be uppermost in my mind. I shall excel because I have worked assiduously to produce a brilliant thesis. My place is assured in the annals of academic excellence, I tell myself firmly Perhaps Akpabio is already looking forward to receiving undeserved cash and material gifts from his students. How sad.

Buoyed by renewed internal confidence, I increase my pace and start to hum R Kelly's "I believe I can fly:"

I believe I can fly,
I believe I can touch the sky

I think about it every night and day
Spread my wings and fly away
I believe I can soar
I see me running through that open door
I believe I can fly

I meet my supervisor talking excitedly with another PhD student, Abdulkadri. He acknowledges my greetings with a wave of the hand and gestures for me to sit. I glance briefly at Abdulkadri but he clearly considers me a distraction. He's holding an MTN recharge card in his left hand whilst another one is on the table in front of him. I peek at the one he's holding as he begins to scratch it: one thousand five hundred. He finishes scratching it, places it down and picks the other. Again, I steal a glance at it and it's the same amount. I lean back on my seat as the import of Akpabio's advice slowly dawns on me. Abdulkadri finishes scratching the second card. He stretches his right hand toward Prof Ephraim and Ephraim gives Abdulkadri a handset. I watch silently as Abdulkadri loads the two cards, one after the other, and politely returns the phone to Prof, who smiles sweetly at him, muttering, "It's very gracious of you, Abdulkadri, are you sure both numbers have keyed in?"

"Oh yes, sir, very sure, sir, you may check your balance to confirm," Abdulkadri says, rising to put the used cards in the waste basket. My heart constricts and my throat tightens. Oh my God, I'm going to cry. Prof and Abdulkadri resume their conversation. I sit still, paralysed with confusion, not listening to a word. What do I do? Should I rise at once and go and buy recharge cards with money meant for my lodging? Would Prof Ephraim not consider it an afterthought, induced by a sense of competition? Do I stand a chance of holding a favourable discussion with him today? I'm still contemplating what to do when Abdulkadri rises to go. I breathe a sigh of relief and resolve to take my chances. Abdulkadri's recharge cards ought to have put my professor in a good enough frame of mind, I tell myself as I brace up to converse with him.

"How is your beautiful daughter, sir?" I ask, smiling sweetly at him.

"She's fine," he answers simply. Not a bad way to start, I mutter under my breath and say:

"I brought my chapter three, sir, in the hope that you might have finished reading chapters one and two. sir." I watch for clues that may help me decipher his likely response. I find none. I choose to be hopeful.

"Let me quickly explain something to you," he says and my hope blossoms. My supervisor has read my work and he's about to give me his impression. How I have looked forward to this moment, this meeting which I can now predict will turn out to be the first truly fruitful and rewarding meeting between us. I adjust my position in my seat, straightening my shoulders and becoming much more attentive.

"I don't have to read any part of your work whilst you write," he says. I frown, not understanding what he has just said, but he's still talking and so I pay greater attention.

"The usual thing is for the student to go on writing until they have written the last chapter of their thesis," he says. Although his expression remains inscrutable, I can't help feeling a frisson of alarm. What does he mean?

"You amuse me when you keep asking me if I have read your chapter this or that. Go ahead and finish your work. Write the entire thesis and when you finish, I will then read and be able to determine the validity or otherwise of your ideas." For the first time today, I think I detect resentfulness in his tone. I don't understand him; I can't make sense out of what he has just said. I go down memory lane and recall that since I started the programme three years ago, my supervisor has not engaged me in any intellectual discussion, apart from when he put me to the test over what he instructed me to read. Each time I request to see him, he demands to know the purpose of our meeting. If I tell him I want him to share scholarly ideas with me, to help me in my research, particularly to sharpen my intellect, he finds reasons not to grant my request. If he doesn't tell me he's busy reading the long essays of final-year undergraduates whose deadline he must meet, he tells me he's occupied with master's students who must complete their programme within a specified period of time. No matter the desperation I put in my voice, no matter how much I plead with him, he paints a scenario of impossibility and I'm always left with no other choice but to agree with him. It's not as if I doubt the authenticity of his claims, but I often feel confused by what seems to me to be his capacity to create time for other PhD students like Agnes, who I am left in no doubt is working at a rapid progress. Why is he treating me differently? Why am I his student if he has no time for me? I want to ask him questions now.

"Excuse me, sir, if you say you don't have to read any part of my thesis until I have finished writing, how would I know if what I am writing is good or not? I have counted on your intellectual guidance since starting this programme, sir, and I'm pained that it has not been forthcoming. For example, sir, I finished writing chapter one and proceeded to writing chapters two and three without any response from you. What if my foundation chapter was invalid, sir? Wouldn't it have been nice, sir, if you had read and corrected the first chapter before I went on to chapter two? I imagine doing so would have given me the assurance that my ideas are valid and if they are not, sir, it would have given the both of us the opportunity to know early enough so that you could guide me properly, sir."

My voice sounds brittle and bitter. I stop talking to regard him. He closes his eyes briefly as if he is trying to control his temper. I swallow and watch anxiously.

"I don't have to read any part of your work until you have finished writing the whole thesis," he says, his voice haughty and scolding but I'm not intimidated. I ask another question.

"May I respectfully ask you, sir, what would be the essence of the supervision if I don't have the privilege of having your input as the work progresses, sir?"

He frowns and I try to rephrase my concern.

"What I'm worried about, sir, is what appears to me to be the absence of real supervision in the writing process. I need your intellectual support, sir."

He squeaks and I know he's angry. Dear God, what have I said? His eyes are suddenly stony, and flashing. Well, what am I supposed to do? Sit here like a buffoon and swallow everything he attempts to feed me with as if I don't have a mind of my own? Oh hell, no! If he has decided not to read my work, then, it's only fair that he answers my questions, every one of them. He seems to be reading my thoughts.

"Your thesis is your work; a supervisor is only an advisor. I'm one of those who have advocated that the nomenclature 'supervisor' ought to be changed to 'advisor' because that is basically what the supervisor does. I won't write your thesis for you and I don't have to read any part of it until you have finished writing," he says with a note of finality.

For a moment, I feel a tiny, fleeting stab of despair but I overcome it quickly. I feel strangely determined to fully engage him.

"I have actually finished writing the entire thesis, sir, but I have been afraid to submit it thinking you might accuse me of being hasty. I have my chapter three with me here, you have chapters one and two, sir, and I shall bring the remaining chapters as soon as you want me to."

He gazes at me. His expression is guarded and unreadable. I tilt my head to one side and smile encouragingly at him.

"I have misplaced the chapters you gave me."

"What?" I glower at him and he glowers back at me. We are now two angry people glaring at each other. He has misplaced the chapters I submitted to him? Doesn't that sum up his disposition to me and my work? Why is he mistreating me? Is this the way he mistreats the other PhD students under his supervision that are not of the same ethnic stock with him? How am I supposed to handle him? I groan in frustration, rolling my eyes heavenward.

"I don't know what to make of this situation, sir. And I'm worried about your attitude toward me, sir. If I have done anything to offend you, I apologise and ask for your forgiveness, sir."

"What do you find worrisome about my attitude to you?" he asks. I don't know how to respond. Isn't it sheer insincerity on his part to pretend not to know that he hasn't been treating me fairly? Well, then, maybe I should tell him.

"You are very brusque with me, sir?"

"I just go to the point quickly," he says. I withdraw my gaze and scan his office for … I don't know, but he's still talking. I listen.

"Talking about going straight to the point, I have a list of books here you must buy. I must warn you, though, that you are not likely to find any one of them in Nigeria. Perhaps you may find a few in South Africa but the United States of America, Canada or England are the ultimate places to find them. Your writing must contain evidence that you have read and used all the books." He pauses before adding, "Now you know you have not finished writing your thesis. By the time you have read those books, you will discover the need to do a rewrite of the entire thesis. Good luck to you," he says dismissively and my tears start to flow. I can't stop them.

Fourteen

I am aware that my supervisor wants me to leave his office right away but I pretend otherwise. I sniff and wipe my nose with the back of my hand, adjusting myself in my seat and gazing at him intently. What else is there to think of him if not as a husk of a man without a heart? Well, it would be good to let him know that I also possess a touch of obstinacy. There's another issue nagging at my heart and I resolve not to leave until I mention it. Fear is a choice; only danger is real, so, I choose not to be afraid of him.

"I want to present my first seminar paper, sir," I say, looking him straight in the eye. He looks surprised. I wonder why.

"You can't make a seminar presentation yet," he says as if it's the most banal of truths. The man baffles me with his utter indifference to my progress but I allow my lip to curl in the semblance of a smile. What exactly does he mean?

"Why, sir?" I ask, he doesn't respond. I won't give up.

"Explain it to me, sir," I insist, trying to put as much defiance as possible into my voice.

"You don't yet have the knowledge required to do a seminar presentation."

"How do you know, sir? How do you evaluate my knowledge and intellectual competence when you have not read what I have written, sir?"

"I have been on this job since when you were in your

diapers, I know when a student is sound enough to embark on what you are proposing and I also happen to know that you are not."

"I beg your pardon, sir!" I straighten up and stare at him, desperately trying not to allow him to shatter my equilibrium. My scalp prickles as adrenalin and fury course through me. How dare he cast aspersions on my intellectual abilities? I have been his student for three years but he has admitted to not having read a single sentence from what I have submitted to him. He gave me an oral test and I gave a good account of myself. What have I done to persistently earn his scorn? Does he know what insanity he is creating out of me by treating me this way? Does he care? I peek at him and he's watching me, eyes wide. He seems to be enjoying my fury and discomfort. Arrogant sadist, I won't let you turn me into an entertaining spectacle. I curse under my breath and glare at him.

"Permit me the indulgence to disagree with you, sir. I find your statement totally unfounded and ill-motivated, sir."

"What do you know about academic papers?" He asks, looking cool and calm. I gaze at him and smile wryly before responding.

"I am sure I know much more than you imagine, sir. And since you say your role ought to be that of a mere advisor, perhaps it would not be out of place if I decline your advice not to undertake my first seminar presentation, sir. Let me write my paper, approve it, sir, even if you would not read it. It would be nice for me to take my chances before the court of scholarly opinion," I say with as much confidence as I can muster. He's silent for a moment. I wait.

"What topic do you have in mind?" he asks. I breathe an inward sigh of relief as I start to tell him. I watch his expression lighten as I continue to speak, and when I finish he says, "Okay, I can see you are well prepared." He stands, effectively dismissing me. I smile a genuine, heartfelt, face-splitting smile and head out the door.

In the corridor I pace back and forth. I'm feeling strangely innervated and restless. I start to sing

Thank you for giving me the morning
Thank you for everyday that's new
Thank you for I can know my worries
Can be cast on you

Thank you for my supervisor
Thank you for I can do my presentation
Thank you for even greatest enemies
I can forgive

Thank you, O lord, your love is boundless
Thank you that I am full of you
Thank you, you made me feel so glad
And Thankful as I do my presentation

Gradually, I'm able to calm my nerves then go in search of the seminar coordinator to request him to put my name on the presentation schedule.

"Do you wish to be the first to present this session?" the coordinator, Dr Mohammed Ibrahim, asks. I beam at him, eagerly acquiescing.

"Are you sure you can get your paper ready in two weeks' time?" he asks and I assure him I can. He puts my name on the schedule. My day is made and I stalk off to the PG School to begin the new session's registration. As I head out of the Faculty of Arts building, I hear my name called. I whirl around to behold

Mrs Korede smiling broadly at me.

"Mrs Korede!" I scream as we rush to hug each other. "I'm so happy to see you," I say excitedly, rejoicing in her embrace and inhaling her sweet, Mrs Korede scent. She looks elegantly sophisticated as always.

"I'm glad to see you, too, Funto, but I'm no longer Mrs Korede, I'm now Dr Korede," she says proudly. I can't help it, my mouth drops open.

"You mean you've had your viva?" I ask, searing, green, bilious envy coursing through me. I look nervous, off-balance.

"Oh yes, sweetheart, my viva held toward the end of the last session. I'm a proud PhD holder."

"Wonderful! Great! I mean, it's absolutely spectacular!" I'm blabbing and struggling to find my equilibrium. Eh-r, Mrs ..., sorry, Dr Korede, how long did it take you to get your PhD?"

"Three years now. Have you forgotten we started together?"

"We did?"

"But of course, we did." She obviously can't contain her happiness.

"I see, this your supervisor has really done well for you o." I'm barely managing to keep up with the conversation and I'm shocked at myself for the pang of envy I feel. How can I allow myself to feel this way? Can't I get a grip?

"You are right, Funto, that man is God-send. Do you know I have also become a lecturer in this same great university?"

What? I choke a sob and lose myself in thought. Here's a woman like me, we started our programme at the same time, three years after, she is being addressed as Dr Korede and I'm still Ms Oyewole. Yes, she may be more stylish, elegant, sophisticated, even more beautiful than me, but can it really be proven that she is also more intellectually sound? That cool, intellectual part of me tells me to understand and not compare or be envious of her because she admitted to having given 'something extra' to her supervisor, something I'm not willing to give even if her supervisor were to be mine as well. Why then do I think I could complete my programme at the same time she completes hers? Besides, she applied for full-time whereas my supervisor made me apply for part-time. No, Dr Korede and I don't belong together. We are different and will always be. Our values, ideals, and, I'm very sure, our life-goals are different. Why do I envy her? Why do I think …?

"Funto, are you alright?" She interrupts my thoughts and I shrug apologetically.

"I'm sorry. I was just a bit absent-minded," I murmur.

"Of course, I understand," she smirks knowingly at me, shameless whore.

"Has Mrs Lawal finished, too?" I ask, diffusing the tension that is threatening to overwhelm me.

"Oh no, poor woman, this will be her sixth registration. I hope her supervisor releases her at the end of this session."

"I hope so, too, and please Mrs… I mean, Dr Korede, please pray for me that I may also have my viva at the end of this session."

"I'll pray for you, Funto, but find a way to make your Oga happy. Your supervisor is the National University of Nigeria. Make use of your brain. Na the money, wey I get na im I borrow you so o," she says jocularly.

"You are serious?"

"Yeah, how else do you want me to tell you?"

"Are you still giving 'it' to him now that you've gotten your PhD?"

"Oh yes."

"Why?"

"He wants us to continue."

"That's dirty."

"That's a perspective but have you considered that every aspect of the sexual act is dirty? I have gotten my PhD on time; I earn a living which goes into the family purse; I don't deny my husband his conjugal rights; what wrong am I committing?"

"You're cheating on him and it's unfair."

"You amuse me with your deliberate naivety and foolishness. Stop acting like a child, Funto. Go and get your PhD and stop lamenting."

I'm far from feeling amused. I stomp off, pouting, my arms crossed like an angry toddler's.

The day arrives for my seminar paper presentation. I scan the filled hall to ascertain that my professor is present. When my eyes find him, I concentrate my gaze on him while my paper is being distributed. I watch as he engages two of his colleagues in light-hearted conversation, very uncharacteristic of my professor, I muse. After a few sallies, he abandons his attempt at banter and sits at the far end of the hall, staring moodily at some unknown point. It's normal for him to feel lonely in a crowd. What is it that grieves this man so and seems to be relentlessly eating him up? I shake my head sadly, but realising that it's my day and that I must not allow anyone to cast blight on my mood, I smile reassuringly at no one in particular. Meanwhile, the moderator announces my name and I rise with confidence. I toss my lovely long weave-on behind me and place my paper on the lectern. I take my time, not intimidated by the people staring at me. I smile when I'm ready, look up at the captivated hall and launch eloquently into my presentation, talking to, rather than reading from my paper. I remain composed and funny throughout my presentation, throwing witty jokes at the audience who erupt on cue at every one of them. Finally, I round off my presentation with a closing remark:

"Distinguished scholars, fellow students, I submit that it is pertinent for Nigerian female novelists to address the Nigerian women's lack of characterisation in public service, the professions and other important sectors of the economy so that Nigerian women may be regarded as participants in the kind of milieu that is fast developing out of the older order of society."

The hall resonates with resounding applause. People are grinning from ear to ear, chatting animatedly with nearly everyone giving me the thumbs-up sign. I smile brightly at the audience, feeling honoured by their reaction. I peek at my supervisor; he is radiating a deadly, brooding silence. What, really, is his problem? I find it strange and unconscionable that my own supervisor, who ought to be interested in my academic progress, and who is duty-bound to mentor me, is acting as if he is at war with me. Is it wrong of me to aspire to a PhD? Why did he consent to be my supervisor if he thought only candidates of his ethnic stock deserved to be his students? I shake my head gravely as a new realisation dawns on me. Prof Ephraim agreed to supervise me and other students outside his ethnic group only to satisfy his employer's requirement of having a specific number of PhD students. It must also be mandatory for him to accommodate students from other ethnic groups in order to conceal his ethnic agenda. Yet, he finds convenient reasons to hold down candidates of other ethnic groups whilst he cleverly promotes his own people. What satisfaction does he derive from ethnic bigotry? What a calamity? What a national shame?

"Ms Oyewole will now answer questions from the audience." The moderator's voice drags me from my thoughts. They ask me intelligent questions and I answer with confidence and good humour. I'm not thrown; I keep up. My confident disposition must be making my professor angry because his face darkens. He raises his hand to ask a question. "I find Ms

Oyewole's presentation narrow and restrictive. One would have expected a senior student of her calibre to have a broader and more expansive presentation," he says and sinks back in his seat. I'm asked to respond. I smile luxuriantly before speaking.

"I understand Prof Ephraim's perspective and preference. However, a more expansive paper would have also borne the additional burden of being nebulous and formless. At this stage of academic endeavour, I would rather focus on the quest for a truly insightful presentation." The hall erupts in a fresh wave of applause. The moderator tells me to take a bow. I do as he says and return to my seat.

Outside the seminar hall, I am surrounded by a sizeable crowd, comprising mostly of PhD students, all requesting my phone number. Some of them want me to throw more light on the ideas I espoused during my presentation, some want me to agree to hold regular academic discussions with them, others simply want to be my friends, describing me as a highly knowledgeable and charismatic budding scholar. I feel like a celebrity on the red carpet. Inwardly, I thank my supervisor for challenging me; I feel grateful for his harshness and lack of compassion, which has motivated me to work harder at my preparation. There is a flip side to agony after all, I muse, beaming at everyone and luxuriating in their presence. I become suddenly aware of Akpabio's presence in the crowd. He winks at me and I mirror his action. I give my phone number to all those requesting it, promising also to make myself available for interactions as regularly as they want me. Gradually, the crowd disperses and I'm left face-to-face with Akpabio.

"World Akpabio!" I hail deliriously.

"Greetings to the most eloquent, intelligent, world-class public speaker of our time! I salute," he says, genuflecting in mock obeisance. Then, his expression changes suddenly from jocular to serious. "There is fire on the mountain, Funto." I gasp.

"What is it?" I ask, my brow creasing.

"Prof Ephraim challenged you at the seminar. Although he failed to achieve his purpose, his action is unusual; it is absurd and frightening." I relax and smile at him, not knowing how to respond. Akpabio amuses me with the way he exaggerates. What could be so absurd or frightening about my professor asking me a question after my presentation? He's a member of the department and has the same rights and privileges as everyone else.

"Look, Funto, you must treat this matter with the seriousness it deserves. Did you buy the recharge cards I told you to buy the other time?"

"Well, I didn't."

"Why?"

"I didn't because I couldn't afford it. I had money only for transport and lodging and I wasn't prepared to take up lodging at the student's union building or a lecture hall as I did the other time. Besides, you warned me never to try it again," I say petulantly. Why is he trying to spoil my good mood? Can't he be happy for me for once and join me in celebrating it?

"You must find a way around this because it's a huge problem." "Why do you like to exaggerate?" I challenge, my mouth still curl up in a smile.

"I'm not exaggerating, Funto. Your supervisor ought to be your own person, the one who protects you from attack and criticism from his colleagues. When your mentor chooses to behave as if he is your tormentor, there is every cause for worry. I smell a crisis." My mood darkens and fear threatens to grip my soul. Is Akpabio a victim of too much knowledge of how to get a PhD or am I actually treating a serious matter with kid gloves?

"Is this really as serious as you make it sound?"

"Get cracking, it's more serious than you think."

"What do I do?" I ask as real panic grips my heart. He's silent. I shoot him a panicked glance; he shrugs in a resigned way. I curse under my breath. What would I do?

"Give me a blue print, Akpabio, you are an expert in what it takes to get a Ph.D." There is desperation in my voice.

"I have no idea at the moment, Funto. We'll keep thinking. In the meantime, try and buy him more gifts if you can afford it." I sigh.

"The money I have on me would be sufficient for my lodging only, perhaps I'll have to brave the odds again by sleeping, I mean, sitting through the night in a lecture hall so that I can save the money to buy him a gift as I did the other time."

"No, you won't sleep or sit in any lecture hall this time. I know a colleague I can talk to who will allow you to use his office for the night. His office is in a basement. It won't be comfortable, of course, but it'll be safer than using a lecture hall."

He looks at me quizzically. I don't want to meet his gaze. I turn away and stare blindly down at my feet. How much more burdensome can life become? My soul wails but then what else can I do? I want a PhD, so I will have to obey Akpabio's instructions. I become his student, listening attentively. First, he tells me to go and have my dinner while he contacts the lecturer in whose office he wants me to pass the night. When I finish eating, I put a call to his mobile phone and he directs me to the friend's office, where I meet them.

"This is Dr Wale Adeleke," Akpabio introduces. Turning to Dr Adeleke, he says, "Dr Adeleke, meet my friend, Funto, the PhD student I have mentioned to you." Dr Adeleke takes my proffered hand, smiling warmly. I curtsey.

"Eh-r, Funto, I have explained everything to Dr Adeleke, and he has agreed to let you use his office for the night. However, he wants to do some work right now and you will use the time to go to the library as you do normally. By the time the library closes and you come back here, he'll be ready to head for home." I'm sure my erratic breathing must be audible. My heart is in a whirl. I momentarily scan the office and observe that its surroundings are sparse. Perhaps Dr Adeleke only recently got his PhD. Well, at least he has an office he can call his own. I peer at Dr Adeleke, he looks cool and calm. Did he have a similar experience as a PhD Student? Is he using his position now to intimidate, harass, punish and oppress his students? I'm a bundle of nerves at the moment but I just have to pretend otherwise. I peek at Akpabio, our eyes lock and I have to tear myself away from his gaze. He's talking to me.

"Look, Funto, this will not be as difficult as you think." Is he reading my mind? How come he knows so much? What difference does it make anyway, whether or not the night turns out to be difficult? I pay attention to what he's telling me.

"I don't want you to travel back to Lagos without taking a bath as you did the other time. Now, listen very carefully. There is a concrete slab in front of this office, beneath it is a gutter. I will bring a jerry can of water, a bucket and a bowl from my house at about 10:30pm tonight. Are you listening, Funto?" he asks, his voice suddenly quiet and soft. I nod frantically. He resumes talking. "You will set your alarm on your handset for 5:00am. When it goes off, you will pour the water into the bucket, open the door quietly, stand on the slab and take a quick bath. It's important you do this very quickly because the cleaners resume work at 6.00am and you know what that implies. There is a couch here that you can manage for the night and when I come to pick you tomorrow morning to buy your supervisor's gift, I want to see you looking radiant and happy. It's no big deal at all, no one gets a PhD without a story, okay?" He winks at me. In spite of my melancholy, I laugh. Akpabio is an actor.

When I return from the library, Akpabio and Dr Adeleke are waiting for me. Akpabio shows me the jerry can full of water, the bucket and the bowl. He also brings toiletries. I tell him he shouldn't have bothered because I have enough in my handbag. Both men bid me a restful good night and disappear. I curl up in the couch and, with the help of the air conditioner, I soon drift to sleep, dreaming about my convocation. How long have I been sleeping? I awake with a jolt, convinced I have levitated. I'm drenched in sweat and it takes several minutes for my breathing and my heart rate to return to normal. What's the problem? What's happening to me? I scramble for my phone to check the time and that's when the realisation hits me: the power company has cut the light. There's absolute darkness and, because I'm in a basement, there's no ventilation. I find my phone. The time is 12:45am. I sit up and search for a book to use to fan my body. I find a book alright, but I'm cascading in sweat and the book is ineffective. My breathing is becoming more ragged and I feel as if I may soon fall into a fit of convulsion. I become panic-stricken, so I rise and move gingerly to the door. I can hear the howl of dogs calling to one another in the night. What am I going to do? I can't bear the heat any longer. I pray frantically that the electricity workers on duty restore power supply but it doesn't happen. I feel faint, weak and life seems to be slipping away. Is this how I'm going to end my struggle? Am I going to stay in this heat and succumb to death? No, I mustn't give in to cheap death without making an effort at self-preservation. But would I be preserving my life by stepping into darkness at 1.00am? I might as well take my chances. A feeling of bravery, or desperation, or both suddenly seizes upon me, I open the door and step into the darkness. A wave of relief instantly sweeps through me as I inhale the cool, fresh air. I'm alive, I murmur. Now I have a chance to continue with my struggle. I close the door gently, holding tightly to my phone. Then I sit, my back to the door, determined to remain in this position until 5:00am unless the power company restores the electricity supply. Darkness and the howl of dogs keep me company throughout the night. Light is not restored.

In the morning, Akpabio comes to pick me and we go shopping. I don't tell him about my experience of the previous night because I don't want him to feel pity for me. What is important is that I survived it and I'm confident I will survive all the other challenges that may come my way. I let Akpabio decide what to buy and he suggests a local fabric. Once we buy it, he tells me to do as I did the last time – go to see my supervisor alone. I agree. My professor collects his gift with the same expression as last time – "That's very gracious of you, Funto." Then, he asks me about the list of books he gave me. I explain that a friend who lives in the United States has agreed to help with them. The truth is that Folake took the list from me and gave it to one of her senior colleagues who travelled to the US on holiday. The man is scheduled to return in a week's time and I have no doubt that he will come back with the books. Folake has assured me that much. I don't waste time at my supervisor's house. I instruct the cab driver who brings me to wait while I deliver my package. I'm out of the house within a couple of minutes, relieved that I'm making progress. I'm just about to exit the campus when my phone rings. Ha, it's my mother. I hope she's alright; it's unusual for her to initiate a call.

"Hello, Funto, how are you?"

"I'm very well, Ma'ami, how are you doing?"

"We are fine, eh-en, you have to come to Ibadan immediately o, you hear? Your father's sister, Mama Abide, yes, she died yesterday night o."

I close my eyes. Why is my life full of complications? My

paternal aunt is dead? Why does she have to choose this time to die?

"Funto! Funto! Are you there?" My mother's voice comes booming back at me.

"I can hear you, Ma'ami. I will come to Ibadan at once." I end the call and burst into full-blown sobs, holding my head in my hands.

Fifteen

JUNE, 2002

My new books arrive, throwing me into a frenzy of excitement. I'm thankful to Folake for her tireless kindness and to my supervisor for giving me the opportunity to enrich my thesis. I take the books to my professor, brimming with joy and reiterating my commitment to work diligently at my research and obey his instruction at all times.

"I have a knack for thoroughness, sir," I assure him with a bright smile and he murmurs his usual, "That's alright." I don't allow his curtness to discourage me. I start a close reading of each of the books, paying careful attention to the ideas that are germane to my research, after which I do a painstaking re-working of the thesis, incorporating new relevant arguments and submissions to my earlier postulations. Finally, I submit the entire thesis, consisting of all the chapters. I'm now basking in the euphoria of my accomplishment and happily looking forward to his response.

Meanwhile, Geoffrey proposes marriage to Folake and my excitement literally hits the roof. I'm not the bride-to-be, but for a self-respecting woman who knows her worth and whose philosophy is to love comprehensively, my friend is eminently deserving of marital bliss and every good thing life could offer. I can't help feeling happy for her and eagerly looking forward to the formalisation of her marriage. I have no doubt in my mind that she will be a true companion and asset to Geoffrey; she will be a wonderful mother to her children, as well. She is compassionate, dutiful, responsible and focused. What else does it take to have a happy marriage? I admit there is a lot I could learn from her, notwithstanding that I am older than her. Anyway, things are looking up for the both of us; I'm making academic progress, and she's taking a courageous walk into matrimony. Everything about us calls for celebration.

My mind drifts back to eight months ago when I received my mother's call informing me of my paternal aunt's passage. I decided to heed my mother's call without letting Folake know about it. I was aware of the financial burden I had brought on her and didn't think it was reasonable to put any further strain on her finances. I got to Ibadan just as the family meeting was being convened. The family would need two hundred thousand naira to organise a befitting burial for our departed relative, Baba Bukola announced and a hush descended on the gathering. He paused to gauge the impact of his words. When no one responded, he went ahead to give details of what needed to be done and why it was important for every member of the family to pay their contribution promptly. Presently, the meeting was over, I called my mother aside and explained as carefully as I could that I had no money and didn't know what to do.

"I understand, Olowo Orimi, the important thing is that you are about to get your PhD. This is your final year and everything will be fine soon."

I felt uncomfortable and afraid about my mother's level of optimism regarding my programme. Poor woman, if only she knew my travails. I contemplated saying something to moderate her expectations but words failed me. What could I say really? Would it be reasonable to dissuade her from holding an optimistic view at this point? Was I not responsible for her feelings? I didn't know what to say, so I brightened and allowed her to go on talking.

"I will pay your contribution and my own together. Don't worry," she said tenderly. I smiled dryly.

"Thank you, Ma'ami, but there is another problem. Because I don't have money at all, I don't want to be around for long because sympathisers will begin to troop in and some of them might make financial demands on me. I want to go back to Lagos immediately, Ma'ami."

"Okay, don't worry, stay here and wait. I will go and check the backyard to be sure nobody is there then I will come and call you."

I waited pensively for about ten minutes before my mother emerged, gesturing to me to come with her. We tiptoed like fugitives to the back of the family compound and, as we approached the back door, she glanced around furtively to ensure no one was in sight. Satisfied that the surrounding was deserted, she unbolted the door gently and gestured to me to step out, bidding me goodbye with her eyes as she closed the door hurriedly. I fled my family compound. When I had walked some distance, I slowed my pace because my heart was beating rapidly, as if I had run an uphill race. I felt like leaning over and grasping my knees, but realising I could still be seen by sympathisers either going into or coming out of our compound, I resumed walking and even accelerated my pace. I didn't look back until I reached the bus stop. I was grateful to my mother for facilitating my escape.

I'm now standing in front of the mirror Folake bought for me, tidying my hair so that it hangs artfully down my back. I'll have a busy and exciting day at the university today, I mutter under my breath as I glance at my reflection. I'm wearing Folake's purple cotton dress and looking radiant, young and pretty. The conductor of the bus I boarded home from the market yesterday hailed me intermittently throughout the journey, addressing me as Maama and making me blush repeatedly. To be forty-two and still radiate youthfulness and beauty is certainly no mean achievement. What more can a woman wish for? I take another look at my reflection and the young woman staring back at me is worthy of the red carpet treatment. With Folake's clothes, I enter an alternate universe any day! Folake is in her room putting money together for my journey. I put finishing touches to my dressing, and when I'm ready to go, she comes to give me the money. I set out with confidence. Agnes and I meet at the university gate and we are immediately locked in a warm embrace.

"Funto, you look stunning, as usual," she exclaims, eyes flashing with excitement.

"What can a poor woman do?" I ask in mock modesty.

"Poor woman indeed!" She mirrors my sense of humour and we laugh boisterously.

"Where are you going?" I ask, still laughing.

"I'm going for shopping."

"Really. May I come with you?" I tease.

"You, come with me, so that you would lead me to the most expensive boutiques in town? No way!" She shakes her head exaggeratedly. It's obvious she is aware of how good I feel about my sense of fashion.

"Why now? I would be glad to be in your company," I pursue, feeling lightheaded.

"You know I can't afford your choice of fabrics."

"I gasp in renewed excitement. If only you knew my secret, Agnes, I mutter secretly, feeling happy that she doesn't. I'm having an aphrodisiac experience and I blossom under her praise. "Really, I'm not as expensive as you think, but since you won't grant me the honour of going with you, let me wish you fabulous purchases as you replenish your wardrobe."

"Who cares about replenishing wardrobe? I'm going shopping as a matter of necessity. I need a skirt suit for my oncoming viva." My mouth falls open. I squeak.

"Your what?"

"My viva comes up next month, July."

"Wow! You are a very lucky young woman." What else could I say? How absolutely easy and anguish-free can getting a PhD be? Didn't Akpabio say no one can get a PhD without a story? What story would be Agnes' story? Would she be forthright enough to recount how she rode on the back of ethnicity and favouritism to get her doctorate? I wrap my arms around myself and stare unseeingly at her.

"I won't call it luck, mine is divine favour from the Most High and I give Him all the glory." Her voice interferes with my thoughts.

"I agree with you," I say absent-mindedly as I feel beads of sweat descend my face, gliding rapidly to my neck.

"If you look at it carefully, however, there's nothing unusual about my programme. This is my third year, Funto. I'm a full-time student and the current academic year ends in July."

"You are totally right," I say sullenly. I wish I could gain access to the inner recesses of Agnes' mind. Does she truly believe there is nothing unusual about her situation, or is she being deliberately economical with the truth? Does she think, for instance, that it's mere coincidence that our supervisor forced part-time on me but gladly consented to her running her programme full-time? Does she think it justifiable that a date has been fixed for her viva whilst I'm yet to have the first response to my thesis? Would my own viva hold next month? Perhaps it would; maybe my supervisor is looking forward to giving me his response today?

"Let me run along now." Her voice breaks into my reverie and I smile awkwardly.

"Congratulations in advance, Agnes, I wish you the best at all times," I say bravely and with as much cheerfulness as I can muster.

I stalk off, half-running and whispering like someone who is manifesting the initial stages of insanity. I arrive at Prof Ephraim's office shortly and knock urgently on the door, turning the knob without waiting for an answer. He raises his head to look at me briefly when I step inside. He is a beacon of hostility. I flinch. Why does he look so stern and hostile? I stand immobilised for some moments, rigid with tension except for my eyes, which quickly scan his office. There's no one with him and nothing to suggest something unusual has happened. I draw a chair directly in front of him, sitting with a thud. Get a grip, Funto! I admonish myself as I try to steady my breathing.

"How is the family, sir?"

"Fine," he grunts. It's not in my character to get easily discouraged by unfriendly responses, I affirm silently. I take a deep, lungful of breath and narrow my eyes at him. He doesn't take any notice because he doesn't look at me. He concentrates instead on a half-open book in front of him and I can't help but wonder if he's actually reading or making a façade. Anyway, I need his attention now, and I must get it.

"Yes, sir, I have come for your response to my work, sir."

"I have not read your work," he says. I stiffen.

"Ha, I'm sorry, sir, but aren't we allowing things to drag for too long considering that I will have correction to do and the session is fast running to a close? I mean, it's my final year, sir." He has previously not looked at me except when I first walked in, but now he fixes me with a cold stare. His stare is intense, almost intimidating, but I resist being intimidated. Instead, my stare meets his and we stare awkwardly at each other for long moments. Then he smiles sardonically before addressing me.

"How many times do I have to tell you that the programme you have embarked upon is a PhD, not a master's degree? I would be surprised if you didn't know that there is no fixed, rigid timetable attached to a PhD programme. You are a part-time student, which allows you to run your programme for between four and six years. Yes, the university closes for this session next month, but that will only mean the end of your fourth year. How did you arrive at the idea of the fourth being your final year?"

He slurs at the last two words to convey his sense of angst or disgust. Suddenly, the room begins to spin. I grab the chair beneath me, holding tenaciously and tightening my grip on it as it seems I'm going to fall off my seat. What's going on? What's he implying? I close my eyes and open them again. Everywhere looks the same. I shift with determination, straightening my encroached shoulders and peering at him.

"Excuse me, sir, I'm aware of the flexibility the university permits in the running of a PhD programme, but you will agree with me, sir, that the same university rule which allows a part-time candidate to spend as many as six years on their programme does not prevent them from finishing the programme within four, sir. This is the reason why Agnes's viva is already scheduled to hold next month, three years after starting her programme despite that she has the liberty to run the programme for five years as a full-time student, sir"

"Don't compare yourself with Agnes." he roars. Really? Why not? I ask secretly but to him, I say:

"Agnes is a student like me, sir."

"Yes, she is a student like you, but she is not the only PhD student under my supervision. Now listen very carefully. It's not yet your turn to finish. I have three other PhD students apart from you and Agnes. The three of them started before you did, they will finish before you. You may recall that you met one of them here sometime ago, you remember meeting Abdulkadri here?" I nod. "That's right, this is his fifth year. That ought to give you an understanding of why you are not on my radar. I haven't looked at your work and I don't intend to do so until I have attended to those three other people who started before you. I hope I have made myself clear."

I swallow hard, trying to contain my emotions and the tears that threaten. Where do I go from here? What do I do? What do I tell my mother who is eagerly looking forward to seeing me resume my responsibilities in the family, including caring for her? What do I tell my daughter who is excitedly looking forward to my graduation this year? I choke and my tears begin to fall freely. I gaze down at my feet, contemplating what to do. By the time I raise my head, I have come to a decision. I sink to my knees in front of my professor.

"Please, sir," I cry, hot tears cascading my face. "I beg you in the name of your Creator sir, let me finish this session, sir. I can't afford to spend six years on the programme, sir. I'm a woman with many responsibilities and no one to lean on, sir. I have no job, no husband, no helpmate, no relative that can assist me, sir. Yet, I have a daughter who I must train, look after, care for, nurture and bring up in a decent way, sir. Have compassion on me, sir. God will reward you with abundant compassion and love, sir May you never be denied anything you seek and earnestly crave for, sir."

I beseech my professor, wringing my hands in my laps. I'm uncomfortable kneeling because the floor is hard against my skin but I continue to kneel, staring tearfully into his stern face as I wait for his response. He says nothing. I renew my plea.

"Please, sir, your dreams, hopes and aspirations shall never be shattered, sir. Happiness will chase and find you, good fortune, abundance, grace, wholesome health, genuine fulfilment and everything you need to make life worth living will never depart from you, sir."

I beg again, and again, and again. It is tortuous to kneel for so long as I have been keeling, but I remain on my knees still, pleading. My professor is not looking at me. He looks askance. I go a step further to demonstrate my desperation. I move closer to him and grab his right leg. He stiffens. I relax my grip slightly but hold him still, clutching the hem of his trouser. I glance up at him; he looks unperturbed. The expression on his face seems to suggest that I'm merely wasting my time and that when I'm tired, I will desist. I feel so world-weary that I burst into a full-scale hysterical wail. I'm crying and begging, tears from my eyes and mucous from my nostrils are being mixed and, together, they are infiltrating my mouth, going down to my lungs. I'm swallowing all. I choke and my tears start anew. Finally, my professor looks down at me and spanks my hand angrily. The impact makes me lose grip of his trouser. I sniff and wipe my face with my hand. It appears he wants to say something. I listen.

"If you say you have finished writing your thesis and you are idle, do yourself a favour, and find something to do. It is not your turn to finish and that is all there is to it. Read my lips: it is not yet your turn."

I blink several times to gather my ravaged senses. I peek up at him and smile sadly. For over an hour, I have kneeled, cried, begged and waited for his response. Finally, he has given it and it's concise though rude and dismissive.

"Thank you, sir," I murmur.

"Thank you, too," he mouths and I head out the door. Our departmental seminar holds today but I can't attend. I'm on my way to Satellite Hotel to pass the night. I don't even wish to see Akpabio.

As soon as I enter my hotel room, I curl up and really let go – sobbing hard into my pillow. Life is truly cruel, isn't it? All I have to show for my effort is an anguished and broken spirit. What would I do? Where would I go from here? My mind drifts back to 1979 during my undergraduate days at Eastern University of Nigeria. I was in 200-level and Dr Ugochukwu Mbanefo took us ENG 205. He wasn't a particularly admired lecturer because he spent half of our lecture period lamenting about how varsity teachers were poorly paid. Although we enjoyed some of his stories and we would throw our heads back and laugh heartily, we were not happy that he seemed distracted and un-coordinated most of the time. Anyway, he came to our class on this particular day, his hands in his pockets and began to tell us about how poor his salary was at the beginning of his career. He said looking at his pay slip nearly always gave him a heart attack so he stopped looking at it. Then, as his career progressed, his pay packet was slightly enhanced and he started to look at his pay slip again. Within a period of six months, however, his needs and commitments escalated and ate up the additional money his enhanced salary provided. He stopped looking at his pay packet again so as to save himself from an untimely death. We were still laughing when, suddenly, he asked if any of us had seen or read a book he came across back in his undergraduate days. I don't recall the title of the book now but I remember he said it was published in 1901. We exchanged quizzical glances but none of us had either read or heard about it.

"Raise your hand if you have read the book," he said, his expression changing from jovial to serious. No one did.

"There is no single person among this multitude that has read this powerful book?" he thundered, all the warmth in his countenance gone. We cowered in silence.

"Well, my dear ignorant students, there is only one copy of the book in the central library. I don't care how you do it, but every single one of you must get a copy of the book, photocopy it, read it, review it, type your review and submit to my office within one week. Anybody who has not submitted their assignment by this time next week should not bother to submit because I shall not collect. For your information, this single assignment shall cover the entire 40 per cent of your continuous assessment. I shall not give any other assignment and there shall be no test. Let me add that if you are unable to do this assignment, do not waste your time sitting for the exam because if you score zero over forty in your continuous assessment, there is no magic that can make you pass the exam. And we have come to the end of today's lecture. I shall see you same time next week to discuss the book which you must have read and reviewed."

He sauntered out of the hall, his hands still in his pockets. The class broke into disarray, each targeting the central library. The class representative wanted to coordinate by collecting money from every member of the class so that he could do the photocopy at once and produce enough copies for all, but most of us were seized by panic and by the time the class rep got to the library, the book had been borrowed by some unknown person. That was how the scramble for the book began, and by the end of the week, a good number of us, including yours truly, were yet to have access to it let alone read and review it. Hours before we were scheduled to have ENG 205, we gathered together and decided to pay Dr Mbanefo a visit to explain that it was not until that day that the class representative succeeded in organising and distributing photocopies to all of us and to plead for more time to do the assignment. He chased us away, saying any student who had not submitted had already failed the course. In the end, the class rep advised us to go and do the assignment within twenty-four hours so that the following day we would go and plead again.

We boycotted the remaining lectures of the day so as to devote the day to reading and reviewing the book. I stayed awake throughout the night. It was not possible to finish reading and reviewing over five hundred pages in one night but I made an effort to read and write my review even though I wasn't quite sure what I was writing. By 5:30am, I had a hand-written review, by 10am, it was typed. A few of my mates were also able to pull it off and we were led by our class rep to Dr Mbanefo's office. We started to beg him but he said he wasn't going to collect it from us. We had already failed the course, he told us. We pleaded but he didn't budge. Many got tired and left but a few of us wouldn't give up. We were on our knees for hours, shedding tears and begging him to have mercy but still he refused. We solicited the assistance of one of his colleagues who came to beg on our behalf but Dr Mbanefo still refused.

Finally, we climbed warily to our feet, wiped our faces and thanked him for refusing to have mercy on us. We failed the course and had to carry it over. We all felt aggrieved, and for the first time in my life I came close to understanding the sense of fury that could precipitate premeditated murder. Some of my mates swore they would send hired assassins after Dr Mbanefo if they could. Others wished they had the power to command lightening to strike him down. I felt certain that most of them might regret taking such an extreme position in retrospect, but they would probably have made good their threat if they could. The power of anger and frustration could be truly boundless. The memory brings a sad smile to my face and pulls me back to the present. Finally, I fall into a wretched sleep which brings me no relief.

Sixteen

I'm back in Lagos but I don't want to tell Folake about my latest experience with my supervisor. She is in a very joyous mood at this period and has every reason to be happy. How could I be so insensitive as to dampen her exuberant mood with tales of my own misery? No, I must begin to learn to manage my unhappiness. I must also be there for my friend as she prepares to walk down the aisle with Geoffrey. Perhaps what I need to do is to create my own happiness by suppressing all thoughts of Prof Ephraim and my PhD. If I could start by acting happy, for example, I might eventually achieve true happiness, I resolve within me as I strategise on how to put thought to action. When Folake asks me what happened in school yesterday, I'm evasive. I merely smile brightly at her, mumbling something about everything being in top form. She smiles back but her eyes crinkle at the corners with concern. I act as if I don't notice.

"I have been thinking about the implication of your oncoming marriage," I say to her, trying to sound as casual as possible.

"I understand how you feel, but I want to assure you that my marriage will not impact negatively on our friendship. We are friends forever, Funto, believe me, nothing can separate us," she says earnestly. She misunderstands me and it doesn't come as a surprise.

"I don't have any fears about us, but I have decided to take your advice by permitting myself the opportunity to socialise, interact with people and seek genuine happiness. I need your assistance because I have been out of circulation from social circles for a while." I pause to regard her. Her expression undergoes a rapid metamorphosis, from calm to cloudy and finally bemused.

"What do you want?"

"I want you to take me to a party. I want to dance, make merry and feel happy. Perhaps, I might find a date." Her face turns cloudy again but I'm past caring. If I can't get a PhD after diligently writing my thesis, I might as well get good sex on a regular basis. Hasn't my professor advised me to find something to do if I was idle? Of course I'm idle and will become even more so after Folake's wedding. I would miss her very badly, no doubt, and who would I talk to? My daughter is in boarding school, I don't have another friend. I'm almost overwhelmed by a sense of the lack of alternative and I don't want to succumb to misery and despair. All that is open to me is to find an easy comforter, and urgently at that.

"Are you sure about this?" I don't like the worried look on her face.

"I have never been surer of anything in my life. The idea is originally yours, remember?" My tone is accusatory.

"I know, it's just that it's kind of sudden."

"Never mind, just help your friend do what you've always wanted her to do and all will be well."

"How soon do you wish to go to this party?"

"As soon as possible, tonight, tomorrow, anytime soon."

"Funto!"

"Folake!"

"Are you okay?"

"Oh yes, I am. Is it wrong to want to be happy?"

"No, it's not. It's just that ..., very well then, we'll go to a party soon."

"One more thing, Folake, would you kindly help me with some money? I want to buy a new dress." She looks shocked, stares at me, wide-eyed. What's wrong with her? Why is she being melodramatic?

"I know you have many beautiful dresses, but I want something different, something new to give me extra confidence." She opens her mouth to say something, then changes her mind and closes it. It's better that way for the both of us. In the meantime, I concentrate all my thought on the party, the new dress I'll buy, how I'll look, who and who I may meet, what kind of relationship I envisage and, curiously, I feel the beginning of happiness, or do I merely imagine it?

Folake provides everything I want and she agrees not to tell Geoffrey that we are attending a party tonight. We have just walked into a night club and the DJ is speaking into the microphone. I can't make out what he's saying but there's a lot of drama in his voice and everybody, including me, begins to clap. I'm wearing a silk, slinking, micro-mini, tight-fitting, spaghetti-stripped dress and my luscious breasts seem ready to pop out. On my feet are a pair of nine-inch pumps and the fragrance I'm wearing is a Coco Channel No. 5. The smell is captivating. I ask for a bottle of big stout. Folake frowns.

"You don't take alcohol, Funto."

"This is a party; I've got to get my groove back."

"Being in a party doesn't mean you have to do outrageous things," she warns but I ignore her, insisting that I want to do something different. What's so outrageous about drinking beer? I don't take alcohol normally but is my current situation normal? Why is she acting as if she's my mother? When I'm served, I down it within a few minutes, grimace and cough but keep my balance.

Folake arches a perfect eyebrow at me. I don't care. I'm on the dance floor all by myself now, She's staring at me in astonishment but I don't let her disapproving stare deter me. I'm here to have fun, be happy, and even more importantly, get busy. I'm in search of an easy comforter. The pulsating, intoxicating music captivates me and I begin to gyrate.

Soon, I become totally loosened, captivated and transported away from myself. I'm in another world now, feeling ecstatic and voyeuristic. In my state of inebriation, I don't notice when a tall, devastatingly handsome man approaches me from the rear but I see him when he faces me and begins to dance with me. Slowly, he comes closer and we are off. Wow! He can dance. He covers the floor, whirling and turning in time to the music. Soon, I lose sight of Folake. I concentrate all my attention on my handsome man and the scintillating dance we are having. I'm grinding him with my derriere now; then, slowly, I come up and he grinds me back. He smiles at me and my excitement blooms. His smile is rare, very gorgeous. This is life, this is fun, and this is enjoyment. It is much more than that; it is true happiness and getting busy. Suddenly, Folake emerges from seemingly nowhere to interrupt my fun by telling me it's getting late and we should be on our way home. How did she manage to locate me? She ought to be as busy as I am. Anyway, I'm not going with her, not yet. She pulls me by the arm when I'm slow in heeding her call and I jerk away. She is stunned. Her look unnerves me. I want to have fun but I don't want to offend my friend. I tell my handsome man to excuse me for a few minutes, promising not to be long, then step out with Folake.

"Folake, I'm sorry, I just want to have fun, pleeeaaase!"

"You've had enough fun for one night; it's time to go home," she insists. I rack my brains for what to say to make her leave me behind.

"I'm an adult and I promise to be safe. I just want to explore the party for a little longer. I'll stay here till morning; that will be safe. Perhaps I might find someone who would prove to be a true friend."

"Someone like the guy you're dancing with?"

"I don't know but trust me, I'll be just fine. I'll see you at home in the morning, okay?"

"Your unusual behaviour scares me, Funto. Is there something you are not telling me?"

"No, nothing, I'm only trying to step out of the box for once. I'll be fine, I promise."

"Be sure not to do anything stupid, it's not necessary," she pleads. I nod, take a deep breath and stroke her cheek.

"That's my girl!" I tease. She agrees eventually to leave me behind. I breathe a sigh of relief and quickly rejoin my handsome man. I feel slightly haunted by the look on Folake's face. I ask for a Smirnoff. I'm served and I take it in quick, large gulps. I feel tipsy, or drunk, I don't know the difference. I have a mission and I need a stimulant to accomplish it; nothing else matters for now.

Apparently encouraged by the interest I show in him, my handsome man, whose name I don't know and don't care to find out, takes my hand and squeezes it gently, running his thumb across my knuckles to and fro and I feel an instantaneous sensuous pull. I like the feeling, so I don't resist. He becomes even more emboldened as he lifts my hand to his lips and kisses each knuckle gently. "Yes," I murmur drunkenly as my heated blood courses through me

"Let's go home," he murmurs. Whose home? I wonder, shaking my head violently.

"I don't want to go home now. I want another drink," I mutter mulishly. I feel free and independent, like a teenager whose mother has gone on a long journey. He serves me two bottles of Gulder; I dink both, after which he doesn't need to do much to convince me to go with him. I don't ask for his name; he doesn't ask for mine, either.

At his residence, I stand swaying at the entrance to his bedroom, in sweet anticipation of what is to come. His arm is around my waist so I don't fall. He looks so gorgeous, so… like Deyemi's father? I don't want to pursue the thought. Besides, I have lost all sense of perspective.

"What's your name?" he asks softly as he unclasps my bra.

"Funto," I murmur.

"What's yours?" I ask.

"Adams," he says.

"Adams," I echo. Well, this man calls out to me in a certain elemental way and I yearn for his touch. He is so overwhelming, so alpha male. I smile secretly. He pulls both straps down my arms, brushing my skin with his fingers and the tips of his thumbnails as he slides my bra off. His touch catapults me to instant ecstasy, sending shivers down my spine. I move closer to him, wanting to feel the heat radiating from his body so that it can warm me all over. Oh, my handsome man hasn't made love to me yet, but I can tell he's delicious by his looks. He's just pulled my hair and it's now hanging down my back. He grasps a handful at my nape and angles my head to one side. I feel I'm in paradise. I'm pleasantly surprised to know that I can still feel the way I feel. Does it mean that I'm still a normal woman, capable of romance? It means that I'm not finished, contrary to what I believed about myself. It's even more interesting that a gorgeous looking man such as Adams finds me worthy of his attention. Adams is now running his nose down my neck, inhaling my smell. I'm thrilled. He runs his nose back to my ear. The muscles in my belly clench; I'm wet and ready for him. Oh, I want this strange man, desperately. What's he waiting for? Why is he wasting time?

"You smell great," he whispers as he places a soft kiss beneath my ear. I explode in giggles.

"Make love to me, my handsome," I plead, desperation in my voice. He gently strokes my cheek with the back of his fingers and, almost suddenly, he's inside me with one swift thrust, filling me, and I'm groaning loudly. I revel in the fullness of his possession as he puts his hands on my head, his elbow holding my hands and his legs pinioning me. I feel trapped beneath him as I feel him everywhere; overwhelming me, suffocating me, but it's paradisial too. It's absolutely wonderful to know that I'm still a woman, carnal, sensuous, intriguing, entertaining and capable of being entertained. My body whispers at me to shut out everything and I obey gladly. What else is there to do in my situation? I shut my handsome man out, the room out, Prof Ephraim out, PhD out, trouble out, heartache out, Folake out, the world out, and I concentrate on how I'm feeling.

My focus right now is on what is inside me, filling me, pounding me and keeping me happily busy. The feeling is out of this world, it is beyond exquisite, it's mind-blowing; my senses are thoroughly ravaged and disconnected. Happiness does not even come close to what I feel now; ecstatic joy may begin to describe it, perhaps. I want this feeling to last forever, but my body betrays me and, finally, it explodes in an intense, body-shattering orgasm and I come gloriously, loudly, sagging weakly. His arms are still around me and I roll my eyes at him in pretended hostility while secretly thanking him for bringing back the woman in me. How would I have thought that I was capable of the kind of sexual performance I have just enacted? Perhaps, I should really thank Prof Ephraim for leading me back to the corridors of ecstasy. My head is against my handsome man's chest and I'm mewing and whimpering as I'm still feeling consumed by the aftershocks of my orgasm. He's holding me close still; perhaps he has fallen in love with me. He's now using his finger to push some escaped tendrils of hair off my face. How more affectionate could a man be? I inhale his unique, Adams scent and nuzzle him. I feel loved and protected in his embrace and I would walk over a broken bottle to remain there forever. I put my hand on his shoulder and grin up at him. He smiles tenderly down at me, murmuring, "You are very delicious, Funto." My joy soars and I gradually drift into sleep, dreaming about my handsome man and how he rescues me from Prof Ephraim.

My eyes flip open. I don't know how long I have been sleeping but there is light everywhere now, bright, warm, piercing light everywhere but I'm struggling to keep it at bay for a few more precious moments, so I shut my eyes back. What I really want is to hide, even if for a few more minutes, although I truly wish I could hide from my failure to get a PhD forever. The glow of bright light is getting too strong, it's penetrating my closed eyes, insisting that I yield to reality and I gradually succumb to wakefulness. It's another morning and it seems to be greeting me, beckoning me to rise and face my challenges. Sunshine is pouring in through the windows and flooding the room. Does it mean my handsome man did not remember to close the window last night? He didn't remember because he was too eager to discover me, savour me? Perhaps he's really interested in me and will keep me busy for the next two years that Prof Ephraim plans to hold me to ransom. Oh, it would be nice to have Adams occupy me, my thoughts, my feelings, and my world. I don't want to climb out of bed yet because I'm still draped in my handsome man; he is wrapped around me like a victory flag. He's still fast asleep, with his head on my chest, his arm over me, holding me close; one of his legs is thrown over and hooked around both of mine. I take a moment to absorb that I'm still in his bed and that we have spent the whole night together.

Then, I lie back for another moment and sigh. Adams is still sleeping and I can't stop my mind from wandering, going over last night. As my introspection progresses, I begin to get the impression that I was in the clouds last night. My reflection suggests also that life in the clouds is unreal because I feel different this morning. My post-coital glow has faded, making me feel almost miserable. Why can't the glow last forever? How I wish I could stay perpetually in the clouds where I would be assured of a life of fantasy, a castle in the air, a drift from the ground and safe from the harsh realities of life. In the clouds, I would be far way from an oppressive and sadistic supervisor, I would be far away from the anguish of having to single-handedly raise a child without gainful employment and I would be far away from the encumbrances of family commitments rooted in age-long custom and tradition, I would only be with my handsome man, making love to me, filling me and moving back and forth inside me. If I took up permanent residence in the clouds, the only quagmire I would be in would be the quagmire of sensation.

Adams is suffocating me with his body heat now and the realisation that he's heavy pulls me out of my reverie. I can't continue to bear his weight, yet I'm reluctant to climb out of bed or wake him, so I change our positions. I shift to remove my body and I'm now lying on top of him, my back to his front. He doesn't wake and I'm glad that my body is still touching his. I want to continue to enjoy physical contact but he suddenly opens his eyes, grins at me and roughly lifts me off him and stands. I'm trying to look at him but he's not meeting my eyes. He doesn't even say good morning, no words of endearment; the man in front of me is not the affectionate and tender-looking man that I danced with and made love with last night. I watch, surprised, as he picks up his trousers, slides them on commando fashion and exits the room. Is the show over? I feel my senses return. My misery returns also in multiple folds. Does it mean I have acted foolishly once again? What do I do next? I'm so mad, scalding tears spill down my cheeks and I brush them furiously aside. Well, I have to get out of this damned bed and go home now. I just want to curl up in my own bed and recuperate in some way, heal my shattered ... what? What was I really thinking? That I could banish the world and it's vagaries from my consciousness simply by having sex? What a blithering idiot I was! Ha-ha-ha, did we use protection? I don't remember. I could easily have gotten my life exterminated in a stranger's bed. How could I have been so stupid? I clamber out of bed, feeling stiff. I put on my clothes, shoes and I pick my bag. He comes in to the room as I'm about to step out.

"Are you leaving? Take care of yourself," he says casually. I peek up at him, wanting to say something then I change my mind. What's really to say? Make a fool of myself further by asking him why he's so nonchalant? Isn't it obvious to both of us? I exit his apartment without a backward glance. He doesn't call after me. I don't expect to find Folake at home at this time and I'm thankful she's not. I need time to think about what to tell her. I enter the shower, rub soap on my face, rinse it off, wash my body, pour water on myself... on and on, all simple mechanical actions, requiring simple, mechanical thoughts. Curiously, I feel much better and able to forgive myself when I have had a bath. I feel convinced that I have effectively washed off the filth of last night. I have washed away Adams and my foolishness. Reality beckons now and I feel ready to embrace it. I'm hungry and there's no food in the house. I need to go to the market to buy some foodstuffs and stew ingredients. The trip will help me further clear my mind and give me an opportunity to test my appearance with bus conductors.

I'm at the bus stop now, ready to start my day on a realistic note. A bus conductor senses my desire to board and tells the driver to stop. "Duro fun joor," he bellows and the driver matches the brake. As I scramble in, the conductor hails, "Maama, wa sere!" I explode in giggles. My day is made. I can face the world! I mutter under my breath as the bus gathers speed. The market is still about five hundred meters ahead but there is a gridlock. Passengers from various commuter buses, including the one I'm in, begin to alight with intent to trek the remaining distance. I hesitate for a few moments and eventually join them. As I cross the road to the median and contemplate crossing to the other side so that I will be facing rather than backing traffic, I hear my name called. I turn and scan the street. A male voice calls my name again and I finally locate him. It's Lekan Babatunde, one of my school mates at Eastern University of Nigeria. He beckons me and I practically race to him, screaming "Lekan!" He's being chauffeur-driven in a posh brown colour Toyota Corolla. He looks calm, confident and self-assured. I stand beside the car, at the owner's corner where he's seated, and we exchange pleasantries. Then an idea hits him. He tells his driver he'll walk the remaining distance and that they'll meet in the office. He opens the door and steps out gloriously. Wow! He looks clean, dressed in black suit which is not a surprise since I'm aware he's a lawyer.

"You look good, Lekan. The law profession is sure treating you well," I say as we cross the road. He leads the way. He's apparently taking me to his office.

"You are not looking bad too," he says and we both laugh. "You are Funto what now?" he asks, smiling mischievously.

"Still Funto Oyewole. How do you mean?" I ask, slightly confused.

"I mean you ought to be Mrs Somebody by now. It's been a long time and we are all aging," he says, stopping in his tracks to look directly into my eyes.

"Well, I guess you are right but I'm not married. Are you?"

"Of course I'm married, with three children."

"Congratulations, Lekan, I'm happy for you."

"Thank you, but why are you still single?"

"Oh, because marriage hasn't happened to me yet."

We arrive at his office. Four people are sitting in his outer office. They greet him in unison. A young man behind a small desk rises to his feet and curtsies, saying, "Welcome, sir." Lekan grunts his reply and tells me to come with him into his office. He removes his jacket and hangs it on a hanger, then walks briskly to his seat and sits with a thud. I draw a chair directly in front of him. I scan his office; his surroundings are sparse but I think it's a design statement rather than frugality.

"Where do you work?" He distracts me with his voice.

"I'm not employed at the moment; I lost my job almost five years ago."

He narrows his gaze at me and I smile. The young man enters holding the visitors' forms completed by the people in the outer office. He places them in Lekan's front and waits. Lekan tells him to tell all of them to exercise patience. The young man says, "Yes, sir," and turns to leave but Lekan calls him back and tells him to go to Mr Bigg's to buy his old school mate a lunch pack.

"Do you want jollof or fried rice, Funto?" Lekan asks. I debate my preference in my mind for a moment before saying "Fried." The young man disappears.

"You see, Funto, we have to meet again so that we can really talk. There are people waiting to see me as you must have noticed and I must attend to them. They are my clients." I nod. Soon, the young man reappears bearing a Mr Bigg's package which he sets down before me. I put it in my handbag.

"Let me have your phone number, so that we could schedule

an appointment," I say, rising to my feet. He dictates his number and I store it in my phone. I'm about to dictate mine but he tells me to hold on. He presses a bell and the young man reappears. Lekan tells him to take my phone number. The young man says, "Yes, sir," disappears and reappears shortly with a sheet of paper and a pen. I eye Lekan in amusement, glancing at the phone in front of him. He follows my eyes but says nothing. I dictate my phone number to the young man; he writes it down and disappears. I smile wryly and exit the office.

Seventeen

SEPTEMBER, 2002

It's the beginning of a new session, my fifth at the National University of Nigeria, Abuja. I'm on campus today for two reasons. One is to start the usual process of registration for returning students, the second to seek an audience with the Head of Department of English. A significant fall-out of my indiscretion with Adams is a no-holds-barred discussion with Folake about the frustration attendant on my quest for a PhD. I expect a full-scale Armageddon over my irresponsible behaviour on the night of the party but she doesn't judge me. Instead, she treats me with more empathy, telling me that people respond to situations differently and that what I did was only my own way of responding to a perceived unpleasant situation. She counsels me not to allow myself to feel so overwhelmed by life's vicissitudes in future and suggests that I seek the intervention of the HOD, whom she believes may be in a better position to appeal to Prof Ephraim on my behalf. I'm about to put Folake's suggestion to use. I believe it will work out well and wonder why I hadn't thought of it before. We have a new HOD, Dr Dansabe Aliyu. I don't know much about him because he's in Language but he looks amiable and pleasant with debonair appearance.

I'm now in the department; the secretary to the HOD is not on seat giving me the excuse to walk straight to the man's office.

I knock gently on his door and he says, "Yes, come in." I open the door and ease myself in.

"Good day, sir."

"Good day, madam."

"Congratulations on your assumption of office as the new HOD, sir."

"Thank you."

"Excuse me, sir, I'm sorry to have to bother you so early in your administration, sir."

"Never mind, madam, I'm here to attend to issues as they arise. You are not bothering me at all." I relax.

"Thank you, sir. It's about my programme, sir. I'm a PhD student, sir."

"I know you, I see you at seminars."

"Ah, thank you, sir. This is my fifth registration. I'm a part-time student but I have since finished writing my thesis. I have also submitted it to my supervisor, Prof Charles Ephraim, but there has been no response from him. Toward the end of last session, I made a passionate appeal to him to kindly let me have his response with a view to rounding off my programme but he declined rather vehemently, sir, I'm greatly burdened by personal challenges, some of which I have shared with Prof Ephraim and on the basis of which I have repeatedly appealed for his compassion. I have come to plead with you to help me appeal to him so that I may not spend more than five years on the programme, sir. I want to state emphatically that I'm not here to cast aspersions on my supervisor's character but to appeal for his kind assistance toward helping me to successfully complete my programme on time."

I pause to regard him with a look of sobriety. He is quiet for a while. I try to calm my nerves.

"I like your tone and attitude, I like your language and it

seems to me also that you are in distress and genuinely in need of assistance. It's only on the basis of these that I shall intervene. Let me make it clear to you, however, that no PhD student has the right to determine when they finish their programme." I nod frantically in agreement, looking at him intently.

"Today, I'm your HOD, but if I start to tell you the trauma I went through before I got my doctorate, I assure you, we would not finish the story today because nobody can get a PhD without a story. My own supervisor held onto my thesis for one whole year without responding and it was agonising, but he did eventually and I finished. That's why I'm here today. You will get your PhD, madam, but you have to reconcile yourself to accepting that you are not in a position to determine when. I like your disposition and candour and, as I said, I'm going to intervene purely on compassionate ground, not because you have any right to question the pace at which Prof Ephraim does his work. He's your supervisor and to you, he's the National University of Nigeria, he does what he pleases, when he pleases and you say, 'Yes, sir,' to him, at all times, no matter what he says. Do you understand, madam?"

"Yes, sir, thank you very much for your kind intervention, sir. Do you want me to be present whilst you speak to him, sir?"

"No. I'll go and see him right away and you may see him thereafter."

"Thank you, sir, I'm truly grateful, sir".

"You are welcome, madam," he says, looking kindly at me as I rise to my feet and head out the door. I go to Akpabio's office but he isn't in. I try calling him but his phone is switched off. Perhaps, I should go to the PG School to start my registration, and then return to the department later to see my supervisor and Akpabio. I feel energised and hopeful as I put action to my plans. Presently, I'm on my way back to the department, singing softly to myself as I walk.

I meet my supervisor in the corridor when I return. I greet him with a smile. He doesn't look at me and, although he smiles back, the smile doesn't reach his eyes. I sense trouble and, silently, I hope that my instincts are wrong this time. I don't want any more trouble from my professor. He turns abruptly and enters his office; I follow in tow, my senses hyper-alert, my subconscious fraught with nerves. He shakes his head solemnly at me and my worst fears are confirmed. I can tell I won't like what's about to come. I try to steady my breathing, to prepare for whatever it is.

"I understand you have been speaking to the HOD about how you want to get a PhD in a hurry and how I have become an obstacle to your majesty's wish," he says menacingly. Stillness comes over me. Good heavens, I'm in trouble. I make an attempt to open my mouth but he holds up his hand. I lower my gaze and stare at my clasped hands.

"I choose not to comment on what you have blabbed to the HOD. Instead, I will tell you three distinct, yet related stories. If you have any more sense left in you, I will expect you to draw the necessary conclusions," he says, looking threateningly at me. I already regret my incaution but of what use is my regret? What I tried to avoid is precisely what I have gotten myself into. I might as well listen attentively to his stories and draw inferences from them. After all, hasn't the HOD told me that it is for my supervisor to do and undo and mine to say, 'Yes, sir,' all the way? By the way, have I said, 'Yes, sir,' to his last statement? I don't remember doing so.

"Yes, sir," I breathe and paste a facsimile of a smile on my face. In my mind, I say, let the stories flow. He seems to take a cue and starts.

"The three stories will exemplify the experiences of

undergraduate, master's and PhD students who have passed through my supervision. I begin with the undergraduate student who imagined she ought to have a smooth sail to getting a university degree and even pass my course without stress simply because her big brother was my colleague. You know, some parents are in the habit of over-pampering their children. This silly girl, the spoilt brat, was the youngest of six children, my colleague and her brother was the eldest. Unknown to her, her brother had regaled us with tales of how their parents often showered her with underserved gifts and pampered her silly on the excuse that she was the youngest child and only daughter. Often, she came to see her brother in his office and I had the opportunity to meet and interact with her. She was thoroughly over-pampered. I hated her with a passion and I always wished she would be taught a lesson of her life because I'm an unapologetic disciplinarian. I don't condone indiscipline. Rather, I insist on raising every child with strong and unwavering discipline. To cut a long story short, she fell into my trap when she was in 400-level. It was during the first semester and one of their compulsory courses was allocated to me. As if to heighten my sense of outrage, she turned twenty-one during the same period and, characteristically, her mother loaded a bus with food and other precious gifts all the way from Lagos to Abuja here, to celebrate her queenly daughter's twenty-first birthday. I was beside myself with anger and I waited to see her performance in my course at the first semester examination. As would be expected from a silly brat like her, her performance did not merit a pass from me. I scored her 38 per cent accordingly. Well, you know the university allows undergraduate students to re-write failed papers. She did a re-sit and I gave her 39 per cent. That was it. Everybody in her family believed she ought to be saved from having an extra semester. First, she went to her brother, my colleague, asking him to come and appeal to me to change her score to 40 per cent so she would graduate. I refused. Next, she went and invited her mother, her father, her uncles, her aunts - quite notable people she has, I must say - but I stood my ground. They begged, cajoled, even hinted at corrupt inducement which they cleverly couched as showing appreciation. Whilst all of these were going on, her brother became the head of department and I threatened that if he or anybody altered my score, I would report the matter to the Senate and they could be sure it would lose them their jobs. I insisted that what they wanted me to do was tantamount to academic dishonesty and I would not be guilty of it, no matter who was involved. I stand and walk on high moral and philosophic principles. In the end, they all realised I wasn't going to play their game. She had an extra semester and, although her brother ensured that the course in question was not handled by me the second time, I had the pleasure of teaching his silly sister a lesson of her life, at least for once."

He pauses. I don't know what reaction my supervisor is expecting at the end of his first story but all I do is narrow my eyes and wait for the second one. Ah, I'm almost forgetting to say, 'Yes, sir.'

"Yes, sir." I murmur and as if that's what he's been waiting for, he launches into the second story.

"The second story involves the daughter of the Vice Chancellor, not the current VC, the one before him. It is a story about the foolery of women, especially when they or their spouse occupies a high position in society. The VC's daughter was running a master's programme in this department and I was assigned to supervise her long essay. I treated her like any of my regular students and that was what her foolish mother could not contend with. As far as she was concerned, her daughter was a special student and ought to be treated differently. Of course, she didn't know the kind of person I am, didn't bother to find out because if she did, she would have been cautioned to tread carefully whilst dealing with me. I don't succumb to intimidation from any quarter. I was busy doing other things and hadn't had time yet to look at the VC's daughter's essay. The girl came to me to enquire about her work and I told her I hadn't had time to look at it. She reported me to her mother; the mother came to confront me. Can you imagine? I called her bluff. I told her to go straight to hell. What did it matter if she was the VC or the president's wife? I would read her daughter's essay when I would read it and no one, not even her husband, could stampede me. She was under the illusion that she was powerful. She reported the matter to the PG School. I was summoned and I told them precisely what I told her. The matter was left at that and I read the VC's daughter's work only when I chose to read it."

He seems to have come to the end of the second story. I rack my brain for an appropriate response. I find none and mutter softly, "Yes, sir." He tilts his head to one side and scowls. I glance down at my feet. He starts to talk again, his voice commands my attention and I raise my head to fix my gaze on him.

"The third story is about a PhD student, someone who interestingly is a lecturer in this department as I speak, but I won't mention his name. He was my PhD student, and as I have mentioned, I work at my own pace. He was quite a diligent student, very hardworking too although I was not very impressed with his output. I was a bachelor then, living outside the campus and he came to my house every weekend to assist me in cleaning my apartment. He would sweep the house, mop the floor, wash and iron my clothes and run errands for me. He was gentle, very obedient, and there was no task that was too hard for him to undertake. In addition to that, his father was a Nigerian 'big man,' if you understand what I mean. The old man was a high-ranking official in a strategic ministry and he was prepared to use his position to advance his son's progress. I was running a conference at some point and the old man ensured my conference got government financial and logistical support. For example, the venue of the conference was booked and paid for by the government, using the old man's influence. The government also facilitated the movement of conference guests and participants. In other words, both father and son did all within their power to encourage me to favour his programme but it all boiled down to a lack of understanding. I was prepared to work at my pace only and no amount of pressure would make me act out of character. Besides, this was a student whose work did not look very good. Although I had not read his PhD thesis yet, but I supervised his master's project and I knew about his academic deficiencies. This was someone who had to do conversion because he was not particularly brilliant. Anyway, I appreciated their good gesture but I was not going to let that colour my perception of reality, so I chose to do as I knew I ought to. When they realised he was not likely to get his PhD at the time they had envisaged, the father accused me of bias. He then used his influence, both inside and outside the department, to persuade another of my colleagues to take over his son's supervision from me. I denied their accusation of bias because it was not true, but I admitted that I was not going to be pressured into helping a student get a PhD simply because he was obedient or his father was influential and had used his position to my advantage. Now you can draw your conclusions from the stories I have told you. I thought I have already told you, but if I did not, or you didn't quite understand, let me repeat, and I advise you listen carefully this time. I have never had to justify my action or inaction to anyone in this university. Not to my students, their parents, my colleagues, the university registrar, the VC, or whoever. Not one person. I do as I wish and I like my autonomy."

"Yes, sir," I murmur.

"No, it does not end there," he says, a sardonic smile playing at the corners of his mouth.

"You have overstepped your bounds and I will ensure that you regret your action. You will look back to your student days under my supervision and weep. The memory of your PhD studentship will always bring tears to your eyes because I will make sure that you suffer. What were you thinking when you went to report me to the HOD? Did you think he was going to pillory me? I am untouchable. I am an enfant terrible, a colossus, a phenomenon, an enigma that is, frankly, too hard for anyone to crack. I am an institution. Who the hell do you think you are? What do I care about your burdens? Do you think I do not have burdens of my own? Could I ask you to share in my life's burdens, my miseries and disappointments? You want to get a PhD in a hurry to solve your problems. What then happens to mine? You do not think I deserve that my own problems be solved as well? Can you solve my problems? You are a bloody idiot, a low-life nonentity. How have you been running your life without a modicum of perseverance? I tell you something, foolish woman, you have come to the right person for tutorials, but I shall even go a step further by teaching you in real, practical terms how to handle delicate affairs of life. I have not decided what your punishment will be, but I can assure you that it will be very harsh and extremely tortuous. I am an unrepentant monster and people like you deserve my maximum cruelty."

My Professor is breathing heavily and he seems to be deploying all his energy into his verbal attack. Saliva is oozing out of his mouth as he speaks. I'm thoroughly perplexed. I swallow a lump that has formed in my throat, then I open my mouth to say something I hope will dissolve his anger but he holds up his hand again. I close my mouth and shift uneasily in my seat. What else can I do other than to listen? Dear God, would I survive this period?

"When I have made up my mind about how to punish you, I will communicate my decision to the HOD. See him, not me, for the details. Get out of my office, this minute!"

I take my leave without another word. I don't want to aggravate his sense of fury.

I break down in tears in the HOD's office as I recount every detail of my session with Prof Ephraim.

"How did you put it to him, sir?" I finally ask. He shakes his head solemnly. "I wasn't trying to report him to you, sir, I merely pleaded for compassion." My tears are pouring in torrents.

"I did not tell him you reported him. You could not have because I am beneath him in hierarchy. He is a professor and a very senior one at that. I was a student in this department when he was already a lecturer. I was only trying to play the role of a facilitator in the realisation of your dreams."

"What can I do, sir?" I sob miserably.

"Wipe your tears, madam. You have to leave my office now since he told you he will communicate his decision to me. He must not find you here when he comes, lest he thinks you have come to report him again. Call me in an hour's time, perhaps he would have made his decision known to me and I will be able to advise you on what to do."

I thank the HOD and take my leave. An hour later, I call the HOD and he says I should come to his office. I'm sitting directly in front of him now, staring anxiously into his eyes. He stares back at me and I can decipher that whatever he's about to say will be far from pleasant. I brace up for the news, no matter how disheartening.

"I'm sorry, Funto, what I have for you is rather bad news."

"Let's hear it, sir."

"Well, I'm sorry, Prof Ephraim says he no longer wishes to be your supervisor." My heart skips a beat and starts to pound.

"What does that mean, sir?"

"It means you have to find a new supervisor."

"Does it also mean that I have to start the programme all over again, sir?"

"That will depend on your new supervisor. As I have explained to you, the wishes and decisions of your supervisor are the major issues to contend with in a PhD programme. Your new supervisor might decide, for example, that they do not even like your current research topic. That would necessitate both of you having to agree on a new field of research. However, if you are lucky, your new supervisor might like what you are working on and agree that you continue to work on it."

"Will I have to go through the process of searching for a supervisor as I did four years ago, or will the department find a new supervisor for me?"

"It is not the responsibility of the department to find supervisor for PhD candidates, but I think you need to calm down and listen to me first because you have not even reached that stage yet. As things are now, you cannot begin to work with another supervisor, even if you find one; not until Prof Ephraim officially communicates his decision not to supervise you. He has to write a letter to the PG School, stating that he is no longer willing to supervise you to enable the PG School amend their records. Until and unless he writes officially to that effect, no one can take over as your new supervisor. Your prayer point now should be that Prof Ephraim does not hold you much longer by not writing the letter. No one can make him write the letter and if he does not write it, your programme stagnates."

I sit immobilised as my world falls away from me, leaving a

wide, yawning abyss. How could my world crumble around me like a pack of cards and I'm unable to salvage it? Where would I go from here? To whom would I turn for succour?

Eighteen

Back in Lagos, the apartment is empty. Deyemi is in school and Folake is at Geoffrey's. I call Folake on her mobile phone, requesting to see her urgently. I want to pour out my mind to her, I want us to think together, chart a new course for me and I need her to comfort me, too, reassure me that all will be well. I need my friend because she's the only one I can really talk to. She answers the phone but tells me she can't come immediately because Geoffrey has been talking about the need for them to spend more time together to plan their wedding. She will come to see me, she assures, however, she might not be able to stay with me for as long as I would wish. I feel mildly hurt by her response but I don't want to add it to my catalogue of woes. I wait pensively throughout the day but she doesn't come. Finally, I manage to take a shower and climb into bed; and as I weep silently into my pillow, reality bleeds into my consciousness. I have failed miserably. I feel a creeping emptiness and desperately wish sleep would offer me an escape but I can't sleep. I climb out of bed. My body is numb and my brain is a vortex of half-formed thoughts. What will I do? Is there a possibility that I can find someone to help me appeal to Prof Ephraim to forgive me? Perhaps his wife may be able to save me; but what if such a step only serves to heighten his sense of outrage as the HOD's intervention did? Where did I go wrong? What must I never do again as a PhD student? More importantly, what must I do?

I start to pace my room, unable to sit, then, I slump, suddenly inert, as though my bones have been sucked out of my body. My thoughts drift to Folake and the telephone conversation we had earlier in the day. I can't believe she would find it difficult to respond immediately to a distress call from me. Is her oncoming marriage beginning to take its toll on our friendship? Is Geoffrey making excuses to keep us apart? Should I run to Shettima for succour? Will he accept me? Has he found another woman since I made it clear to him that there was nothing he could do to make me accept him? If I go to him, would I be doing so because I love him or because I'm desperate for a comforter? Have I become an unbearable burden to Folake? Self-pity is threatening to envelope me. How could I have failed to realise it? Folake and Geoffrey are living with a purpose; I must recognise that and avoid becoming a nuisance to them. I climb back to bed and eventually fall into a wretched sleep that brings me no relief.

When I open my eyes, light is filling the room, making me blink. My head is fuzzy. I sit up in bed and try to stretch and I'm aware that I ache all over. Are my aches a result of the journey or they are purely in my mind? I stagger out of bed and make my way into the bathroom while going over yesterday's events in my mind. I have no idea yet how to go about my problem. When I come out, I head straight to the largest mirror in my room. I stand in front of it and gaze at my reflection. My eyes are flat; there is no life in them at all. What I have always known to be my beautiful face is now pale and etched with sorrow. I look old and dishevelled. Dear God, don't let me slide into the abyss. I dress quickly, still contemplating what to do without coming up with a concrete idea but essentially waiting for Folake. She doesn't come and she doesn't call. I don't want to put pressure on her by calling again. I decide to pay Lekan Babatunde a visit at his law chambers. I'm in luck, he tells his secretary to let me in as soon as my name is announced. He sits comfortably behind his large desk and chuckles as soon as I enter.

"Good to see you, again, Funto," he says with a smile.

"Good to see you, too."

"How are you?" he asks. I close my eyes momentarily and open them again. I can't help feeling melancholic.

"I'm fine," I mumble with a forced smile.

"You don't look fine to me; you don't even sound like someone who is fine."

"Really?"

"Seriously, Funto, you know you can talk to me. We've come a long way."

"I know, and I'm fine, you have to believe me." Do I believe myself? "How is the law practice?" I ask to distract him. He ignores the question.

"Your eyes are filled with silent tears," he says softly. He's definitely not going to play my game. I shrug my shoulders but say nothing.

"Okay, tell me, why aren't you married?" He wants to talk about marriage again.

"Because it hasn't happened yet."

"When will it happen?"

"I have no idea, perhaps tomorrow, maybe the day after, probably never. I can't tell." He's about to say something but changes his mind. He presses the bell on his table and his secretary walks in.

"Go and buy lunch for my friend at Mr Biggs. Be quick about it."

The young man says, 'Yes, sir,' and turns on his heels, but Lekan calls him back. "Have you asked her what she wants to eat?"

"I'm sorry, sir," he breathes, then turns to me and asks:

"What would you like to eat, ma'am?"

"Fried rice and fish."

"Yes, ma'am, do you want Coke, Fanta or Schweppes?"

"Bottled water is fine, thank you."

"Yes madam." He stalks off. Lekan and I turn to gaze at each other.

"I want you to be married, I want to see you looking happy, not the way you do now."

"You amuse me. Why do you associate my mien with my marital status?"

"Why else would you look so downcast? Anyway, thank God our paths crossed. I'll take it upon myself to ensure that you are happily married." For how long is he going to be going over the same subject?

"You got it wrong. I'm unhappy but it has nothing to do with my marital status."

"I don't believe you, I feel certain that…" His secretary walks in, bearing a Mr Biggs meal pack and we pause in our conversation. I start to eat and then make up my mind to open up to him. I need to unburden my heart to someone. I'm beginning to fear that I could drift into insanity if I don't ventilate my frustration. Lekan listens without interrupting me. He tilts his head to one side and narrows his eyes. I tuck my loosened hair behind my ears while waiting for his reaction, which is long in coming. I feel strange, nervous. He seems to be weighing his thoughts. I don't even know what I'm expecting from him but I need help and who knows? He might be able to help although I still can't figure out how. Finally, he starts to speak and I listen as though he were my teacher.

"You are an exquisite woman, Funto. You are honest, strong and beguilingly innocent. I used to be in awe of you way back in our school days. You deserve to be happily married and to have all the good things of life." I frown. What has marriage got to do with it? I wonder silently, but he ignores my frown and continues talking.

"Your story makes sense to me in a lot of ways because I can connect with it at a deeper level. I will tell you a short story to illuminate my point. You were a witness to my sound academic prowess when we were in the university. I need not belabour my point in that regard except to add that it didn't take me long to secure a job in a famous law chambers after national service. I thought it was the beginning of a glorious career for me but it turned out to be the beginning of a life of vicissitudes and nightmares. Enemies of progress rose with a strong determination to clip my wings. I began to struggle but the more I struggled, the more they came at me with their demonic and oppressive powers. It took me a long time to realise that I was battling with forces greater than me. I kept moving from job to job as I was either sacked or summarily dismissed from the previous one. The curious thing was that each circumstance seemed perfectly explainable such that if I was unable to think deeply. I could easily have dismissed my predicament as normal and probably blamed myself for my endless woes. Then, there was this particular job I lost that nearly put me on the brink of madness. It was in a high-profile law chambers, very upscale. My office directly overlooked the Bar Beach but, like every comfortable seat I sat on, satanic and powerful forces swopped on me, pulled the chair from beneath me and I fell miserably. Fear, anguish, despair and desolation characterised my life throughout this period. It was as if there was no hope at all; worst of all, I became the laughing stock and butt of jokes among supposed friends and relatives. No one wanted to be associated with me."

I stare frigidly at Lekan as he speaks and my appetite is ruined. I start to perspire. I wrap my arms around myself. Maybe

I should say something, tell him to get to the point. What's he trying to tell me? I have been told that hitherto despondent people tend to feel their mood being positively altered when they have reasons to believe that other people they assume are free from problems actually have worse problems than theirs. I recall the tremendous effect of the title of a Mexican soap, "The Rich Also Cry," on Nigerians, including people who were not regular television viewers. They would rush home and stay glued to their television screen to watch the soap, not so much because they were taken in by the plot or storyline or even the characters, but simply because the title offered them some form of succour. They were always eager to find out how the rich could suffer and shed tears like poor, ordinary folks. I don't know Lekan's intention for telling me about the difficulties that attended the early years of his career but I'm happy that he has overcome the horrors of those years because the man sitting in front of me has no trouble at all. Perhaps that's precisely the point he's trying to make; to let me know that I shall overcome my own problems someday. If this is his point, then, it's a point being well made because I feel like the sun has set for me right now. I even have strong doubts as to the possibility of it ever rising again.

"Funto!" His voice distracts me from my introspection. "I want to help you, if you would let me." I straighten up, becoming more alert.

"Of course, I would let you; I'm in search of help," I quip, trying not to sound too desperate. He lowers his voice to a whisper although there are only the two of us in his office.

"I'm doing this because I care about you. You are a brilliant woman and you deserve to be accomplished." I'm urging him, with my eyes, to save me from further suspense. It's awfully agonising.

"I'll take you to a place and you'll be amazed at the outcome.

Your supervisor will be the one to send for you. He'll ask your forgiveness and you'll get your PhD within the shortest time possible. It's a wonderful place I'm taking you where all problems are solved no matter their magnitude. This is not about religion, Funto, it's about recognising that certain things have to be done at a certain stage in the life of an adult in order to forge ahead in life and having the courage to do them. I don't do this for every friend I have but I will do it for you. After you have gone there, and you have done all that is required of you, if you fail to get your PhD in a year's time, and if you don't find a man to marry you within six months, you would be at liberty to call me a bastard."

Lekan fixes me a hard stare, my entire body trembles as an alarm bell sounds in my brain. I retrain myself from telling him straight off that I'm not interested. I climb wearily to my feet before muttering, "I must thank you for the food and especially for the invitation, but I would like to think about it." He senses my discomfort.

"Is anything the matter?" he asks.

"No. I just need to get somewhere before the evening traffic begins. I'm very grateful for all," I say in a rush and turn on my heels. He stands to walk me to the door.

"How? How soon would I have your response?" he asks. He doesn't get it, does he? I'm not interested. Back off! I scream inwardly, but to him, I say, "As soon as I decide. Once again, it's very thoughtful of you to have offered to assist me. I appreciate."

I open the door and practically take flight. I'm panting by the time I reach the bus stop. Am I afraid, angry, surprised or shocked? I don't know but I want to get away as fast as possible. One thing I need to do quickly is find a way to impress upon myself that I haven't heard Lekan's proposition. That he hasn't said anything like that at all. It was all in my dream, a huge, lousy dream that I ought to treat without regard. I open my bag to check my phone for missed calls. Folake hasn't called; no one has. I can't take it anymore; I will go to Geoffrey's to find her. She's the only person I can talk to without being afraid that she could come up with some weird and outlandish idea.

I arrive at Geoffrey's residence three hours later. His niece tells me her uncle and aunty are in the middle of a discussion and that she will announce my presence shortly. I sit tentatively on a couch, trying to fix my gaze on the television but I fail. My mind is in turmoil. I want to talk to my friend. I try to nudge Geoffrey's niece into letting Folake know about my presence without further delay but she's reluctant. I become more restless and rise impulsively to my feet. I start to pace the room and, without thinking of what I'm doing, I make my way to the passage with intent to knock softly on the door of any room where I hear their voices. I take a deep, precious, lungful of air, trying to calm my panicked breathing. Why am I suddenly panicky? I move steadily but slowly, listening in, then I hear Geoffrey's voice and halt instinctively.

"The time to do it is now. You have to summon the courage to tell her. I mean we have tolerated her for too long and it can no longer be business as usual."

"What you are asking me to do is unreasonable, insensitive and wicked," Folake says.

"Your friend is a sponger and you know it. I don't understand why you keep wasting your hard-earned money on her. She is a miserable, low-life parasite who will go on feeding fat on your sweat and mine for as long as we let her. You no longer need a friend like her, especially now that you will be my wife. I have allowed you to feed her and her bastard daughter because I saw how you enjoyed doing it. That's okay for as long as you are a spinster. Now that you will be my wife, our wealth has become a commonwealth, the same goes for our purse, and it's time to put her precisely where she belongs – on the street."

"I can't do it because it would be callous and unfeeling. I won't do it; it's unfair."

"Then you leave me no choice than to do it myself. What's the big deal? By the way, do you suppose she can afford to renew the rent on your apartment when it expires? It's only a matter of time before she hits the streets because I won't let you spend another dime on her. You no longer need the apartment, period!"

That's all I can take from Geoffrey, otherwise I will combust and explode and it will be ugly. I turn the door knob and it opens. I stand awkwardly, gazing at them in turn. Folake's eyes widen and her mouth opens. She takes in a huge breath, as if wounded. She looks tortured. Geoffrey glares at her and I regret my incaution. I have no right to burst in on them in this manner. Folake looks uncomfortable and I cringe inwardly. I have overstepped the mark.

"I'm sorry," I mouth at Geoffrey, who shrugs nonchalantly. I turn to leave. In the passage, I'm momentarily lost, my heart pounds and my blood races through my veins. I feel panicked and out of my depth. What would I do without Folake? She's been more than a friend to me; she has become my sister, my confidant, my support, my pillar, my hope, my ally, my all. Who would replace her in my life? As I stand in the passage, they continue their bickering. The tension is too much for me to bear. I don't want to be here; I don't want to witness this encounter. It was wrong of me to have intruded and still be eavesdropping because I can hear every word they say. I'm intruding, I want to vamoose, but I'm stuck, my limbs refuse to move. I just want to understand what's going on so as to know what to do.

"See what you've done; are you happy to make a poor woman miserable?" Folake asks.

"I don't give a damn. Besides, it's good that she has heard it directly, let her get it into her skull that it will no longer be possible for her to sponge off you. You are now mine and whatever you have belongs to me, also."

"Let's help her, Geoffrey darling, she is a human being like us, it's just that she's been rather unlucky in life. Life deals us blows sometimes and I admire her tenacity."

"Life's blows my foot. The reason why her life is the way it is can only be because she fails to plan. She doesn't deserve your pity, Folake. Besides, we don't run a charity. Let her go to some NGO for assistance or, better still, relocate to a village. She can't survive in Lagos."

Bile rises in my mouth. I should not be here. This is one of the most excruciating conversations I have ever had to endure. I scamper out of the passage, out of Geoffrey's house. Outside, I'm frozen to the spot. Tears begin to ooze down my cheeks and I dash them away roughly with the back of my hand. I gaze down at my feet, tears still trickling down my cheeks. I don't know for how long I have been gaping unseeingly at my feet, but someone sounds a car horn which startles me. I look up to find a Toyota Avensis beside me. There is only one occupant in it and he beckons me, urging me to either come close to talk to him or come into the car. I choose the former, resting my elbow on the front passenger's door.

"Any problem, madam?" I shake my head slowly without speaking.

"Why, but you are weepy." Fresh tears pool and trickle down my cheeks.

"You know what, madam? I didn't stop to chase you, okay, and I hope you believe me. I see you are in distress and I want to help. Why don't you come in? Perhaps I can help you to a point."

I open the door and climb in.

"Where are you going?"

"Bode Thomas, Surulere," I mumble.

"Well, let's see how far we can travel together," he says. I'm quiet.

"You are really distraught," he observes tenderly, glancing at me briefly and returning his eyes on the road. I don't know what to say, so I say nothing.

"Perhaps a soft drink will help calm you a little," he says kindly and although I feel grateful for all his effort, still I'm mute. I'm pre-occupied by the thought of what my life would be like from now on. He seems to realise that I don't feel like talking. We travel in silence until we arrive at CMS. He finds a place to park and beckons a woman bearing an array of soft drinks on her head. She attempts to cross the road quickly but a speeding taxi appears to be dangerously close and she slows. My benefactor is holding out a five-hundred naira note in his left hand, his right hand on the steering wheel. Suddenly, a shirtless man who has been standing close to the soft drink seller makes a spontaneous dash across the road and heads straight in our direction. He reaches where we are, practically snatches the note from my benefactor's hand without uttering a word and quickly crosses the road back to the soft drink seller, who must now be thinking that the shirtless man wants to help my benefactor with his purchase. We are stunned and confused at the same time, too. We watch the unfolding drama. For a moment, I allow myself to believe that the man wants to do us the favour of buying the soft drink or save the seller the trouble of having to cross the road. But there's something about his manner that makes his intention unclear and this is what we have to be patient to find out. Meanwhile, the shirtless man is now standing next to the soft drink seller and she is giving him all her attention. He selects a bottle of Coca-Cola, gives her the naira note, she issues him the balance from squeezed naira notes lining her left palm; he collects the balance and approaches another woman selling Gala. He carefully selects two and pays. He's now trying to cross the road again. What a good and responsible Nigerian! He's merely trying to help us. Then, it occurs to me that we didn't request for Gala; we didn't request for anything because he didn't give us a chance to. Anyway, he crosses the road swiftly and is once again approaching us. We are watching and waiting to see what he wants to do. He reaches where we are and stretches his right hand containing the balance from his purchases toward my benefactor without saying anything. He doesn't give my benefactor the soft drink or the Gala. My benefactor takes the money, looking bemused. Then, the shirtless man turns back abruptly and finds a place to sit by the side of the road. He uncorks the Coca-Cola bottle, takes a long sip from it, unwraps one of the Gala and begins to munch, eyeing my benefactor coldly. I find my voice.

"I think we should leave here, now." He turns to look at me, our eyes lock and we hold each other's gaze for the first time since I came into his car.

"I think you are right." He mutters, putting the gear back in drive.

As we drive off, we take an involuntary look at the shirtless man. He continues to munch on his Gala and sip from his Coca-Cola. He looks calm and unruffled. My benefactor and I exchange glances and start to talk.

"Thanks for helping out," I murmur.

"The pleasure is mine. Do you want to talk about it?"

"Yeah, it's a long story really, but I will summarise by saying that I'm a PhD student in dire need of a source of income.

"You ought to be celebrating. You have a promising future."

"Really?"

"Yes of course, all you need to do is approach any of the

existing universities, polytechnics or colleges of education and apply for a part-time teaching job. That way, you'll be earning some income and will have enough time for your research."

My mouth falls open in sudden realisation. Why haven't I thought about it? My situation is not as hopeless as I imagine, after all.

"Thanks for letting me know," I murmur.

"The pleasure is mine. You may try Clamorous University of Nigeria for example."

"Indeed you are right. What's your name?"

"Pitan Badmus."

"I'm Funto Oyewole."

"Good to know you, Funto. I won't be able to take you as far as Bode Thomas but I can take you to Costain bus stop."

"That'll be just fine, thank you."

"This is my complimentary card; don't hesitate to call me anytime, so that we can gist. In the meantime, don't worry yourself unduly. Go to Clamorous University and give me a feedback on how it goes, okay? "

"Thank you very much," I say, smiling shyly and taking the card from him.

By the time I alight from Pitan's car, my mood has moderated. I'll go to Clamorous University tomorrow, I mutter under my breath.

Nineteen

A persistent knock on the front door jolts me into wakefulness. I feel disoriented for a moment but I manage to climb groggily out of bed. Folake stands at the door. We stare silently at each other for some moments, both of us filled with unspoken recriminations. Then, suddenly, we start to grin at each other like two idiots. I make the first move, whirling her around as if we are on a dance floor.

"Welcome home, baby girl," I mouth. My words are her undoing. A strangled sob escapes from her throat and she starts to cry.

"No, Folake, don't cry," I say, reaching over to curl my arm around her as she sobs quietly into my shoulder. "We don't need this, and you know it," I murmur, struggling to hold back my own tears. She is holding me tighter now. I'm taller so she buries her head in my chest and wraps her arms firmly around me. I wipe her face with the back of my left hand and use my right hand to clean her nose. After a while we sit together on the same couch, neither of us saying anything. I feel guilty; I feel ungrateful. Perhaps Geoffrey is right. I haven't quite planned my life. What efforts have I made to earn a living since the sudden loss of my job? My life is truly beginning to resemble that of a sponger. The only thing I have done has been to put all my energy into pursuing a doctorate which has amounted to putting all my proverbial eggs in one basket. Is it reasonable for a grown adult like me, and especially one with responsibilities, to attempt to place my burden on another individual as if that individual does not have their own responsibilities? What effort have I made in the last four years to source for a means of livelihood? Now that the doctorate ambition has clearly become a mirage, isn't it about time I took the proverbial bull by the horns by learning to stand on my own feet? I feel utterly foolish and irresponsible that Geoffrey has to remind me to plan my own life. Folake does not owe it to me to cater to my needs. Why have I continued to shamelessly live off her?

"Funto?" She snaps me out of my reverie. "I'm very sorry about yesterday. You know Geoffrey is …"

"No, Folake, there is absolutely nothing to feel sorry about. I ought to apologise for barging in on you two because it was wrong. Maybe I was beginning to take your kindness for granted and I needed someone like Geoffrey to caution me."

"No, don't talk like that. Geoffrey's argument is faulty and I have told him as much."

"I know he's right, Folake, but whether or not he is, you and I have come a long way and you mean a lot to me."

"Same here, Funto, and please don't believe the trash Geoffrey said about you. You are an intelligent and highly knowledgeable woman. I admire you greatly. As for Geoffrey, I will continue to work on him. These things take time, as you know."

"Of course, I do understand, and as I mentioned, his reprimand is a necessary and timely wake-up call to me. I need to find something to do to earn me an income."

"I think you are right about that. Geoffrey wants us to relocate to England. We will have our wedding there also."

"Oh I'm so happy for you, Folake. You deserve all these good things that are coming your way. I hope you don't change your ways. I want you to continue to be as kind-hearted as you have always been."

"You amaze me when you describe me as a kind person because I don't see myself that way. I'm just me, living the only way I know how to live."

"I know, and I'm very proud of you. How soon are you two leaving us?"

"In a matter of weeks, Funto. I just missed my period and Geoffrey wants our child to have British citizenship as well."

"What! You are pregnant? Wow! Congratulations, dear friend. This is terrific news and it calls for celebration," I say, laughing heartily as my mood brightens. My spirits are lifted. I spring to my feet and rush to the kitchen to make tea. As we wait for water to boil, I tell her about the latest problem with my PhD. Suddenly, the heavens open and it starts to rain. Folake clutches her hands together in her lap, keeping still, apparently not knowing how to respond to my catalogue of woes. The water boils, I make tea and we drink in silence. I don't want to make her unhappy.

"I need to have a bath and get dressed," I announce cheerfully.

"Where are you going?" she asks.

"I'm going in search of a job."

"You have a place in mind?"

"Yes. I met a guy yesterday who advised me to try applying to Clamorous University of Nigeria for part-time teaching."

The rain stops. We walk back to the sitting room.

"A guy? Be careful, Funto." She cuts me an eye and follows it immediately with a smile to take the sting out of her rebuke. I feel like a wayward child. I withdraw my gaze from her and sit quietly for a moment.

"It's not what you think. I have learned my lesson, or at least,

I'm trying to. I imagine he's just a kind-hearted 'Lagosian'. He gave me a ride and when I told him about what's been happening to me, he suggested I try Clamorous University."

"Indeed, you need to take a step. The rent here will expire in two months' time and although I will find a way to give you some money regardless of how Geoffrey feels about it, it won't be sufficient to renew the rent, let alone take care of your other needs."

My heart skips a beat and then starts to pound furiously. I haven't thought about Folake's planned emigration from Nigeria in all its ramifications. I feel naked and world-weary. How much would she give me? How long would it take me and how soon would I pick a job? I look at her uncertainly. She doesn't know how to respond, merely narrows her eyes and looks thoughtfully at me. My mind is in fresh turmoil. Oh, I'm so confused. After a while, she finds her voice.

"Everything will be alright, Funto. I wish you would believe me when I say that you don't need me or anyone else for that matter to survive, and even thrive. You never cease to amaze me with your innate strength. You are a strong and self-contained woman and your future is sparkling bright as long as you don't permit negative thoughts about yourself. Get a grip on your mind, face the world with the boundless courage that you possess and everything will be just fine."

I smile kindly at her. My mind is still foggy but I find her pronouncement about my potential quite believable. I watch as she speaks and observe that she doesn't seem uncomfortable making those positive comments about me as she would have if she were hiding the truth. A warm glow spreads slowly through my veins. We hug each other tightly and when we disengage, we smile broadly at each other. It's a cathartic experience for the both of us as we realise we have come to the end of an era. From now on, we have to live our lives without each other and I'm undoubtedly the worse hit. Life has to go on regardless.

The road is wet after the rain, but I set out on my mission to Clamorous University of Nigeria. Two-and-a-half hours later, I'm at the security office of the Central Administrative Block. I'm trying to convince a security man to allow me access into the human resources unit.

"Who do you want to see there, madam?" A scruffy looking man asks.

"The personnel manager."

"The personnel manager is on leave."

"Alright, let me see whoever is sitting in for him."

"You don't even know who you want to see," he says rudely.

"I'm here to make an enquiry."

"In that case, we are the people to see, ask us anything you want to know."

"No, I don't think you would have the information I require; let me see an official of the human resources or personnel department."

"We can't do that, madam. Visitors are allowed in strictly on appointment."

"Why are you being difficult?"

"There is no vacancy at Clamorous University, madam, No be wetin you wan know be that?" another man interjects, smiling mischievously. Perspiration breaks out on every part of my body as my brow creases and my jaw clenches in anger.

"Is this how you are trained to address visitors to your university?"

"Hey, Olufunto Oyewole the queen!" a female voice booms at my back, I turn and my eyes settle on Adaora Nwankwo.

"Oh my goodness, Ada!" I scream as we rush into each other's embrace.

"Welcome, madam, welcome, madam," virtually all the security men in the room are mouthing and jostling to make their voice the loudest. I watch the frenzy with suppressed amusement. Ada acts as if she doesn't hear them.

"You look prettier than you did back in our undergraduate days, Funto, what's the secret?"

"See who's teasing," I mumble, tingling at her touch. She takes my hand in hers and we walk out of the security office, first into an open space, then into the reception and finally we head straight to her office. It's large, spacious and well furnished. My eyes involuntarily settle on the name-plate on the table: 'Deputy Vice-Chancellor, Administration. I feel a familiar, faint stab of envy but I don't allow it to show on my face. Ada is bubbling about the office, apparently glad to see me. My mind drifts back to our undergraduate days when she and I were course mates. We couldn't be described as friends and I don't remember us going beyond acknowledging casual greetings from each other throughout the duration of our stay in the university. She was a member of a group of four girls who played a lot and were seen 'everywhere.' They were beautiful, trendy, vivacious, boisterous and care-free. They were chatty and incredibly fun-loving but they also appeared vain and attention-seeking. I smile at the memory of our lack of relationship back then and find it almost unbelievable that we are now acting as if we are long lost friends.

"What are you doing here?" Her voice brings me back to the present.

"I came in search of a job," I mutter, still feeling bemused.

"A teaching job?"

"Oh yes, I see your name hasn't changed," I murmur, indicating the name-plate on the table.

"Yeah, baby girl, it hasn't changed because I'm not married."

"Me neither," I say and we laugh loudly.

"Why?" she asks, eyeing me mischievously.

"I ought to be asking you the same question."

"You are very pretty, Funto."

"And you are even prettier, Adaora." We burst into another riotous laughter.

"I see you are doing great here," I observe, changing my expression from jovial to serious.

"Yes, o, my sister, it can only get better."

"You are now the Deputy Vice-Chancellor, Administration? How did you climb the ladder of success with such amazing speed?"

Well, I have a master's degree in Public Administration but I admit that I don't owe my meteoric rise to my qualification only. You know this is not a conventional university, so things are done a bit differently here."

"How do you mean?"

"I mean things are slightly more flexible."

"I see; how has the flexibility in the system helped your career growth?"

"Hmm, I'm related to the Vice-Chancellor from my mother's side. He brought me here when he was appointed about six years ago and has been responsible for my rapid career growth."

"The Vice-Chancellor was appointed six years ago? I thought university VCs serve a single term of five years only."

"You are forgetting that this is not a conventional university. He asked the president to give him three additional years to serve when his term expired. He will spend eight years."

"He's truly powerful." The words are out of my mouth before I realise it.

"You know he's the pioneer VC. He has a lot of ideas he wants to bring into the system and he doesn't trust that the next man would understand them. He's also interested in leaving a solid legacy and firm administrative structure that will be difficult to dismantle."

"It's very thoughtful of him, I must say, and I'm glad you are doing well for yourself."

"I'm doing super-fine, my sister. In fact, my promotion to my current position was announced only two weeks ago and it threw most of my colleagues off-balance. A majority of them felt so envious and bitter that they couldn't congratulate me, but as I said to you earlier, it can only get better."

"Whoa! I wish you the very best in your new position."

"Thank you joor. A beg don't mind me ojare; I'm so selfish just talking about myself. Let's talk about you, what have you been up to?"

"Well, I worked in the public service until I was laid off some years ago and I'm now trying to acquire a PhD."

"Hey, Professor Funto Oyewole!"

"Abeg, leave that one, my sister. I'm happy to have found you and happier now that you are a 'big woman' here." I flash a mischievous smile and quickly restore my candid expression. "Seriously, Ada, would it be possible for you to help me secure a teaching appointment here at Clamorous University?"

"I can help you but I must explain certain things to you. Clamorous University does not engage its teaching staff on a permanent basis. Don't forget that the Federal Government established this place to cater to the needs of working-class people who desire greater academic knowledge but are unable to achieve this through a conventional university since they have to combine work with study. Therefore, because our students are expected to be experienced people who wish to update their knowledge, they receive lectures sparingly because they are expected to depend more on their study materials. Lectures hold between four and seven o'clock in the evening and their teachers, known as instructors, are paid on the basis of courses taught only. Also, instructors are required to teach for a prescribed number of hours only. For example, a two-unit course attracts eight hours of lectures only for an entire semester. If an instructor chooses to engage their students for longer than eight hours in the semester, they do not get paid for the additional hours. The effect is that the remuneration is very poor, I must warn you because you are my friend. It is good for people who have a full-time job and only wish to supplement their income. However, since your situation is as you have described, the stipend here may be able to take care of your transport fares to Abuja whilst you intensify your search for a well-paying job."

A feeling of disappointment threatens to overwhelm me but I don't permit it. There must be a beginning with every life's journey, I counsel myself. Whoever climbs a mountain from the top? I straighten my shoulders and smile brightly at her.

"Thank you for being honest, Ada, I will give it a shot. How many courses may I be given to teach?"

"I'm afraid I can only get you one slot for now but I'll see what I can do to increase your slot as we go along."

Again, despondency threatens but I don't give in to it. I resolve to banish all negative feelings and emotion from my psyche from now on. I have what it takes to thrive; Folake says so; surely, she can only be right. I will give it my best effort and who knows? The management of Clamorous University might soon find me worthy to be given more courses to teach. The thought brings a smile to my face.

"I'm grateful for your honesty, Ada. What do I do next?"

"I will give you a sheet of paper on which you will write your application for the position of an instructor. Leave the rest to me."

I can hardly contain my excitement mixed with relief. I take the sheet of paper from her with both hands and begin to write. She tells me letters to Clamorous University are addressed to the VC, not the Registrar. I do as I am directed and when I finish writing, she directs me to another office to submit it, promising to start work on it immediately and telling me to check back in two weeks' time for my letter of appointment. I can't believe my luck. I thank her profusely and head out the door.

As I climb down the fleet of stairs of the reception building into a terrace, I sight a posh car with a chauffeur holding one of the back passenger's doors open. I'm intrigued by the spectacle and I instinctively look around for the owner of the car whom I'm sure must not be far away. My face breaks into a wide grin when Ada emerges and our eyes lock. Her reaction, however, surprises me for she hurriedly looks away and walks briskly to the waiting car. I'm also walking toward the car because I must necessarily pass it on my way to the gate. We arrive almost together as she climbs in. The driver genuflects and closes the door after her before hurrying to the driver's side. He climbs in. I wave and smile brightly at Ada but she doesn't acknowledge me. I move to one side to allow the car pass but it remains stationary. After pausing a moment, I resume my walk and exit the premises. Standing outside the gate waiting for a bus, I decide to pay Pitan a surprise visit at his office. The day has been more successful than I could have imagined possible. I feel like celebrating my accomplishment.

"See who's here," Pitan says softly when I'm ushered into his office. He smiles sweetly and gestures for me to sit down.

"I came to thank you for the ride and, more, for your advice. It paid off," I say breathlessly.

"Have you visited the university already?"

"Oh yes, and I'm happy to let you know that I met a former school mate who has promised to facilitate my engagement on part-time basis."

"I'm very happy for you."

"It's you I must thank. You made the suggestion."

"Have you had lunch?"

"No."

"There is a restaurant in the next building; we could go there to eat," he says. At the restaurant, we both order rice and plantain. I eat with relish, more out of excitement than real hunger. Life will not be as difficult as I have imagined, I assure myself yet again with a smile.

"You look happier than yesterday," Pitan observes and my smile booms.

"I'm trying to be happy," I quip, only to notice worried lines on his forehead.

"Is everything alright?" I ask. He hesitates before answering. I let my cutlery drop and gaze at him tenderly.

"Something is on your mind," I challenge and he sighs in a resigned way.

"Come on now, it's definitely not as bad as it seems, whatever it is," I chastise.

"It's my mother, she makes my life miserable and, frankly, my life would be less complicated if she were no longer around."

"That's uncharitable. How could you say such a thing about your own mother?" I'm angry at him and I can't hide it.

"I'm sorry if I shocked you, but why do some women choose to go to war with their son simply because he has taken a wife? What's the rivalry in aid off? It's not as if I can marry my mother." My frown dissolves and I start to relax,

"Your mother does not approve of your wife?"

"Apparently so, but what irks me is that she doesn't have anything concrete against the poor girl other than cheap blackmail, all in a bid to cause disaffection and disharmony in

222

my home."

"I understand your frustration but your mother remains your mother. You must find ways to affirm your love for your wife without being disrespectful to your mother. You must strive at all times to honour your mother, provide for her and be a good son whilst also finding ways not to allow your marriage to suffer. Your ability to juggle both successfully is what makes you a real man, if you ask me. And you must not be afraid to tell your mother the truth at all times. That's why she's your mother."

"Thanks, Funto."

"The pleasure is mine," I murmur, narrowing my eyes. He reaches over, takes my hand and squeezes it gently. I gently withdraw my hand. Pitan will be my friend and we will keep it very safe, I resolve within me.

"There is another area you may wish to explore," he says, dousing the tension.

"Yes?"

"I think you should register a business name; it doesn't cost much and I could assist with finance if you know a lawyer who could do the registration with the Corporate Affairs Commission."

"That'll be very kind of you. I know a number of former schoolmates who are practising lawyers in Lagos." I do a quick mental rundown of the lawyers I know and decide to go for Ikhidero Egharevba. I must avoid going to Lekan lest he reminds me of his invitation. I beam at Pitan.

"I know a lawyer that can do it fast."

"Good, then, I will give you some money at once. You can use the certificate to get small jobs, such as a supplier of stationery in offices. It may not fetch you a regular income, but once in a while when it does it will help to cushion your financial difficulties."

"I can't thank you enough, Pitan," I say, feeling happy and rising to my feet as we finish our food.

Outside Pitan's office, the evening traffic begins to build up but I don't let it discourage me from taking the next step. Lawyers are usually in their offices in the evening. I will go to Ikhidero's office at once and pay for a business name registration. Life can get truly exciting with just a little effort. I smile broadly and start to hum a song as I walk to the bus stop.

Twenty

JULY, 2003

I turn and stretch. I have been lying on the couch since morning, gazing unseeingly into space. I feel an aching emptiness. Folake and Geoffrey have since left for England. I have moved out of Surulere and now live in Mushin. I don't know how Deyemi will feel about our new neighbourhood when she comes home on holiday. Well, at fifteen, and with just one more year to complete her secondary school education, she is no longer a child from whom I need to hide the sordidness of our situation. I glance at my phone for a sense of time. It's now nearly 1.00pm, time to prepare lunch. I have become acutely aware of meal times since I hardly have anything else to do apart from going to teach at Clamorous University, which is only once a week. I haven't been paid since I started teaching but I continue in the hope that I will get paid soon. Meals have now become more than punctuation marks in my life; they have become events in themselves. When I was writing my thesis, there were times when I would forget to eat. Most times, I would only manage to run across the road or send for snacks if Deyemi happened to be around. These days, however, I prepare all three meals a day and the more I eat the leaner I become. I climb warily to my feet and move to the large mirror on the wall. I stand and take a long, hard look at my face. I'm pale; dark circles are around my now too-large eyes. I look gaunt, haunted. I need to learn to use make-up. I sigh. My phone rings. It's my mother. Why is she calling me? She doesn't initiate a call to me unless absolutely necessary. I'm afraid to answer it but I can't possibly ignore it. I press the green button.

"Hello, Ma'ami," I breathe.

"Hallo, Funto, How are you? Come to Ibadan today, I want to see you."

My heart jumps. I have deliberately neglected to call or visit her for some time now because I don't know what to tell her. I'm aware she thinks I ought to have finished my PhD. How can I bring myself to explain that not only have I not gotten my doctorate but also that I'm no longer certain I will ever do so? She would look me in the eye and say, I did warn you, didn't I?

"Hello, Funto, are you there?" Her voice snaps me out of my reverie.

"Eh-r, yes, Ma'ami, but I can't come today. I will come tomorrow morning."

"Ha-ha, come today so that you will spend the night with me."

"No, Ma'ami, I will come early tomorrow," I insist. How will I tell her that I can't even afford the transport fare unless I ask a friend for assistance?

"No problem, Olowo ori mi, you Lagos people are always busy. I will expect you tomorrow."

"Okay, Ma'ami. Bye." I sigh and stare blankly at the wall. What would I do? Even if I'm prepared to face my challenges with stoicism and ignore hurtful comments from her, what about the implication of my failure on her life and health? How would she feel when she finds out that I have failed miserably in my attempt to earn a PhD? It'll only break her heart. No, I must find a way to shield her from the oppressive truth, protect her and avoid doing or saying things that could cut short her precious life. I run through the list of contacts on my phone and locate Pitan's number. I dial it; mercifully, he answers.

"Hello, Pitan, are you at work?"

"Yes, Funto, are you alright?"

"I'm fine. It's just that I need to see you, if you don't mind."

"Of course not. I'll be here till six o'clock."

"Good. I'll be on my way shortly."

"Cool."

I dash into the bathroom for a quick wash. Three hours later, I'm in his office.

"You care for a late lunch?" he asks as soon as I arrive. I nod. He takes the lead as we walk to the restaurant.

"I don't like the way you sounded on the phone," he says after we have placed our orders.

"I got a call from my mother. She wants me to come and see her in Ibadan tomorrow. I know why she wants to see me but I don't want her to know about my challenges. It would crush her."

"You need some money?"

"Yes, please, if you could help."

"That won't be a problem, but do you really think it's reasonable for you to lie to her? I thought you said mothers deserve to know everything. And just for how long do you figure you can continue to pretend all is well?"

"Well, y-yes, I mean n-no, when we know the things we tell them would only hurt them gravely."

Pitan's face clouds in confusion but I act as if I don't notice. He doesn't understand what has transpired between my mother and me over the subject and I don't want to go into the details. As for my mother, I must continue to keep an 'all is well appearance' until they truly become well.

"How much would you need?" He pulls me out of my thought.

"Well, what can I tell you? I need transport money and maybe a little extra to give to her as gift."

Pitan cheerfully gives me more than I could have hoped for and I return home to prepare for my journey.

In Ibadan, my mother takes a look at me and frowns. Why didn't I remember to apply make-up as planned?

"Olowo ori mi, why didn't you tell me yesterday that you are sick? I would have travelled to come and meet you in Lagos instead of you doing the journey in this state," she asks, her eyes crinkling with motherly concern. Do I look really so bad or is my mother exaggerating?

"I'm not sick, Ma'ami, it's just the Lagos stress," I mumble, but I don't sound convincing even to myself.

"Are you a stranger in Lagos or new to its ways? How come you are suddenly feeling so stressed? I don't know why you don't want to leave Lagos and come to Ibadan."

"You worry too much. Why did you ask me to come?"

"Eh-r, I asked you to come when I realised that you are no longer talking to your mother about your PhD. How far have you gone?" My heart skips a beat. I swallow hard, try to calm my nerves, then quickly paste a false smile on my face.

"I have finished my programme, Ma'ami," I declare falsely.

"Eh, eh, eh, my very own hard-working daughter, I trust you! Olorire omo ni e lojo-kojo, iwo o ki nse alaseti, come hug your mother, suck my breast all over again. You deserve it. You are the true daughter of your father and I have always known that you are destined for great things. I know there is no ambition too huge for you to accomplish. You are success incarnate."

She scoops me into her arms. She is chanting, her breathing is getting harder by the moment and I'm scared that she might convulse out of excitement but I can't stop her. I remain in her embrace, trying not to succumb to my own emotions, which would only out me to her. I can't afford to cry for the sake of my mother's phantom happiness. Then, suddenly, she disengages from me and starts to sing and dance.

Mo sorire o
Eleda mi modupe o
Mo sorire o
Eleda mi modupe o
Mowa dupe ore ana
Baba Modupe o
Mo wa dupe ore eni
Baba Modupe o
Motun dupe ore ola o
Baba Modupe o
Baba Modupe o
Baba Modupe o
Baba Modupe
Bi mobaji l'owuro kutu-kutu ma d'ori mi mu
Mo sorire o
Eleda mi modupe o

I look nervous, off-balance, but my mother takes no notice. She is in her element. I shake my head sadly. If only you knew the truth, Mother, but I won't let you know. I won't let you know because I don't want to spoil your happiness. I promise to protect you even if I have to lie and deceive you in order for you to stay in a perpetual joyous mode. Ignorance is bliss, Mother, and you deserve nothing but a blissful experience, no matter how illusory it may be. You deserve to be looked after, cared for, because you've been through so much. Why should I bring you more pain? Why should I tell you what would make you despondent, even if it is the truth? No, I shouldn't do it and I won't. So, go on, Mother, rejoice. Perhaps in your rejoicing, God may have mercy on me and touch Prof Charles Ephraim's heart. But even if he does not have a change of heart, even if I never get the PhD, I will go on lying to you for as long as it makes you this happy. I watch her dance and, as I do, allow myself to feel a modicum of excitement. In time, I become enthralled and I rise, yielding slowly to the melodious rhythm of Paul Play Dairo's song: Mo sorire o Eleda mi modupe o. I give her the money I got from Pitan.

Back in Lagos, it's vacation time for my daughter. Students bubble about at Maryland Secondary School, excited at the prospect of a long vacation. Deyemi tells me she would like to introduce me to one of her friends.

"How many friends do you have?" I tease,

"Mummy, I can't count them because, in this school, everybody has to be everybody's friend."

"Okay, okay," I enthuse, raising my arms in mock surrender. "Where is this friend so that we can get going?"

"She's over there with her father, come, let's go and meet them." She drags me along by the arm. I surrender, giggling. Her friend is enjoying her father's attention as he puts his arm around her shoulder, talking excitedly and smiling at her. He stops talking when they notice our presence.

"Good afternoon."

"Good afternoon, madam," the man responds, smiling.

"Mummy, this is my friend, Susan, and this is her dad," Deyemi introduces.

"Susan, how are you?"

"I'm fine, ma."

"I'm Dolapo Adeoti," her father offers.

"Glad to meet you, Mr Adeoti, I'm Funto Oyewole, Deyemi's mother." He takes my proffered hand, shaking it warmly.

"Same here," he says. I glance briefly at Deyemi to confirm that I have done as she pleases, then turn to go but Dolapo clears his throat and I halt.

"Are you driving, madam?"

"No," I answer simply.

"In that case, we may all go in my car. In which direction are you going?"

"Mushin." Deyemi looks at me questioningly. I cut her an eye before returning my attention to Dolapo, who seems eager to have us in their company.

By the time Deyemi and I alight two bus stops from our residence, her friend's father and I have interacted well enough for me to know that he works with a commercial bank on the Island and in a position to assist in my job search. He lifts my spirits considerably when he tells me to bring my CV to him the next day, promising to submit it at their corporate headquarters. Deyemi is taken aback by our new neighbourhood and is initially disconsolate, but when I explain carefully to her all that has happened, especially Folake's relocation to England, her mood brightens and she renders her mantra.

"Don't worry, Mummy, everything will be alright."

Of course, everything will be alright, my subconscious echoes cheerfully. Folake has just sent me some money through Moneygram. Besides, Dolapo seems genuinely interested in helping out. He paints a picture of someone who is close to the decision-makers of the bank he works in.

"I will personally take this up and ensure that you become gainfully employed within the shortest time possible," he assures again and again. I beam at him appreciatively.

The next morning, I'm in his office at 11:15am to keep a noon appointment. He smiles and tells me to exercise a little patience as break time is at noon. I haven't considered the likelihood of his wanting to hang out with me during his break. I'd thought I was coming to merely hand over my CV to him. I wait patiently. He hasn't asked for the CV but I don't think I need to pressure him unduly. I'm sure he knows the purpose of my coming.

At exactly noon he saunters through the reception door, hands in his pockets. He smiles warmly, gesturing to me to come with him. He leads me to a restaurant within the bank's premises. Everywhere is bustling with activity. There is something about his demeanour that I don't quite understand but I don't pay it any mind. We make our orders and set about our meal.

"I hate to see women suffer," he declares seriously.

"That makes you a kind and compassionate person," I say, nodding vigorously in agreement. "If I had the executive fiat to cause a letter of appointment to be written for you today so that you start work immediately, I would do it without reservation," he says, pointing a finger heavenward to indicate his earnestness. I nod vigorously in concurrence. I glance at the large envelope containing my CV, which I place on the table. He follows my eyes, muttering, "I will take it from you when we finish our food." I smile. My subconscious is insistently suggesting that this man has designs on me but I tell myself that he's just being nice although he appears tense and uneasy. Do I intimidate him? We finish our food and he gives me some money, which he says is for my transport fare, and takes my CV. I thank him profusely as he walks me back to the reception area after we exchange our phone numbers. I'm about to step out when he suddenly asks:

"What are you doing this weekend?" I pout but quickly pull myself together. This is where all this is leading to, after all. Well, I could play your silly game.

"I don't have anything in mind at the moment."

"I would like us to meet and spend some time together." This is getting really interesting. "Really?"

"Yes, I want us to get to know each other more, we need to talk more and exchange ideas."

"Very well, then."

"If you would be free around 4pm on Saturday, I could pick you up and we could go somewhere special."

"I would be free at 4pm, Mr. Adeoti."

"Call me Dolapo, please."

"Well, see you at 4pm on Saturday, Dolapo."

A playful part of me looks forward to my date with him, as a kind of sport, and he doesn't disappoint. At precisely 4pm, he calls to say he's parked in a filling station close to where Deyemi and I had alighted from his car. I dress quickly. I wave down a passing commercial motorcycle, hop on it. I'm with Dolapo in a jiffy.

"I'm glad you could make it," he says, smiling sheepishly. I smile back, mumbling something about having looked forward to seeing him, too. I regard him briefly in silence. He's fidgety. What makes him so ill at ease?

"Where is this special place we are supposed to be going?"

"Eh-r, I want us to go somewhere very private, a place where we can talk without disturbance."

"What do we want to talk about?"

"Be patient now, when the time comes, you'll be the first to know." I sigh, feigning resignation. He takes my hand and squeezes it gently. I don't react.

"Do you know any decent hotel in your neighbourhood?" Hotel? Do I look like a slut? I'm shocked but I don't want to show it. I want to see just how far he can go with his foolishness.

"No, I don't," I reply simply.

"Don't worry, we'll drive around and I'm sure we'll find one."

A sardonic laugh etches at the corners of my mouth but

Dolapo is too self-absorbed to notice. His ignorance serves my purpose. He laughs with me, thinking I'm enjoying whatever it is he imagines he's doing. Well, he's right in a way because the game promises to be far more entertaining than I thought. We soon locate a hotel and he drives into the premises smoothly. A young man standing as if he's been waiting for us directs the car into a garage. I hear the garage door close as soon as Dolapo drives in. He appears to be quite experienced about everything. He leaps out of the car and meets the young man who is already by the driver's side. They take turns to speak in low tones. Dolapo follows the young man into the hotel, telling me to wait in the car. I remain on my seat, humming quietly to myself and enjoying every moment of the game. Dolapo is back; he opens the passenger door for me and tells me to follow him. I'm giggling from ear to ear, like a toddler about to be served a candy. We are now in the hotel room. He orders a drink for me.

"What about you, won't you take something?"

He looks confused momentarily but recovers in time to smile his thanks, then orders a beer for himself. Our drinks arrive; he uncorks the bottles in turn, fills our glasses and starts to unbutton his shirt. I can't hold my laughter. I throw my head on the pillow and surrender to convulsive laughter. Just how far can the fool go?

"You are a very funny woman and I'm enjoying your company," he says happily as he rises to hang his shirt in the wardrobe.

"You are the truly funny one," I manage to say amidst laughter, wiping my face with the back of my hand. "You said you wanted us to talk," I remind him.

"Oh yes, Funto, you see, eh-r, I want you to listen to me."

"I'm listening. Isn't that what I came here to do?"

"Yes, yes, eh-r, you see, you need a man, o ye e?"

"What gives you the impression that I don't already have one?"

"Ha-ha, you are looking for a job now. If you already have a man then he does not deserve you because he can't take care of you. Any man who has a beautiful woman like you and can't take care of her needs is not a serious man."

"I see. So you think you can take care of me because you work in a retail bank?"

"Eh-r, listen eh, any woman who is in this type of your situation needs a man to survive."

"What situation?"

"Ha-ha, situation of need now." I squeak but if he notices, he pretends otherwise. "Eh-r, I will give you money, huh? I will take care of your needs but I will 'pound' you very well o. When I 'pound' you, eh, I think you understand what I'm saying? When I 'pound' you very well, then I will give you money. I just want to help you."

I can't believe what I've just heard. How could a supposedly educated, grown man living in Lagos be this crude? What has come over him? I shake my head solemnly but can't help the wicked gleam in my eyes. It's a chance for me to have some entertainment and a foolish man like Dolapo is just the right ally.

"So, do you propose to 'pound' me today?"

"Yes o, what else are we waiting for?"

"I like your type. That means you have plenty of 'action', so, why don't you go ahead and undress fully?"

"Eh-hen, that means you are 'on fire', too."

"Well, whether or not my body is 'on fire', I'd like to see what stuff you've got if only to be sure it can 'pound' as well as you claim. Size is a factor, you know."

I'm struggling to smother a grin that is threatening to split my face into two. Like one possessed of a strange illness, Dolapo removes his clothes and stands naked before me. Good God, what a man!

"Are you ready for 'action'?" I tease.

"Yes, now."

"You won't use protection?"

"Do you want to feed me with unpeeled banana? I do skin to skin, my queen."

"With every woman?"

"I know you now; you are the mother of my daughter's friend."

"You don't know anybody when it comes to sex, Dolapo. Where is your condom?"

"I don't have; I want to enjoy you."

"Put on your clothes and come and sit down with me for a minute. You brought me here so that we could talk, remember?"

"I don't want any long talk, Funto. I want us to really get down."

"I insist we talk before anything at all."

"Okay, but be quick." He sits down beside me. His breathing is audible.

"How did you come about the notion that you have to screw any woman that approaches you for help? You wouldn't even be patient enough to do what she's asked for before demanding for gratification."

"Eh-r, I'm only trying to help here and you should know also that there is no free lunch anywhere."

"You are the most despicable clown I know. Now, you will put on your clothes, open the damned door and take me back to Mushin. And let me make it very clear, if you attempt anything funny, I will destroy you with my bare hands. If you have any doubt as to what I can do, go ahead and try, okay?"

He opens his mouth to say something. I hold up my hand,

he closes his mouth, puts on his clothes and opens the door. We drive in silence back to Mushin. And I climb out of his car without muttering a word.

In the morning, I visit Ikhidero's office with intent to collect my business registration certificate, but he's a way to court, so I wait till he returns. He smiles brightly at me when he walks in, taking my proffered hand in a warm handshake and enquiring after my wellbeing. We chat generally about everything except the subject of my visit. I don't want to be forward, but I'm wondering why he's acting as if he doesn't know the purpose of my visit. Or is he expecting me to broach the subject first? We go on chatting for a little longer until it seems obvious to me that he's not going to mention it if I don't.

"I'm here to collect my business certificate," I announce casually, smiling sweetly at him.

"Oh, your business registration, I haven't done it." I frown. Do I detect nonchalance in his attitude? Is this how he treats his clients?

"Why?"

"Well, because I haven't got round to it, that's all." Anger is welling up inside of me but I don't let it show.

"I paid you for it, didn't I?"

"Yes, you paid me. How much did you pay me? Did you also pay for my office rent? Do you have any idea how much it costs me to maintain an office here on Allen Avenue? Look, Funto, I have bigger issues to deal with. I'm looking for a big brief, do you understand? I want to be given briefs that would help me meet my huge financial commitments, not petty jobs like business registration."

I'm shocked at his response. In what way have I offended him? Maybe I should ask him.

"Have I offended you by giving you a small job and paying

you to do it?"

"I'm not saying you have done anything wrong; but you are my friend, you should understand."

"You didn't do the job because I'm your friend?"

"Not exactly."

"Why didn't you tell me not to pay you because I'm your friend? Why didn't you even charge me less amount than what a non-friend client would have paid because I'm your friend?"

"Look, Funto, I don't really want us to argue, okay? I haven't done it. I haven't even applied for it at the Corporate Affairs Commission, so don't waste your time coming here soon. I have your phone number; when I do it, I will call you. I may even come to deliver it at your doorstep because you are my friend."

"When may I look forward to this August visit?"

"I don't know and, as I said, I don't have time yet for that kind of small job."

Ikhidero is clearly the limit; I get to my feet and head out the door.

Twenty-one

SEPTEMBER, 2003

It's been five years since I started my PhD journey and one agonising year since my supervisor refused to continue as my supervisor. I'm still awaiting his official pronouncement without which I cannot make a new beginning. I visited the university a number of times during the last academic year and the HOD told me on each occasion that Prof Ephraim was yet to put his decision in writing. It's the beginning of a new session and I'm getting ready to pay my HOD another visit. I towel-dry my hair and run a comb through it, then gaze at my reflection in the mirror.

Alas! I can hardly recognise the gaunt, sunken-eyed, hollow-cheeked, old woman staring back at me. My hair is turning grey. Arrgh! How on earth did this happen? I can't contain my emotions; I sink to the floor and surrender to overwhelming, chest-wrenching sobs. I miss Folake. It's been only a year since she left within which period she has sent money to me twice but so much more has happened, especially to my appearance. Outside, I flag down a passing danfo. The conductor is muttering something and smiling at me. I walk as quickly as possible toward the bus. As I attempt to climb in, the conductor screams at the driver, who seems to be in a hurry to speed off: "Ni suru fun o, agbalagba ni o/ be patient o, this one is an elderly person o." I shake my head sadly as the conductor relieves me of my handbag, ostensibly to make it easier for me to settle in. "E pele, Iya/ sorry, old woman," he says, returning my bag. I lower my head to hide my tears.

The HOD smiles kindly at me when I walk into his office, but the way the corners of his eyes crinkle with concern tells me my supervisor is yet to put official effect to his verbal declaration. How could a man take such absolute delight in torturing another soul? Why is Charles Ephraim doing this to me? I turn and walk out of the HOD's office in search of Akpabio. I find him in the corridor walking toward the flight of stairs to the basement. He stops in his tracks, folds his arms against his chest and shakes his head solemnly. My tears flow unrestrained.

"You look awful," he breathes.

"I know. I'm at my wits end, Akpabio, what must I do?"

"Let's find somewhere quiet to talk," he says, pulling me by my arm. A breeze toys with the hem of my dress as we walk but I'm neither amused nor angry. I'm numb. Akpabio doesn't take me to his office. We keep walking until we find a secluded place, then he puts his hand on my shoulder and lowers his voice.

"Funto, your PhD problem has become serious. You need to do something drastic."

"What do you suggest I do?"

"Look, you need spiritual intervention; you need to engage the services of a powerful spiritualist." My mouth falls open involuntarily. He frowns.

"I don't want this kind of reaction from you. I'm only trying to help. Prof Charles Ephraim is a hard nut to crack."

"Prof Ephraim is difficult, I agree, but what has spirituality got to do with it? I don't see the connection, Akpabio," I blurt out and I almost wished I could take my words back when his frown deepens. I'm morose.

"Listen to me, Funto, I know what it takes to have a PhD because I already have it. Why won't you let me help you?"

"I came to you because I know you know what it takes, but I can't make sense out of what you are telling me. I'm on the verge of a mental breakdown."

"Don't be, just listen to me," he says. The concern I see on his face commands my obedience. Besides, every time I have turned down his advice, I have regretted doing so. Maybe I need to take him more seriously.

"Talk to me, Akpabio." I breathe.

"What I'm asking you to do is not strange. I did the same thing when I was about to have my viva." Really? Why didn't he tell me this before now? He sure knows how to get a PhD.

"What did you do?" I ask, fear gripping my soul.

"Do you know Prof Tejumola Adaranijo?"

"Yes, the former sub-dean."

"That's him!" he exclaims dramatically, eyes suddenly glinting with excitement. I'm confused. "He's a very wicked Professor and he was to be a member of the panel of examiners at my viva by virtue of his ad-hoc position as sub-dean at the time."

"You feared he could prevent you from having a successful viva?"

"Fear? I knew he would if I didn't take a proactive step."

"What step did you take?"

"I consulted a spiritualist who assured me that Prof Adaranijo would have a sudden engagement that would keep him away from the campus during my viva."

"Are you kidding me?"

He burst into a throated laughter; apparently enjoying the sensationalism of his story.

"Well, I, Dr Akpabio Asuquo, can confirm to you that Prof

Adaranijo was not anywhere near the department until past 3pm. My viva held between 10 and 12 noon." He erupts into another round of laughter. I stare at him frigidly for some moments and he goes on laughing. Then I find my voice.

"That could have been a coincidence."

"Oh, you are so naïve and foolish, Funto. Anyway, do you want help or not?"

I bow my head in thought. What do I do? I have never heard anything more senseless. But then, what do I really know? Maybe I should acquiesce to his weird proposal. After all, was it not the same Akpabio who told me five years ago that I would need to conduct research into several other areas apart from my PhD topic? Well, I'm truly a research student

"I'll do it," I murmur.

"Are you ready now?"

"Why not?"

"That's cool. The man of God who helped me is currently out of town but I know another just as powerful. His name is Prophet Tosin Idowu."

"You mean you patronise marabouts on a regular basis? Akpabio, what happened to your education?" The words are out of my mouth before I can stop them. He eyes me disapprovingly.

"Prophets are not marabouts. They are men of God. Besides, nobody wants to engage in this kind of a thing but their circumstances and frustrations keep leading them to it. Are you not on your way to doing the very thing you condemn now?" I lower my head instinctively, awash with shame and embarrassment. Akpabio puts his hand on my shoulder.

"I'm sorry to make you feel bad. In the past, I had no regard for prophets, marabouts or even people who call themselves men of God with power to solve other people's problems. I used to think that somebody who wants to proffer solutions to my spiritual problems would have solved or be seen to have solved their own. Such people should no longer have physical, financial, spiritual or any problem whatsoever because they would have become self-sufficient. Physician, heal thyself used to be my philosophy. But that was the cynic in me. I have since realised, sadly, that things are not what they seem. You often find out, for example, that the person who is supposed to be helping you is the same person who is hindering you. They want to keep you in a perpetual state of dependency so that you can worship them for saving you, but you will never exit the maze. I have learned my lessons in this regard, Funto. I banish my cynicism whenever I have overwhelming needs. I overlook the unmet needs of people who lay claim to the ability to help me solve my problems. I seek solutions to my problems." Akpabio's words move me to tears but my feelings are mixed. I don't know whether to feel sorry for him or for myself.

We meet Prophet Idowu in his sitting room with a woman I presume to be his wife. She rises and disappears through the adjourning door as soon as we take our seats. Akpabio introduces me and tells him my problem. The man rises and begins to move about, shifting his weight from side to side, whispering incoherently. After awhile, he calms down and looks at us in turn.

"Before we can do anything, we have to pray," he says and immediately breaks into a song: "Osuba re re o, Baba. Osuba re re o, Oba t'ao ri, t'anrise owo re, o, Osuba re re o."

After the song, he tells me to fall on my knees. He puts his right hand on my head and starts to pray. I shift uncomfortably on my knees. I peek at Apkabio. He's also kneeling and his eyes are closed. I don't close my eyes. I watch the Prophet as he whirls around. Then he starts to dance and clap his hand.

"Oh God, Almighty, we bring your daughter, Funto, before

you. We want you to touch the heart of her supervisor because you alone possess the anointing that breaks the yoke."

When he finishes praying and reciting some Bible passages by heart, he tells us to return to our seats. He addresses Akpabio.

"Brother Akpabio, the Lord revealed everything to me as I was praying. Sister Funto's supervisor is really a terror but the Lord is able to deliver His own. Sister Funto will come back tomorrow morning alone. She will need some items that we shall use to break the yoke. Eh-r, she would have had to go and buy them from outside, but my madam has them here on sale, so all that Sister Funto needs to do is to buy from my madam."

"How much will everything cost?" Akpabio asks, taking out his wallet.

"Eh-r, it's three thousand naira, but as I said, it's my madam that is selling the items, not me. I don't charge people who come to me for help; I know they will come back to testify to the glory of God."

He smiles self-righteously. Akpabio nods vigorously and proffers the three thousand naira.

"Help us give it to madam, sir, so that by the time Funto comes tomorrow morning, everything will be ready."

I rise, feeling groggy. What am I trying to do? Am I still in control of my senses? Do I really need to get this desperate? Tomorrow I will come here, without Akpabio, and will put myself at the mercy of this strange man. Is there any way I can predict what he might do to me? Do I retrace my steps, tell Akpabio and the Prophet here and now that I'm no longer interested? What, exactly, does the Prophet have in mind? Should I just be patient enough to find out? Well, I have less than twenty-four hours for the great reveal. Maybe it makes more sense to wait till then. Besides, Akpabio would think me an ingrate if I fail to follow this through.

"Funto! Funto! Funto!" Akpabio distracts me from my scattered thoughts. The Prophet walks us to the door and reminds me not to be late for our 8am appointment.

The next morning, at exactly 8:05am, I stand uncertainly in front of what I think ought to be the Prophet's apartment. There is a Nissan car parked in front which wasn't there when we came yesterday. Perhaps the Prophet has a visitor. I knock timidly on the door and he opens it immediately. He comes out holding a small polythene bag. He moves with a swag that doesn't seem characteristic of his persona. I try to smother an amused grin but fail miserably. He strolls importantly to the driver's side and gestures to me to get into the front passenger's seat.

"I didn't notice the car yesterday," I observe after closing the door.

"Actually, it's not mine. I went to take it from a friend early this morning," he explains, and adds, "for your convenience."

"I see," I mutter, wondering why he thought he needed to borrow a car for my 'convenience.' Anyway, I don't know where we are going but the Prophet is driving and he seems to be in an exhilarating mood, chatting away excitedly. A part of me is amused but another part is apprehensive

"Where are we going, Prophet?" I ask, trying not to sound frightened.

"Don't worry, Sister Funto, we will soon get there and I will explain everything to you."

I take a deep breath and focus on the road. We are soon driving out of town. Again, I feel a frisson of alarm and contemplate calling Akpabio. Eventually, he parks by the side of a bush. He turns to me, smiling, I return his smile.

"Yes, we are there," he says softly but I don't respond. He collects the polythene bag from under his seat and brings out a sponge, a tablet of Lux soap and a bottle of olive oil. I look at him quizzically. He smiles.

"Yes, Sister Funto, as I explained yesterday, your supervisor is a very wicked man so you need powerful forces from heaven to rescue you from him." Rescue? I ponder this in my mind but I don't talk.

"These are the items Brother Akpabio paid for yesterday. I brought you here because you need to take a spiritual bath. We are already by the side of a river. Can you see the path?" He shifts his gaze toward the bush path. I follow his eyes and nod. "That is the road that leads to the river. Don't be afraid; I will be there with you. You will use this sponge and the soap to wash your body thoroughly after which I will personally help you rub this oil on your body, and I mean every part. But that is not the end o. After you have bathed, you will close your eyes and I will help you put a 'small something' in your private part." My eyes flip open wide, involuntarily.

"Excuse me?" I cry hoarsely but he holds up his hand and I try to calm down. He may be a bloody nonentity but he's right about the need for me to calm down and hear the entire garbage.

"You see, I only want to help you, so I will be very gentle while I'm inserting the 'something' into your private part."

"I thank you for the great effort you have put into helping me, Prophet, but could you kindly show me the 'small something' you want to insert into my private part?"

"Don't be in a hurry, sister, it's a spiritual 'something' and it's in my pocket. I will bring it out at the appropriate time."

I fear I could explode in anger right now but I'm aware that it could turn out to be the costliest mistake of my life. I'm in the middle of nowhere with an obviously deranged man. Do I know what he's capable of doing? And who would know what happened to me if I failed to handle the situation with caution? I clear my throat and smile suggestively at him.

"Prophet, don't you think this place is rather too exposed for what we plan to do? I mean, someone might just choose to pass and happen on us while we are at it."

"Don't worry at all, Sister Funto. This place is safe o. Many women have taken their bath in this same river and received their miracle."

"I believe you, Prophet, but I have a better idea. You know we 'acada' people are very particular about the way we do our things. So, let's go back to town and look for a hotel. I will pay and we will have our privacy. I'm a 'big' woman in the university; I mustn't be seen taking a bath in the bush," I say calmly and pray silently that he finds me believable. It works! He smiles coyly at me and puts the car in motion. We are heading back to town now and I'm quietly planning my offensive. The Prophet seems to be a man about town; he doesn't ask questions and he knows where to get what. He drives into a hotel and parks. Then he hesitates for a while before telling me to give him money to pay for 'short time.'

"How much do they charge?" I ask.

"It depends, five hundred naira for one hour and eight hundred for two hours." You even know the rates, I mutter under my breath but to him, I say:

"Do you suggest we pay for an hour only? You are the one who knows how long the exercise may last."

"Let's pay for two hours so that we can relax well," he says and I smile in agreement. I act as if I want to open my handbag; then, suddenly, I open the car door and climb out of the car. He mirrors my action, frowning. We are both standing by the car now, regarding each other.

"Mr Prophet, I want you to explain to me what bathing in a river and inserting a 'small something' in my private part has to do with earning my supervisor's favour?" I demand tersely.

"I just want to help you."

"Exactly the same way you've been helping other women who run to you because all problems require the same method to solve them?" I snarl, my indignation burning inside of me as adrenaline surges through my body. "How dare you tell me this crap?"

"You see, Sister Funto, this is a spiritual warfare which ordinary people like you cannot understand. Brother Akpabio brought you to me because he trusts my work." Curiously, the mention of Akpabio's name seems to calm my nerves. I sigh.

"You know what we are going to do, Prophet?"

"No."

"You will give me the items, including the 'small something' in your pocket." His countenance changes, but I act as if I don't notice. "I assure you that I will take the bath and someone will help me to insert it in the appropriate place."

"An ordinary man cannot do it; it has to be a man of God."

"In that case, you are a buffoon. Surely you have more sense than you are portraying, don't you? I advise you start applying it by making sure you size up your next victim well enough before running off to borrow a car. Bloody bastard!"

I stalk off, leaving him open mouthed.

When I recount my experience to Akpabio, he accuses me of bias. "That's what happens to people of little or no faith at all," he insists. I laugh derisively.

"What has faith got to do with the matter at hand, and faith in what, Akpabio? Is it in the 'small something' the silly man wanted to insert in my wherever?" I challenge him fiercely.

"I know your problem, Funto."

"What's my problem?"

"You were suspicious of the man from the beginning. You doubted the efficacy of his power so it was easy for you to ascribe wrong meaning to his intention. Anyway, I will take you to a

Prophetess now. At least you can trust a woman like you."

I don't argue with him. What's the point? I'm getting more confused about everything; even as I can't shake off the feeling that Akpabio and I are engaged in a senseless mission that could only yield more confusion. I feel a creeping emptiness. This is a time I would have loved to talk to Folake, seek her opinion. Is my life truly jinxed, as Lekan Babatunde tried to make me believe? All I feel is anguish. My struggle is futile and it breaks my heart. For someone who feels as helpless as I do, and without a sphere of reference, what else could I do in the circumstances but succumb to the suggestion to consult another spiritualist. A choking fear claws at my heart as we go but I struggle to be hopeful. I want to get a PhD, I remind myself for the umpteenth time and 'the end justifies the means' is a well known maxim. If I have to fraternise with prophets and prophetesses in order to achieve my goal, I might as well go the whole hog.

"Madam, I can see you are under a serious attack," the Prophetess says as soon as Akpabio introduces me. Attack, I echo in confusion, wondering what she means but I don't react. I don't want Akpabio to accuse me of bias or lack of faith. Akpabio senses my discomfort. He takes his time to explain in great detail what I have been through with my supervisor and how we want the Prophetess to help us make Prof Ephraim put his decision into writing to enable me start afresh.

"Where do you work, madam?" the Prophetess asks. I don't know how to respond, Akpabio intervenes by explaining that I don't have a job at the moment.

"You have worked before, madam?" she asks.

"Yes, I have, but I was retrenched some years ago," I explain.

"Did your former employer pay you some money as severance package when you were disengaged?"

"Oh, yes, they did."

"How much were you given, madam?"

"I was paid the sum of three hundred thousand naira."

Akpabio shifts uncomfortably in his seat. I glance briefly at him. His face clouds in either worry or confusion, I don't know which.

"Ah, that is very good, madam, three hundred thousand naira is good money," The Prophetess says, her face lightening up. I shoot Akpabio a quizzical look. He shrugs resignedly. I hang my head in frustration.

"Madam, your problem is very serious. The Lord has revealed it to me but I don't want you to panic. I want you to believe that there is no mountain too high that our Lord cannot climb. Let us pray."

My senses are thoroughly ravaged and disconnected but Akpabio gestures to me to fall on my knees. I obey. The Prophetess picks the Bible from a wooden table and begins to read from it. She seems to half-read and half-recite as she appears to know the Bible by heart. Occasionally, she peeks at us as she reads. Finally, she stops, places the Bible back on the table and tells us to close our eyes. I half-close my eyes. She starts to pray, raising her face to the ceiling as she does so and shaking her body violently. I shift uneasily on my knees. After a while, she finishes praying and starts to sing, spinning and dancing whilst Akpabio and I watch, exchanging glances occasionally, especially as she appears to be doing a kind of performance. She's completely absorbed in it. A hush descends on the room when she brings it to an end.

"The Lord says He will solve your problem but you have to make a sacrifice. Do you understand me, madam?" she asks. I nod, wondering where this is leading.

"You will go and bring one-hundred-and-fifty-thousand naira, after which you will leave the rest to the Lord because the battle is the Lord's to fight." I open my mouth to say something but no words come out. I close it and just gaze at nothing. Maybe I'm in shock. Akpabio clears his throat and starts to talk.

"Eh-r, thank you very much, Prophetess. We will go and look for the money. We shall return."

"You people have to be fast about it because the attack is raging," The Prophetess says, furrowing her eyebrows.

"We understand, Prophetess. One-hundred-and-fifty-thousand naira is not a small amount but we shall raise it."

"Madam was paid three hundred thousand naira by her former employer. You mean she can't take half of it to solve a serious problem?"

"That was a long time ago, Prophetess, but we shall raise the money and come back," Akpabio pleads. The Prophetess is visibly disappointed and her interest in our presence wanes by the second. We take our leave. Akpabio pulls me by the arm as soon as we step out.

"Funto, how could you have told her that you were paid three-hundred-thousand naira? Don't you understand the psychology of these people?"

"How would I understand when I don't know them?"

"Sorry about the embarrassment, okay? I think you should go back to Lagos now. Let us wait until my own man comes back from his journey. The man is so powerful that they invite him from across the country to help solve their spiritual problems. I will call you when he is in town; we will visit him and you would be glad we did."

I don't know what to say. I return to Lagos; depression gnawing at my heart.

I awake with a jolt. I pick my way through the house to the toilet. By my reckoning, it's between 2am and 3am. This is the fifth night since I returned from Abuja and have been suffering from insomnia. It's beginning to tell on my health. My mind drifts to my supervisor and tears roll down my cheeks. How could the thought of an individual evoke so much anguish and pain? I'm staring up at the ceiling and I can't stop my tears from flowing. Perhaps I should talk to my Creator.

Dear God, please do not allow me to inflict pain on people I ought to help

My Dear God, may I not be an architect of pain or sorrow to anyone.

I ask this because I'm aware that to inflict sorrow on others is to inflict sorrow on myself May I be a catalyst of joy, love and progress, not an obstructer, God.

In your love, God, let me find strength to face the pain of the stone in my shoe

You who know the goings on in the dark and in the light

In due time, remove the stone in my shoe

I am getting wary, God, I am getting tired, I am getting discouraged, I can't take it anymore

I turn to you, God, it is getting late.

Do not abandon me to the whims and caprices of my supervisor.

Dear God, and may I not in turn be that which I pray against

May I not be a tormentor of my students because vengeance is yours God

Help me, God, because I ask all these in your name. Amen.

Gradually, I don't know when, I drift into sleep.

Twenty-two

JULY, 2004

I'm in an extremely jubilant mood this July as my daughter graduates from secondary school. She is now preparing to go into the university in September. My joy is further swelled by her physical, mental and psychological growth. It's amazing how, at sixteen, Deyemi has all the attributes of an adult. We relate more as friends now than as mother and daughter. I don't want to worry about how to find the funds for her university education. It would simply be part of my existing struggle to which I have grown fairly accustomed. Besides, Folake sends money to me from time to time. She never ceases to encourage me when we talk on phone, telling me to hold on to my dream and not falter. She has an adorable daughter, Princess, whose photographs adorn my bedroom. Princess looks a splinting image of Geoffrey. Folake is pregnant again. I'm very happy for her and Geoffrey. I'm standing at Kofo Abayomi Bus Stop on Victoria Island after teaching my students at Clamorous University of Nigeria. The evening traffic is in full swing but I'm not perturbed. Deyemi will be busy preparing dinner and all I'll be required to do whenever I arrive home will be to shower, eat and hit the bed. The commuters around me look frantic, agitated and restless. Suddenly, someone sounds their car horn with a persistence that commands my attention. I locate the lone occupant beckoning me. I walk slowly toward it, wondering who it could be.

"Funto Oyewole, the great!" the man exclaims dramatically. I smile. He looks faintly familiar.

"Come right in, joor." he says jocularly, visibly excited, I open the passenger door and climb in, feigning as much excitement as I can.

"How have you been? Where are you going?" he asks in a rush.

"I'm going to Mushin."

"It's been a long time, you know. The last time we met was when we went to collect our original certificate at the Grammar School and we didn't really have time to gist." I'm glad he's helping me to remember who he is but I still can't recall his name. I warm up to the conversation regardless.

"So, where are you now? What's been happening to your sweet life?" he asks.

"Well, I used to work with the Federal Government but I'm not in a regular employment at the moment. What about you?"

"Me? God forbid that I, Femi Alawiye, at forty would be employed by anyone, be it an individual or organisation, private or public." Well, thanks for reminding me of your name, I mutter under my breath.

"You mean you are self-employed?"

"Of course, Funto, we are no longer kids now. We are over forty and I would find it utterly humiliating to have to answer, 'Yes, sir,' or 'Yes, ma'am,' to anyone at this age."

"That's interesting. I like your spirit. So, what do you do on your own?"

"I'm an hotelier. I own and manage my own hotel. When I was working in my twenties and thirties, I was also saving money with determination so that, once I turned forty, I would become my own boss."

254

"Congratulations, Femi, I'm very happy for you," I say, feeling genuinely impressed with his achievement and sense of purpose.

"I want you to come and see my hotel."

"Really?"

"Yes, why not?"

"I would be glad to come around?" He opens a compartment on the dashboard and brings out a complementary card

"I will definitely come to pay you a visit," I say, peering at the card on which is written: Chief Femi Alawiye, Director, Alawiye International Hotel. Phone 0800 – 123 – 456.

"When may I expect to see you?"

"When do you wish to see me?"

"Today, tomorrow; I want you to come as soon as you can make it."

"Let's leave it till Saturday," I murmur, amused by his enthusiasm.

"Saturday it is, then. I will be waiting."

Alawiye International Hotel sits comfortably on an acre of land. I glance at my watch: 5:03pm. I take in a lungful breath of air as I walk to the reception.

"Welcome, madam," a young lady greets me with a warm smile. I smile back.

"I wish to see your director, please?"

"Any previous appointment, madam?"

"Oh yes, I'm scheduled to meet him at 5pm, I'm sure he's expecting me." I beam at her.

"Your name, madam?"

"Funto Oyewole."

"Ms or Mrs?"

"Ms"

"Alright, madam." She lifts the receiver of the intercom on the desk and punches a number "Yes, sir, there is one madam here, her name is Ms. Funto Oyewole, she says she has an appointment to see you at 5pm, sir." She's stealing glances at me intermittently as she listens to the voice on the other end. Suddenly, her brow creases. She replaces the receiver, clasps her hands and sighs as her expression darkens. What could be the problem with her? I wonder silently but I don't react. I fix my gaze on her, waiting for her to lead me to my friend, or tell me something. She takes her time, as if she's trying to arrange her words before speaking.

"Sorry, madam, the director says he is sleeping. No, he says he's having his siesta and if you would exercise patience and wait for him."

"I see," I breathe and immediately turn on my heels. I'm exiting the hotel premises.

"Excuse me, madam, please wait." I turn to face her.

"Aren't you going to wait? I mean you came all the way to see him."

"Never mind, my sister, and thank you very much for your time. Tell your director to enjoy his siesta; I will call again another time."

I'm walking briskly toward the gate. I'm almost at the gate when I hear my name called. I whirl around and it's Femi. He's standing outside the reception hall, beckoning me to come back. I stand rooted to the same spot for a moment, contemplating whether to do as he asks or simply ignore him. Get a grip, Funto, a voice whispers from within and I walk slowly toward him.

"I'm sorry, Funto," he apologises with a smile but I'm far from being amused.

"What's the bravado in aid of?" I query and his smile broadens. I can't hold my own, I burst out laughing as he stretches his right hand in a gesture of reconciliation and I shake it warmly.

He leads the way. He takes me to a garden shed, ordering one of his workers to bring us chairs and a table. We sit facing each other.

"What would you like to drink?" Femi asks.

"Malt would do," I murmur.

"Why malt? Why not beer? It's going to be on me, you know?"

"I know. I'd rather have malt than beer."

"Okay, if you insist."

"I do," I mouth.

"Life is truly interesting, Funto," he says as we await our orders.

"Absolutely," I mumble.

"Some things happen in life and give you an indescribable feeling," he says but I don't respond because I don't know the appropriate response to give. Something seems to be giving him a high.

"I can't believe it, Funto." He winks at me. I squeeze my face in confusion. He's about to say something when his worker brings our drinks. He sets them down, opens them in turn, bows and takes his leave.

"You wanted to say something," I remind him, although I don't think he needs reminding judging by the flash in his eyes. He's obviously having a swell time but I'm slightly irritated because I can't wrap my head around his source of unbridled excitement.

"I can't believe I'm sitting right here in front of you."

"Really?"

"Yeah, if anybody had whispered it in my ears, a moment before I saw you a few days ago, that I would come in contact with you soon, and that you would even pay me a visit, I would not have believed it."

"That must be truly interesting," I comment lamely for want of a better thing to say.

"Yes, you are right, but that's not the only reason why I said what I did. You see, life is actually much more interesting than we are aware of."

Why won't he make his point clearer? What's wrong with him and why is he going round and round in circles, almost exasperating me?

"Don't be obtuse." I'm unable to hide my disdain.

"Okay, I'll be explicit. You see, way back, when we were in secondary school, I was enamoured of you but I never had the courage to express my feelings. You were tall, beautiful, distinctively classy and the dream of many of us male students. I wanted you to be my girl and although we were young, I daydreamed about how, one day, I would hold you in my arms, cuddle you, kiss you and be intimate with you. Unfortunately, you walked around with a certain no-nonsense, almost arrogant mien that sent jitters down my spine and prevented me from making my intentions known to you. One day, I made up my mind to banish my fear, vowing not to allow you to intimidate me any longer. I was going to brave the odds at all costs. I resolved firmly and went ahead to tell my friends and even dressed up specifically for the occasion. I told Banji and Seyi that the day had finally arrived and that I would not let it pass without making my intentions known. As they rang the bell for our first break that day and students trooped out to buy one thing or another, I was in company of my friends and they were teasing and asking me if I really felt bold enough to carry out my plan, I was still assuring them of my determination when suddenly you emerged from seemingly nowhere. I promptly gave the books in my hands to Banji, adjusted myself and straightened my shoulders. They goaded me on, telling me not to back off. 'This is your chance,

Femi,' Seyi said, gesturing for me to walk ahead of them so as to meet up with you. I took a cue, taking long strides and out stepping them. Moments before I came close enough to be able to say something to you, you dramatically increased your pace and raised your face heavenward. My confidence dissolved irretrievably and I stood, immobilised, as you walked past me. I didn't need to turn to look at my friends; I heard their voices as they erupted in laughter. I took to my heels, their voices trailing me. I didn't have the courage to go back to the dormitory until very late in the night and, of course, that put paid to my grand plan to approach you for a relationship. From then on, you simply became a phenomenon whose abode I could not tread, let alone conquer. I know you are eager to say something, but permit me to explain that what I find interesting today is that a woman, whom I held in awe years ago, is not only paying me a visit but now needs my assistance. What an interesting world! The tables have turned, Funto, in my favour, and it intrigues me no end."

I stare at him for long moments, not knowing whether to congratulate him or be sorry for him.

"You are a comic actor, Femi. You truly amaze me."

"Is that all you can say?"

"What would you like me to say?"

"I want you to dignify me with a proper response."

"Well, at least you've given me an idea how your mind works. So, all that rigmarole about you having a siesta was orchestrated to achieve some cheap revenge?"

"You would never know how much you intimidated me, Funto, and, honestly speaking, it felt good to want to hit back at you now that things are not very good with you, but when I was told you declined to wait, I said to myself, the woman is as arrogant as ever."

"You see how foolish you are?"

"What am I foolish about now?"

"Everything, but if you would pardon my immodesty since you want a proper response, even if you had summoned the courage to speak to me then, you would have met a brick wall. Also, whilst I would be very grateful for your kind assistance in my current situation, it's never going to be sufficient to put me in a compromising situation with you, so, your revenge is needless."

"Why?"

"You are not my idea of a lover boy."

"Is it because I'm shorter than you?"

"Go and look after your wife and stop clowning," I say in mock chastisement and we both laugh.

"This girl, you are still as impossible as ever, Funto the Great! But you look like someone who really needs help," he says, suddenly radiating a sober countenance.

"I have some unresolved issues that are threatening to destabilise me," I murmur.

"What issues?" he asks. I give him a brief history of my PhD struggle and my inability to secure a worthwhile means of livelihood. When I finish, he doesn't immediately respond. We sit in silence for a while; he, in thought, I, staring into space.

"The solution is for you to get your PhD," he murmurs. I nod. "Once you have it, you will have a respectable job as a varsity teacher."

"I know, but the PhD has become elusive."

"Let's work on your supervisor."

"How?"

I will take you somewhere," he says and an alarm bell sounds in my brain. Not again.

"Huh?"

"I will take you somewhere," he repeats.

"I don't want to patronise any more marabouts. I have done it but it didn't work," I say with a raised voice.

"Calm down, Funto, you haven't been to the man I want to take you to. He's special. He has no rival, no equal." I hang my head low. What's going on? Why does everybody seem to think they can't exist without either getting involved in voodoo or patronising religious charlatans?

"Don't fence yourself off from the opportunity to achieve your life goals simply because some persons have disappointed you in the past." His voice cuts into my thoughts. I raise my face and stare blankly at him.

"Life is uncertain, yes, I agree, but in the midst of the uncertainty also lies certainty. Take your chances, Funto. Let me take you to Baba."

"Baba!" I echo in fright.

"Yes."

"Who is he? What's his brand?"

"He's a powerful Babalawo, a traditional medicine man to the core. You would be amazed by his power."

"Your description scares me," I say, unpleasant memories of my previous experience ravaging my soul. I shake my head to gather my wits.

"Scared? You ought to be intrigued." His eyes glint with fresh excitement.

"Are you sure your plan is not to get me to swallow some love portion to enable you achieve your childhood dream?"

"Forget about the past, Funto, we are adults now. Frankly, you've made me realise my foolishness. I regret playing the siesta trick on you and I truly want to make it up to you," he says and I detect earnestness in his words.

"I will believe you."

"Please do, for I speak in earnest. Besides, we can always be useful to each other. It's my turn to help you today, it may be yours tomorrow. I will always admire you but I will respect your wishes at all times as well." Maybe because my frustration has gotten the better of me, making me to lose all sense of perspective, I agree to go with Femi to Baba's place.

Baba looks fearsome. I imagine he must have been huge when he had use of his limbs. He's not crippled but I don't understand why he crawls in the manner of a snake. My entire body is cascading in sweat. I'm in a wrong place. My heart is pounding. What am I doing to myself? How could I have allowed anyone to convince me to come here? I ought not to be here, I say regretfully under my breath, but it's certainly too late for regrets. Unbidden tears pool in my eyes and I wish the ground would open and swallow me up; at least it would end my misery. Who would then take care of my daughter, my breath and the only hope I have for a happier future?

"Kneel down and greet Baba," Femi whispers in my ears. I do as he instructs.

"Good afternoon, Baba," I murmur amidst sobs. Baba thinks I'm overwhelmed by my problem. He's looking at me intently, smiling.

"Sit down, my daughter, don't cry. I know your problem already," he says. I'm flabbergasted. He knows my problem? How? I haven't said anything. Is he really as powerful as Femi says?

"I will help you overcome that man, that your Oga that is troubling you and debarring your progress." Good heavens! This is certainly beyond a guess. He seems to know my problem truly. I cast a confused glance at Femi as my heart pounds away furiously.

"Yes, let me see how to handle him," Baba murmurs and I watch him, fear-stricken, as he searches for … I have no idea.

Finally, he finds it. It's a little stick, about the size of a standard ruler. He stretches his hand toward me, using his eyes to tell me to take it from him. I'm trembling all over. I try to stretch my hand, I'm shaking violently. I'm thoroughly drenched in my own sweat now. What am I doing here? I ask myself for the umpteenth time.

"Take the stick, my daughter," Baba whispers tenderly. The tenderness in his voice is soothing. I take the stick but I don't know what to do with it. He calls out a name and a young boy appears in the doorway.

"Get me the white basin, half-filled with water," Baba says and the boy disappears. Seconds later, he reappears. He sets the basin before Baba and leaves.

"My daughter, the power to deal with your Oga is in that stick and the stick is in your hand. What it means is that you hold the power to deal with him as you wish. I'm going to summon his spirit here shortly, and you are at liberty to do what you please with him."

What does he mean? I don't understand but I'm not in a position to voice my confusion. I'm peering at him and at the stick in my hand intermittently, hoping the mystery would unfold soon. Baba starts to chant incantations and Femi grins. How come he's enjoying this weird performance? Baba finishes chanting and tells me to look into the basin. Femi and I take a cue simultaneously. What? Am I in a trance or something? Right here in front of me, in the water inside the basin, Prof Charles Ephraim's image looms large. Ha! My supervisor! In Lagos! All the way from Abuja! How did this happen? I fear for my sanity now. I start to shake violently. Femi is holding me by my arms, whispering to me to be calm. I look furtively at Baba; a soft smile plays at the corners of his mouth.

"Listen carefully, my daughter, your Oga's life is in your hand now. You can choose to eliminate him through any of his body parts. If you want him to go blind instantly, for example, simply use the stick in your hand to chuck his eyes, one after the other, and he goes totally and incurably blind. If your wish for him is instant death, use the stick to chuck his chest and if you want him paralysed, target his waist. He will become paralysed from the waist down. Even if you want to break his skull, the same stick in your hand is what you will direct at his forehead."

I peer surreptitiously at the water; Prof Ephraim seems to be staring back at me. I hold his gaze for some moments. He looks calm, innocent, without the air of a professor. Good heavens! I shift my gaze to Baba. He's looking at me intently, urging me to make up my mind how I want to end my supervisor's life. I find my voice.

"No, Baba, I didn't come here to kill my Oga. I want him to live, thrive, be happy and successful in all his life's endeavours. I have only one wish, I want him to soften his mind toward me and take pity on me. I don't even want to insist that he continues to be my supervisor, but I want him to be kind enough to put his decision into writing so that God may look down on me with compassion and direct me to another lecturer who would agree to supervise me. I want my supervisor to set me free, Baba."

I notice Baba frown as soon as I start to speak. His frown deepens as my speech progresses; by the time I finish, he's pouting. I'm bewildered.

"Why did you come here if you knew you didn't want to kill him?" he demands tersely, eyes blazing in fury. I freeze. "You came here to waste my time?" he challenges.

"Ah, no, Baba, I'm sorry, I didn't mean to offend you." I'm weeping profusely; Femi quickly colludes in my denial.

"Eh-r Baba, she is sorry, we are sorry. Actually, she didn't know how powerful you are."

"If I make my Oga blind, who would read my thesis, Baba?

If I killed him, who would write the letter I desperately need him to write to set me free?"

"Shut up your rotten mouth? How dare you come here and talk about God? Who is interested in your God?" Baba barks and I cower. I want to say something but he isn't done yet. "They talk about God and heaven as if this life means nothing. Well, I don't give a damn about their paradise but I know this world is mine to live to the fullest. I have the wherewithal to maximise all it's got to my advantage and I will live it and use my power to the benefit of those that value it. Now, listen to me carefully, you little rat, don't you ever go near the owners of the world without having made up your mind to live in their likeness. If it were not for Femi, I would have taught you the bitterest lesson of your miserable life, such that you would never again dare to waste an old man's time." He eyes me malevolently, letting out a prolonged hiss.

I rise swiftly to my feet and take flight. I keep running without looking back until I reach a bus stop. I don't ever wish to set my eyes on any of them again.

Twenty-three

NOVEMBER, 2004

It's been two whole months since a new academic session began at the National University of Nigeria and I haven't been to school at all. Much as I hate to admit it, I'm no longer enthusiastic about my programme. Each time the thought of going to school crosses my mind I perish it as quickly as it occurs, preferring to occupy my mind with other things. Perhaps I shouldn't feel proud to admit also that most of my mental preoccupations have become largely frivolous but I embrace these frivolities nonetheless, essentially because they don't give me irksome feelings. What could be exciting, for example, about the prospect of travelling all the way to Abuja only to be told that Prof Ephraim is yet to put his decision into writing? What would be the purpose of my journey? I don't want to get upset, especially now that there are heart-warming occurrences in my life. One of them is Deyemi's admission into the university to study mass communication.

Then there's my chance meeting with Shettima during Deyemi's matriculation ceremony which has surprisingly uplifted my spirits to unimaginable heights. For reasons I can't really explain, I find that my feelings have moderated toward him. Do I feel guilty that I have hitherto been unfair to him? Do I consider my prolonged nonchalant attitude immature, unreasonable and foolish? I don't know but Shettima and I are now the kind of friends we've never managed to be and I still feel as if I'm having a dream. What is really responsible for my new feeling about him? Is it real? He came to the matriculation ceremony with a friend whose daughter is also a fresh undergraduate and we got talking while haggling with a photographer who had come to do business. He was as gentle as ever and I found myself gravitating toward him. Everybody was in a joyous mood, which must have been responsible for the ease with which I responded to his fresh overtures.

I'm lying on a couch in my sitting room right now, drawing a mental picture of Shettima. Why does he occupy my mind so frequently these days? Is it not the same Shettima I met years ago and told myself I didn't want? What in heaven's name is new about him? I don't really know since I didn't permit myself the chance to know him earlier on. Well, I'm all alone in the house as Deyemi is in the university. I haven't found another job, either regular or part-time in spite of my efforts. My teaching slot at Clamorous University has also remained just once a week and I haven't even been paid for the period I have taught. It was with Pitan's kind assistance that I was able to pay Deyemi's fees two months ago. My thoughts drift back to Shettima and his face blooms before me; a handsome, fiftyish man who my instincts have always told me is uncomplicated and easy to be with. I still don't wish to probe into his personal life as I have no intention of leading him on beyond mere friendship. That's what I'd rather believe at the moment. I must keep it safe, I can keep it safe, just as I have done with Pitan. I tell myself firmly. What I find a bit worrisome and somewhat embarrassing is that there are times when I'm desperately lonely, such as now, that I start to think about relating with him in a way that is different from the way I do with Pitan. A few nights ago for instance, I …

Ah, perhaps I shouldn't pursue the thought any further

because I'm not sure about my feelings, really. Curiously, the more I try to avoid thinking about him, the more I do and that is exactly my problem. Oh, my goodness, could my problem just be loneliness and nothing more? That explains everything, then: loneliness. After all, I successfully resisted him while Folake was around. I feel a rush of relief gradually surge through me as I realise now why it always seems as if I want to be with him since we met at Deyemi's university two months ago. It certainly is not because he now holds some strange spell over me or something like that. Another reason could be ... lack of sex? Ha! Do I want to admit this much? Well, I have to so as to be true to myself. Otherwise, why should I feel so out of control, anxious and vulnerable? Shettima is not my boyfriend, for crying out loud, I say emphatically under my breath to assure myself that I'm in control of my emotions.

But there is something that baffles me still. I'm unable to take him as any kind of friend and that is the real reason why I have struggled to shut him out of my life since our first meeting many years ago. There has always been something very tempting about him; something because of which I felt I needed to run very far away from him. I don't know what it is or what I want him to be presently but... I sigh heavily. Shettima and I need to talk. That's the honourable way to go about solving the problem. There are issues we need to discuss, I murmur aloud as I rise to pick my phone from the dining table. I can dismiss a lot of things from my mind but since it's getting increasingly difficult for me to dismiss my feelings for him, the only reasonable thing to do is to iron out whatever it is that is causing the complications in my mind. I dial his number and he responds.

"Hello, Shettima, I think we have some issues to discuss when we meet this Saturday," I mouth, trying to put a bit of nonchalance into my voice.

"Saturday is a whole two days away, I could come to your place right away if you don't mind." I'm quiet for a moment, weighing his words.

"Funto?"

"Very well, then, I'll be waiting," I whisper, hoping I didn't sound too eager.

"See you shortly," he says cheerfully and hangs up. I rise swiftly to clean the apartment and take a bath. I feel excited already. I apply some make-up and hold my hair back in a ponytail. For some time now, I have made deliberate effort to avoid checking my reflection in the mirror. Today, however, I stand confidently in front of the largest mirror in my room. My eyes glitter with lustrous good health and the warm smile that greets me melts all my concerns. I gaze endlessly at my reflection, a tiny smile playing at the corners of my mouth. There has always been something going on between Shettima and me that neither of us can deny. Maybe we are both having a little problem facing it; but its existence is unmistakable. A soft knock on the front door makes my spirit rise as I walk toward the door to admit him. At the same time, I feel slightly angry at myself at the sense of expectation firing my blood.

"Welcome," I breathe, stepping aside to let him in.

"I'm here," he says unnecessarily, trailing a cloud of cologne in his wake. Its scent wafts upward, thick and sweet and clogging. It seems to mask everything else and I realise, belatedly, as my stomach jolts, that I haven't eaten all day. Shettima reaches out for my hand but I disengage gently and lead him to a couch before dashing to the kitchen to fetch two bottles of Coca-Cola.

"To us," he breathes. We clink the bottles but this makes me feel slightly awkward. I lower my gaze.

"You wanted to talk to me," he says, putting down his drink and placing his hands on my shoulder, making me to turn fully to him. Yes, that's what it is, too stripping. It's not that I feel as if he undresses me with his eyes, although there is an element of that, too, but because I feel he looks right through me, into my soul. I feel totally naked in front of him now, all manner of deceptions and pretensions lost to his knowing eyes. I have been feeling this way since two months ago when we reconnected at Deyemi's matriculation ceremony.

"You wanted to see me. Is something wrong?" he asks. My answer is a long sigh. I feel suddenly numb. He looks at me and shakes his head. Then he runs a hand around the back of his neck in a peculiarly sensual movement that makes my eyes follow his movements hungrily. Hum, I don't know what to do with Shettima.

"Well, I guess I just realise how little I want to be involved with you. May be the guilt I feel about the way I have behaved to you in the past is giving a wrong impression of my current feeling, so, I want to explain my position but I want you to tell me more about yourself regardless," I manage to articulate, not believing the first part of my declaration. He slides me a look that sends shivers through my veins.

"Lets' go for lunch," he murmurs. I glance away, afraid he will see through my pretence.

"Sure," I breathe. I'm relieved, I have no wish to tread into areas that I 'm not ready for.

One-and-a-half hours later, we sit across from each other at a Sweet Sensation outlet. I try to reflect inwardly about our sudden intimacy. For two months, we have led the semblance of companionable but separate lives and it's seems as if we are both in a dream, a holding pattern, a cocoon and it doesn't seem as if either of us wants the real world to intrude.

"You already know that I'm a northerner from Adamawa State. What else do you want to know?"

"I want to know more about you. I want to know why you are not married. I want to know about the mother of your son and why you didn't marry her. I want to know why you have persisted in your desire to have a relationship with me even when I told you I wasn't interested. I want to know anything and everything about you."

"Fine. Are these the only issues you wanted us to discuss? You sounded on phone as if there's something you really wanted to tell me; something that is gnawing at your heart and you've spent a greater part of this afternoon looking confused and lost in thought."

"Yes, I have something to tell you."

"Let's hear it first then; thereafter, I will tell you everything you wish to know about me." Silence stretches between us during which I rehearse in my mind what I want to say. Finally, I look him straight in the eye like someone who is ready for a final showdown.

"I want our friendship to run on a smooth course, Shettima. I don't want complications. I told you years ago that I didn't want to be emotionally attached to you; my position remains the same. Maybe I now want fun but I'm certainly not searching for a husband or a father-substitute for my daughter. I mean, I want this to be a nice diversion for the both of us. I just want a little time with you, that's all." I peek up at him, his face clouds in confusion. In the meantime, I concentrate on devouring the fried rice and chicken in front of me. I won't permit any further complications in my life, not even with the long-suffering Shettima, I swear beneath my breath.

"Look, I can understand why you are so paranoid, Funto, but do you really think it's necessary for you to tell me what you've just said?" I shrug, feeling trapped. I'm making an effort not to squirm in my chair.

271

"I don't know," I mumble, not meeting his gaze.

"You were very difficult if not downright impossible for many years; but we've acted almost like a couple in the last two months, Funto, and I thought we have both been taken in with each other at last. You even told me three weeks ago that you loved me." I said that much? What was wrong with me? How could I be so unguarded? I hang my head low in embarrassment.

"I was under the influence of my own loneliness, Shettima," I say stiffly.

"Do you say this to every man?"

"I haven't had a man in my life in a long while, even all through the time that you relentless showed interest in me. But I managed to carry on regardless." I blurt out, summoning the courage to meet his gaze. "Maybe I'm just needy now."

"I'm sorry," he murmurs. I feel suddenly drained. We finish our food.

"Do you want us to go to your apartment or mine so that I can tell you all that you wish to know?"

"Let's go to yours."

We walk to the car. Why am I struggling? Why does it seem as if I'm pretending? And for how long do I really want to keep acting this way? This man can ask anything of me, anything at all, and I wouldn't deny him. Is this love or infatuation? I wish it's the later so that I can hope to recover but I know how I feel and it's deep and impossible to ignore. We are now in the car together and Shettima is driving to his residence at Adeniyi Jones in Ikeja. The atmosphere between us has been stifling since my confession about my sexless life. He's remarkably quiet. Perhaps he now understands my disillusionment and pain. He knows why it seems I'm just looking for an excuse to throw it all away. The truth is that I can't just jump into a sexual relationship with him. I don't deny that once in the past, with Adams, I have responded to some aching need and have thrown caution to the winds. At that time, I hadn't really cared about my own future; I had given in simply to assuage the terrible pain and disappointment my supervisor was meting out to me. Now, however, it's a whole new proposition, I'm not willing, ready or able to embark on a sexual exploration with Shettima. I cast a brief, furtive glance at him. He seems to be concentrating on the road, his hands gripping the steering wheel. Looking at him just now makes me realise that the dialogue going through my head is all academic. Perhaps I'm under the influence of my PhD thesis right now because, if this man sitting next to me asks me for sex, I will say yes. Finally, we are in his house. We go straight to his kitchen, where I bring out a packet of lemon juice from the fridge and pour two glasses for us. We don't leave the kitchen; we sit across from each other on a plastic table and chairs that serve as an emergency dining set. He doesn't want me to remind him of his promise. He starts to talk.

"I had lofty plans about marriage and family life as a younger person. I was in love with my son's mother, we were engaged and she was already pregnant with our son. The only mental picture I had of our future was one of a strong, united, loving and happy family. But life is full of twists and turns." He pauses and sighs, his brow creasing.

"So, what happened?" I ask with trepidation.

"I have a heart condition," he says out of the blue. My eyes widen in shock.

"I called off our wedding," he says in distress, staring at me with eyes so dark they look bottomless with hurt and pain.

"Were you in Lagos or Yola at that time?"

"Yola. That's why I left."

"Oh, Shettima," I breathe.

"I couldn't stay in Yola any longer, I couldn't stand it. I decided to relocate to Lagos, to die far away from home."

"Your son's mother refused to marry you because of your health condition?"

"No, she didn't refuse to marry me. I didn't tell her."

"What?"

"I couldn't bring myself to tell her. It would have crushed her and she would have lost her pregnancy."

"What did you do?"

"I picked a quarrel, made it irresolvable and became generally impossible. I insisted that the marriage plans had to be cancelled."

"Did you have any inkling of what you were doing to her by shattering her hopes and dreams?"

"I knew she would recover. Anger, a sense of betrayal and other negative emotions she would feel toward me would all combine to hasten her recovery process and I knew she would get back on her feet and move on with her life. In my view at the time, that was far preferable to turning her into a widow at a very young age. She was twenty-two. I didn't want to punish her with my death because I didn't know I would be alive till now. I thought I was going to die sooner."

"How correct were you in your presumptions? Has she truly moved on?"

"Oh yes, she has, she's married with two other children, apart from my son. She lives in Yola with her family."

"You didn't think you deserved to be loved and to have a family because you have a heart condition?"

"There is more."

"More?"

"Yes, the doctor said it was congenital, not correctable and terminal, so, to me, it was like a death sentence. I'm surprised I'm still alive." My head reels.

"When you found out your death wasn't going to be as

quick as you ..." He interrupts my question.

"I haven't found out anything. The condition can't be wished away; I take every day as a gift; that's all."

"I'm sorry, let me rephrase. What I meant to ask was whether or not you tried to get in touch with her after a while; after you overcame the initial shock of your condition."

"What would have been the aim of such an attempt? To try to make her feel bad or to try to constitute a distraction to her marriage? Such a step wouldn't have been fair to her."

"What about your son? Does he know you?"

"Oh yes, he does. I'm responsible for his education and upkeep and his mother and I relate in respect of him."

"I'm sorry about it all."

"There's nothing to be sorry about. Are you satisfied now?" I don't respond and he draws a harsh breath and sits back in his chair, his jaw tightening.

"That's why I left Yola," he says grimly.

"Did the doctor tell you how long you have to live?"

"I don't remember him saying so, but then, it can happen anytime."

"Anybody can die at any time, Shettima, heart condition or not," I whisper.

"Well, you are right, but not everybody carries death like an atlas." I slip my hands across the table, reaching for his. I clasp them tightly, silently offering all the prayer, love and support I possess. Shettima looks down at our entwined hands. To my utmost surprise, he leans down and kisses my fingers. When he lifts his head, my heart is beating like a drum, my pulse hammering inside my veins, my chest heaving as if I'd run a marathon.

"Make love to me." He breathes. I'm a little hesitant, but thrilled. The silence between us now is intense. I'm not quite certain what I'm going to do but I know I want him and he wants me, too. What more can I ask for? The tiny portion of my rational mind that still functions is trying to remind me of the complications that could arise if I fall in love with him but I ignore all entreaties. I know there is no retracing my steps. I'm completely done for. Something in my face must have registered because Shettima takes the glass of juice from my unresisting hands and pulls me toward him, his arms surrounding me, his chin resting on my head. I count my heartbeats, aware that there is no going back. With a sigh of surrender, I press my cheek against his babanriga. Fleetingly, I warn myself not to ever again tell him that I love him, but then he stirs, his mouth pressing kisses against my temple and the lobe of my ear and all conscious thoughts flee. My fingers dip into the soft fabrics of his babanriga, bunching it spasmodically as his teeth bite the lobe of my ear, tugging gently and causing curious sensations to swirl inside me.

I have had a child but I'm still inexperienced when it comes to sensual pleasure. Deyemi's father was quick in his lovemaking, almost clinical sometimes, apparently because his mind was unable to disengage from his family back in America. So, he couldn't spend a lot of time pleasuring me. I felt this was the way it was supposed to be, except for that encounter with Adams. I remember now how his hands and mouth and body and overall need worked their magic to turn me into a quivering mass of desire. My mind goes back to how I cried out with his plunging thrust, begging for more even while a distant part of me marvelled at my own wantonness. In my alcoholic state that night, I wrapped my legs around him and urged him onward. My only regret is that the experience was over much too quickly. Right now, with my flesh shuddering and my lips reaching up to meet Shettima's, those thoughts are distant little pinpoints of light, fading away into a black vortex. I meet Shettima's kiss urgently and when he groans softly, pressing my weight against the kitchen wall, his own weight hard against my yielding contours, my knees turn to jelly.

"Funto," he murmurs, his hands sliding into my hair, holding my head hostage to his plundering mouth and tongue. His tongue stabs between my parted lips, then the lip of my own tongue tentatively reaches forward and he sucks it between his own. A whirling sea of emotion overtakes me, weakening my already puny resistance. Resistance? I laugh in my heart! I want him as much as he wants me, more probably. Although there is no future in this relationship, no positive ending, but I can't stop myself because I want it too, badly.

"Don't stop," I whisper when he draws back to look at me.

"I can't," he admits simply. Then he starts to unbutton my blouse. I watch it fall away. I peek up at him. He sucks in a sharp breath.

"Don't look at me like that," he says.

"Like what?"

"Like you sympathise with me," I laugh loudly.

"You are reading me wrongly. My goodness, Shettima, I want you," I say matter-of-factly and that does it. Whatever eleventh hour nobility that may have possessed him is shattered. With vein and vigour, he kisses and caresses and presses his body against mine. His hand cups my breast, kneading it, his finger and thumb rubbing the hard button of my nipple between them. His hips pin me to the wall and there is no mistaking his urgent arousal. With a feeling of stepping outside myself, my fingers reach down and slide over his sex, cupping it. A moment later, his hand comes to help, rubbing my fingers over his manhood in a smooth motion that quickens my blood. I gasp, shocked by the stab of pure sensation I feel when his hand insinuates itself in my most feminine area, sliding beneath the band of my cotton panties and touching the hub of my pleasure. I put my hands on his shoulders, pulling him closer even though our bodies are practically fused. When his head bends to my breast, my hands curl in his hair, pulling and releasing rhythmically. Sensations run from my breasts to the core of my feminity as if pulled by strings. I want to lie down on the kitchen floor and let him have his way. I want to moan and writhe and cry out like a primal animal. I will go all the way with him regardless and make the most use of every moment I'm privileged to share with him. It doesn't matter how brief.

"Shettima, … Shettima…" I breathe. And when his head bends lower, his tongue licking a trail over the soft hill of my abdomen, his fingers parting the way for his intimate penetration, I simply lose all strength. I slide down to the floor and, as his hot tongue teases and torments, I let out a sound between a scream and a whimper, reaching a climax so fast my body convulses in wild ecstasy.

"I'm a shameless woman and I hate myself for what I've just done," I mumble in giggles of laughter.

"True," he agrees and the amused look on his face slowly dissolves into an urgent hunger that makes me catch my breath. I want him to do something more, in the bedroom. Slowly, we find our way there. It's been a long time since I made love and I have forgotten the sweet feeling of possession and desirability it engenders. Shettima takes me on a slow rhythm and soon my head tosses about on the pillow. It is sweet torture. I can't stand it. I cry out, begging something unintelligible and when I come, it's a skyrocketing climax, my whole body convulsing, and my words sweet declarations of love, in clear violation of my earlier resolve. Then I hear his tense voice.

"Do you want us to continue?"

"Is that question really necessary? What does it look like to you?"

"You are not afraid that I may die today?"

"Nobody is God, Shettima. No one has the time table and every life experience is a moment in time. Let's make the best use of every moment we have."

He doesn't respond. I know I can't leave Shettima. In some ways, being with him is absolute paradise, the fulfilment of my fondest, most impossible fantasy. I'm aware, though, that in another way it's like embarking on a journey to nowhere because, deep down, I know it's not real, it's not even good and it doesn't make sense as there's nothing to build on, no future to plan for, so that leaves me up the proverbial creek without a paddle; but then, what do I do?

Twenty-four

I had a long telephone conversation with Deyemi yesterday, telling her all that has happened between Shettima and me. She was quiet all through my narration and, when I finished, she said I should be careful not to get hurt. Her comment made me feel like I was the child and she my mother. I managed to assure her that Shettima is a good man.

"Do you really know a good man, Mum?" she queried. I couldn't give a straight answer. Instead, I found myself pleading desperately for her approval but she wouldn't give it. She said I have to wait until she comes home and holds a discussion with him. It's amazing how children grow very fast and start to control their parents. Dear God, let my daughter approve of my relationship with Shettima because, if she doesn't, I would have no choice but to kiss my sweet boyfriend goodbye. We were about to end our conversation when she asked if there has been a development regarding my programme. I told her I haven't been to the university since the new session began.

"Go to school, Mum, and find out what has happened," she told me. I promised her I would. Then she said I should promise not to cry regardless of the situation. That I promised also. That's the reason why I'm getting ready to go to school today. Thoughts of Shettima fill my heart as I dress. I don't really feel like going but I agree with Deyemi. It's beginning to look like I've developed a phobia about visiting my department and I don't think it's the best way to handle the situation. Besides, with Shettima in my life and sweet thoughts of him in my consciousness, I ought to have the courage to face a thousand demons.

I'm standing happily at my bus stop now; waiting to board a bus to Ojota, from where I will board an inter-state bus to Abuja. A bus has just pulled up a few metres away from me and I'm walking as fast as I can toward it. The conductor notices me and starts to bang repeatedly on the body of the bus, screaming "duro fun, oga mi, j'eko wole joor / Stop for her, my boss, allow her to come in." I increase my pace, and when the conductor steps out to allow me climb in, I grab the door of the bus for support, especially as I'm aware that the impatient driver could move any moment. "Nisuru fun o, arugbogidi ni eleyi o/be patient with her o, this one is very old o," he yells at the driver who obeys. I smile sweetly rather than scowl at the conductor. What does it matter what he thinks of me and my age? My Shettima doesn't think I'm old and finished and that's all that matters to me. I climb in majestically and find a seat. I don't care what you think, lousy conductor, I mutter under my breath as the bus gathers speed.

I'm now in the secretary's office, waiting to see the HOD. My phone rings.

"Hello, Ms Oyewole, my name is Bimbo Atanda from Clamorous University. The director says to inform you to come for a meeting of all instructors next tomorrow at 10am."

"Very well, I'm actually not in Lagos today, but I will return tomorrow."

"Okay, bye."

"Bye, thanks."

"Madam?" I turn to face a thick set man sitting next to me.

"Did you just tell someone on phone that you came from Lagos?"

"Yes, why?"

"You live in Lagos?"

"Yes, I do."

"How come you are using a Nokia 3310 phone?"

"What's wrong with it?" I don't understand him.

"Don't disgrace Lagos o, madam. Those of us who live in the provinces can be excused but there is no excuse whatsoever for anyone who lives in Lagos to use a cheap phone now." I open my mouth in surprise. What has living in Lagos got to do with my choice of phone?

"But my brother, this phone works very well o, probably better than some expensive ones. I make and receive my calls, I send and receive messages and I even play games on it. How am I disgracing Lagos?"

"Madam, please change your phone o, unless you are not from Lagos," he insists, shaking his head vigorously to emphasise his disapproval. I shut my mouth, then open it, trying to articulate something but there's nothing there. I smile a sphinx-like smile. Soon, it's my turn to see the HOD. I take a deep breath before knocking softly on the door. I turn the knob to admit myself in.

"Good day, sir."

"Good day, Ms Oyewole. Please sit down." I draw a chair in front of him and sit.

"I have good as well as bad news for you," he begins. I'm surprisingly composed. No fear. I give myself a mental pat on the back for my courage.

"I'll start with the good news. Prof Ephraim has decided to continue to be your supervisor rather than write to inform the PG School of his disengagement from your work." He pauses to see my reaction. If he expects me to jump up in jubilation, he's definitely got it wrong. I don't feel excited at the prospect of being Prof Ephraim's student all over again. I'm not sure I care about anything any longer. I remain calm on my seat, staring impassively at the HOD. When he's ready, he'll break the supposed bad news. He senses my lack of interest and smiles wryly.

"Well, Ms Oyewole, the bad news is that there is a letter for you from the PG School, informing you that you have spent the maximum period of six years allowed to run a doctoral programme part-time and that since you have not finished, you are advised to withdraw from your current registration and reapply for a fresh period, if you so wish." I plaster a sardonic smile on my face because I don't know the appropriate response to give.

"I know how you feel, Ms Oyewole," he says tenderly. Still I say nothing and he resumes talking.

"These things happen. I want you to focus on the good news, which is that you still have a good chance to earn a doctorate." All my pain suddenly resurfaces. I don't even know how I feel. I have been confounded and frustrated by every turn of events since this programme started.

"Go to the PG School to obtain the registration form." His voice snaps me out of my reverie. "Then go to your supervisor and fill the form in his presence. Remember not to do or say anything to pressure him this time around. Pray very well for God's favour and everything will be alright." I sigh heavily, climb groggily to my feet, mumbling my thanks. I turn on my heels but the HOD calls me back.

"This is the letter from the PG School; it's addressed to you. I know its contents because they also copied the department." I take the letter and head out the door. Thirty minutes later, I'm back in the department and in front of Prof Ephraim's office. I hesitate for a moment, allowing Deyemi's admonition to run through my brain. "Promise me you won't cry, Mum, no matter what happens." I paste a semblance of a smile on my face and brace up to face my professor as I knock gently on his door. I hear his voice, telling me to come in. I enter boldly and greet him cheerfully. I sit directly in front of him, placing my registration form on the table.

"I have here the registration form for fresh students, sir. I now know how to fill it, except for the part where I have to indicate whether I wish to run the programme on full or part-time basis, sir," I say with as much calmness as I can command.

"Put part-time," he says. I peer at him and smile. He doesn't return my smile.

"That's alright, sir, I'll do precisely as you say." I finish filling the form then I append my signature and give it to him. He signs after confirming that I have ticked the right box. I return to the HOD's office to hand over my form to Mr Oragui, who will pass it on to the HOD for his signature.

"This is my form, Mr Oragui. Do you think the HOD will sign it at once so that I may take it to the faculty today?" I ask. He takes the form, eyeing me with pity. His countenance is almost my undoing but I hold my ground, refusing to succumb to my emotion.

"There is no advancement form here, madam. You didn't collect it from the PG School?" he asks and I laugh, but my laughter is off, forced. I tilt my head to one side.

"I filled and submitted advancement form for four consecutive years, Mr Oragui, yet I made no progress in my programme. I didn't know how right you were six years ago when you told me only my supervisor could determine my progress, I have learned my lesson, even if belatedly. I won't bother with the so-called advancement form henceforth." My tone is clipped. I'm bristling with tension in spite of Deyemi's warning. Calm down, Funto, I admonish myself inwardly. I break eye contact with Mr. Oragui to gather my composure. He rises swiftly to his feet, telling me to sit and wait for him. He enters the HOD's office, holding my form in his hand and is out again in a jiffy, returning the form to me with a sombre look. It has the HOD's signature.

"Take it in your stride, madam; and believe that this is the time God has appointed for you to run your programme." I stutter and head out the door.

I have just submitted my form at the PG School and I'm contemplating going in search of Akpabio or simply retiring to Satellite Hotel. I'm still standing in contemplation but I don't seem to understand how I'm feeling right now. I clutch my hands together, trying to keep as still as possible because the ground beneath me and everywhere else seems to be spinning. God! I'm feeling dizzy. Am I swaying like a drunk? Am I about to fall? My whole body tenses in apprehension. I take quick, panicked steps toward a long bench in front of the records' office, sitting with a thud as everywhere continues to oscillate around me. Dear God, don't allow me to die like this.

"Are you alright, madam?" I hear a voice call tenderly to me. I haven't noticed a youngish looking man sitting beside me.

"I'll be fine, I just feel slightly dizzy," I murmur.

"You don't look okay to me. Let me get you something to drink, then I can accompany you to the campus clinic."

"That would be very kind of you." I unzip my handbag to bring out my purse, bringing out a two-hundred naira note.

"A malt drink will be fine." He takes the money and scurries off. I hold my head in my hands and start to cry. He's back within a few minutes with my drink. He uncorks the bottle.

"Sorry," I murmur as I take the drink, embarrassed by my crying.

"Don't worry, madam, you'll be alright." I down the malt in a quick gulp and curl up with tension.

"Are you sure you can walk to the campus clinic now?" he asks and I nod.

"Let's go, then."

At the clinic, an attendant in the card room brings out my card and tells me to come with her to see a doctor. I follow her meekly. It's my first time in the clinic since my registration six years ago. I remember how a majority of my fellow PhD students circumvented the aspect of our registration that mandated us to register at the campus clinic. They were uncomfortable that they had to tender their urine and blood for test and analysis, fearing that they could test positive for HIV. How on earth did they expect us to surrender ourselves to that kind of comprehensive medical examination? they queried, and when I pointed out to some of them that they ought to see the requirement as a privilege to undergo a free medical check-up, many of them openly laughed at what they insisted was an unnecessary risk on the part of those who surrendered to the test. "How would you feel, Funto, if they found out through their test that you had AIDS?" One of them asked. "Well, I would go for counselling and start to do everything that people who are living positively with HIV virus do," I replied and they laughed. It would be far better not to know, they insisted, arguing that ignorance is bliss and that it's no use killing oneself before one's time. I recall arguing further that being aware of one's health status was important as it could elongate life and promote healthy living. Again, they faulted my argument, saying it was not about how long but how well, and that no matter how short they lived they would prefer their life to be devoid of anxiety and fear. It was an argument I couldn't win because a majority was against my line of thinking. I gave it up. But as I walk behind the clinic attendant holding my file, I secretly praise myself for not succumbing to the view of the majority. Who knows what could happen to me today if I don't receive medical attention.

"Sit here, madam, I will take your card in and when you

hear the sound of a bell, go in," the attendant tells me. I mumble my thanks. My benefactor has since left.

"Good day, doctor."

"Welcome, madam, how may I be of assistance to you?"

"I woke up this morning feeling well and healthy. Well, at least that's why I was able to travel down here from Lagos. However, I was at the PG School this afternoon when I was suddenly overtaken by a dizzying spell. A fellow student advised me to come to the clinic."

"That was good advice indeed. Do you still feel dizzy now or the feeling has abated?"

"I feel dizzy still, although not as gripping as it was when it started."

"Are you on any medication?"

"No."

"Any other complaint apart from dizziness?"

"I feel faint, tired and weak."

"Your record shows that you are a PhD student."

"Yes, doctor," I eye him questioningly.

"Well, that provides us a sort of guide."

"Really?"

"Yes, our experience shows that a majority of PhD students that visit the clinic have blood pressure-related issues. It has become so rampant that we have had to institute a counselling unit for PhD students. However, we are not going to conclude that you are one of them until we have carried out some preliminary tests. Let's check your BP for a start."

I surrender myself to the test and it turns out that the doctor's guess is right. He says my blood pressure is through the roof. I'm utterly embarrassed but he doesn't seem to feel my embarrassment. He scribbles on my card, telling me an attendant will lead me to the counselling room and that I will be given some medication thereafter. I mumble my thanks, rising clumsily to my feet. The woman I meet in the room tells me tenderly to take a seat. My card is placed in front of her. She reads through it quickly before looking up to hold my gaze.

"I'm going to start by showing you something, madam," she says as she brings out a large book from a drawer.

"This contains the names and departments of students who have received treatment for blood pressure issues in the last six months and about 90 per cent of them are PhD students. Are you experiencing problems in your programme or are there factors such as genetics that could predispose you to high blood pressure?" I gaze at her, not knowing how to respond.

"Have you been encountering problems in the course of running your programme, madam?" I nod repeatedly, blinking back the tears that pool in my eyes.

"Would it be of any help to you, madam, if I told you that you are not the only one? Although some PhD students are lucky to run their programme without stress, many of them are overwhelmed by situations they had not anticipated. You must learn to manage whatever difficulties and disappointments that come with your programme without harming yourself. I understand that you set out to sacrifice three or four years of your life, full of fervour, to hard work and difficult study, so as to be able to carry out the responsibility you have set your heart on. I'm also aware of your ardent desire for swift achievement. Then, you suddenly realise that things are not what they seem. I know how disconcerting it can be but tell me, madam, what would be the use of your doctoral degree if you suffered paralysis before you had a chance to earn it?" I shudder in fright. "Go home, take the medication you will be given, take plenty of rest and, above all, steel your mind to the vagaries of your programme. Don't ask yourself when you will finish; be content with knowing that you will get your PhD eventually." I manage a smile and my mood actually brightens a little. I thank her profusely and climb to my feet.

I'm outside the clinic now, walking toward the university gate. I wish I could return to Lagos today but it's already too late to travel. I want to be in Shettima's arms, I want him to cuddle me, kiss me and assure me again of his love for me. In the meantime, I allow my mind to go over the last time we made love. My sweet and delicious Shettima, I stop in my tracks and close my eyes momentarily as erotic scenes play in my mind, wishing that when I open them, it would be daybreak and I would be with him. I open my eyes, I'm still in Abuja. I decide to call my daughter, just to hear her voice.

"Hello, Deyemi, how are you doing today?"

"I'm fine, Mum." Did she just snap or am I mistaken? I don't know what to make of her response but the tone of her voice contradicts her words. Or could something be wrong with her and she doesn't want me to know about it? Is she really fine? Dear God, please don't let anything untoward happen to my daughter. I need to find out. I'm suddenly overtaken by a feeling of dread. I'm afraid for her. Please God, help me look after my only child, my succour, my hope, my breath, my life. My hand is shaking as I re-dial her number.

"Hello sweetheart, are you sure you are fine? You sounded dull and tired. Please talk to me." My tone is desperate.

"I'm okay, Mum. It's just that I'm very busy right now." Busy? What does that mean?

"I'm sorry," I mutter. I'm beginning to feel like a pest. "Do I call you too often?"

"Eh-r, not exactly, Mum, but ... yeah, you do some times. You called me three times yesterday, for example, and you make me wonder if you don't get tired of calling." I'm awash with embarrassment mixed with anger and I feel the beginning of a headache. I try to pull myself together. What else can I do in the circumstance?

"I'm sorry to have disturbed you. Do have a great day." I end the call but she calls me back immediately.

"Mum, I'm sorry. I didn't mean to be rude. It's just that I have assignments to do and deadlines for submission."

"I'm not angry. We'll talk later." I don't know whether or not I'm still angry but what difference does it make?

In Lagos the following day, I squint at myself in the mirror as I dress to go to Shettima's house. I look pale. I start to sing a soothing melody, vowing not to allow my unsatisfactory look blight my day. There's something mesmeric about Shettima and I smile as memory of our intimacy floods through me. When I finish dressing, I pick my handbag without checking my reflection. I don't want my fears to escalate. At the bus stop, danfo buses are unusually scarce. I become tired after waiting for fifteen minutes without being able to get a bus. I don't know why I feel this tired really. Is it because of my high blood pressure or my eagerness to see Shettima? Anyway, I resolve finally to take a molue, the long, usually decrepit, train-like commercial truck. I clamber in as soon as one arrives and I'm lucky to secure a seat before it fills up to the brim. Many people are standing in utter discomfort, clutching the rusty rails of the truck even as more commuters continue to troop in, as if they can't see that it's already full. I poke my face through the window and beckon a yoghurt seller. I select a strawberry one.

There's noise all about the vehicle. Some passengers who are sitting are quarrelling with those standing for attempting to lean on them for support. Some of the people standing are fighting their fellow standees for suffocating them. I watch them with detached amusement, their bickering reminding me of a story a former school mate told me. He had said he was going to Oshodi from Lagos Island during rush hour traffic one evening and could only secure a standing position in a molue. He was dressed in a local fabric known as ankara which was sown in a loose style of sokoto and dansiki. The journey started smoothly and continued without a hitch until the molue came upon a deep pothole, causing passengers to bump into one another involuntarily. That was when he noticed a fair-skinned, pretty teenager standing directly in front of him. From the moment he became aware of her, his manhood stood in stubborn turgidity, threatening to pop out of his loose trouser. He tried unsuccessfully to press it down but it was as if it had assumed a life of its own. To make matters worse, the road became increasingly bumpy and the molue continued to sink and rise from the endless potholes, making him surge forward involuntarily and hitting his menacing manhood against the young girl's derriere. It wasn't long before the young woman became aware of the assault and glanced back with a deep frown. My friend muttered his apology. When he failed to prevail on his organ to behave, he had to quickly climb down from the molue at the next stop in shame before he had reached his destination. The memory brings a smile to my face. I'm happy I'm comfortably seated by the window, no offending member stabbing my behind and no one is leaning on my shoulder.

Shettima's face lights up when I arrive. "How are you?" he asks as he puts his arm around my waist. I tingle at his touch. I don't waste time reeling out all my experiences since yesterday. I gaze down at my feet when I finish and he gently covers my hands with one of his. When I glance up at him, he's smiling at me.

"Congratulations for having a chance to re-start your programme. It means you've been given a fresh opportunity to live your dream and you will live it. It doesn't matter how long it takes your supervisor to read your thesis, you have written it, okay?" I nod uncertainly. "And l want to assure you that you and your daughter will not lack for food, clothing or shelter for as long as I live. Do you know how happy I'm to be in your life? I feel highly privileged to care for you and if I can succeed in wiping your tears, in making you genuinely happy, then my life would be halfway well lived."

I break into sobs but I don't know why. Is this what I have been reduced to in spite of the efforts I have made in the last six years? I'm now starting all over again and as a burden to another friend? For how long will I continue to look up to friends for my basic needs? Shettima cups my chin in his palm, raising my head up so that my eyes might meet his but I avert my eyes. How can I bear to hold his gaze, I, who has just been confirmed a liability and drainer of his purse? There ought to be a better way to live than this.

"I'm not coming at you from the perspective of pity," he says sombrely, as if reading my thoughts. I shrug my shoulders. What difference does it make, anyway? I'm numb but he seems to want to talk, so I listen.

"I'm coming at you from the perspective of deep, genuine affection. I love you and I would crawl over broken bottles to prove just how I feel about you. Let your supervisor take all the time in the world while I still have breath. I have vitality, I have abundance, you and Deyemi will not lack and you will not have to beg me for anything. Just ask me and I'll do whatever you wish me to do. It's that simple." His gaze holds mine now. He's utterly sincere. I blink at him as my heart expands.

"Well ..." I swallow, fighting the knot of emotions that catches in my throat. I don't know what to say. He senses my confusion and nods slowly. His lips twitch with an amused smile. When my brain finally connects with my mouth, I voice my concern.

"I appreciate your love and kindness, Shettima, but being an absolute liability to a man does not sit well with me. I want to be accomplished as me, Olufunto Oyewole; that's why I have deployed all my energy and focus into working hard to achieve my goals. What do I have to show for my efforts other than myriad challenges that have continued to portray me as a tramp, a loafer and now a ...." I stop. I can't bear to say the word. Oh, I feel awful. He smiles and shakes his head at me.

"Relax, you've more than risen to the challenge. You have done very well indeed," he says and there's a hint of pride in his voice. His sincerity is almost my undoing.

"Oh, I..." I choke a sob.

"Listen to me, Fnnto. I'm going to sever your relationship with those bus conductors. I will buy you a car and move you out of Mushin to a neighbourhood of your choice." I gasp in disbelief.

"What? Are you crazy?" I ask and he props himself up on his elbow and gazes down at me before answering.

"Yes, I'm crazy for you," I snort because it's the only expression I can manage. Why does he want to do so much for me? Why does he hold me so high in his regard? I put my head in my hands to break eye contact with him and gather my ravaged senses. I'm silent for a moment and when I look up, I straighten my shoulders.

"No, I won't let you do all you've promised for me, it'll hurt my pride as a woman."

"Don't sweat this, I'm your lover and I want to be in your life in every way I can." He kisses me chastely, then, skims his thumb down my cheek. I feel like I have been run over by a freight train.

"I'm sorry." I murmur, trying to sound contrite.

"I know you like jeans because they are convenient but I want you to start wearing more of our fabrics from now on. I will do the buying; all I want is for you to wear them, okay?" I nod, smiling sweetly at him. After dinner, I climb into his bed and wait for him to join me. Later, when he climbs in beside me, wearing only his boxer briefs, I move so that I'm lying on my side, propped up on my elbow. I caress his face. He takes my hand and places it on his chest. I lean down to kiss him.

"You are my miracle," I whisper.

"I love you. I will always love you," he says, moaning loudly as he makes love to me.

Twenty-five

I'm eager to attend the meeting of instructors at the Clamorous University of Nigeria today. Perhaps the university management has finally concluded arrangements to pay us for the over three years of teaching. It baffles me that semester after semester, courses are being allocated to instructors without remunerating previous work. The university management doesn't seem to consider that, apart from their time, instructors spend money on transportation and sundry other expenses in order to be present in the classroom. I often have to resort to borrowing and sometimes outright begging just to be able to transport myself to the venue of the lecture at Ikoyi. Anyway, I'm dressed now, ready to set out and grateful that I'm in Shettima's house and so have no opportunity of looking endlessly at my reflection in any of the mirrors in my bedroom. Besides, if sex is as therapeutic as medical science claims, I ought to look good today and shouldn't need a mirror to tell me so. I use the small mirror in my handbag to apply mild make-up and that's it. I don't want any negative emotions to blight my day. When I'm paid today, I'll buy some vegetables and fresh fish, then I'll garnish them with plenty of onions and tomatoes. I wish Deyemi was around to partake of the sumptuous meal of amala that will go with it. Thoughts of Deyemi remind me what she told me during our telephone conversation a few days ago. She said she now has a boyfriend. Can you imagine? Does that mean that I'm no longer the only one who knows about 'it'? I still, my whole body tensing. No! Not yet, I declare firmly under my breath. I smile and my mood brightens.

"His name is Nathaniel, Mum, you will like him!" she said excitedly and we burst into a boisterous laughter.

"I trust your judgement, sweetheart. Do you want to tell me more about him?"

"Oh yes, Mum, he finished from this university and is currently on national service."

Minutes after our conversation, I remained seated, processing the information she had just given me and marvelling at how my little girl has suddenly grown 'big' enough to have a boyfriend. It was a mixed feeling for me. I felt a rush of warm emotions flooding through me but I couldn't help feeling old as well. Then, I called Folake to intimate her of the development. Silly girl, she congratulated me and sounded genuinely happy about the news. I didn't know how to feel really and Shettima didn't help matters by calling me a grandmother-in-waiting when I told him. Time to go! I chastise myself, bringing my thoughts back to the here and now as I finally leave the house. Shettima has since left for his office.

I'm taken aback by the huge crowd of instructors I meet at Clamorous University waiting for the meeting to begin. Are they this many? How about the strange faces I'm seeing? Who are they and from where have they suddenly surfaced? I stand in front of the hall, unable to hide my surprise. People are buzzing around, some trying to find space to sit while some of those already seated are engaged in light conversation.

"Funto!" I hear my name called. I curl my lips in an amused smile while scanning the hall to locate my caller. My smile blooms when her gaze meets mine. It's Chidimma, my closest associate at the university. She is married with three children and holds a master's degree in political science but doesn't have a regular job. She told me she has never used her certificates to work and that when her husband's relation who works at the university suggested she teach part-time, she grabbed it with both hands. "There's nothing more dreadful than having to rely on your husband for all your needs, my sister." She once told me, matter-of-factly and although I had no experience to share since I have never been married, the hint of sadness in her eyes validated her story. "I'll do my utmost to keep this job, Funto, so that I, too, can at least bring something to the table and earn some honour," she added seriously. I didn't know what to say, I merely patted her on her back and smiled up at her. I'm picking my way carefully now through the multitude and soon I'm by her side. She creates a space for me. I sit beside her feeling well received and warm in the inside.

"Do you know why the meeting was called? Are they going to pay us?" I ask.

"Funto, you too like money," she croons, slapping my back playfully.

"That's what I thought, too, but it doesn't look so. Besides, I came pretty early and was able to ask questions from some of their staff. They told me that they merely want to distribute examination scripts to us," she explains. I frown.

"Na wa oh, these people know how to share work but they don't care how you get the work done. What kind of people are they?" I grumble.

"Na condition make crayfish bend, my sister. I'm sure they are aware that we don't have any worthwhile engagement. What can we do other than continue to hope that their consciences will disturb them one day?" Chidimma asks, her eyes frosty.

"I didn't know there are so many instructors," I mouth, changing the subject.

"Do not say I told you," she says, lowering her voice conspiratorially. "More than half of the people in this hall are not instructors. They are people connected to members of the university staff who want to do or return favours done to them by friends and relatives. Some of the men you see are here because they happen to be brothers-in-law to some people and there are many housewives around, too, who know next to nothing about teaching." I can't believe what Chidimma has just said. My frown deepens as I wonder how much of her information could be true. Perhaps Chidimma is more frustrated than I imagine and maybe she's already feeling threatened by a sense of competition by the multitude present.

"How would they know how to grade scripts, then, if they are as ignorant as you imply," I query.

"When you ask me, what do you want me to say?" she retorts, half-playfully, half-seriously. Perhaps I should let the matter drop; she seems a bit edgy and sorrowful and I don't know what to make of her story.

"Distinguished and valued instructors," the director's voice booms over the babble of voices and a hush immediately descends. Most of us didn't see him enter but now we concentrate all our attention on him. I straighten my shoulders and adjust myself in my seat.

"The management of Clamorous University wishes to thank you all for your continued cooperation and hard work. We are aware that we have not been able to fulfil our own obligation to you because we haven't been able to remunerate you for upward of two or more years now. However, we wish to appeal for your understanding and patience. We wish to state emphatically that all arrears owed will be paid in due course. What we cannot tell you is when. However, we strongly advise and appeal to you all to see your yet-to-be-paid remuneration as savings which will continue to accumulate and all of which shall be paid eventually. We want to assure you, also, that we have records of work done by each and every one of you and your labour shall not be in vain."

A loud murmuring fills the hall with some people raising their hands to speak. The director is frantically appealing for calm. There is palpable anger on the faces of many and they appear desperate to voice their displeasure but the director seems to want to resume talking. Finally, a level of quiet is achieved and the director's voice bellows.

"I am afraid we do not have time to entertain questions today because the task at hand is urgent. As you are aware, the semester examination has been concluded with some of you serving as invigilators. In a short while, my staff will bring the scripts to be shared among you and you have one week, I repeat, one week, to turn in your graded scripts. As usual, adequate records of the number of scripts marked by each of you shall be diligently kept and you shall be paid in the nearest future. Thank you all for your cooperation and patience."

He heads out the door as the hall erupts in murmurings. Within a nanosecond, some officials of the university emerge, each dragging the largest size of 'Ghana must go' bag containing the scripts. They ask instructors to move to particular parts of the hall in accordance with their department. Suddenly, I don't know how it happens, but a scramble ensues. Everyone seems to be eager to get as many scripts as possible since remuneration will be calculated on the basis of the number graded. Good gracious God! What is this? Suddenly, everything seems to be a battle of physical strength as people, but especially men, hijack scripts from those deemed to be weak and incapable of fighting. I stand rooted to the spot, open-mouthed and wide-eyed, taking in the unfolding drama. What's going on? Why are people desperate to have scripts to grade when they do not know when they will be remunerated?

"Funto! Are you going to stand there like mumu instead of fighting for your own scripts?" Chidimma admonishes but I'm unable to move. I shift my gaze to her as she dashes across the hall to a section I imagine is her department and, to my utter astonishment, she immediately begins to drag a large envelope containing scripts with a man. The man is mouthing invectives at her but she doesn't seem the least bothered. She is dragging and the man is dragging. Finally, she wins! My eyes are threatening to pop out of their sockets. Chidimma has just 'conquered' a man! I watch, enthralled, as she quickly puts the seized envelope into her large handbag, which she clutches protectively on her left arm. Then she moves swiftly toward another man and starts to drag a bigger envelope with him. Chidimma challenges me. I feel suddenly possessed by a strange energy. I take quick steps toward the section I recognise as my own department, stepping on toes as I walk and not bothering to offer apologies. I target a man holding a huge envelope marked Use of English 101 and begin to drag it with him, summoning all my strength.

"You want to try me? You witch!" the man lashes out at me.

"Arrgh! How did you know? Let me tell you more. I'm not just a witch; I'm a ruthless sorceress and I will kill you within the hour if you don't leave this envelope for me." I widen my eyes dramatically at him and it works. He relinquishes the envelope. I struggle not to laugh so as not to demystify my imaginary sorcery.

"Okay, you have collected it but can you grade them? Do you have the knowledge?"

"How dare you accuse me of incompetence? Do you know who I am?" I challenge fiercely.

"Are you educated? Aren't you just a miserable, sex-starved

housewife taking undeserved advantage of your relative working with Clamorous University?"

"You are the lowlife relative of a staff here. Let me introduce myself properly. I am the foremost concubine of the vice-chancellor and I apply my witchcraft to make him leave his wife's bed to give it to me regularly. I'm not sex-starved, you wretch!"

I turn my back on him, searching for another victim. I glance surreptitiously at a tall, thirtyish looking man holding an envelope marked GST 102. I contemplate snatching it but before I make up my mind, my victim alerts the man.

"Hold tightly to your possession, this deranged woman is about to snatch it," he warns.

"She wouldn't dare!" the man boasts. Really? Is that a challenge? I charge at him with the envelope in pretended fury, rough-handling him and murmuring like a demented animal. "You don't know the stuff I'm made of. You haven't heard about my power," I blab. My first victim colludes in my bragging.

"That woman is a vicious witch!" he screams and my second victim automatically lets go of the envelope. I hold up the seized envelope with my right hand, cupping my waist with my left and shaking violently and daring them to come near me. Both men eye me malevolently for a moment before letting out a long, contemptuous hiss. I continue to stand menacingly, totally fearless and I'm wondering silently what has come over me. Could this be an aspect of me I hitherto didn't know existed? They walk away and I smile contentedly at my sheer bravado. I'm on my way out of the hall now. I look for Chidimma to thank her for lending me her courage but I can't find her. Maybe she has left.

In less than a week, I finish grading and I dutifully return the scripts to the university but, as usual, no mention is made of remuneration.

"We have the record, madam," the official assures me when I express concern over non-payment of arrears of previous scripts graded and non-disclosure of a specific time of payment. Soon, another semester exam is approaching and it seems I'm going to be unusually lucky this time. A senior member of my department has just requested me to set examination questions for Literature 103 and I'm delirious with joy. He assures me that management policy is not to lump payment for exam questions with teaching. It's a specialised service, he reassures me, adding that examiners are promptly paid immediately after the examination. My academic worth is gradually but surely being appreciated. I'm no longer a mere instructor but an examiner as well. I beam with satisfaction and regale Shettima with an exaggerated account of the meeting between me and the head of unit of English. I apply myself to diligent reading of the area in question and, within two weeks, produce what I'm convinced is a high-quality, academically sound examination questions which the official say I must submit through him and not directly to the head of unit. Two weeks after the examination, I receive a call from the departmental official, Mr Jagun Bodunde, informing me that the university may pay me a meagre one or two thousand naira for the exam questions and that he will collect the amount on my behalf. I don't understand him and I'm not shy to say so.

"Yes, madam, I want to help you to collect the money so that it doesn't delay. The university will pay either one or two thousand, I can't tell you precisely how much it will be, but it will be between one and two thousand. I will collect the money on your behalf and hand it over to you. I'm making this call in advance because I don't want anyone in the department to know about the transaction, okay? This person is my brother in the department; therefore, I must tell him about it, I don't want that.

Or, that person is my sister, therefore, I must intimate her with the matter; I don't want that at all, am I clear enough, madam? You know I did it to help you, so let the transaction remain strictly between us. Do you understand me, madam?"

"Thank you very much, Mr Bodunde, I understand," I mutter with guarded politeness but I can't help feeling there is something fishy about the call and his manner of speaking. What's so secretive about doing a job and getting paid for it? I turn the telephone conversation over in my mind for some time, wondering what to do. Does Mr Bodunde want to short-change me? Is he playing some kind of crooked game with me? Well, it may not be a bad idea to find out. I put a call across to a clerical staff of the department, Mr Boniface.

"Good day, Mr Boniface, this is Ms. Funto Oyewole, one of your instructors. Do you have an idea of how much the university pays for setting examination questions?"

"Do you mean per exam paper, madam?"

"Yes, per paper."

"Fifteen thousand." My eyes widen in surprise,

"Thank you very much, Mr Boniface."

The morning after, I walk straight to the office of the head of unit to demand for my money. His face clouds in confusion when I introduce myself.

"Well, I'm surprised you are here because Mr Bodunde says you travelled out of Lagos and asked him to collect the money on your behalf."

"Actually, I did travel, sir, but I'm back in town now." He sends for Mr Bodunde, who shows annoyance at seeing me. I flash him an enigmatic smile. He pouts.

"Ms Oyewole is back in town," the head of unit quips innocently.

"Ah, welcome, Funto, how was your journey?" Mr Bodunde

asks. I manage to respond without giving anything away. The head of unit gives me fifteen thousand naira. I thank him profusely and take my leave without looking in Mr Bodunde's direction. Later in the day at my residence, I recount the day's activities to Shettima and he convulses in laughter.

"You are a proper Lagos woman," he teases and we erupt simultaneously. "But you need to watch out for that Bodunde of a man o," Shettima notes light-heartedly. "Make the man no go put sand-sand for your gari for that place." I dismiss his fears with a wave of the hand but his observation turns out to be prophetic. When I arrive in Ikoyi to teach the following week, I find some of my students idling away in the corridor. It's unusual for them to act in this manner. Normally, I would find them sitting quietly in the hall, waiting for me. I am even more surprised and a little confused when they show no interest in entering the hall even when they see that I have arrived. Some of them mumble their greetings and promptly resume whatever it is they seem to be doing while others pretend not to notice me. My mind doesn't go to Mr Bodunde; I just don't understand what could be responsible for their unusual behaviour. Anyway, I don't show my surprise or displeasure; I respond cheerfully to those that greet me as I make my way to the hall. Perhaps they are just being students. They will join the rest of the class in no time. I'm in the hall now and, although I meet a sizeable number of students who look happy enough to see me, I'm still racking my brain for clues that will explain why those outside don't seem to be in a hurry to join their mates.

"Can anyone tell me what's going on? Some of your mates are playing outside," I ask, now visibly puzzled. The class rep responds.

"Excuse me, ma, Mr Bodunde came to address us earlier today and what he told us is responsible for the attitude of some of our mates." Bodunde has something to do with this?

"What did he say?"

"We are really sorry, ma."

"You haven't told me what Mr. Bodunde said, what are you sorry about?"

"Eh-r, he kind of said that you are not qualified to teach us, ma." My mouth falls open. "Sorry, ma, a majority of us don't agree with him because you teach well, ma. We just think maybe you guys ..." Words fail him. He stares blankly at me.

"What else did he tell you?" I ask. My voice is soft, tentative. The class rep is quiet for a moment, as if contemplating how much of the information at his disposal he should divulge. "Eh-r, he said you got the job out of pity, not on merit and that he decided to tell us because he pities us, having to be taught by an unqualified lecturer. He said he will organise tutorials for us just to help us and that he will ensure that the university dispenses with your service in the nearest future."

I try to articulate something but I can't find my voice. What could I possibly say to these young, innocent souls that would give them a clearer picture of the truth and take away the embarrassment and shame I feel right now? I'm boiling with rage but to what end? Bodunde has an upper hand over me already. I feel thoroughly disgraced and humiliated. How would I ever be able to look at these students in the eye, either inside or outside this classroom, from now on? Bodunde has dealt me a hard blow. In spite of my pain however, I resolve firmly not to descend to his level by sharing the dirty details of what transpired between us with my students. Let them believe whatever Bodunde has told them. I'll go home and recuperate from my disgrace. Without uttering another word, I pick my papers with my head hung low as I try to make my way out of the hall.

"Excuse me, ma, sorry, ma, please come back, ma," I hear a

305

babble of voices behind me. I'm compelled to stop in my tracks, smiling wryly to hide my embarrassment. Everybody wants to talk at the same time. When I raise my face, the concern I see on their faces nearly moves me to tears but I'm determined not to betray my emotions. I listen calmly. The class rep leaps up to his feet, displaying about four sheets of paper filled with names and signatures. I don't know what it's about, but he's trying to prevail on his mates to let him have the floor. A hush descends shortly.

"We appreciate you, ma, and we don't agree with Mr Bodunde and we don't believe his claim because we are the ones you've been teaching. It is true that some of us, like the students that have refused to come to class, are of the opinion that since Mr Bodunde is a staff of the university, whereas you are a part-time instructor, he must know what he is saying and that he can use his influence to make all of us fail your course, especially as we believe that you must have offended him somehow. Those students want us to obey Mr Bodunde who told us to walk out on you once you enter the class today and that we should all say that you don't know how to teach. But a majority of us don't want to obey him. We want you to continue to teach us and that's why we have gone ahead to compile our names and signatures which we intend to submit to the university management. We have decided to let the school authority know that it's Mr. Bodunde that is instigating us to say what we don't want to say. The students who don't want to cooperate with you are only afraid that Mr Bodunde can victimise us and that we cannot challenge him and win since we are students."

The class rep looks thoroughly flustered and disconcerted; my heart goes out to him and all his mates. Those of them who have decided to play safe by avoiding my class are right. Who knows how far Mr Bodunde could go in his crazed quest for vengeance? Would it be fair then to allow the students to be at the receiving end of our senseless fight over money? No, I can't afford to trifle with their promising lives by putting their education and destiny in jeopardy.

"Your mates who have decided to play safe by avoiding my class as instructed are right," I tell my students with all sense of sincerity. "It makes sense for you all to do precisely as Mr Bodunde has instructed because he's a staff of the university and he understands the system," I mouth, walking out briskly without a backward glance even as several voices call after me, appealing to me to come back and teach.

I receive a telephone call from Chidimma a week after, informing me that a fellow instructor told her in confidence that a select number of instructors who have found 'favour' with some officials of the university are being paid all the arrears of their remuneration. A select few? What does that mean and how does one find 'favour' with the officials? I ask.

"My sister, I understand those being paid are those who offered monetary inducement, bought gifts or gave an undertaking to the officials to return an agreed percentage of their earning as bribe as soon as they receive their money."

"Have you been paid?"

"No."

"Have you bought gift or paid bribe?"

"No, my sister."

"What do you suggest we do?"

"I think we should go there and demand for our own money."

"When?"

"Why not tomorrow?"

"What time?"

"Ten o'clock in the morning will be okay."

"We will meet there."

In the morning, Chidimma and I are on time. We go straight to the office of the director and we are ushered in. Chidimma gestures to me to speak. I clear my throat.

"Yes, sir, we have been reliably informed that instructors are being paid and we are here to collect our arrears, sir." He doesn't respond immediately. Chidimma and I exchange glances and watch him quietly. After staring into space for a while, he brings out a bound document glittering with official finesse from one of his drawers and places it on the table. Chidimma shoots me a confused glance. Finally, the director speaks.

"We have paid all our instructors without exception. Here is the record, the list of all instructors with the amount paid to them." He tosses the document toward us, as if asking us to verify his claim. I don't think either of us can make sense of what he just said but, like automatons, we act in accordance with what seems to be his wishes. We painstakingly go through the long list, which is arranged according to units. We find our names, neatly typed, with different amounts purportedly paid to us. Everything bears an undisputable official stamp with a final remark indicating, 'Paid.' I blink repeatedly when my eyes settle on my name and the amount I supposedly received. I'm utterly stunned.

Twenty-six

SEPTEMBER, 2006

It's the beginning of a new academic calendar and two years after Prof Ephraim agreed to resume supervision of my thesis. He told me two years ago that he would contact me when he must have finished reading my work. I interpreted that to mean that I was not to ask him about it. Well, I haven't asked him since then, I haven't even been to the university, but two years after, would it be too early for me to want to find out how far he has gone? Would my presence constitute an affront? Would it be tantamount to wilful disobedience of his instructions? Am I to simply fold my arms and pretend as if all is well, even if he doesn't respond till eternity? I don't think it would be out of place to visit my supervisor at this time especially as I haven't heard from him in two whole years. A lot has changed about me and I can say with some measure of confidence that they are mostly positive. I no longer live in Mushin for example. I now live in Opebi, close enough to Adeniyi Jones where Shettima lives because the two neighbourhoods are in Ikeja. My daughter's education has not been truncated, contrary to my fears. Shettima has taken absolute responsibility for all her needs. As for me, he has bought me a Toyota Camry with which I cruise around the city and I no longer use my 3310 because he also bought me a Motorola phone. I'm now an authentic middle-class city dweller.

What else can I ask for, and why should I be afraid to visit my supervisor?

However, I have resolved not to re-introduce gifts, recharge cards, cash or any form of corrupt inducement as a feature of my relationship with my supervisor. What do I have to show for the past efforts I made in that regard? Perhaps I'm as much to blame as my supervisor. Why did I believe, for instance, that calculating pushfulness or any skill in ingratiating myself into his favour or relying on Akpabio's knowledge of how to make my supervisor like me could earn me a PhD? Well, perhaps it's good to be taught the kind of lesson I have learned through experience. Notwithstanding my gaffes, however, I ought to have the right, as a student who has continued to pay school fees as and when due, to want to know the progress my supervisor has made on my work. Let him be the one to tell me he has made no progress and I shall accept it.

"I want to travel to Abuja to see my supervisor," I announce simply to Shettima.

"Has he called you?"

"No."

"I thought you said he told you not to bother him."

"Yes, he did, but for how long would I continue to be afraid to make a simple enquiry? Besides, there may be a miracle waiting for me in Abuja. Maybe he has finished reading and hasn't found the time to call me. Perhaps, he has forgotten completely. I need to go there to find out the true position of things."

"Why do you always talk about miracles?"

"Because miracles do happen, Shettima."

"I don't agree with you on that. I'm a realist."

"You've told me that often enough, but deep in your heart, you know miracles do happen, don't you?" I ask, disapproval radiating off me. He smirks.

"I always find the strength and the ability not to believe in miracles," I frown but he ignores my expression.

"However, if I'm faced with a miracle as an undeniable fact, I'd rather disbelieve my own senses than admit the fact."

I want to say something but he holds up his hand and continues talking.

"If I admit a miracle, I will admit it as a natural fact hitherto unknown to me. For example, if on your arrival at the national university, you found that your supervisor had read your work, you would like to regard it as a miracle, right?" I nod.

"You see, there would be nothing miraculous about it, he would have read it if he had anyway, only that you were not aware of the fact."

"Do your health issues have something to do with your philosophy?"

"I don't know really but I don't think so," he says honestly. I gaze intently at him, not knowing what to think or how to feel. I do know one thing, though, and it is that my Shettima is a lover par excellence. I know also that he doesn't look sickly, pale or emaciated. On the contrary, he looks a picture of health. He is a slender but well-built, clear-eyed man. He's of medium height, very handsome with an elongated oval face. My Shettima is very well composed and I love him to pieces.

"Going to Abuja may mean an overnight. I want to come with you." His voice interrupts my reverie.

"No, that won't be necessary. I'll be fine."

"I can't trust you on that and you know why."

"No, I don't," I lie.

"You shed tears nine out of every ten meetings you have with your supervisor. I'm not saying that my presence will prevent you from crying, but I want to be there this time to give you my shoulder to cry on." He shows great emotion as he speaks, with the corners of his mouth trembling. I hug myself momentarily, marvelling at how nice it feels to watch him fusing about me. I agree to let him come with me. Being in his company is fun and relaxing and makes me feel much younger. I feel as if I'm just seventeen, and in my imagination Shettima is only nineteen. Life can be incredibly sweet sometimes!

By mid-day the following morning, Shettima and I are sitting in front of Prof Ephraim. I introduce my friend to my professor and he responds to Shettima's greeting with a smile that doesn't reach his eyes.

"It's been quite a while, sir," I quip, looking at him intently to gauge his mood and hoping silently for a warm interaction. His look is impassive.

"I thought to come around to find out how far you have gone with my work, sir," I say, flashing him a warm smile.

"I have just returned from a sabbatical leave and haven't had time to look at your work," he says without interest. My heart contracts painfully. The absolute lack of empathy which I detect in both his words and mien wounds me. I feel as if he has just pounded me in the stomach. I put my head in my hands to break eye contact with him. I try to swallow but it's hard with a dry mouth. I raise my head and sigh heavily, running my hand through my hair. I don't know if I imagine it but my supervisor now wears what seems to me to be a permanent scowl. He rises on his feet and walks to his book shelf to pick a book. Shettima and I follow him with our eyes. He carries himself with deliberate arrogance; although I suspect he imagines it to be with more dignity. A sardonic smile is playing at the corners of Shettima's mouth but I'm far from being amused. The truth is that I'm finding it really hard to tolerate the caprices and reproofs of my professor. He's so mean, so insufferable and tyrannical. What a man!

"There may be a way out for you very soon." His voice interrupts my inner turmoil. "You recall that ASUU did a warning strike earlier this year?" He wants to use the Academic Staff Union of Universities' strike to do what now? I wonder inwardly. Well, I know about ASUU's strike profile just as I'm aware also that apart from declaring strike actions, members of the public don't seem to think that the union has any other motive for being in existence. The public's cynicism may be a little overstretched but I often find myself in a dilemma regarding whose side to place my sympathy when I consider that I started my PhD programme in 1998 and since 1999 till present, ASUU has embarked on national strikes for at least three days every year except one. What I don't know right now is how my professor intends to use the union's strike to my advantage. I look questioningly at him.

"I'm sure you are aware also that the government has always shown partial or no interest in meeting the demands of our union, so pray that a more comprehensive strike holds and lasts for a long time to give me time to read your work." What? Raw anger surges through me but all I can do is gape at him, open-mouthed. I can't believe my professor said those words. I should fall on my knees and pray for the mutilation of the academic calendar of my dear country's universities? I take a long, steadying breath to calm my fraying temper before responding.

"My daughter is an undergraduate, sir. I don't want her education to be truncated," I say with all the calmness at my command.

"Then it's left to you to prioritise your needs. Let your utmost desire determine your supplication to your creator." He sounds vaguely affronted but I resolve quietly to ignore his tone.

"Do you really think it's possible, sir, for any parent to pray that their undergraduate children would be sent home from school to roam the streets and probably get into crimes and other negative activities even if it would enable their supervisor to read their PhD thesis?"

"Yes," he answers, serious and straight-faced. Bile rises in my mouth and I struggle to fight it down but fail. I'm about to start sobbing in hysterics and shrieks when Shettima gently slaps my back and clears his throat to speak.

"I thank you very much for your time and kind attention, sir. I will join Funto in praying for a speedy declaration of a long and protracted strike by ASUU, and I trust you will have found time to go through her work before our next visit." I turn to glance at Shettima with astonishment. I wouldn't have believed he was capable to such refined and polite sneers. We both rise to our feet as if on cue and exit Prof Ephraim's office. Shettima confronts me fiercely as soon as we are on the corridor.

"When are you going to learn to let your supervisor be? Can't you see that the man is an ill-natured clown? Do you think you can change him?" he asks in real or pretended anger. "Why would the foolish man tell me to go home and pray for a prolonged ASUU strike when he knows my daughter is an undergraduate?"

"Why should that surprise you knowing your supervisor? Can you stop ASUU from embarking on a national strike because you have an undergraduate daughter? Let your mind be at rest, Funto, Deyemi is only eighteen. What I don't understand is why he needs your prayers to achieve his sadistic aim. He's a member of ASUU, you are not, let him impress it on the ASUU executive and congress to ensure another strike is called and prolonged. I'm sure he also wields enough influence to make government ignore their demands. What I want you to know and believe firmly in your heart is that as long as I have breath, you and Deyemi will neither hunger nor thirst. You will lack nothing because I have taken you two to my umbrella and no one who is there shall be in want, Insha Allah. By the way, it's nice meeting your supervisor. Can we go back to Lagos, please, madam?" He genuflects in mock obeisance.

"Shettima…look …" I start to say but I'm unable to mutter anything coherent. The trustful expression on his face distracts me. It's amazing that it hasn't really been long since he entered silkily into my life but it feels like a century. Or, was he already in my life during all those years that I discounted him? I want him so badly that it's embarrassing. I can't think of one single thing to say to him right now. I peek up at him, still racking my brain for something to say, and eventually, I find my voice.

"I love you," I whisper. He holds my arm at bay.

"You are making a bigger deal of your supervisor's antics than you need to,"

he says softly.

"I know. I'm sorry," I mutter, trying to sound contrite.

"Can we go now?"

"Not immediately. I want to see my friend, Akpabio."

"Sure."

I lead the way to Akpabio's office after confirming his availability. He's still sharing an office with a fellow lecturer but he's alone when Shettima and I arrive.

"World Akpabio!" I hail. "Shettima, this is Akpabio, Akpabio, meet the man in my life," I introduce. They shake hands warmly.

"Funto has told me a lot about you," Shettima says.

"I hope they are positive things?" Akpabio asks with a smile.

"Oh yes, they are. I must thank you for looking after her."

"Why are you still sharing an office? I thought you would have had an office of your own by now," I remark although I can't truthfully claim to be ignorant of what goes on in the university system. Am I excited at having Shettima around me, or am I just being mischievous?

"You just want to mock me in Shettima's presence. Who am I to complain of sharing an office when some of my colleagues who joined the university more than eight years ago are still sharing offices?" Akpabio says well naturedly and his response makes me feel foolish. What's wrong with me? I'm racking my brain for something to say to redeem myself in his eyes but there's a soft knock on the door. We all whirl around to behold a middle-aged man who walks in.

"Good evening, sirs, good evening, ma, please, I wish to see Mr Akpabio Asuquo." He has hardly stated his request when Akpabio explodes in surprise anger.

"You address me as Mr? Oh, hell, no! Do you know what it takes to have a PhD in this country?" Shettima and I exchange glances but Akpabio's sense of outrage doesn't allow him to notice. He's boiling over with rage. It's curious how a man who, only moments ago, was full of smiles and good humour could fly off the handle so quickly with so such frenzy.

"I'm very sorry, sir, I meant no disrespect, sir."

"You will do more than apologise. You will go right back outside and look at the name on the door, do you hear me?" he fumes, saliva oozing out from the corners of his mouth. I glance in Shettima's direction but he's not looking at me. His head is hung low. I shift my gaze to the man who looks visibly embarrassed.

"Go out and check the name on the door!" Akpabio roars. The man rushes out and is back within a second.

"I wish to see Dr Akpabio Asuquo, sir," he corrects himself. Shettima gives me a rude tap on the shoulder and rises swiftly to his feet. We bid Akpabio a hurried goodbye and exit his office.

"There's no need for us to spend the night in Abuja. We return to Lagos at once," he says. I don't respond. My mind is busy processing the day's events.

****

We are now on the Lagos-Ibadan expressway, glad that we will soon be in Lagos. Then, suddenly, I don't know if my eyes are playing tricks on me but there seems to be pockets of flash lights emanating from the belly of the bush about one hundred metres ahead of us. I have lost count of the number of times I have travelled on the expressway and have never noticed the existence of a hamlet or village inside the bush in this particular part but then it's my first time of travelling on this road at night. I glance at my mobile phone: 7.45pm. That explains it then. There's darkness everywhere and maybe what I'm seeing are lights from local lanterns. I take a deep, reassuring breath to convince myself there's no cause for alarm. Ah! What's wrong with them? The three vehicles in front of us are driving dangerously, swerving recklessly. Something seems to be wrong somewhere but I can't put my finger at it.

I glance at Shettima for a clue and my fear escalates. Is it panic I see on his face? Is it confusion? I don't have time to decipher what it is because ... Ha! Mo Gbe, t'emi bami ooo, a staccato of gun shots suddenly rent the air. I shoot Shettima another quick, panicked glance but, again, I don't have enough time to gauge his reaction. Like a dream, masked men carrying what looks like AK 47 rifles jump out from the bush, into the middle of the road. They are many and they are everywhere, pointing their guns at us and ordering us to stop. Will Shettima run over them, killing as many as possible? Or will he consider it in our own interest for him to stop as being ordered? Oh my goodness! They are shooting and shouting at the same time. It's doomsday for Shettima and me and there's no escape! Is this the end of my dream? Is this how Shettima's life will be rudely terminated? Where are our guardian angels? What wrong has Shettima committed by offering a helping hand to a troubled

317

woman? The masked men are fiercely warning Shettima of their intention to kill us if he doesn't stop. Shettima brings the car to an abrupt halt. They surround us in a jiffy, even as they continue to shoot into the air. I cower in my seat, contemplating briefly whether to flatten the car seat so as to duck, but I reason that might be foolish considering the vehemence in the hoodlums' voices as they order us to "come down." We climb out of the car obediently.

"Bring your money or we kill you!" one of them says in faltering English. Without as much as a whimper, Shettima and I surrender all our valuable items. Shettima opens a compartment on the dashboard and brings out a wad of naira notes. He also gives them his two mobile phones, his wrist watch and his briefcase while I tender my handbag, jewellery and mobile phone. Then, they order us to lie on the express way, face down, to be searched.

"If I search you and see any money, I kill you." one of them warns harshly. How could we still be keeping cash or any valuables on us with the kind of command they have given us? We proceed to the middle of the road, where they order us to lie down. I don't know if this is part of their original plan or if they are acting on impulse but they are ordering us to undress now. We begin to remove our clothing. I remove mine until I'm only in my panties and watch Shettima remove his until he has only his boxer briefs on. We make to lie down but one of them barks at us that we have not finished. Shettima is the first to remove his boxer briefs and then I remove my panties and we both stand in absolute nudity before persons whose voices suggest are our children's contemporary in age. But they are not just young people; they are our tormentors and they feed their eyes on our nakedness for a brief moment before they order us to lie down. I didn't notice until now that they have rods but they start to lash us. Neither Shettima nor I make a sound; we take the lashing with equanimity. However, probably because we remain quiet in spite of our pain, they interpret it to mean that the pain we are receiving is not enough, so they slap our backs in turn with the blade side of the machete. Shettima and I intuitively understand the message. We start to scream as loudly as we can.

Some of them appear to be ransacking the car while others are searching through our clothes. All this while, gunshots ring out intermittently. We remain face down, half-dead on the road. The thought in my heart is that they will eventually either open fire on us when they get all they want or allow on-coming trailers to crush us. Fortunately, their gunshots have warned other road users to stay away. It's about thirty minutes' ordeal which ends with a command from one of them who says: "Let's go." We wait for about three minutes to be sure our tormentors are gone before we rise from the ground and scamper to find our clothes. We stand confused, scared and traumatised for a while. Neither of us speak. Slowly, Shettima's arms stretch toward me, folding me. I make no move. His arms tighten around me, squeezing me and that's when my tears start to flow freely. I don't recall if I have ever felt this kind of anguish in my life.

Finally in Lagos, we go to my residence in Opebi, where Shettima intends to spend the night.

"We need to talk," Shettima says solemnly as soon as we are in my apartment. My heart leaps into my mouth. Is he angry with me? He looks roughed-up and a little dishevelled. I don't know how I look, probably worse but I'm in no mood to check my reflection in the mirror. "We have to talk," he repeats.

"I know," I whisper, expecting to hear the worst but he proceeds to fold me into his arms and my fear dissolves.

"I have been thinking of what could have happened to us," he says in a whisper. A stark silence stretches between us. He sighs heavily as if he's weighing what he's about to say. All I want is for him to hold me tighter, squeeze me real good to drain me of this misery that is threatening to overwhelm me. I wait for him to do as I wish but he doesn't. I take him by surprise, kissing him passionately and clinging tightly to him. He doesn't push me away. He's not angry with me, I reassure myself and relax. After a while, he folds his arms tightly around me and buries his nose in my hair. I inhale his sweet Shettima smell.

"I want you to promise me that you will not visit, call or by any means attempt to contact your supervisor until he calls you as he has promised he will whenever he finishes reading your work. You can't change the man and a PhD is not half as important as your life and mental wellbeing."

"I promise," I mutter softly.

"Apart from our encounter with the armed bandits, did you know the way you reacted in his office?"

"I'm sorry," I whisper, trying to calm him. I wrap my arms around his shoulders and grind my pelvis against his.

"Oh, Funto," he murmurs, his voice rough and low." I'm happy about what I'm doing to him. I want him to make love to me now. I want to heal him and me too. My body is desperate for him.

"I need you to be in my life," he says tenderly.

"Me too," I mumble as his hands reach down to loosen the rope of his trouser. I use the opportunity to remove my clothes, flinging them in different directions. We could have been killed cheaply a few hours ago. We are fortunate to be alive and it's worth celebrating. What better way to celebrate than to make sweet love?

"Take me, Shettima, please," I breathe, my voice hoarse and needy. He responds in one swift move, burying himself inside me. "Arrgh!" I cry out from surprise at his alacrity. My Shettima is wonderful.

When senses return, we realise the house is in total darkness. Perhaps, the Power Holding Company of Nigeria has seized electricity, as they often do; but there appears to be light in the adjoining building and everywhere else apart from the four flats in my block. What could have happened? I don't keep my electricity bills longer than twenty-four hours before settling them.

"Why don't you find out from your neighbours?" Shettima suggests. I hurry into a T-shirt and a pair of jeans. "Don't be long, I want us to go and buy Suya.

"Sure, I'll be back shortly," I mouth and head out the door. I'm in luck; I notice a rechargeable lamp in my immediate neighbour's sitting room. I knock on the door. He opens it immediately.

"Good evening, Mr Fehintola."

"Good evening, madam."

I notice we don't have light whereas everyone else does and I'm wondering why."

"Well, some PHCN workers came here earlier in the day and disconnected our electricity from the pole."

"Why would they do that? I mean, we don't owe them."

"Some of us do owe them, madam. I owe them," he says simply.

"I see." I don't know what to say. I remain standing although I'm not clear as to why. Maybe I'm waiting for my neighbour to make me a promise that he will pay tomorrow so that we will have electricity restored. He seems to read my mind.

"I'm afraid we'll have to manage without electricity for a while, madam."

"Why?" I ask, desperately, trying to hold on to my fraying temper.

"Because I'm not going to pay quickly."

"I'm sorry, Mr Fehintola, but I think we ought to treat utility bills with a little more seriousness so as not to inconvenience ourselves and others."

"I know where you are coming from but, unfortunately, you do not have the right to tell me when to pay or not pay my utility bills. I owe PHCN, not you, and I will pay only when I choose to or I'm able to. Now, if you'd excuse me, I have things to do. I don't know why some people who came to Lagos from remote provinces would choose to carry themselves like Oyinbo, even when their miserable villages are not yet connected to the national grid." He bangs the door in my face. I turn on my heels and head back to my flat.

"The Federal Government has just introduced pre-paid metre system, go to PHCN office tomorrow and apply for one," Shettima suggests when I recount my encounter with Mr Fehintola. I acquiesce.

At the PHCN office the next morning, I'm directed to an office when I state my mission.

"Welcome, madam, it will cost you thirty-five thousand naira. You are obviously one of the wise ones to have come quickly. The procedure is that you will pay the amount to a commercial bank, you will then bring the bank teller to us and we will issue you a form. You will also bring two passport photographs with the bank teller, madam."

"Thank you very much."

"You are welcome, madam." I step outside to call Shettima. He tells me to meet him at a First Bank branch on Allen Avenue. When I arrive, he withdraws the money.

"There might be other contingencies you haven't factored into your request. Later, baby," he quips and is about to drive off but seems to remember something. "Kilishi or Suya, which would you prefer today?" he asks.

"Suya, with plenty of onions." He drives off. I proceed to the counter to make the deposit and within an hour, I have the bank teller and two passport photographs in my hand. I return to PHCN office.

"Here it is, sir," I say.

"Eh-r, madam, you will have to pay an additional five thousand naira."

"For what, sir?"

"For stamp."

"What stamp?"

"Ha-ha, see this madam o, won't we put an official stamp on your form, or you don't want your boys to eat again because government has decided to give you people pre-paid metre?" he asks jocularly.

"You want to collect five thousand naira just to stamp my form? Does the stamp not belong to the government? That's plain thievery and you know it's not good."

"No problem, madam, in that case you will come back next month. Actually, there's no ink in our stamp pad," he says and turns his back on me. Realising that I may not make headway otherwise, I curse under my breath and pay. He puts the money in his pocket and stamps the form. Then, he tells me he needs to open a file for me, which I have to buy. No more surprises.

"How much?"

"Fifty naira."

I pay and continue to stare at him.

"Yes, madam, you can go."

"Go? What about the metre? He permits himself a prolonged laugh before answering. "Madam, you are funny o. You mean you didn't know that the pre-paid metre is not available yet? It may take up to six months or even a year. Look at these files."

He points to a heap of files resembling the one he just opened for me. "They have all paid and filled the form as you have just done. When the metres start arriving from Abuja, we will give to them before you because they paid before you did. So, it's turn-by-turn."

"Why didn't you tell me this before? Why did you ask me to go and pay for something you know is non-existent?"

"Are you blaming me? See this woman o, am I the government that made the announcement on radio, television and newspapers that prepaid metres are now available?"

"What do I do? I need a metre of my own desperately."

"That's what you should have said now. You should have explained that you need help."

"Alright, I have explained and I'm still explaining. I need a metre, it's urgent."

"Okay, madam, the only thing you can do is to pay for an old one, unofficially o, I hope you understand me? Eh-hen. You know it is now illegal for us to give electricity consumers old metre since government has introduced pre-paid ones. But since the new, legal one is not available, I can help you to get an old one from our store. It will cost you money o, eh-hen, because I have to tell you. So, when you and I have agreed, I will get it for you, and then you will buy your own wires and connect light directly to your flat from the pole. That way, nobody can disconnect you as long as you settle your bills promptly."

I sigh heavily.

"How much would you take to get me an old metre?"

"It's twenty thousand naira, madam, not negotiable because I'm not the only one that will take the money. The ball is in your court, madam." I don't have any more energy for talking. I walk groggily out of the office.

Twenty-seven

SEPTEMBER, 2008

Deyemi is preparing to go back to school in the hope that it will be her last session as an undergraduate. She ought to have graduated since last July but for the instability in the university calendar. She says she is eager to graduate so that she will be able to use her NYSC allowance to contribute to my school fees. I don't know whether to laugh or cry. This is the same girl because of whose education I embarked on a PhD programme. How am I supposed to react to the idea of her becoming my sponsor?

"I want Uncle Shettima to have some respite, Mum," she says, looking at me piteously from the corners of her eyes.

"Uncle Shettima won't need a respite through your NYSC allowance, he's happy paying our fees. Besides, your graduation will serve as a good enough relief for him," I insist. My feeling about the role Shettima is playing is mixed. On one hand, I'm happy that he came into my life and saved me from what would have been a calamitous existence. What would have become of my daughter and me if not for his kind intervention? What about my mother? She still doesn't know that I have not yet obtained the much-touted PhD. Folake still sends me money from time to time but Shettima has since assumed full responsibility for my upkeep, insisting also that I placed my mother on a monthly stipend to keep my secret from leaking to her. He has also ensured that I don't fail in paying her regular visits and keeping a good appearance each time. I'm happy and grateful for all of these and even more. One the other hand, however, I can't help feeling how woefully I have failed as an individual and, more especially, as a parent. The pride of every parent is to be able to cater to the needs of their children. That's what I see every parent around me do and that was what eluded me.

"Okay, Mum, I will be using my allowance to take care of your lodging at Abuja and to put fuel in your car." Her voice cuts into my introspection.

"You will spend your allowance on yourself, sweetheart, to buy shoes, bags and jewellery."

"Nathaniel takes care of that and he says he'll do even more now that he's gotten a job with Nestle Plc."

"Nathaniel is a very fortunate young man to have found a good job shortly after his national service. I'm so happy you two are making out fine in your relationship."

"Yes, we are, that's why I want you to permit me to offer my NYSC allowance to assist you as soon as I start serving, mum."

"I can do without your NYSC allowance still."

"How about buying gifts for your supervisor?"

"You don't give up, do you?" My phone rings. It's Folake.

"Hello, Folake baby!"

"Hi Funto, take a guess on the name Geoffrey gave our new baby boy."

"It shouldn't be a hard guess, should it?"

"I'm waiting, madam Sabi."

"Geoffrey Junior."

"Well, you are kind of close, shows you are still as smart as ever."

"I'm not correct?"

"Not exactly. My son's name is Geoffrey the Second of

Nigeria, can you beat that?"

"Wow! What can I tell you?"

"Say it the way it is, Funto, Geoffrey is a clown. By the way, I just sent some money to you and Deyemi."

"You did what? How could you put yourself through so much inconvenience after all my explanation that Shettima is picking practically all our bills? Listen Folake, you have to stop sending money to me, not unless I request it of you. You've done so much and now Shettima is to the rescue. You've got to plan for those kids, you know."

"Hello madam preacher. Yes, you told me to stop sending money, and I told you I won't. At least not until you obtain your PhD. Give me a call the day you hold your PhD certificate in your hand, then, I will stop sending you money. We started this project together, remember? I will continue to support you in any way I can until you achieve your dream. As for Shettima and the role he's playing, I'm very happy for you and you deserve all the love and attention he's showering on you. You are a great woman. You deserve care, fun and happiness. My only regret is that you wasted so much time; you punished yourself and poor Shettima for too long. Anyway sha, be sure to cover lost ground o. I will personally ask Shettima to update me on your performance." She laughs a throated laughter and I reel in delight. Folake is an angel, I mutter under my breath but to her I say:

"You are a spoilt girl. A beg no spoil me for my mama o.

"Aren't you going to ask me for the test question and answer, abi how you wan take collect the money?"

"Yeye girl, what's the question?"

"Daughter's boyfriend's name. And the answer is Nathaniel. I will send the number to you by text."

"You are truly silly."

"I have to go now. Tell Deyemi to expect my call in two

hours' time. Bye."

"Bye."

" Folake says she will call you in two hours' time and she has sent money to us again. I say to Deyemi

"Your phone is ringing again, mum." I snatch it from her hand. Good gracious God, it's my supervisor!

"Hello, sir. Good day, sir, how is the family, sir?" I'm breathless. Has my supervisor ever called me?

"I have read your work. You may wish to come over so that we can discuss it."

"Okay, sir. Alright, sir." The line is gone. I sit paralysed with excitement, grinning at my daughter.

"Finally, Mum?"

"Finally, sweetheart," I breathe. I put a call across to Shettima to inform him of the happy development and when he suggests travelling with me, I decline vehemently.

"I need to go alone, please," I plead and he reluctantly agrees, warning me to make sure I don't lose my composure. I promise.

I'm now sitting in front of my supervisor; my thesis is on the table and he's expatiating on his comments and observations as we go chapter by chapter.

"I find it laughable that you refer to Buchi Emecheta's heroine in The Joys of Motherhood, Nnu Ego, as a young woman from Eastern Nigeria. It's a shame you didn't know that Ibuza is in the west of the Niger," he says coldly.

"I'm sorry, sir."

"Of course you ought to be very sorry but then poorly educated Nigerians with parochial turn of mind behave like that all the time." There's undisguised contempt in his voice. I turn over his words in my mind as I stare at him. It's interesting that my professor thinks I'm parochial. Perhaps, I am truly so, wouldn't it be more interesting to subject our minds to scientific investigation with a view to finding out which is more parochial? Maybe I should ask him.

"I think most of us in this country merely manage, not to use the word pretend, not to be seen as parochial, sir. I thought I was managing quite well, but now that you have drawn my attention to what may appear to be my failed attempt, why do you think most Nigerians are parochial, sir?" I stare at him and he holds my gaze. His eyes give nothing away. Even as I ask the question, deep down, I know the answer. He tries to say something but the words wouldn't form. His mouth hardens and I feel a sudden pang of pity for him.

"You will agree with me that it's been quite some time since you wrote your thesis and that there have been many more publications after you finished. Therefore, there is the need for you to update your work by consulting relevant publications and incorporating new ideas into your thesis. You have six months to do this and submit back to me."

"I will do as you have instructed, sir."

"Remember that you must be very thorough."

"I will keep your warning in mind, sir." I'm out of my supervisor's office and on my way back to Lagos. I haven't seen or spoken to Akpabio in over a year. He hasn't called me, either. I contemplate going to his office but discard the idea. It'll be a happier time for both of us when my thesis secures my supervisor's final approval. In the meantime, it's in my interest to return to Lagos at once and concentrate on re-working my thesis.

I finish my re-write in three months but wait for another three months before reverting to my professor. My thesis defence is scheduled to hold in July, the same month Deyemi will be writing her final degree examination. I'm eagerly looking forward to my viva but I'm far more excited about Deyemi's forthcoming graduation. Perhaps I would have the opportunity to write my story some time, and it would be an amazing success story of a helpless parent flown sky-high by friends and associates. What would have happened to my daughter and my dreams if it hadn't been for the likes of Folake, Shettima, Akpabio and Pitan? I would most probably have been long forgotten in the trash can of history. Thinking about it makes me feel like calling Akpabio and Pitan. It's a shame that I have remained in close touch with Folake, who is far away in the UK, but have not spoken with Pitan and Akpabio, both of whom are in Nigeria for God knows how long. Shettima is undoubtedly keeping me happily busy. He dominates my universe and I'm proud to be his woman.

"Hello, Pitan, how have you been?"

"Hello, Funto, it's good to hear your voice."

"Indeed. I have missed you."

"Have you?"

"Oh yes, I have. It's just that one thing keeps happening after another and time keeps slipping by. Don't mind me, joor."

"You sound so different, Funto, so confident; your boyfriend is looking after you very well."

"Shettima is a great guy," I admit, giggling.

"What does he do for a living?"

"He's a government contractor."

"No wonder. Government is never broke."

"I don't know about that but I'll sure visit you one day soon and I'll bring plenty of Suya and Killishi for you. It's a promise."

"Now I know you've been thoroughly 'northernised.' Anyway, I'm very happy for you and it would be my pleasure to receive you, as always." Minutes after ending my conversation with Pitan, I continue to grin stupidly at my phone. I try Akpabio's number but it's switched off. I send a text message, promising to see him when I come for my viva in July. I'm happy to be 'northernised' by my sweet and delicious Shettima.

Twenty-eight

JULY, 2009

Deyemi is back at home. Her degree examination has been put on hold just as my planned viva has been postponed indefinitely because the now familiar crisis in the country's tertiary education sector has reared its ugly head yet again. ASUU has embarked on what they say is a total, comprehensive and indefinite strike. Hopes for a quick resolution is slim as both the government and ASUU have resorted to trading blame. The teachers are asking for autonomy, increased funding of tertiary education up to 26 percent of annual budget as recommended by UNESCO, improved infrastructure in all the nation's ivory towers and payment of earned allowances of lecturers, among other demands. The lecturers' body accuse the government, and particularly the law-makers, of awarding themselves outrageous salaries, describing their action as an unnecessary plundering of the nation's resources. The lecturers' union go as far as supplying figures of what they claim are the law-makers' jumbo pay packet. A senator earns eleven million naira as regular monthly salary and allowances and twenty-seven million naira as quarterly allowances, such as estacodes and duty allowances.

The senate leadership, comprising ten principal officers, draws over one billion naira as quarterly allowance, higher even than the President of the United States of America. A House of

Representatives' member also earns a total sum of one hundred and forty-six million naira per annum. The lecturers say the senators can afford to send their children and wards to Ivy-League universities from the proceeds of their ill-gotten wealth, yet they don't care if the doors of the country's underfunded, mismanaged and deteriorating universities remain eternally shut. The government has, characteristically, called their bluff, describing their demands as unreasonable, highly provocative, unmerited, self-centred and impossible to meet. It agrees that it is reasonable for them to ask for well-equipped libraries and laboratories and a more conducive learning environment; but criticises them for always asking for increased salaries.

As both parties trade blame, it is the students and their parents who are once again at the receiving end of what promises to be another protracted battle. The parents are on bended knees, appealing to striking lecturers to take pity on their innocent children who have, once again, begun to roam the streets or loaf about at home. The dons are busy trying to educate the parents on the difference between being in school and receiving a good quality education. They are telling the parents to direct their appeals to the government whose officials, they say, literally swim in money.

My daughter and I are stranded but neither ASUU's position nor the stance of the government is my focus right now. I choose to preoccupy my mind with the happy expectation of my daughter's twenty-first birthday, which comes up tomorrow. I have every reason to be in a joyous mode - with or without a PhD. Deyemi has been the soul at the heart of my worries. She is the soul that is my life and death. And now that I have been rescued from the indignity of not being able to take care of her, now that she is about to become a full grown adult, what else do I have to worry about? My sweet, tall, slender, beautiful daughter will be twenty-one tomorrow. My heart expands. Deyemi stands at exactly my height but she is far more beautiful than me. Her skin is supple and tender, unlike mine, which is dry and coarse. And she has her father's oval face: absolutely gorgeous! My daughter is a child to be proud of any day. Apart from her mesmerising physicality, she's also loving, caring, good-natured, well-mannered, intelligent and hardworking. I love her with such intensity that the feeling threatens to suffocate me at times. My daughter will go far in life; she will achieve much and reach mountain peaks that will make it possible for her not to have to depend on anyone for her existence. I'm also proud of my modest accomplishments, regardless of what may look like the ASUU/Federal Government conspiracy to thwart my dreams. No amount of negative currents can smoke my spirit and vision of existence. I may have experienced difficult times and deprivation, but I'm also an enlightened woman possessed with a deep sense of achievement. With my daughter's twenty-first birthday tomorrow, I have not only tasted success; I have become the epitome of successful parenting, notwithstanding the insensitivity of those privileged to hold positions of responsibility. Education is acknowledged all over the world as one of the most powerful weapons against poverty; but if they insist on not letting us have it, then we will look in other directions to give meaning to our existence.

"Hi, Mum." Deyemi breezes in, snapping me out of my thoughts.

"Hi, sweet angel, have you checked on the caterer?"

"Oh, yes, I have, everything is going on smoothly, but that's not what I wanted to discuss with you."

"Really? What's special?" I ask, my face lighting up in joyous anticipation.

"I have decided to go and learn photography after my

birthday because there's a rumour that the ASUU strike will persist for the next six months."

"What? When did labour unions begin to set a time-table for their industrial action?"

"I don't know, Mum, but I have decided not to allow ASUU to frustrate me."

My heart glows with affection. How very thoughtful of her.

"What informs your choice of photography?"

"It's related to my field of study, Mum. I'm studying mass communication but beyond that I want to use my camera to record not only the 'what' but also the 'why' of a scene. I hope to record powerful images that will expose the problems confronting my environment and the Nigerian society at large. I want to strive for excellence not only in academics, but also in photography."

"Come here, come and embrace your mother," I quip, feeling absolutely proud.

"I have something else to tell you."

"I'm all ears."

"Nathaniel will be here tomorrow, to see you."

"Of course he'll be here tomorrow; it's your very special day."

"He wants to see you for a special reason."

"More special than your twenty-first birthday?"

"Yes."

"Give your mother a hint."

"Well, he wants to marry me, Mum, and, I have said yes."

"He wants to marry you? You mean, Nathaniel loves you enough to want you to be his wife?" I ask incredulously. I can't help it. A small, nervous, disbelieving giggle erupts from deep inside. I bite my lips in a desperate attempt to stop it from turning into full-scale hysterical laughter but I don't succeed. I lean back in the chair and surrender myself to the blissful laughter. I drape my arm across my chest as my laughter gradually turns to scalding tears. This is too much for me to handle. Soon, I'm sobbing and shrieking and Deyemi is holding me in a tight hug.

"Stop crying, Mum, or I'll start my own." She wipes my face with a handkerchief and when we look into each other's eyes, we erupt into simultaneous laughter. We are still laughing when we hear a knock on the door. Deyemi goes to open it, retrieving the Mr Biggs lunch packs from Shettima. There's another pack, containing Killishi. I'm salivating.

"How is it going with my beautiful girls?" he asks jocularly.

"Nathaniel will be here tomorrow, to ask for Deyemi's hand in marriage," I announce breathlessly. Shettima gathers Deyemi in his arms, lifting her off her feet and swaying her in the air. I watch both of them with quiet amusement.

"What are you waiting for? Let's start the celebration at once!" Shettima exclaims, heading toward the door. He returns shortly with an audio CD and slots it into the sound system. It's the Kool and the Gang's 1980 classic: CELEBRATION.

Yahoo!
Celebration
Yahoo!
This is your celebration
Celebrate good times, come on!
(Let's celebrate)
There's a party goin' on right here
A celebration to last throughout the years
So bring your good times and your laughter too
We gonna celebrate your party with you
Come on now, celebration
Let's all celebrate and have a good time

Celebration
We gonna celebrate and have a good time
It's time to come together
It's up to you, what's your pleasure
Everyone around the world come on!

It's like the three of us are in a dancing competition, we are digging it real good and sweating. On impulse, I stroll into my bedroom to check my appearance in the mirror. What a difference a day can make! I'm brimming with joy, a wide-mouthed grin on my face. There's a glow on my face that wasn't there before. My eyes are bright and shinning. How am I ever going to sleep? I saunter back into the sitting room; Deyemi and Shettima are still dancing and screaming joyfully. Shettima draws me into his arms; he raises my hand to his lips and plants a soft kiss on my forefinger. I close my eyes as my heart expands.

"You are my miracle," I breathe.

"I'm your Shettima. Thank you for sharing this moment with me," he murmurs. Later that night, as Shettima sleeps peacefully beside me, his arms draped loosely over my body, I lie back and stare at the ceiling, marvelling how my life of drudgery has transformed into sheer bliss. The world has righted itself, I mutter under my breath as I slowly drift into sleep.

Twenty-nine

DECEMBER, 2009

The Academic Staff Union of Nigerian Universities suspended its strike two months ago. I have had my viva and I'm still basking in the euphoria of my achievement. Deyemi's degree examination has also taken place. She has been posted to the Presidency in Abuja for the mandatory National Youth Service Corps programme. I'm in my house in Lagos, savouring my accomplishment on both fronts and preparing for my graduation ceremony, which holds next week. Whoever says life is full of highs and lows could not have put it better. This is – supremely - one of the high points of my life. I'm alone in my Opebi home at the moment; Shetima will be coming over later in the day, when we'll go out to make purchases for my graduation party. Our plan is not to travel to Abuja with a lot of stuff since Deyemi is on ground to handle the greater part of the preparations. However, we'll buy the souvenirs we plan to give our well-wishers from Lagos.

"Dr Olufunto Oyewole!" I hail myself with a throated laugh. I can't keep record of how many times I do it daily since my viva. The truth is that I'm trying hard to put my excitement in check but it's not been easy; the more I try, the more I fail so I let it be. I deserve the accolade anyway. It's unbelievable that I have finally become Dr Funto Oyewole. I'm hailing myself yet again, am I not? I am restless with uncontrollable happiness. Maybe I should rise on my feet to distract me a little. I stand. It doesn't help much. I sit, then, stand again.

It's just eight in the morning but sunshine floods my room already, brightening my life and sending a soft, enveloping breeze to warm the morning air. Outside, the smell of fried plantain is just around the corner. I turn slowly to pick the remote control from the table. I switch on the TV. 'Good Morning Lagos' is on air. The anchor is saying many things but I can't pick out a word. I stand, gazing unseeingly at him for long moments. "This is absolutely amazing," I mouth aloud, glancing at the mirror. I check my reflection. I look younger, more vital and full of strength, almost the image of myself at thirty-five. Dimples play beside my mouth. Am I seeing them for the first time? They look so sexy! Gosh! I smile, throwing my reflection a flash of white teeth that melt my feminine soul. My phone rings. I jump. It's Folake.

"Hello, Dr. Funto Oyewole!" her voice booms.

"Yes, the doctor is greeting you," I say with exaggerated importance. We laugh heartily.

"How prepared are you to receive Her Royal Highness, the Princess, and His Majesty, Geoffrey the Second of Nigeria?" she asks.

"Are you kidding me? What you are saying is that you are coming for my graduation, all the way from London, and with the children?"

"We've started packing already, if it pleases the doctor," She answers, picking her words carefully.

Folake never ceases to surprise me. Minutes after our telephone conversation, I sit motionless, overwhelmed. She is the only one I know who makes a promise and stands by it.

Some of her former school mates once unfairly described her as a saintly fool who does not know the value of money simply because she gives it away at the first demand. But I know she is no fool. She is a kind-hearted, compassionate woman who is not as sensitive as most of them are where money is concerned. Folake did not finish her studies in the university. Barely a year into her programme, she suddenly told her course-mates that she did not see herself as academically inclined. She gave them all the money on her as a parting gift and left, much to their disappointment. She returned to her parents and declared that she was ready to start a career using her ordinary national diploma. Of course, they were distraught but could not dissuade her from the path she had chosen. In the end, they learned to respect her decision, especially since she had demonstrated honesty by coming home rather than running off with some man.

I glance at the wall clock. It's nearly ten. I have to shower quickly. Shettima will be here any moment. My phone beeps. It's Deyemi. It's unusual for her to call this early. I dial her number. She scarcely allows it to ring before answering.

"Hello, Mum, I need your help urgently."

"Out with it, my sweet girl."

"I want to apply for a workshop in America. Application entry has been on for some time but I didn't get to know about it until this morning. The closing date is tomorrow, Mum, and I need someone to fill a reference form for me as part of the application. I've tried to reach your friend, Dr. Akpabio Asuquo, but he doesn't seem to be available as his phone isn't connecting."

"Akpabio travelled for a conference. Send it to me by e-mail immediately."

"That's the problem, Mum, it mustn't be filled by anyone who is family. Moreover, the referee must be either an academic or someone working with a non-governmental organisation. Oh, Mum, you have no idea how interested I am in sending my own application. This is one opportunity I'd hate to miss." I can almost feel her pulse. My palm is sweaty. I rack my brains for a solution.

"Entry closes…"

"Tomorrow, Mum. Surely you know people in the academia or the development world who can help?"

"I know a few people alright, but whether or not they will treat the form with the urgency it requires is what I don't know."

"Oh, Mum, you have to work hard at this. This is very important to me."

"Okay, darling, send it immediately, let me get to work."

"Straight away, Mum, you are the best!"

She hangs up. I start to perspire. I do a quick rundown of the relevant people I know. I know Prof. Thompson at the University of Lagos. He's a very kind person who has done me favours in the past and can be counted upon to do more. I know Mr Tomori in civil society. He would be glad to be of assistance. And how can I forget the adorable Mrs Gbajumo of Mental Development Initiative? Yes, I even know Dr Chidi Okafor of Lagos State University, an amiable and easy-going fellow who never ceases to offer a helping hand whenever necessary. Why am I worried? Deyemi has no problem at all. My phone beeps with an incoming e-mail. I download the form, read through it and send to all my contacts with the same cover note:

I'm writing to seek your urgent assistance to serve as a referee for my daughter's application to a workshop in the United States of America. The application requires that she provides a letter from a referee either from an academic advisor or someone affiliated with an NGO. The letter is to be written with your organisation or institution's letter head. She is also required to submit a short PDF form filled by the referee. Please help my daughter, you are her last hope on this and she's very keen in participating in the exercise. I would appreciate if you would kindly fill the form and also write a referral letter and send both documents to me or directly to my daughter, Deyemi Isaac, today. Her email address is deyemiisaac@ gmail.com. The application deadline is tomorrow. Thank you for your time and assistance.

God bless you.
Your friend,
Funto Oyewole.

I sit, casting intermittent glances at my phone for an early response. I'm oddly agitated. I'm yet to take my bath when Shettima arrives. I tell him about the development and he suggests we suspend our planned outing till tomorrow.

"Your shopping can wait. Let's give the day to our American workshop-loving Deyemi," he says jocularly. It's almost noon already. No word from any of them yet. Shettima calls Deyemi to enquire if any of them has been in touch with her and she replies in the negative. One o'clock, two o'clock. I become frantic. I dial Prof Thompson's number. Perhaps he hasn't checked his mail box. Why didn't I think about that? His phone rings but he doesn't answer. I dial again and again and again. No response. I try Mrs Gbajumo's number. An automated voice croons from the other end: "The number you are trying to call is not available at the moment. Please try again later. Thank you." I hiss and try Dr Okafor's number. "The user is busy on the other call. Please try again after some time. Thank you." Mr Tomori is my last hope. Why is my hand shaking? "The subscriber you are trying to call is not available. Please try again later. Thank you." Damn! I glance up at Shettima, feeling utterly drained. He places his hand on my shoulder. I shudder.

"What's the matter?" he asks, alarmed.

"I can't help my daughter," I groan.

"Calm down. There'll always be a way out."

"But there's absolutely no way in this matter, can't you see?"

"Who says? Look, we'll try your former Oga."

"Which Oga?"

"Your PhD supervisor, of course."

"You are kidding, right?"

"Do I look like a jester? Of course, I'm not kidding."

"You can't be serious."

"What's wrong with trying him? He is a human being and an academic. Thinking about it now, I'm convinced he's in the best position to assist given the very short time at our disposal."

"If I didn't know you, I would think you were high on stimulants. How can you even think of him?"

"Why not? Is he not an academic?"

"You don't know what you are saying," I charge angrily at him. Surprisingly, he meets my match.

"You are the one that is being unrealistic here. Prof Ephraim is in Abuja. Deyemi is in Abuja. She needs the assistance of an academic. What could be wrong with her going to see him on campus and asking for his assistance face to face?"

"Shettima, you are the limit. What you are saying is completely inconceivable, thoroughly outlandish," I almost shout.

"Outlandish indeed! I'm aware you just got your PhD so your head is swirling with big grammar. Why am I even wasting my time talking to you? Deyemi is the person I ought to be speaking with."

"That man is wicked, Shettima. He's not capable of doing anything good," I cry in exasperation.

"I won't hold further conversation with you on this matter.

Back off, okay?" He snaps but I don't give up.

"Prof Ephraim doesn't know Deyemi. He has never met her. How do you expect him to render such a huge assistance to a stranger?"

"Prof Ephraim has never met Deyemi, I agree, but he knows about her. That's enough for our purposes. All Deyemi needs to do is to go to him and introduce herself as your daughter and ask for his assistance. Look, stop distracting me, I must talk to Deyemi at once."

"You are about to engage on a wild goose chase. Prof Ephraim won't help."

He ignores me. Moments later, he's talking to Deyemi.

"You've got to try because it can never be wrong to make an effort. Yes. Prof. Ephraim can help you. Go and introduce yourself to him. Tell him you are the daughter of his former PhD candidate. Beg him to help you. The worst he can do is say no. You've got nothing to lose. No, no, no, your mum is making efforts here in Lagos but I want you to complement them. I'll refund your taxi fare next week when we come for your mum's graduation. You'll go now? That's my girl. Hurry, talk to you soon." He hangs up. I arch him a perfect eyebrow. He smiles contentedly.

"I'm hungry," he declares.

"Who cares? I thought Prof. Ephraim can solve all your problems."

"Don't be mad at me," he says softly, taking my hand. "I just want us to try all possibilities. Whatever he does or fails to do can't be new to you, but it's worth trying."

"Okay, okay, Mr Possibility."

I walk groggily into the kitchen to start preparing a meal of amala and okra. I'm still cutting the okra when Shettima breezes into the kitchen, brandishing his mobile phone like a trophy.

"I just received a text message from Deyemi," he says, eyes glinting with excitement.

"What does it say?"

"It says..., I mean ..., okay, I'll read it to you."

What has come over Shettima? I don't remember ever seeing him act this way, like a teenager.

"Deyemi writes: 'Uncle Shettima, I'm sitting in front of Prof. Ephraim, he is busy working on his computer, writing a reference letter for me. He has already finished filling the form. He's so kind. I'll call you when I leave his office.'"

Shettima grabs me from the waist and hugs me. I surrender to him, my head on his broad chest. My feelings are mixed. A part of me is overwhelmingly joyous at my daughter's breakthrough. But there's another part that feels oddly embarrassed. Have I been unfairly judgemental about my professor? I want Shettima to hold me tighter, squeeze me real hard and purge me of all personal vendettas. I want him to rid me of my fallacies, especially the one bordering on hasty generalisations. He appears to read my thoughts.

"The man was unkind to you," he reminds me softly. I know he just wants to make me feel better. I try to say something but I can't. My lips twitch.

"Don't blame yourself. Your experience made you overtly judgmental," he says, relaxing his hold on me.

"I'm surprised to find that my professor possesses some degree of humanity," I manage to whisper. Shettima meets my gaze, his eyes narrow, hunger flashing in their depths. Hunger for what: Food? Sex? I can't tell. What I do know is that I'm overwhelmed. I don't know what Shettima is up to. He captures my lips with his, the force of his body pushing me toward the kitchen door. He keeps pushing until we reach the sitting room. When my knees encounter the cushions, I slip down with a thump.

"Not fair!" I declare harshly but I know my outrage is more pretence than real. He grins wickedly and sinks down beside me. One of his hands clasps my outer thigh, twisting me until I face him, our knees touching. The same hand starts a bold foray across my leg. I stop him.

"You are heading toward dangerous territory," I warn softly.

"Tell me about it, doctor. How dangerous?" His phone rings. We jump up simultaneously.

"It's Deyemi," he exclaims triumphantly putting his phone on speaker.

"Yes, uncle, I've just left Prof. Ephraim's office. He did everything for me," she says excitedly.

"I'm happy you have a chance to put in your own application," Shettima says. "I will make a deposit into your account tomorrow to defray your costs. Well done, Deyemi. I'm very proud of you," he adds, joy oozing out of every pore. I feel like an outsider. "Ah, thank you, uncle, that'll be great. I'm really looking forward to it. Eh-r, tell Mum not to bother again, okay? I'll call her later today. I need to go to a cybercafé right now to send my application. I miss you guys, as always. Bye."

"Bye."

I leap to my feet and dash to the kitchen to resume my cooking. Shettima must be very hungry.

Thirty

The big day arrives at last! Shettima and I came into Abuja yesterday. On our arrival, we went straight to the campus to pay my convocation fee. Deyemi joined us thirty minutes ago, beaming with excitement. There's something about her looks that suggests that she's enjoying her national service at the Presidency. She makes my heart expand with pride. We are at Chelsea Hotel, putting finishing touches to our preparations. Folake will fly in with her children at 8 a.m. From the airport, we'll all return to the hotel for a quick breakfast before heading on to the National University of Nigeria. Lunch will be brought to the convocation arena by the caterer Deyemi contracted. I look forward to savouring every minute of my much anticipated great day. I take a deep lungful breath and smile secretly. All is well that ends well, I mutter as my mind drifts to my mother. She's unaware of today's event and part of my heart bleeds at the thought. How complete I would have felt if my mother were with me? Here I am, having one of the biggest events of my life, and I can't invite her. Whenever I think about the lie I told her in respect of my PhD journey, I feel like flogging myself and jumping up in jubilation at the same time.

On one hand, I feel awful that I have had to tell such a gargantuan lie to the woman that birthed me; on the other, I give myself a mental pat on the back for successfully hiding my pain from her and thus shielding her from agony. What would have happened to her if she had been privy to my anguish all through the years? Perhaps, such knowledge would have despatched her to an early grave and I would have blamed myself for her death. I did what I had to do to protect her, I tell myself firmly as fresh doubts threaten to engulf me. Is this true or am I merely looking for undeserved understanding? I'm probably a psychological coward who is unable to admit that part of my reason for lying was also to avoid the 'I warned you' chastisement. Or why do I find it necessary to constantly reappraise my actions? But even in spite of my frequent attempt at self-justification, I have come to agree with Aminata Forna's view that all liars lie to protect themselves from the pain of truth. The challenge for all, she further opines, is to discover the purpose served by the lie and this is where I find the greatest justification for my decision to hide the sordidness of my situation from my mother. I lied to her for the sole purpose of protecting her, not to escape the pain of 'I told you so' syndrome, I remind myself for the umpteenth time.

"Mummy, I thought you would like this lip gloss." Deyemi's voice pulls me out of my introspection. I seize it from her with drama, my mood brightening.

"Let me try it. Looks like it's a natural colour." I stand in front of the mirror and apply it.

"Wow! I love it. Thanks darling."

"You are welcome, Mum." Shettima smiles coyly at me. I ignore him. My mind is on Folake's children right now. I can't wait to see my dear Princess and Geoffrey the Second of Nigeria. UK has been good to my friend, without a doubt. She left Nigeria with a pregnancy some years ago and she'll be home today for my graduation ceremony with two absolutely adorable children. I beam. We are all dressed now, ready to go.

We make it to the airport in less than thirty minutes. I

marvel at the pleasure of driving in Abuja. Will Lagos ever succeed in solving its traffic problem? Folake's flight is shortly announced. The three of us are now on our feet, eagerly waiting to sight our returnee and her children from the multitude filing through the arrivals lounge. Deyemi is the first to see her. She screams excitedly and I instinctively follow her eyes. Then, I see her and the children. But they are not alone. What! Am I seeing clearly or am I in a trance? I blink several times as my eyes again settle on him. Good gracious Lord! Geoffrey! Is this not him? He seems to have sighted me, too. He's smiling broadly. I don't know what to feel. I stand rigidly on the same spot; Shettima and Deyemi rush to embrace them. I'm numb with elation. Why didn't Folake give me a hint? This is the most pleasant surprise of my day! I still can't move. I stand open-mouthed then start to grin from ear to ear. Geoffrey comes to my rescue. He moves swiftly and folds me perfectly in his arms. I surrender to his warm embrace, Folake, Shettima and Deyemi form a ring around us. We disengage slowly. Geoffrey wants to talk and, as if on cue, we turn to him.

"You are a survivalist, Funto. I love your irrepressible spirit. You are a woman of exceptional courage and determination. I admire your tenacity. I like the way you insist on what you want. I love your boundless energy, enthusiasm and perseverance. Come on now, you deserve another hug." He folds me in his arms again.

I want to say something, I'm frantically searching my brain for the right words but I seem to have become tongue-tied. I have to respond; I must say something.

"Eh-m, you know, Geoffrey," I stammer but I'm determined to speak so I pull myself together and finally find my voice.

"I'm sorry for all the misunderstanding between us, for thinking that you hated me, for not making enough effort to understand you," I say in a rush.

"You don't have to apologise for anything, Funto. I never gave you a chance, either. I misjudged you and misunderstood what you represented, but all that's in the past now. What we have today is overwhelming joy and the celebration of a monumental success. I want to be part of it. I'm already part of it. Look at you; see the way you're glowing. And I'm even happier that you have found true love at last." He looks in Shettima's direction. My gaze connects with Folake's children and I rush to them. Now I know why Geoffrey named his son Geoffrey the Second. The boy is a younger version of his father. I marvel at the wonders of nature, sometimes so comical, other times seemingly spiteful. What has my friend done to deserve the glaring alienation? I shoot Geoffrey an accusatory glance but he's busy talking with Shettima. I look questioningly at Folake. She doesn't have my time, either. She and Deyemi are engrossed in some gist. I turn my full attention to my goddaughter and her brother.

On our way back to the hotel in Shettima's fully-loaded SUV, Deyemi regales us with the story of Prof. Ephraim's kindness to her.

"He wrote everything for me and then gave it to me to read, asking if I liked it," Deyemi says. We exchange glances. Deyemi is obviously enjoying the attention.

"He said many kind words to me. He told me I'm prettier than Mum, for example."

"That goes without saying, Deyemi," Folake says with exaggerated earnestness. "Funto would be disqualified in the first round if the both of you were the only participants in a beauty pageant and it won't be on account of her age," she adds.

Inside the campus of the National University, we have

hardly alighted from our vehicle when my friends command me to put on my academic gown. I do as I'm told and we are soon surrounded by a horde of photographers. Akpabio joins us, looking resplendent in traditional Efik attire. What else can I ask for? I grin from ear to ear, feeling like a new bride. The photo session has hardly begun when a faintly familiar face walks briskly toward us, wanting to speak to me. I can't hide my eagerness and flash him an encouraging smile.

"Congratulations, madam, it's really a glorious day and I'm truly happy for you," he quips, radiating genuine warmth. I stretch my hand. He takes it enthusiastically.

"Thank you, my brother," I say, adding, "You kind of look familiar, but I'm sorry I don't remember when and where we last met."

"Oh, you are very correct, madam. We met at the Post-Graduate School during our registration many years ago."

"Is that so? You must have graduated a long time ago and, I must say, it's very kind of you to come around to rejoice with us late bloomers." My body vibrates with excitement as I speak but I can't help noticing that his expression suddenly darkens. It seems I have touched a sore spot. I regret my incaution. Comport yourself and act with decorum and maturity, I admonish myself silently. I try for distraction.

"Eh-r, remind me of your name, please?" I say tentatively, hoping that I succeed in clipping the excitement in my voice."

"My name is Wale Balogun. Actually, I have not finished," he declares grimly. I feel his pain.

"I'm sorry. Your supervisor is making things difficult for you?" I ask, putting as much sympathy as I can in my voice.

"No, no, no, it's not my supervisor's fault at all. Give it to the man, he's very hardworking, diligent and kind. Most of the people who started the same time as I did under his supervision have since finished. And even many who came after me have graduated as well." He confuses me.

"What then is the problem?"

"I am the problem, madam. I don't have the time for my research. I have since found that research is a difficult venture to engage in and writing even more so. My supervisor encourages me, he challenges me, threatens me, talks to me and uses all kinds of methods to make me take my studies seriously, but I can't find a way around it. I feel utterly helpless and irresponsible." He sighs.

"How have you managed to remain a student for so long? Your registration ought to have lapsed if you've been around for as long as you describe."

"Oh yes, the PG School has advised me to withdraw twice and I have done so and re-applied on each occasion. My supervisor is a patient man. Most of his colleagues would not tolerate that from any student." It's my turn to sigh. I don't know what else to say. Mercifully, I find one more question to ask.

"How far have you gone with your thesis?"

"Madam, I haven't tried at all o. I'm even ashamed to mention it." He's ashamed to talk about his thesis? How else does he want us to keep the conversation going? I yawn to express my boredom.

"OK. How long have you been on the programme?" I ask.

"Ah, madam, I have done like… let's see now…, eh-r…, I have done up to eleven or twelve registrations." I gasp but he doesn't notice. "If only I can just finish my chapter one, then I can move on quickly from there." My mouth falls open. He hasn't written the first chapter in twelve years? How long does he plan to spend on the programme? And why is he telling me all this? As if reading my thoughts, he suddenly looks up, his mood brightening.

"Eh-r, madam, can you spare your academic gown for a

moment? I'd like to take some pictures with it," he says, smiling sheepishly; then, as if embarrassed, adds quickly, "Maybe the photographs will ginger me to work hard from now on."

"Absolutely," I mouth, hurriedly pulling off my gown. He takes it in both hands and skips off like a teenager. I gape at him from a distance.

By the time Wale returns, it's time to go in for the day's ceremony. As we stroll leisurely toward the venue, Shettima whispers in my ear:

"We are paying Prof Ephraim a thank you visit after the ceremony." I nod vigorously and then go on to demonstrate my acquiescence with an open kiss, feeling completely unabashed.

www.ingramcontent.com/pod-product-compliance
Lightning Source LLC
Chambersburg PA
CBHW030154200626
46812CB00017B/1901